Other publications

Educational
A colour-coded study-aid for examination students, up to and including A-Level,devised for Henderson Publishing plc. 1995. Texts include: *Othello, Macbeth, Romeo and Juliet, Pride and Prejudice, Jane Eyre, Great Expectations.*

Fiction
Maddy and the Captain.

Acknowledgements

The Picton Library for access to archive material pertaining to the Liverpool Blitz, 1940; the E. Chambre Hardman Trust for the cover photograph; Stephen Gavin for his design; Christopher Norris for his invaluable help with editing; the wonderful people who provided the background to Merseyside in the Thirties; Joanna Markham, for her marketing expertise and my readers, Ann Green and Angela Awbery White for their unstinting support and encouragement.

Crossings

Jeannie Heppell

Published by
Lady Spring Publications,
Holgate's House,
18 Town Street,
Old Malton,
North Yorkshire,
YO17 7HB

ISBN 0-9542776-1-9

Cover photograph
'Schoolboys on the Ferry'
by kind permission of
The E. Chambre Hardman Trust,
59 Rodney Street, Liverpool L1 9ER

Cover Design by Stephen Gavin, Zero/Zero
www.Zero/Zero.co.uk

Printed in 11 on 12 point Plantin Typeface
by Sessions of York
The Ebor Press
York, England

For my parents,
with love.

Also by this Author

Maddy and the Captain

This fascinating and absorbing story starts in 1913 and is a vivid and sometimes moving account of the impact of the First World War. But unlike many books that explore this area, Jeannie Heppell has shown us an often forgotten side of the war, that of the women: mothers, sisters, fiancées and sweethearts left behind while the men were away fighting. Her carefully drawn characters, especially young Maddy, give us a glimmer of understanding as to what life was really like in those turbulent times and how the young were forced to grow up very quickly. Because she lives in Yorkshire, the author has also based some of the novel in our fair county. An excellent and engrossing read.

Marie Clapham for *Yorkshire Life Magazine*, May 2003

PART ONE

THREE CHILDHOODS

1. Summer's End
1926

SHAFTS OF PALE light were flickering on the wall. From her bed, Stella could just make out the gap in the curtains which had allowed them in, to flutter there like so many elongated moths. Fretting. Disturbed. Frightened. As she was.

There must be a wind. The light would not flit from place to place with such agitation if the tree was not in motion out on the green.

The child straightened herself rigid on the bed and pulled the covers up to her nose. From this position the intrusive light shivered on the ceiling. She screwed up her eyes so tightly that her top lip pulled upwards and her teeth touched the starched smoothness of the sheet. The leaf patterns still twitched in a pool of bluish light behind her eyes.

She knew the tree well. It was the focus for every house that formed the little community around the green, not just the children who lived at the Stanhope Foundation. Its metamorphoses throughout the seasons had become part of the pattern of their own lives. It made them feel more special for having it. 'The People Who Lived On The Green.' That is how they thought of themselves.

At present the tree in the centre of the green was just about to change its colour. It had shaped itself throughout the summer into a great shaggy bear, its branches sweeping the ground. Underneath, it could form a cave, a house, a hiding place. A fragrant, earthy haven which crunched under the children's feet; for it was only the children who crept inside, to find themselves whispering at the wonder of it. Every time.

The tree was useful too. In previous autumns, Stella had disappeared under it, virtually camouflaged, the colour of her hair mingling with the coppery, dark red foliage. She would kneel amongst the heaps of fallen leaves and collect in her apron scores of little beech nut cases to be painted silver by the children in preparation for Christmas time. They would be hung on the tree in the dining room of the Foundation. They would be strung on silver thread to create garlands to decorate the dormitories. Thousands of little stars to comfort them in the middle of winter. But this year she would not be there. Someone else would have to do it.

She turned over on to her side and rummaged under the pillow for her handkerchief. But she was in a strange bed. The hollows and troughs in this mattress were as unfamiliar to her as the sheets, shiny with starch. She gave up the search and rubbed her nose on the sleeve of her nightdress, snuggling right down under the bedclothes.

In fact, she was staying with her aunt Maddy. Aunt Maddy had set up the Foundation towards the end of the war, in the next house along. Stella had been there all her life, as far as she knew, with all the other children who had lost a parent then. Aunt Maddy had looked after them all, with Miss Sefton who ran the part which was the school and Liddie who cared for the babies. And her mother flying in whenever she had time off from the hospital where she worked; almost literally flying in on her motor-cycle. They could hear her coming for miles.

Her mother was extraordinary. No-one else had a mother who rode a motor cycle or got covered in oil taking motor cars to pieces and never seemed to mind. No-one else *could* take an engine to pieces that she knew. And Stella thought her the most beautiful mother in the world. Aunt Maddy did too.

Aunt Maddy was not really her aunt but her mother's closest friend, but she was better than a real aunt to Stella. She loved her dearly. She loved them all, even Aunt Maddy's husband who was always getting into difficulties one way or another. The greatest trouble he got into was when it looked as though he was going to take Maddy away to Stowe soon after their wedding. Fortunately, he got a job at a school near Lyndhurst instead and all the children began to talk to him again, forgiving him for marrying her and posing such a threat. They had stayed at The Green and everything had remained as it was. Until now.

Now her own mother was married and it was Stella who was going away. Hundreds of miles away. Her newly acquired stepfather was a doctor who had gone off to lecture in a university in the north. They had been married that summer and her mother had arrived at The Green the night before to collect her and take her back to Liverpool. It seemed like the end of the world.

When she appeared for breakfast her heart rose. The trains from Lyndhurst were not running. There was no coal that day. The miners were still on strike and the coal for the railways had at last run out. Lou Bundenell was vastly annoyed despite her sympathy for the cause of the inconvenience. Perhaps if they could get to London somehow the main line trains would be running. Surely they would have emergency supplies? Aunt Maddy would not hear of it. She pointed out that she and Stella could be stranded anywhere, for hours, if not days. Why did she not borrow a car? It could be returned, one way or another, at a later date.

Lou began to express various objections, as if to herself, mulling over the options. It was Lonsdale, Aunt Maddy's husband, who stepped into the breach. He would drive them to Liverpool, but Stella's luggage would not fit into the car as well as the three of them, he pointed out. Her trunk would have to wait until it could go by train.

He looked across at Stella.

'If you want to raid it first to retrieve your best treasures, do it straight after breakfast, little lady, but...' he was smiling as he went on, 'make sure that you have something to depend on for when I get us all hopelessly lost. Bear that in mind when you choose, would you? Will you do that for me whilst I go and check the petrol situation?'

Stella nodded solemnly. Of course he would not get lost if her mother was with them. She *never* got lost. On the other hand, unlikely things were sure to happen if they were with Lonsdale.

She thought about what she should take. Books were the obvious thing and perhaps she ought to slip Tilly in, in case there really was an emergency. Tilly was an ancient, much-loved rag doll who was so soft she would fit inside her coat and no-one could possibly guess she was there. Stella liked to curl her fingers round the strands of wool which served for Tilly's hair. And suck her thumb if no-one was looking, as she had done for as long as she could remember, except that now she knew that she was far too old for such babyish practices and would be chastised for it if she should be caught..

She gazed at Lonsdale with half-hooded eyes as he crammed a piece of toast into his mouth before disappearing out of the door. Tilly was uppermost in her thoughts as she recalled the endless, sleepless hours of the night just gone. Then, inevitably, a choking sound came from somewhere in the region of the outer door. She could hear it clearly. That, and Aunt Maddy's voice, brought her back to reality.

'Well, that's settled then. Crisis over.' Aunt Maddy smiled benignly round the table but Stella knew that she was waiting for her mother to explode. And then she would defuse it, as she always did, by laughing at her. No notice at all had been taken of Lonsdale's predicament.

'It's a bugger's muddle, all the same!' Her mother pushed her plate away in irritation. 'But I suppose I should have anticipated it.'

Aunt Maddy nodded, ' But it doesn't matter. There's nothing lost,' she said calmly to Stella rather than to Lou.

Stella never ceased to find it amazing that no-one, not even Liddie who was very old, reacted to her mother's bad language. If *she* had said 'bugger' or even 'damn', she would have had her mouth washed out in soapy water until it foamed. When her mother said it and even worse things, not an eyelid flickered. Aunt Maddy now was folding her napkin as if her mother had made a comment on the weather. No, that wouldn't be it; her language when referring to the weather was usually unrepeatable. It was more as if her mother had said 'That was a nice breakfast.' Stella looked at them both as she finished her glass of milk. It was bemusing.

She supposed she ought to ask if she could get down and have the key to the trunk.

* * *

After the dismay of all the goodbyes, the journey seemed interminable. They had started off in mist but even when it cleared Stella could not bring herself to become interested in the scenery. She sat miserably in the back jammed between two suitcases and eventually fell into an uncomfortable doze, Tilly's hair wound round her thumb.

She woke to find that they had stopped for lunch and the sun was turning the inside of the vehicle into a greenhouse. Her mother and Lonsdale, (she never questioned why he was always called Lonsdale, he just was) were laughing as they struggled to open the sun-roof. It gave way suddenly and they fell towards her in a heap. They all tumbled out of the car with a great deal of noise and a certain lack of grace and Lonsdale and she wafted the doors to and fro whilst her mother spread out the picnic.

When they packed everything back into the car half an hour later, Lou suggested that Stella might like to sit in the front with her for a bit. She wanted a cuddle, she said. Stella knew that her mother had sensed that it was, in fact, the other way round. She, obviously, was not the only one conscious of the miles and miles that now lay between her and the only place she had known as home.

So it was that she was sitting on her mother's knee with her head sleepily cradled against Lou's shoulder when they both found themselves, with extreme suddenness, ejected from the seat and half-way out through the roof. Whilst they were suspended there for a split second, they had a magnificent view of the surrounding countryside. Then they descended rapidly with a serious bump back on to the hard seat.

Fortunately Lou was winded and therefore, temporarily, speechless. It was Lonsdale who spoke.

'Good God! Are you alright?'

He had skidded the car to a halt on the verge of the road.

'I am sorry. I had no idea that the crest of the hill was so hump-backed. I'd got plenty of speed up you see, the old girl might not have made it otherwise, I...'

'Bloody Hell, Lonsdale, just shut up will you!'

Lou gently ran her fingers along Stella's limbs, checking that there were no bones broken. By the time the expert inspection was over Lonsdale had rushed round to the passenger door and opened it in order to lift Stella out.

'It was wonderful, wasn't it Mummy? It was just as if we were going up in an aeroplane.'

'Exactly, darling! ' She kissed her as she was set on firm ground.

'You are damned lucky Lonsdale! You could have killed us.'

He had that look of utter disbelief on his face which he always had when such things happened to him, as they often did. He never related the consequences of his actions to himself, for instance on one occasion he had been attempting to ascertain whether the school chimney was on fire and had walked backwards, straight down an open manhole. As he clambered out to the cheers of the audience of boys, all he said was, 'Who put that there?' His escapades had become legendary. There was no jeering in the response of the boys to his idiosyncracies. They found him hilarious but they also knew that he had returned from Flanders having been decorated for bravery several times over and that he had recovered from wounds which would have killed a lesser man. In addition, however clownish he purported to be, he was one of those rare creatures, a born teacher, and they held him in the highest esteem.

So did Lou, despite her opinion that Maddy stood in line for canonization for the way in which she tolerated his eccentric and often dangerous behaviour. And if he did not make Maddy dazzlingly happy, as her first love Dennis Stanhope had done, he made her content and she protected him as he, in his strange way, protected her. Poor Maddy, who had lost Dennis and her brother Jimmy on the same day in 1918; poor Maddy who had been in need of more solace than Lou could give her, and who had ended up with Lonsdale and his propensity for disaster. But he loved her. She was the whole focus of his existence. He loved her more than all else and Lou was thankful for it on behalf of her friend.

And now she saw the funny side of this latest escapade and she laughed, standing on the grass verge with the sweep of a spectacular valley below them. Her laughter was infectious and she and Stella became helpless at the recollection of their surprising ejection from the body of the car. They only sobered up when Lonsdale partially exonerated himself by pointing out that if the sun-roof had not been open it could have been much worse. Stella was tucked safely on the back seat before they set off again, Lonsdale forgiven, but a wary Lou keeping an eye on her daughter's safety as they continued on their way.

The weather and the scenery altered as they drove further north. A bleakness appeared in both and fog was threatening. It was in this misty atmosphere that Stella first became aware of the groups of men collected on the corners of the streets in the towns they passed through. Even she registered the hopelessness in the way they stood. Like horses who knew they were sick. *They* stood like that, with one leg bent.

'What are they doing, Mummy?'

'Nothing. That's the trouble.'

'What's the matter with them?'

'Nothing's the matter with them darling. They haven't got a job, that's all.'

Lou hated the way that she had said that. 'God forgive me!' she said to herself, 'but how is an eight-year-old to be told how millions of men come to be without work? And that it does matter, it matters more than anything.'

Her short experience in the north had saddened her immeasurably. During the war there had been something to fight against; she certainly had: against the deluge of wounded, the shortages of everything, the cold, the grieving. But how did one fight this? How could anyone have predicted that it would end up like this?

'They haven't got any work, you see. They haven't anywhere else to go.'

Stella did not ask any more questions. She knew by the tone of her mother's voice that it would be useless to do so. It was the same deadness which came over it when she asked about her father. No, better to leave it and find out for herself.

It was very late when they arrived at Stella's new home and pitch black. She was only vaguely aware of being carried through a panelled hall and up a great staircase. Her clean nightdress felt cold, but someone had put hot water bottles in her bed and she was sound asleep almost before she hit the pillow.

A clock was chiming five with a delicate, unfamiliar tinkling. It was immediately followed by a deep-throated bellowing noise coming eerily through the dark, as though it was part of it but at the same time, far away. Stella woke up in terror and then she realized where she was. The mournful sound must be the fog horns on the river. Her mother had said that the house looked out over the mouth of the river. On a clear day you could see the coast of Wales. But when you couldn't, the foghorns would sound.

Curious, she slipped out of the high bed and felt her way across to the window to see what was behind the curtains. There was nothing. A blanket of thick fog enveloped everything. It was not even swirling. It was a murky grey screen which beaded the glass and muffled the keening of the injured sea-creatures which the fog-horns pretended to be. It would not be that morning that she would see the Welsh coastline.

She sat back on her heels, her chin drooping on to the buttons of her nightdress, all her misgivings about the new life she had been pitched into compounded by the ghostly hooting.

She didn't care about Wales, or anywhere else. She wanted to go home. She just wanted to go home.

* * *

On the other side of the channel the mist came creeping from the water, sweeping in gradually, curling off from the impenetrable block of greyness which the river had become. It was as if the Mersey did not exist; just solidity.

It smothered the outlines of the coastline so that the great ships in various stages of construction, propped up in the dry-docks, could almost be mistaken for the ruins of the ancient priory just down river from them, if, at five in the morning, anyone cared to make a distinction. Nobody did.

The few people who were about in the region of Monk's Ferry had better things to do. The ferrymen, for instance, were busy preparing for the first crossing, cursing the fog, the damp clamminess of everything they touched, the slippery decks. They could only hear each other; they would have had to bellow with the strength of the intermittent fog-horns if they had meant their complaints to reach any further.

In the back entry of Monk Street a small boy struggled to get his bicycle through the doorway from the yard. He was only half-awake and the bicycle was too big for him. But he was determined to do it. He had to get the coke. The queue began to form at the gasworks at five and the Town Hall clock was already striking. If he was late the sixpence in his pocket would be useless. All the coke would be gone.

It wasn't far, just a few streets beyond the Haymarket, but he needed the bike to bring it back, slung across the handlebars. He had been going for the coke since the miners' strike had started. It was the only way to get fuel on any regular basis.

His breath came in spurts as he pedalled along standing up. If he sat on the seat he could not get enough power. His legs were not quite long enough. But it made his thighs ache to go slowly in that position; he could hardly see through the reluctant daylight and the ashen swirl which enveloped everything. It made him want to cough.

'Bugger off!' he muttered to a scrawny-looking dog which had materialized from nowhere and was yapping at the rear wheel. The thing had made him jump and now he felt vaguely silly.

'Get lost, will you!'

The dog sidled away into the gloom. Jack tried to pedal faster but he was coming up against the tramlines.

The fog-horns boomed from out in the river. He was so used to them that they were almost comforting. He thought of the slow ships creeping up the channel, sending out their warnings to each other as they groped their way through the water. He was groping too at this point, to avoid getting his wheels caught, but he knew the way well and even if he did come a cropper, he reminded himself, he wouldn't hurt anything which wouldn't mend. And the trams would not start to run for another hour. With luck, the fog should have lifted before he was on his way home.

It did not occur to him that he really ought to be there still, tucked up safely in bed, the sound of the fog-horns encroaching on his uneasy dreams. His friend Pinny had recently enlightened him as to the facts of life. Jack had not believed him. 'Don't be daft! It's for peeing with,' he had said, and Pinny the Omniscient had snorted. 'You'll see,' he had smirked over his shoulder as he had swaggered away. And recently Jack had been having the strangest nights. He wondered if he ought to mention it in Confession but he went cold at the very thought. Last night though, he had dreamt about making a fool of himself on his first day at his new school. Letting everyone down. He didn't like letting anyone down, particularly his father. As he toiled along, the familiar boomings nudging him on his way to the gasworks, thoughts of his father were uppermost in his mind.

In his time, David Jamieson had walked from the Clydeside shipyards to Birkenhead in one pair of boots, well-patched by the end, in order to fend for his wife and young Jack. He had walked all the way, when there were fewer and fewer ships to be built in Glasgow, after the war had ended. And now, having suffered all the privations leading up to the General Strike, Cammell Laird had laid off men and if Jack shut his eyes as he pedalled on, he could conjure up the picture of his father sitting rigidly in his chair by the fire. Not seeming to see anything. Knowing that there was nowhere to walk to this time if things got worse. It was as if the man was visibly shrinking .

His perception of his father's state was intuitive. He could not have articulated why he felt as he did, had someone asked him. He just knew that he had to get back with the coke; that it was his responsibility, to keep the fire going; that his father had a need to direct his unseeing gaze into it; a need that seemed even more paramount than his mother's who cooked on it; a need greater than his own longing for warm porridge before he went to school, and that of his little sisters jostling for the best position to put on their woollen stockings which had been drying on the fender overnight. Although he did not understand it for what it was, his father's increasing hopelessness was a great motivator for Jack. At ten years old, he was trying to compensate for it. His other troubles and embarrassing little shames he tried to push away but they were not quite so accomodating as the yappy little dog he had just dealt with. They kept coming back.

He could smell the baker's before he could see it. Warm yeast and the smell of coffee from the sacks stored in the main shop reminded him that he was hungry. The faint light that was coming from the basement turned the mist a creamy yellow as he approached. He stopped for a moment above the windows. He liked to watch the bakers working down there beneath his feet. Busy with trays, stacks of them, they glided in and out of his vision oblivious of his fascinated scrutiny of their dusty-white world; unaware of the grumbling in his, as yet, unfed stomach and the watering in his mouth as the crusty loaves emerged from the ovens.

He hurried on not allowing his gaze to fall on the notorious chewing gum machine which was positioned to one side of the main shop. That had almost been his undoing, that machine, in the recent past. It had suddenly opened a little door in its front and spewed out coins when he had automatically hit it, passing by on his way to serve at Mass two Sundays ago. He had not been able to believe his luck. He had tentatively scooped up the pennies and put one back through the slot. It produced a stick of gum. He tried another one. Same result. He had rushed on to impart the splendid news to Pinny in the Sacristy whilst they struggled to get the lace-edged smocks over their heads. 'We'll go back and get the rest,' Pinny had whispered, his face alight with the joy of it, 'as soon as Mass is over.' And in between the tinkling of the bells for the consecration, 'You lucky sod, Jack Jamieson...you lucky, lucky sod!'

And once they were done, they raced away from the church with more than usual desperation, anxious to know if the little door was still ajar. It was, but there was no more money in it. 'Look! We can get all the chewing gum out if we put one of these pennies through the machine over and over again,' Pinny had shouted, his fervour for the scheme making him shiny-eyed and high-voiced. He put that into speedy effect while Jack had counted the coins from his pocket and handed Pinny his share. They had nearly two shillings each. Jack had treated his sister Molly to the Music Hall. He had bought a seat in the Gods for each of them and a whole tin of toffees and felt the goodness of giving. It hadn't lasted. Molly had been so overwhelmed with it all that she had not been able to keep her mouth shut and had blurted out the whole story to their mother and Jack had been locked in his room without supper. 'It's *The Lives of the Saints.* you'll be reading, my boy,' his mother had shouted at him. 'Twice mind! And I'll be testing you in the morning!' He had not split on Pinny. His friend would have been beaten. He was glad that he hadn't, he thought to himself as he turned into Jackson Street, Pinny had enough to contend with in a family of disorderly brothers as it was. Pinny, however, did not ever go for coke. He was at least spared that.

Jackson Street was where the gasworks were, at the bottom end. The familiar, nauseating smell insinuated itself through the rawness of the mist. The fog, it seemed, became the smell clinging to Jack's clothes and hair, even the hair under his cap. He hated it. There was no smell like it: sulphur from the gasworks, the salty cleanness of the sea overpowered here by the stench of leaked oil, a vague hint of decaying effluent and, as he joined the queue which shuffled against the great high wall, the acrid stink of unwashed people. He hated it.

He had to wait for the gates to open. His bicycle was awkward to hold and got in the way of others. Most of them had small hand carts made out of bits of wood on axles and wheels from long-discarded prams. Cardboard boxes were balanced on top; Sunlight Soap in the main. One of the carts had two pieces of wood nailed to its sides for handles. The spokes of Jack's wheels caught on one of these as it rested on the ground,

'Watch what you're doin', yer dozy bastard!'

Jack moved sideways and the speaker, a largish man with a chipped front tooth, took the precious place in the queue without so much as a by-your-leave.

'You go to Hell,' Jack muttered to the back of the man's coat.

'Kick a hole in his box,' came the whispered advice from the boy behind.'Smash his bloody box in. Go on!'

But before Jack's indignation could manifest itself physically or otherwise, the wide metal gates opened and the queue shuffled forward, sacks in hand.

The trolleys, and Jack's bike, had to be left near the gates. When his turn came, he handed up his sack to a workman on the platform above a big chute. He also handed over his sixpence. The man filled the chute and the coke tumbled noisily down; choking, filthy dust coming with it.

He could go then. He dragged the heavy sack to where his bike was and fished in his pocket for his bit of string to tie it up. There were women around him scrabbling amongst the bits which had fallen on to the ground, scraping them up with their blackened hands cupped together and then throwing them into their box. A little extra for free. The man on the platform turned a blind eye.

'Here, love, let's give you a hand wi' that.'

It was one of the women. She helped Jack to hoist his bag across the handlebars. Her fingernails were all broken and cracked; the black had got underneath. He tried not to notice. He was embarrassed for her. He thanked her quickly and moved off, pushing the bike with its cumbersome load.

He would have to scrub himself clean in the scullery before he went to school. He wanted no such signs to remain of his early morning activity. Not that he cared if anyone at St. Aidan's knew that he had been at the gasworks since five o' clock. He was the eldest. His little sisters could not be expected to take a turn. 'It's my way of looking after them,' he told himself. 'My way of making sure that they're alright. As the eldest....I don't mind, I really don't mind,' he repeated. But as he made his laborious way home, the heavy sack exerting its arbitrary will against that of his bicycle, he nevertheless offered up a fervent prayer that the strike would soon be over.

The Town Hall clock was striking seven as he carefully negotiated the back gate into the little yard of the house in Monk Street.

* * *

Number 5, Oakshot Road was where the Reynolds children lived. They had been travelling since well before dawn, crammed into the rear of an old-fashioned Bentley alongside their cousins and the two majestic aunts whose responsibility they had been all summer. The vehicle having pulled to a stop, the three of them piled out, somewhat stiffly, and raced up the steps to the front door, not waiting for either of the aunts to give them permission. Once they were safely inside, their father drove the rest of his passengers on to their destination a few streets away.

The ensuing excitement in Oakshot Road was not just because the children had returned after being away since Easter, in the family's Welsh farmhouse, but also because they were all due to go to a very special wedding on the coming Saturday.

They had an inkling of the almighty fracas that this pending alliance had caused, despite the fact that they had been away from home so long. Fran had eavesdropped on the mutterings of the aunts and had reported her findings to her siblings. They were aware, therefore, of the dreadful snub to their mother Izzie when an invitation had failed to arrive at the appropriate time from her Mackenzie cousins. These particular Mackenzies were intent, it seemed, on pursuing their elevated isolation. The children were astonished then to hear that they were actually going and had been avid with curiosity ever since.

The facts behind the matter were that, in her turn, Izzie's mother had blotted her copybook. She had married a man much older than herself. This would have been overlooked by the family had he been a Rear Admiral, or even to stretch a point, a Colonel in the army, but he was most decidedly no such thing. He was a policeman. The Mackenzie girls had always seen themselves as having the monopoly on sea captains. It had established itself as a tradition in the family, both in Scotland and later when they had migrated to Liverpool. No trudging on foot from Glasgow for them. They had travelled first class, on the train, their boots not only intact but still impeccably shiny on their arrival.

Not only was Izzie the daughter of an ordinary policeman but to the eternal horror of the family, his career soon came to an abrupt and ignominious end. He was a bridge fanatic and played once too often whilst on duty. It had come to the notice of his superiors that, should the Station itself be broken into when he was involved in a game, the likelihood was that his sole reaction to the intruders would be to ask them not to make a noise on their way out. The concentration on his hand was legendary. Izzie's side of the family had been kept at a cautious distance ever since, despite the fact that the ex-policeman had subsequently made a great success of the small business which he had started with the help of his wife and ultimately left her very comfortably off when, aged ninety nine, he had fallen off a roof he was repairing and transformed her into a far-from-reluctant widow.

Izzie, however, had no intention of letting her superior relatives continue this tiresome feud, nor was she prepared to allow them to get the better of her on this occasion. It was her parish where the wedding was to take place after all. It was a matter of principle on her part. Didn't she run the social side of the church virtually single-handed? Didn't the vicar repeatedly tell all and sundry that he would not know what to do without her?

Her cousins and her aunts had, therefore, been besieged with a vengeance. She had insisted that an invitation was issued. She would not become the focus of neighbourhood gossip and, she had added, neither should they. Their ill-gendered spite would not do them any good to be broadcast throughout a parish in which she had such standing. Eventually she had won. An invitation had grudgingly arrived and for Izzie it was an opportunity not to be lost. Her young daughters were soon to find that out to their great delight.

Once inside the house, they dashed straight upstairs to inspect the rumoured, now actual, new clothes, yelling 'hello!' when they remembered, which was not until they were halfway up, on the first landing. Izzie, they soon discovered, had made them each a new dress and a velour coat in peacock blue trimmed with ruby red. They had never seen anything quite so beautiful, nor ever possessed anything so grand. New hats from the local milliners were there to be tried on, under her supervision, and they were even invited to look at themselves in the big Cheval mirror in their parents' room, should they refrain from dancing around and pull themselves together.

There, carefully laid out on the bed, was the outfit Izzie had made for herself and the hat ordered, most definitely not from any local source, but specially from Bond St. in London. The girls were not allowed to breathe on it, let alone touch it. Izzie had felt that it was on her head, literally, that the honour of the Reynolds rested and she had spent a small fortune in addition to working her fingers to the bone.

Izzie was a capable woman. She was also a strong woman. When, in 1917, she had received the telegram that her husband, Fa, (not a sea-going man as it happened), was missing, presumed dead, she had refused to believe it. All his brothers had been killed, all his sisters were widowed. He *had* to come back. She was so convinced of this that she had refused to take the miserable twelve shilling pension due to her as a war widow. In addition, she considered the amount a total denigration. His life must have been worth more than that. She would not demean him or herself by accepting it.

Together with her sister Alice, she immediately took the lease on an empty shop and stocked it up with wool. It prospered, for she had a good head for business and wool she knew about. It was also in great demand. She gave up the house where she had gone as a bride and moved in to the rooms above the shop.

This was where she was, with her two children, Neville and Dorothea, when in August 1918 she received a letter from Fa's friend Joe. He wrote that he had seen Fa! Joe had actually seen him in the P.O.W. camp where he had been taken. He had had no idea that Fa had been there too, in the hospital. But they had been attacked, from the air, bombarded by their own Air Force and the prisoners hurriedly evacuated. That was when he had seen him, marching away from the burning huts, his eyes and head heavily bandaged, but Joe had called to him from his line and the unmistakable, distinctively cheeky wave had come back. Fa was alive!

It was proof of a sort but the reason Izzie had been convinced that the contents of the letter were true was that there was no-one else called Fa. He had been called by that name for as long as anyone could remember. Nobody knew when it had first started, probably when he was at school. His initials were F.A.R., a fact likely to have proved irresistible to his peers. There was not a time when he had been called anything else. What other man would have answered to that name? None!

And it had been true. He had come back almost a year later, having taken all that time to recover from his wounds, and their third child, Fran, had been born in the rooms over the shop before they had moved to the big house on Oakshot Road. The business which he had inherited from his father was run from there and Izzie had helped to get it back on its feet with the proceeds from her particular war effort. It was now booming! Hence the Bond St. hat.

She shooed the girls off, back to their own room. When she was alone she tried it on again and admired the velvet flowers adorning the front of it. If it had had a feather she would have cocked it in the direction of the Mackenzies. She and Fa had come through and business was better than it had ever been. The miners' strike had meant that hauliers and carriers were in great demand and hauliers and carriers was the business that they were in. She was looking forward to the wedding. She did not often show off but she had every intention of doing so on that day.

She prayed that Fa would not be late. If the trains started to run again before the weekend there would be all that extra on top of everything else. She fussed and fretted about it, although there was not the slightest hint that the miners intended to inconvenience her by returning to work within the week. She had persuaded herself that Fa would undoubtedly be kept late and she was already seriously put out. She had coped with his purported death like a heroine; she had been overjoyed at his return and was able to sustain the pretence that his scars did not exist as if she had been a euphoric young bride, but she would not have him exposing her to a whiff of criticism from the Mackenzies. Particularly not on Saturday, when they would all be out in force. *That* she could not cope with!

Practicalities, however, had to take precedence over her self-inflicted anxieties.

'You must be hungry,' she said to the rosy-faced girls. 'I've done a second breakfast for you downstairs. Be quick now or Neville will have eaten most of it, knowing him.'

* * *

Meanwhile, in the house on the Esplanade, Stella had resumed her look-out post at the window whilst she awaited her call for breakfast. She dare not go down on her own.

The fog had begun to lift and the Wirral emerged as a long dark strip across the water with mounds of grey behind it. She wondered whether that could be the mountains of Wales, but it was probably just clouds.

Her mother had said that she would take her to Wales.

She sighed again. It was a bad thing to wish that she could have stayed behind. She would hardly ever see her mother if she had, and she didn't want that. But neither did she want to be with this stranger that her mother had married. Her new stepfather.

She was not used to men. She knew Uncle Lonsdale and Mr Mason, of course, who did the caretaking at the Foundation and cooked the food for them all. He had been there since Aunt Maddy had started the Foundation after the war. Stella was used to *him;* she loved him, and his son Dee, who was really called Dennis, after the Captain who had been killed. The Captain had been Mr Mason's commanding officer. He had also been Aunt Maddy's fiancé, Dennis Stanhope. She supposed that the Foundation would not have been there at all if he had not been killed. But nobody talked about it. Nobody talked about anyone who had died then. Dee Mason, for instance, had lost his mother. No-one had told them how. He just didn't have one. It was mostly fathers whom the children had lost. They had all lost someone, that was why they were there, but she could not recall any of them ever *finding* a father, or a mother. Except herself.

‘Good morning, darling. Oh, splendid, you’re dressed! Quickly now, come down to say good-bye to Uncle Lonsdale. He’ll be off soon.’

Her mother had her head round the doorway. She was smiling. That, and the brightness of her pale gold hair, was as good as a light in the darkness of the room. Then she came forward and kissed Stella as she helped her down from the window seat.

‘Hurry now, we have to go and fit your new school clothes this morning as well, remember.’

Stella did remember. Her heart sank at the thought of a new school. But there was another week yet. She would not think about it for another week, this day-school where she might, or might not, fit in.

Wishing desperately that she could actually go with him, she ran down the great stairs to have her last hug from her mother’s friend. They stood at the front door to watch Lonsdale drive away. It did not take long for the car to be out of sight, yet they remained for a while on the doorstep, each tightly holding the hand of the other. Then they turned and went into the breakfast room.

Dr. Bundenell was standing to one side of a sturdily burning fire, his hands behind his back. He was a slightly built man with a lean, classically handsome face. But only his mouth seemed to smile, revealing small, even teeth. His eyes were not smiling. They were not looking at her. Not directly.

Stella shuddered involuntarily, as if she were cold.

He motioned to her to take her place at the table. She shifted her gaze to the rest of the room: a large, heavily curtained window, two green leather chairs by the fire, a gleaming brass fender and, to one side of that, a brimming coal scuttle. She wanted to find out where it had come from. If there was no coal for the trains, where had that come from? But she didn’t dare to ask.

She was unsure where to sit. Her mother caught her eye and patted the seat of the chair next to her.

During breakfast, whilst the doctor talked with her mother, she pecked intermittently at a piece of toast. She took tiny little bites, nervous about making a noise as she chewed. Compared with the dining room at the Foundation, this room was echoingly empty, apart from the sound of Dr. Bundenell’s voice as he deplored the iniquity of the miners in holding the country to ransom and congratulated himself on his foresight in filling the cellar with coal during the summer when, apart from anything else, it was cheaper.

Stella was glad that she hadn't asked him herself. She had not understood most of the words he had used, in fact, but she knew that she did not like the way he said them. And he would not look at her. His eyes slid away from her face as though she had some ugly mark there which was causing him offence. She found herself dabbing at her mouth with her napkin, constantly.

An unfamiliar clumsiness took hold of her in proportion to the incipient dread creeping through her limbs. 'He is not *nice,*' she thought. 'This new father I have found, I do not think that he is really very nice.'

The rest of her uneaten toast remained on her plate.

* * *

The fog had lifted by the time Jack arrived for his first day at St. Aidan's, resplendent in his brand-new uniform recently acquired from the local Gent's Outfitters, (modestly named 'The Grand Clothing Hall'). His mother's admonitions as to preserving its pristine condition were still ringing in his head, his skin rosy from the energetic scrubbing it had recently been party to.

The school was highly prestigious and places were scarce, but Jack was now part of it. Its boys were the pride of the city. One of them was the organist at the Anglican cathedral in Liverpool, even though he was a Catholic. More importantly, its football team won every championship for miles around.

St. Aidan's had once been a manor house which had been given to the priests after the war by a grateful Catholic family. Jack knew that there was supposed to be something interesting about the circumstances, some 'When you're old enough' story, about which the boys had created various implausible myths. It was now a bit scuffed and shabby in places from a generation of schoolboys going through it but the first impression that Jack got on his arrival was unexpectedly mundane. It was the all-pervading smell of wax-paraffin which had been used to transform the wooden floorboards into a hazardous skating rink, a fact which Jack discovered when he attempted to walk on them.

Running was forbidden. Genuflection was essential when passing along the chapel corridor. At the exact spot where the Sacred Host was housed inside, on the alter, priests, masters and pupils alike had to halt their progress to the classrooms and cross themselves as they bent one knee to the floor. Boys had been expelled for forgetting to do so. On the plus side, it was a good wheeze to get into the chapel choir because you went round the feeder schools on a rota and you always got a good cup of tea and a bun with jam and cream in it. Jack knew about that, he had heard the St. Aidan's boys sing at his old school. He had never seen them getting cream buns though. All he had ever got from singing in the choir there was a packet of Pontefract Cakes for being the best soloist. He had eaten them all at once and the prize had turned on him. It had given him the runs for days.

All essential information was imparted to him by Pinny McLaughlin. Once, when they had both been in the Junior School together, Jack's friend had swallowed a safety pin with spectacular effect and had been called Pinny ever since. Nobody remembered his real name, which was just as well as he had always hated it. He had not enjoyed being a Mick. It had been apt to draw unsavoury epithets to it on more than one embarrassing occasion.

Although a year younger than Pinny, Jack was in the same form. He had been allowed to go up to St. Aidan's at ten because he was clever. Pinny had forgiven him for this distinction a long time ago. Besides, it had its advantages; Jack thought up such good ways of keeping out of trouble. Ways to avoid getting caught, for instance. But he hadn't this time! It was Pinny who had wheedled out of the older boys all the unspoken rules which one usually learnt about only by breaking them; those traditions and rituals which new boys were expected to know by telepathy. Pinny held no truck with telepathy. He had done his ground work thoroughly.

As they were coming out of chapel, Pinny signalled to Jack to meet him outside at breaktime. Jack, equally surreptitiously, signalled confirmation.

When he got out there, groups of older boys were in the courtyard throwing stones at the huge pear tree which dominated the area of space. The pears were hardly worth the squabbling effort of collecting once they had dropped to the ground. They were not yet ripe and were small, bitter and hard. The tree was decidedly ancient and had almost given up the contest with the hundreds of boys who had attacked it in its time. Nevertheless, the barrage of stones went up in waves, almost as if there had been a given command. The boys on the sidelines shouted encouragement to those with artillery. Jack was with them, hardly daring to join in, not having been invited to do so and knowing his place as a new boy. Not so Pinny. He was in there with the best.

Jack was looking upwards, attempting to trace the success, or otherwise, of Pinny's stone.

'You lads there! The boldness of you, you creatures! Will you stop that now?'

It was Fr. Cyril. The boys disappeared as fast as bread off a plate in any one of their houses with a family of growing boys in it, but one stayed behind to have a last fling, hoping there was time. It was this boy's sharp-edged stone which hit Jack a stinging blow on the side of his head and knocked him down. He had not seen it coming. Blood was trickling down to his ear, threatening to ruin the collar of his new green blazer.

He was holding his hand over the wound in a vain attempt to stop the flow when Fr. Cyril reached him. He ducked, half expecting a cuff from the priest but it didn't come.

'Will you get along upstairs with you now and have that seen to? Do you know where to go?'

'No, Father.'

'For the love of God! It's a fine mess you're in!'

He pulled out a rather grubby handkerchief from the pocket of his cassock and put it to Jack's head.

'Here. Will you straighten up now. Your head's not going to fall off at all!'

Jack had no intention of straightening up. Even if his head stayed to one side forever he was not going to get blood on his blazer. He was convinced that his mother would add a few of his brains to the unforgivable stain if he did. As the priest bent towards the boy, Jack noticed that there were the remains of several days' dinner on the loose panel of his habit which fell towards him. Round blotches, each the size of a half-crown. Probably soup.

Fr. Cyril obviously did not get it in the neck for making a mess of *his* clothes. Jack felt that life was decidedly unfair.

The priest straightened up to his full height.

'Danny McGuire! I can see you there behind that wheelbarrow. Jesus, Mary and Joseph! The first day and some eedjit's left a barrow in the yard. Lord help us all, it never gets any better! Will you be out of there now and take this youngster up to the labs to Mr Rimmer.'

There was no movement from behind the wheelbarrow. Fr. Cyril took a step towards it, dragging Jack with him.

'Out of there, you young divil, before I have the life out of yer!'

Danny McGuire emerged, looking sheepish, his jaws still working the residue of stolen fruit. He was a handsome boy when his cheeks were not puffed out like dormouse pouches. As Jack did, he also wore a new blazer, still looking shop-fresh, not incipiently scruffy and creased as those were which were on the backs of the more belligerent First Years. He had new boots as well, good boots; ones made of real, supple, shiny leather. His father owned a pub. They were just about the only ones who were not distressed by hard times: publicans and bookies. You could always tell who they were.

Fr. Cyril gave Danny a smart smack on the ear; leather boots or no leather boots, it did not impress him one bit. A spray of half-chewed pear shot out of the boy's mouth like spit. The priest grunted and shoved them both off and then stood by whilst Jack was escorted inside the school building through the side entrance.

The two boys made their way to the top of the house to the First Aid Post in the laboratories. Danny McGuire did not just think himself superior, he *was* superior. He knew the way for one thing. But he was not renowned for any graciousness in his nature. He did not consider it fitting to apologise to Jack for causing his injury. He did condescend to speak to him on this occasion, however, for what it was worth.

'What are you doing hanging around with that scruffy-looking bugger, Pinny McLaughlin?'

Jack took this to be a rhetorical question, had he known what a rhetorical question was. In the event he decided that it did not deserve an answer. Traipsing upstairs behind Danny it seemed to him that even the twinkling boots had a sneer to them. Forcing his head to stay on one side made him feel vaguely sick as he struggled on. He pondered to himself what would have happened if he had broken his leg. It was a long way up. The labs were on the third floor. Still, it would have saved him the problem of the spreading bloodstain.

When they arrived, Danny pushed Jack through the door and made his escape. He was not going to hang around to be in line for any blame which might come his way.

Mr Rimmer was at the far end of the room, setting out test tubes on a long bench. They stood in neat rows in a wooden frame. He looked up and noticed Jack.

'Been in the wars, have we sonny?'

Jack nodded.

'Yes, sir.'

Mr Rimmer took a big white box with a red cross on it from one of the cupboards.

'Let's see what we can do for you then.'

He examined Jack's head, gingerly removing the blood-sodden handkerchief and poured iodine on to a piece of cotton wool. It stung madly as it came into contact with the wound and it stank enough to make Jack sneeze. When it was all over and Jack had a startlingly white pad strapped to his temple, the master indicated that the boy should sit by the window whilst he filled in the form to explain why Jack would be late for his next class.

'Your name?'

'Jamieson, sir.'

'You can straighten your head now, Jamieson, now that I've finished. What form are you in?'

'1 Alpha, sir.'

'Thank you, Jamieson. Now sit down for a bit, you look quite done in.'

The boy did look done in the master thought, as he studied the slight, thin figure in front of the window, the green blazer swamping him. 'First Year,' he concluded. 'Young for it too. Probably all a bit much to take in, a new school all at once. Probably didn't sleep half the night with the excitement and everything. That would explain the dark shadows under his eyes. And it is a nasty cut he has there.'

Jack did not sit down even though he was thinking that it had been such a long day already and that he was so tired he did not know how he was going to get through the rest of it. His legs felt *ancient* ! He flicked the dark lock of hair away from his forehead with a toss of his head and winced. It was a gesture which was habitual to him but he would have to remember not to do it. It made the sticking plaster pull.

He leaned on the window ledge and looked down into the courtyard below. He was directly above the pear tree and he could see, amongst the branches, the top of Pinny's head. He was stuffing pears into his pockets with one hand, precariously balanced on one of the branches, his other hand holding him there.

Jack moved quickly across to Mr Rimmer's bench, his legs miraculously re-energised. He did not want to risk the master having to come across to him. Pinny would inevitably be caught in the act if he did.

'Thank you very much, sir.'

But his plans were thwarted. There was a plopping sound from outside the window. Pears dropping! The master moved across and leaned out.

'You boys! Get to your classes. The bell's gone. And I thought Fr. Cyril had already told you not to throw stones up there. Get along with you!'

He shut the window. Pinny had obviously not been spotted.

Jack had no need to search far for a diversion. An overriding thought, other than the plight of his friend, had resurfaced and visions of his mother having a fit to beat all fits wafted graphically into his mind's eye.

'Please, sir. Is there any blood on my blazer, sir?'

He positioned himself so that the master had to have his back to the window.

'Bless you, no. There are a few drops on your shirt but a bit of a soak will get that out in no time.'

Mr Rimmer smiled at him.

'Now run along, my class will be here in a minute.'

'Yes, sir.'

Jack went down the stairs two at a time. He was anxious about Pinny. Could he still be stuck in that wretched tree? He hadn't been caught though, as far as he knew. He offered up a quick prayer to St. Jude in thanksgiving for blinding Mr Rimmer when he had looked out of the window. St. Jude was a really dependable cove if you could get a line to him.

When he reached the bottom he realized that he hadn't the slightest idea which room he was supposed to be in, or where. He fumbled in his pockets for the timetable card he had been given that morning. It wasn't there. Panic struck despite the fact that Mr Rimmer's note would have got him off lessons for the rest of the morning.

By some miracle, or the further intervention of that dependable cove, the patron saint of hopeless cases, he eventually found himself in front of the master-timetable in the main corridor. He was squinting at it in a futile attempt to unravel its mysteries, when Danny appeared again, this time on his way to the Headmaster's study with a message. He had no difficulty in telling Jack exactly where 1 Alpha was and what they were doing... Maths.

Danny saw the main chance as soon as he spotted Jack peering at the inscrutable hieroglyphics high on the wall. Helping him out would put off the evil moment when he had to face the Headmaster. He was only taking a note from Fr. Michael but one could never tell with Heads in his experience. He might give him an arbitrary cuff over the ear for no reason at all and then inform him that that one 'Was in the bank for next time'. It was a hazardous business taking messages to headmasters. He decided to prolong the discussion with this fortunate boy who had had the accident. Fr. Michael would be sympathetic to that. He was a rare old soft touch, in Danny's opinion.

He searched the notice board for something to prolong the delay. He found it.

'Have you seen that advertisement from those fellows up at Leasowe?'

Jack looked at where Danny's finger was pointing. It was a neatly written postcard requesting boys to offer their services as caddies at the golf club. The payment was 1/6d. per round. It was a small fortune. If Jack could offer that to his mother, the fact that he had got blood on his shirt, even if she did insist on believing that he had been fighting again, would be forgiven. His heart lifted. He could walk to Leasowe. He could go across the fields. It was only a mile or so.

'When do they want them?'

'Weekends, you eedjit! When did you think?'

Jack would go on Saturday. He was saved!

'Thanks, McGuire, I'd better be getting along now.'

He flicked his hair back in involuntary joy and immediately regretted it.

'Well, thanks again. Thanks a lot.'

He ran off, effecting a reasonably decent slide on the polished floor as he went. It left an imposing skid mark on the patina which had been laboriously acquired by the sweat of one of the lay-brothers. Jack failed to notice.

* * *

Stella, new to the neighbourhood, took every chance to wander about exploring in that first week before her school started. She would let herself out through the end of the garden which led directly on to the sea shore and walk for miles through the dunes and along the wide stretches of remarkably firm, ridged sand. She was used to pebble beaches. It amazed her how the sand stuck to her feet even when dry. She would dawdle home along the front, trusting that her shoes would be kicked clean by the time she got back. She was fascinated by the rows of houses along the front, and did her best to spy on the people who lived in them. She tried to be still out at dusk when the curtains had yet to be drawn or the blinds pulled down. Then she could see inside if the lamps were lit. Scores of little mimes enacting themselves just for her or, more often, only empty rooms waiting for something to happen.

The houses were all different in one way or another but what stamped them all, without exception, was that special something that is only be found in seaside towns. Stella could not define it exactly. She thought that it might be something to do with all the different shapes, as if some had been squashed in among the others in a determined effort to get their share of the view. Some had balconies with wrought iron railings or verandahs with slanty roofs supported by pillars of delicate tracery. Tall, thin houses with elongated windows, or fat, squat houses with shutters faded by the sun. She liked these better than the ones at the far end of the front where the promenade, having been called Marine Drive for most of its length, inexplicably changed into Beach Lawn. There were big solid houses there, painted white, dazzling in their immensity. These had a little park between them and the shore. You had to have a key to get in and the high retaining wall on the other side, facing the sea, was also impossible to breach. Stella had tried it with a singular lack of success. There were iron railings cemented into the top.

Once, when she was wandering along the front hoping for an unlikely gap in the railings, she saw an intriguing sight. A massive old motor car drew up ahead of her. The hood was down. Several small heads formed two perfect rows in the back until the vehicle stopped and they all emerged to wait demurely on the pavement accompanied by two very large ladies in suitably imposing hats, one of whom had the key to the gate. The whole group disappeared inside the park and the car drove away.

Stella ran as fast as she could back to the beach wall and climbed up, clinging on to the bottom of the railings for dear life. From her vantage point she could see the children in the distance, playing now, their elders walking sedately along the winding path behind them. Stella hung on as long as she could until the ache in her arms became unbearable. She dropped down on to the sand and examined the condition of her shoes. Sitting with her back against the wall she took out her hanky, spat on it and attempted to disguise the scuffing which had appeared all round the toes. She did not care about the dressing down she would get on her return. It would be worth it. She had liked watching the children in secret.

She was coming to depend on spying and she did it because she was lonely. She had always been one of many, loved and cherished by the adults who ran the house on The Green, the focal point of the little Hampshire village where she had spent most of her young life. It was a strange feeling to be one on her own. Mourning for the loss of her friends, she tried hard to tell herself that it was wonderful to be with her mother every day, which it was, but her mother was bound up with her new husband.

Stella considered it a great bonus that the doctor did not seem to be at home very often. He was besotted by his bugs in his laboratories; he had promised to take her to the University to see them. The Bug Man in his Bug House. She was positive that she did not want to go. She prayed that she would not be obliged to. When he was at home, she tried to avoid him whenever she could. If he took hold of her hand she wanted to snatch it away. It didn't feel right, the way he did it. Nor did the tickling fingers creeping across her knee, hidden by the cloth, when she was sitting at table. It made her want to kick out and hurt him. She didn't of course. She had been well taught not to be hurtful to others. Aunt Maddy had instilled that into all of them from their earliest days. The worst thing that one could possibly do was to hurt others, she had said. One had to be polite at all times, even to people one did not necessarily like. That injunction was a bit of a burden for Stella at the moment. It even made the imminent arrival of her trunk less exciting than it would ordinarily have done, it seemed to her.

The house on the Esplanade, and the one adjoining it on the other side, was back to front. The imposing features, in terms of large windows and the doors on to the terrace, faced the sea. What one saw from the road was what would, in the natural order of things, have been the rear of the house. The breakfast room window overlooked a patch of garden, the kitchen and service wing jutted out at right angles from the main bulding. There was a long path to the entrance door and a smaller, tradesman's entrance near the gate. It was through this gate that Stella's trunk was actually delivered just as they were starting breakfast on the following Saturday. The trains had started running again and, once she had heard that, she knew that it would not be long in coming.

She sat near the window and watched as the trunk was rolled in. She could hear the jingling of the bits as the blue roan cob, which pulled the cart, tossed its head in the morning air. It was a pretty cob, perfectly well-behaved except for an impatient little stamp of its hoof when its master disappeared through the door.

He was only a minute or two and then Lou arrived back at the table and Stella could no longer see the little mare as it trotted away from the gate, nor her master as he urged her to 'Look lively, or we'll both be for it!' heading for home at an urgent pace.

Stella too wanted to stamp her foot in impatience as the meal went on interminably. She was desperate to get away and for once she had the perfect excuse. She needed to unpack her things. And she really did want to see if there would be any messages from her friends.

There were. Several. They all said much the same thing; that they missed her very much but were sure that she must be the luckiest girl in the world to have her mother to herself all the time. They envied her her new life but were glad that she was so very, very happy.

She pushed them deep into her pocket after she had read them.

The best thing was a present from Dee Mason: a drawing of the beech tree on the green, rather violent in colour but the shape was exactly right. His scribbled message on the back contained no assumptions as to how she was supposed to be feeling, to her immense gratititude. She put it carefully against the mirror on her dressing table where she could see it all the time.

It then took her half the morning to sort everything else. She and Lou together. Then she said she would go for a walk.

The tide came right up to the dunes when it was in and on this particular Saturday this was the case. A beach walk was out of the question. She decided to venture instead among the patchwork of roads behind the Esplanade to see what she would see.

She was aware that there was a wedding long before she reached the particular church gate. There were several cars festooned with white ribbons and a crowd of people waiting around to see the bride. She waited too, on the opposite side of the road, sitting on the parapet of a low wall to someone's front garden, a cluster of blue hydrangeas behind her head. She sucked one of the pear drops which she had bought from the little corner shop. Her stepfather had forbidden her to go into shops on her own so she had made a bee-line for there first. The pear drops immediately acquired an added piquancy.

Eventually the bride and groom emerged. Her dress was worth the gasps of admiration it elicited from the onlookers but Stella felt that she did not compare with her own mother in terms of looks. Her mother was unique. There was no-one to match Lou in Stella's experience, not even Aunt Maddy, and she was very pretty in a different sort of way. She thought that this bride was very ordinary, but then Stella was biased.

The guests were emerging from the churchyard. Stella stayed where she was for longer than she had intended. Several of the gentlemen were wearing kilts and black velvet jackets and the bridesmaids had the same tartan round their waists as sashes. The younger ones were jumping about, looking for notice; in vain however, as most of the adults were talking and laughing at full pitch, in competition with the pealing of the bells. The little tots had to resort to a one-foot-on, one-foot-off-the-kerb game before a disembodied arm appeared out of the crush and hauled them in, one at a time. Several of the male guests were sidling, rather furtively, Stella thought, to a point further along the railings in order to smoke a cigarette. It was obvious that they were delighted to be released from the confines of the church. Their feet shuffled as they laughed amongst themselves but Stella could not make out a word of what anyone was saying. She did not need to; she was fascinated by the scene just as it was, especially the vicar resplendent in his embroidered cape, talking to a lady in a very expensive-looking hat who did a lot of smiling.

Into her line of vision came two girls in matching blue coats making their way towards the edge of the crowd. Their faces were vaguely familiar. When their brother joined them in his stiff new suit and the big, handsome man who was obviously the father, she knew exactly who they were. It was the family in the car which she had seen at the key park the other day. To her astonishment, she realised that it was the father who had delivered her trunk that very morning. She was tempted to run up to them and tell them who she was, ask them where they lived, but she knew she couldn't. It simply wasn't done. She would have to wait for some sort of introduction but she could not see how that might come about. Dr. Bundenell worked at the University, in the Department of Tropical Medicine. The father of this family delivered trunks. There would be no occasion when they would meet. That impediment was rather more difficult to conquer than defying an instruction about not frequenting corner shops!

A bustle of adults crowded round the girls as a further surge came out of the church. Stella made a decision to go. It was getting cold and she was very conscious of having been sitting on the stone for a long time. She looked back as she got to the turning. The smaller of the sisters had come out beyond the edge of the group and was looking straight at her. Instinctively Stella waved. The girl waved back. A mass of blonde curls framed her face under the peacock blue hat but it was her eyes which were the most striking. Even from that distance, they were the most alert and lively eyes Stella could ever remember seeing.

She turned quickly into the side road and ran home, her hand already in her pocket to touch the carefully folded drawing from Dee. It reminded her so much of Hampshire that she had immediately changed her mind about leaving it to grace the dressing table. From now on it was going to go everywhere with her. She must write to Dee, to thank him, as soon as she got back.

⋆ ⋆ ⋆

Where Jack lived they were surrounded by golf courses, (away from the docks, that is). Leasowe was one of the better ones. That Saturday, bright and early, he had walked across the fields, sure that he would not miss it because it was near the hospital at Leasowe Castle. He had bounced along confidently, swishing the long grass with a stick which was long enough to make-believe it was a golf club, full of delight at the thought of the precious 1/6d. and interpreting the beautiful morning as a sign, a good omen. It was exciting to be facing something entirely new; something which had been beyond his imaginings before this.

Now he was not so sure. He had not known where to go until one of the other boys who had also arrived in good time, told him to tag along with him to the Pro. Shop. There was a kiosk to the side of it. That was where the caddies collected. As the members arrived, they would take their clubs to the Pro. or his assistant, and he would go to the window and request a caddy. The boys would put their hands up and when they were chosen the gentleman's golf clubs would be handed out through the window and off they would go to the first tee. This had been going on all morning and Jack was still standing there. The other more experienced boys had commandeered the bench, as of right. It looked as though he might never get a turn. Disconsolate, he made patterns in the sandy soil with his stick and pondered on the obstacles attached to ambition.

Towards late afternoon, just as some of the boys coming in with the returning players were handing over their irons across the bench inside the window, a latecomer arrived and asked for a caddy. Jack was asked to come forward. His heart beating fast and an unwelcome flush darkening his cheeks, he stepped up to the kiosk and the bag was handed out.

'Just a minute, sonny.'

He had the bag halfway out of the window.

'Put it down, put it down.'

Jack did as he was told, trying not to look too awkward as the unaccustomed weight of the clubs shifted and the bag tried to swing away from him.

'Now then, laddie, have you caddied before?' The bulky man who might, or might not have been the professional, the Pro. himself, filled the space of the opening and looked at him with an amused smile turning up the corners of his mouth.

'Yes, sir.' Jack mentally crossed himself. That would have to be accounted for in Confession next week! He was not accustomed to telling deliberate lies. He felt bad about it and prayed that it did not show on his face.

'Have you now?'

The golfer was looking away. He seemed to be examining his fingernails. Jack hoped that he was not looking at his watch.

The Pro., (because it was he), leaned his arms on the wooden ledge.

'Well, pick me out a mashie.'

Jack looked at him in disbelief, panic flickering in his nether regions.

'A mashie?'

The man nodded.

Jack tried not to shut his eyes as he appealed, most urgently, to St. Jude for help. He stared at the bag and tried to read the names which were stamped on the back of the clubs. It seemed to take him an interminable age. He could feel both their eyes upon him. If the golfer began to tap his foot he would die of shame. Then, there it was... Mashie!

He pulled it out, relief mixed with a modicum of triumph flooding over him as he held it up.

'You're sure you've caddied before?'

'Yes, sir.'

'Well, go and tell that to the Marines!'

The two men laughed, as did the boys who were still hanging around. Tears of mortification threatened to sting Jack's eyes. He was confused, puzzled. Surely he had got it right?

'Off you go now, my laddo.'

He was being dismissed!

'Harrison, we'll have you.'

As he made his slow way back across the endless fields, he broke the stick across his knee and threw the two pieces as far as he could into the undergrowth. He had not been chosen.

He was not chosen for several weeks but he kept on going up. Not on Saturdays any more. His mother had made a fuss about his absenting himself when there were chores to be done and little ones to be looked after, so he had felt duty bound to stay at home.

Sundays were different. He could go after church if he could swap to early Mass. Jack had been an altar boy since he was eight and he had always served at High Mass at eleven o'clock. He delighted in it. He loved the swinging of the incense, the peculiar odour which lasted and lasted, almost to the end of the week when it would be renewed. He loved the choir and the plain chant, the familiarity of the Latin words, which he had been hearing since he was a babe-in-arms. He would have to sacrifice his coveted place at High Mass and serve at the early morning one where Fr. Coogan got through it as if his life depended on speed-speech! Jack did not approve of Fr. Coogan. He felt that he was lacking in reverence. It was not good enough. Still, he would have to put up with it if he wanted to spend the rest of the day at Leasowe. He would have to sacrifice his dinner too but that was a minor issue under the circumstances.

One of Jack's dominant characteristics, which in many ways had everything to do with the strength of his faith, was what Pinny called his stickability. If he set his mind to something, or he felt that it was incumbent on him to do it, nothing would stop him. Both aspects had attached themselves to the issue of the golf. He had become fascinated by the whole scene, he wanted to be part of it, but most of all he wanted earnestly, wholeheartedly, with every fibre in his body, to go home with the 1/6d. in his hand. He wanted to see his mother's face light up. Things were hard for her and she did not deserve it.

So he sat on the caddies' bench week after week, hoping to be chosen. Sometimes he took a book with him to while away the time but it soon became too cold to sit without gloves. (Reading with one's fingers encased in wool was what he referred to as, 'a mug's game' so he abandoned it).

During quiet periods, the experienced caddies cleaned the irons in the hut. He tentatively offered to help and was told, in terms that verged on the trenchant, that he would have to supply his own emery paper if he was really serious about his offer. There was no payment for the work. He couldn't expect a reward of any kind.

Jack was so relieved to be out of the cold that he would have paid them for the privilege if he'd had the means to do so. The next weekend he turned up with his sheet of emery paper carefully folded in his pocket and set to with a will.

Scraping mud off golf clubs and then rubbing up the irons until they shone was warming work but it was, by its very nature, a mindless task. The other boys were wary of him. They did not understand why he was doing it when he was bound not to get anything out of it. Their gentlemen might give them a tip if they noticed the effort which had been made, (they didn't always!) but Jack didn't have a gentleman. He was doing it for nothing. They found that strange, so they told him what to do and then kept their distance, exchanging telling glances over the bent head of this infiltrator.

Jack, as he worked on, thought about the elusive fee. It began to acquire an almost mythical significance, especially in relation to his mother.

She was no stranger to privation, Jack's mother. She had been brought up on a small farm in Machrihanish. Her grandparents had found they were no better off at all when they had chosen the west coast of Scotland to flee to from Ireland, during the time of the famine. It had been no less a struggle for her parents in their turn. Jack had been told many times, especially when he or Molly asked for anything extra, how hard it had been. And the babies had kept coming, there were four below him and his nearest sister now. Perhaps if he could contribute a bit extra it would mean that she could have something nice for a change, for herself. But she never would; she never did. If there was ever anything to spare it went into the Poor Box in church. It pleased her to do that. Jack didn't mind if the whole 1/6d. ended up there. At least she would have been able to make the choice. It was important to Jack, that after all she had gone through, was going through, his mother might have a choice.

He rubbed on vigorously, the effort and his hopes keeping out the seeping cold.

Gradually the other boys learned to trust him. They realized that he had no designs upon their territory. He was as straight as a die. They began to include him in their conversations. This was how he came to learn what all the clubs were and how he had made the mistake that had perplexed him since that first, disappointing day. He had picked out a mashie alright, but a mashie niblick, the wrong one altogether. He blushed to think of it. They talked about the game: which club was best for what, the areas of the course that caused most trouble, the players who were the best to caddy for and the ones whom they had cause to dislike. Jack's solitary thoughts became a thing of the past. He felt that he belonged.

But he still had not earned a penny piece.

One Sunday, late on, just before the last round could hope to be played before darkness fell, he was sitting on the bench with Teddy Marwood. Even though Teddy was what was termed a first class caddie, he condescended to talk to Jack. He had watched the boy over the weeks and he could not help but admire his pluck in sticking to it. He was a good 'un, he had thought to himself. He was worth bringing on. When his booking arrived, a Dr. Davis, he had brought a companion with him. Jack was the only option open to this guest if he wanted a caddie, which he did.

'Stick with me,' Teddy whispered to him out of the side of his mouth as they made their way to the first tee. 'I'll see you right.'

He not only saw Jack right, he coached him as they went along, Jack frantically trying to remember it all and wishing that his boots did not leak.

When they returned almost three hours later, with the night closing in fast, Jack waited behind Teddy at the kiosk for his payment. He saw what Teddy got: 2/6d ! And the doctor gave him 6d. as a tip.

To Jack's eternal gratitude, Teddy shared his tip with him. He was worth dying for was Teddy, he thought, as he stumbled home, tired as a dog, but happier than he had felt for years. He had 1/9d. to hand over to his mother!

That day was the turning point. Next time he was asked for specially and before the month was out his good manners had attracted a Mr. Whitmore. The fact that Jack always said, 'Thank you' and stood quietly by concentrating on the swing with never a fidget had impressed him and Jack ultimately became his 'permanent'. Mr. Whitmore played in the team and when Jack caddied for him during matches, he was invariably given two Three Castles cigarettes and two Glacier Mints. The Three Castles cigarettes were luxurious; they were ten for 8d., hand-made. Jack knew that, and appreciated the fact, so his two were put carefully in his pocket and taken home for his dad. He never broke one, not one; only sometimes did they get a bit crushed and then he meticulously straightened them out before handing over his prize. The Glacier Mints he ate on the way home. Mr. Whitmore was The Tops.

2. Music Making
1927

JACK'S HEAD WAS always full of music. The house had resounded with it all his life. His mother's singing was with him wherever he went, the refrains repeating themselves in the recesses of his mind. She sang haunting Celtic melodies even when she was happy. She had been happy in Glasgow in the prosperous days. The Clyde had been alive then, the shipyards ringing with activity day and night and the men full of pride in what they achieved. They had achieved such miracles. Warships were turned out as if they had been toys for Christmas and damaged ones refloated in such a short space of time that no one could believe it. One of the first things she had bought, when she was newly married at the beginning of the war, had been a gramophone. It had been an enormous extravagance at the time but she had exonerated herself by quoting the Chinese proverb, 'If you have the money to buy two loaves, buy one loaf and a hyacinth.' The precious machine, together with the wax recordings of operatic arias, had travelled down with the furniture when his father had ultimately been able to send for them. That was long before his four sisters and his little brother were born. It was when ships were no longer the dependable lifeline they had always, always been. And the men were on the move, pinning their hopes on the demand for ocean-going liners to provide them with work, bemused and troubled by the unprecedented inactivity in the yards.

Jack had been two when he and his mother had come down by train to Merseyside. He did not remember it but he sensed that he must have been singing. He was always singing; so was his mother. When they weren't singing they hummed bits from the arias or popular symphonies: Beethoven, Rossini, Brahms; and Jack could whistle before he could walk. The story went that on that momentous journey he had refused to wear the little hat that matched his sailor suit and he had insisted on keeping it on his knee. By the time they had reached Liverpool, Lime Street it was brimful of silver sixpences, with only an occasional copper to disturb the sheen. His talent had never since reaped such rewards.

He was about to sing for his supper at the golf club concert however. Each year the caddies put on the entertainment for the Members' Dinner and this time Jack had been included. It had not gone without notice that he had the ability to mimic the swing of every member of the club with startling accuracy. The potential for a great deal of fun at the members' expense had proved irresistible to the top caddies who were organizing the event. One or two had old scores to settle and they looked upon Jack Jamieson as a gift from the Gods. He, in his innocence, had little idea of what they were up to when they presented him with the list of victims. He just earnestly practised, evening after evening, in the field behind the rows of back gardens belonging to the houses in his street. He practised with the most treasured possession he had ever had, his first club, an ancient cleek which he had swapped the previous June for The Chatterbox Annual one of his Scottish aunts had sent him for Christmas. From then on he had lived with that club in his hand. The Chatterbox Annual was still going the rounds of the other caddies, more dog-eared and tattered by the day.

The request to represent the less-than-perfect characteristics of his betters for the amusement of the audience at the concert had a lasting effect on Jack. For one thing it taught him what not to do and the quality of his own swing became cause for comment, not only amongst the caddies, but the Captain himself. The other was as a result of the awkward nature of the field. He had to drive on the diagonal if he was not to lose the one and only ball which he possessed. He watched that ball like a hawk. For ever more he was renowned for the accuracy of his 'eye'.

Besides being the unwitting instrument of the caddies' revenge, he had been asked to sing. He had chosen the 'Londonderry Air.' It was one of his favourites but he felt that it was all spoilt by the fact that the boy in the song was called Danny. The McGuire of that name had just got him into terrible trouble at school and if the song had not been printed in the programme as sung by Jack, he would have refused to do it. He would have changed it to something more appropriate: one of the other Irish songs about betrayal and such-like disloyalty. There must be one that would fit the case.

Danny McGuire was not worthy of the 'Londonderry Air' this week. He might possibly have redeemed himself by the following week or Jack's good nature might have overcome his fury with him by then, but Danny McGuire was certainly not Jack's 'Danny Boy' at this particular juncture.

There were two gardens surrounding St. Aidan's, one belonged to the school and was cultivated by a team of boys who sold the produce to augment the school funds. (They were famous for it.) The other belonged to the house next door. It was a large garden which contained a line of greenhouses behind the high wall which separated it from the school. Unfortunately the height of the wall did not prevent balls of all kinds finding themselves on the wrong side of it. The gardener quite understood this phenomenon but was not prepared to spend a large proportion of his time returning them. Instead he collected them in an old barrel and when he was ready, he would distribute them. The boys could never be sure when this would be. It was entirely according to his whim.

Danny and Jack had become bosom pals throughout the year since the propitious pear tree incident and the tip about Leasowe. At this point they were exasperated. They had been reduced to playing marbles for weeks and seemed to have been waiting for the gardener's share-out for ever. There was nothing for it. They would have to go over the wall. *They* would retrieve the balls. If they could reclaim enough they might become legends in their own time, Danny had stated conspiratorially. According to him this would stand them in very good stead for future favours from the rest of the school. Jack was a bit sceptical about this element but he was prepared to go nevertheless. He was sick of the sight of marbles.

They chose the far end which was in shadow and over they went with consummate ease, Danny's exceptional boots looking rather more commonplace once he had reached the top. They had no difficulty in locating the barrel. With the speed of light, dozens of tennis balls were under their jerseys, the hems tucked firmly into their trousers and the belts pulled in a notch and then they were on their way back. Jack had rolled over the parapet of the wall, his jersey bulging out in the most extraordinary, uncontrollable manner and had landed on his feet. That was when he, and everyone in the whole playground, heard the crash. Danny had put his foot through a pane of the greenhouse.

What followed next was inevitable. Danny was caught sliding back down the wall, balls dispensing themselves from his clothing as if from a machine designed for that sole purpose. The duty master's hand had him by the scruff of the neck as he was dragged along, his shirt-tails flapping in a most uncharacteristic fashion. Jack had merged into the crowd of boys milling round the scene competing for the trophies so unexpectedly made available to them. Danny's fate, it seemed, was of secondary importance. Jack felt safe for the moment. His confidence was further enhanced when Danny, as he was being marched away, mouthed over his shoulder, 'I won't give you away!'

Jack had let the balls in his possession surreptitiously join the others on the ground, slipping only two into his own pockets. He sauntered casually across the square of yard whistling the high notes from 'Danny Boy', thinking about how lucky he was to have been chosen to sing in the concert on the coming Saturday.

'Jamieson!'

A first floor window had been opened with considerable force. Mr Murphy was framed within it.

'Up here, NOW!'

It had obviously taken him less than ten pathetic seconds to break Danny down. Mr Murphy wasn't even frightening. He taught English and in Jack's opinion, was a very sensitive man. Danny should be ashamed of himself. Jack would fight to the death rather than tell a tale on a friend. He had almost done that in his time. He would have faced Commander Stewart, the most formidable of the lay staff, and protected Danny had he been called upon to do so. Giving in to Mr Murphy indeed!

It was thoughts such as these which filled his head during his solo on that Saturday night. There was a heart-melting quality in his pure soprano voice at the most ordinary of times. That night, mixed with just a hint of anguish at his loss of faith in his friend, the stinging around his left ear, (not a second of Jack's earlier exposé of the members' foibles had escaped the Pro. and he had taken prompt action), Jack's rendition of 'Danny Boy' brought tears to the eyes of more than one of the judges. He won the prize for Best Performance.

More than one influential member was to recall Jack's name in years to come as a result of that night. Unbeknown to Jack, Danny MacGuire and the gleefully triumphant caddies had done him sterling service. He forgave them just the same.

* * *

The piano teacher's house was just round the corner from where Stella lived. It was the prime reason that the woman had been chosen; Stella could walk there and back. It was a dark house, the front rooms facing north, and full of dismal, lumpy furniture, an inheritance of which Miss Blanchard was proud. She saw no reason to change anything.

Stella did. She hated going there. For a whole year it had depressed her and this particular morning had nothing to recommend it. It was a miserable, louring day. The sky sagged with impending rain. Through the window of the upstairs sitting room where the piano was, Stella could see great, heavy, pendulous clouds. The lesson was not going well.

'Pay attention, Stella! The nocturne please!'

Stella placed her fingers on the keys and peered at the sheet of music on the stand. Miss Blanchard was sitting next to her on the double piano stool and she was intensely aware of the slightly unpleasant odour emanating from the knitted frock. She could not define it. It was like ancient mouldy apples. It was nothing like the smell of Edward Bundenell, not at all, but it made her want to squirm away just as she did when he would steal quietly up behind her and she would jump as his knee pressed itself between her legs. She would smell his smell then: soap and a faint odour of formaldehyde, his whole body covering her, his breath wafting her hair. The terror was where his hands would search. And she could not cry out. The smell of him suffocated her then.

Her playing detiorated into a series of desperate thumps. She should not be here. She needed to get into a bath. The need was urgent. She should not be here.

'Stop! Stop at once! Now, begin again, please. With more soul, girl! Where is your soul?'

Miss Blanchard rapped Stella's knuckles with the little baton which she used for pointing at the notes on the sheet music. Stella turned resentfully, wondering what this particular woman might know about soul.

She gazed blankly at the thin face glowering into hers. The colour of putty. A lack of charity about the lips. It was a frowning, dissatisfied face which could never blossom.

Stella dropped her eyes and attempted to play.

She was frightened of the music. If she played it properly it threatened to reveal what actually *was* in her soul. She did not want Miss Blanchard to know that. She didn't want anybody to know that. Truthfully, she did not want to know herself. She did not understand why that was. But she would try to play this piece respectably. Then perhaps, she could go home.

She hit a wrong note. The baton came down again across her fingers, more sharply this time.

'Again!'

She prepared to start once more, then an angry defiance took precedence over her need to get out of that suffocating room.

'No!' she said.

Stella, flushed and challenging, was also frustrated by her own lack of control. She should just have gone on with the game. The game she played all the time, of pretending that everything was alright. She sat bolt upright staring unseeingly at the sheets of music.

'No. I won't!'

Miss Blanchard turned a storm-cloud purple. In truth, she disliked Stella. She envied her striking looks and her youth and her endless future. She envied the house where she lived and the fact that her stepfather was a university man. Stella had everything. Miss Blanchard saw herself as having lost whatever might have been.

'You baggage! You spoilt, impudent baggage!' It was a shriek, so strident it was offensive even to her own ears.

She was given to the histrionic gesture. Being dramatic appealed to her sense of outrage at the injustice in the world. Her back arched, her eyes turned upwards to the ceiling, she spread her fingers along the keyboard and hammered out a dramatic chord.

Stella, before she knew what she was doing, slammed the lid down on to Miss Blanchard's hands.

Lou was immediately called for. There was no question that the woman was in hysterics. Even so she managed to convey that Stella was a monster, an impossible pupil; her fingers, her only means of livelihood, had been viciously broken. She would not consider being in the same room as the girl for another moment. Stella would have to go.

Lou established that the fingers were not in fact broken but she had to concede that they were badly bruised. She paid Miss Blanchard for the whole term and Stella was sent downstairs whilst she offered placatory apologies. When Lou left, she was in no doubt as to Miss Blanchard's opinion of the fiend which she had spawned.

Mother and daughter did not exchange a word on the way home and when they reached it, Stella went upstairs without prompting. Lou could hear taps running.

She went into the drawing room and looked out across the grey water to the darker grey of the headland of the Wirral. Streaks of silver appeared in the sky as the rain clouds moved off towards Wales but it was almost monochrome, the view from the window, with a solitary dredger on the skyline.

She shook her head in incomprehension. She was at a loss to know what to do about Stella. She was not even sure that she actually knew her these days.

When the child had been born, Lou had been alone in London. It was during the last days of the war and it had been Maddy, and Maddy's Aunt Hart, who had rescued them. They had taken Lou 'in hand' and it was their love, their kindness, which had dispelled all the rage and the overwhelming sense of hopelessness which had possessed her. If Maddy could cope after all she herself had lost, then so could Lou. Not long after, Maddy had turned her father's house into the memorial to her dead fiancé, a kind of permanent residential school, for children whose only parent had been widowed, or, in some cases, abandoned. Stella and Dee Mason had been amongst the first occupants.

Lou was free then, to train properly yet spend all her time off at The Green. She had shared in Stella's growing up as the other parents did with their children. Maddy made it all happen. The weekends seemed like one huge, great party with all the comings and goings. Stella had been happy, well-adjusted, gregarious; without a care in the world. And then Lou had met Edward.

The child had not been the same since they had left Hampshire. She had gradually become silent, secretive almost, and she obviously loathed the select little private school which Edward had chosen. He had strongly disapproved of Maddy's progressive ideas, of her insistence on educating boys and girls together, but more particularly, her lack of discrimination when she took in children regardless of their class. In Edward's opinion, his wife's friend was asking for trouble and he had been quite plain with Lou when he had insisted upon Ince House for Stella. He wanted the best for her he had said. Lou could not understand how she had allowed him to do it, at the time.

Yes, she did. She understood it too well. She had not begun to cross him then. She had been basking in the euphoria of the newly-married. Any thoughts which were in opposition to his she had initially witheld. His consuming interest in finding cures for tropical diseases for instance. She had interpreted that as an interest in humanity at large; a desire to make the world a fitter place. She had been wrong. It was the research that obsessed him and if the results happened to bring him a major prize then that might be considered a real bonus. Edward was ambitious; ruthlessly, coldly ambitious. Nothing, no-one, especially she, was to get in the way. She had retreated in confusion, into herself. Stella, it seemed, had now added violence to *her* withdrawal.

Lou turned away from the window decisively. She would find a new piano teacher immediately. Today.

She had heard about a Mr Morris who, although blind, was rumoured to be excellent. She would find out where he was and hope that he would take Stella on. The more she had to occupy her, the more friends she could make, the better. But, Stella was refusing to make friends; she was hanging on to her Hampshire connections. Here, she remained solitary and would walk for miles along the shore following the tideline, contemplating the debris which had been washed up from the boats, as if it might contain the answer to all that troubled her. Lou would watch her from the upper windows of the house, with an overwhelming sadness which turned her body heavy, her heart to lead.

The incident with the music teacher had produced the same debilitating effect. The finding of Mr Morris became imperative.

Lou decided to take Stella with her and to her relief there was immediate compliance. She explained that the best place to find out the address would be the main Post Office. It was to prove exactly right. The man taught from his house off Crosby Road, they would have to take a taxi. Stella looked suitably remorseful all the way.

They were welcomed in by Miss May, Mr Morris's daughter, who explained that her father was in the middle of a class but if they crept in and positioned themselves on the window seat at the far corner, he would know that they were waiting.

They were shown into an enormous room containing three grand pianos and heaps and heaps of music piled high on every available surface.

Mr Morris was sitting to one side of the piano nearest to the fireplace, his predictably fine-boned hands resting lightly on the well-polished arms of a mahogany carver chair, the inevitable baton held loosely in his fingers beating the time. Sitting at the piano, with her back to them, was a curly-haired girl who was obviously having difficulties with the piece in front of her. On the window seat were the rest of the morning's pupils, there for their edification obviously. Stella immediately recognized that amongst them was the girl she had been seeking for almost a year.

Stella and Lou found a space at the end of the row and waited.

'Hello,' whispered the girl, moving back a place whilst everyone was shuffling up to make room. 'I'm Fran Reynolds and that is my sister Dodo who is making such a mess of that piece at the piano.'

She smiled at them as she squashed in beside Stella.

'She doesn't do her practice.' A slightly breathless pause, 'I've seen you before, I think. Several times. Are you having classes here?'

'I hope so,' was all that Stella had time to say before, 'Shhhhhsh' came whistling towards them from Mr Morris's chair.

He continued to painstakingly explain how the piece should have been handled, drawing in the other pupils by advising them to remember the points he had made. His voice was deep and soft, suggesting endless patience.

'Now Dodo, again.'

To Stella's astonishment, Fran slipped off her shoes and crept quietly from her chair and she was standing next to her sister within the blink of an eye, her right hand resting on her shoulder. As Dodo began to play, Fran played the left hand for her. Both sisters looked amused. Suddenly, with alarming accuracy considering his blindness, Mr Morris's baton was across Fran's fingers.

'Back to your place, imp. Far too clever for your own good!'

Stella flinched, but this had obviously happened before. It looked as though it had become a standing joke. The other pupils were smirking. The sisters laughed out loud. Mr Morris turned his head towards the window and the newcomers.

'Mark that young lady; she will go far.' He paused. 'But not today!'

Everyone shuffled again; this time in amusement.

Before Fran went up to the piano for her lesson, she rummaged through the pocket of her skirt and brought out a stubby pencil. On the back of her music book she wrote: '*He is playing in a concert on Tuesday at St. George's Hall. Will you be able to join us?*'

Stella looked at Lou who nodded. She smiled at her mother with genuine delight and nodded vigorously herself when she turned back to Fran.

By the end of the morning Mr Morris had agreed to take on Stella as a pupil and was highly impressed that she had already arranged to hear his concert.

The following Tuesday, Dodo, Fran and Stella were escorted by the two aunts. They travelled on the overhead railway. It was a new experience for Stella. The concert itself was a revelation.

As the programme progressed she thought that she recognised what Miss Blanchard had meant when she had referred to 'soul'. Mr Morris had revealed his soul through his playing. And it was as if he knew what troubled her own, as if he was trying to tell her. Just her. No-one else.

Guilt began to tarnish some of the enchantment of the evening and brought tears into the corners of her eyes. She had behaved unforgivably to Miss Blanchard. She had allowed her own unhappiness to turn her into something mean and she had hurt an old lady. Miss Blanchard could not help being old and maybe it was some dreadful, appalling thing in *her* past that had made her as she was. Stella decided that she must try to make it up to her in some way. As she surreptitiously blew her nose, she decided that she must apologise, at the very least.

It was the furtive movement of the handkerchief coming from inside Stella's sleeve that caught Molly's eye from across the way. But that wasn't what kept her staring for a second or two. The fascination of two identical peacock blue coats on the companions of the red-headed girl seated along from them on the opposite aisle was what attracted her attention. She nudged Jack for his approval. A severe frown from their mother soon put a stop to any response her brother might have had. The playing of the blind pianist, a phenomenon so enticing to Mrs Jamieson that she had decided to treat her two eldest that night, reclaimed much of their former concentration. Stella, ignorant of the momentary interest she, Fran and Dodo had elicited, continued with her immediate preoccupation. She must, somehow, make amends to the music teacher.

But what she had sensed in the first instance was correct. Miss Blanchard did not possess the remotest hint of a 'soul'. When she used such a term it only referred to the pose of the thrown back head, the hiatus before the removal of fingers from the keys, the over-use of the sound pedal and the swaying of shoulders, the latter preferably clad in a silk shawl, should one be to hand. Miss Blanchard thought that such things represented soulfulness. That was her interpretation of it. She had always lacked perceptive intuition. Had she had it, she would have been other than she was.

That was why, when a pretty posy of flowers appeared on her doorstep with a genuine plea for forgiveness enclosed in the wrapping, she threw the lot into the wastebin. She had no perception of a child's capacity for suffering either.

3. Protests
1932

FRAN AND STELLA, since that chance meeting in their childhood, became an established duo. They went everywhere together, particularly as they rapidly approached the threshhold of being 'grown-up.' More often than not, Dodo would be with them when she got the chance. Compared to the other two she really was a dodo. She fluttered indecisively over every decision and came to depend on the two younger ones as a matter of course. They in turn, protected her from the effects of her intermittent silliness.

In time, this became less possible. Dodo went off to Secretarial College and ultimately to a job. She worked in Southport. The other two often cycled out to join her after work in the summer and they would go to the Lido. Sometimes they went on Sunday mornings but activities on a Sunday were not looked upon with favour by Izzie. They would soon be women, her girls, and she was over-protective. Whilst she was in control, they would be within her sight on a Sunday. Preferably, for part of the day at least, in church.

Stella spent more and more time at the Reynolds' house. Izzie often arranged a party on a Saturday evening when lots of the cousins came. The Mackenzies had grudgingly conceded that the Reynolds had come up in the world. Fran would be at the piano most of the evening so that they could dance, or when the boys preferred to play billiards in the big room at the back which had had the fireplace removed so that there was sufficient room to manoeuvre the cues, the girls played cards. There was always a delicious supper. It was all designed to persuade the girls that it was much more fun to be at home.

Sometimes though, they went to the parties organized by the vicar for what he called, 'the youth' of the parish. These were not really parties but decently chaperoned dances designed to bring the young people together once a month or so, and they were held in the church hall.

Officially, Stella should not have gone. She went with her mother, when they went to church at all, to another parish further along the sea-front, St. Faith's. This was not because her mother was unduly religious but because that was where the piano teacher played the organ and they liked to listen to him. Notwithstanding, Fran insisted that Stella should be included in the Reynolds' contingent for the evenings at St. John's and she was.

These were a constant source of hilarity for Fran and Stella. The aunts, by whose ubiquitous presence the Reynolds offspring and their cousins had long been dominated, were duchesses in aspiration as well as in demeanour. They insisted that the Reynolds girls travelled the two or three streets (certainly no more than five hundred yards) to the church hall in a taxi. The first time Stella had seen them alight from this prestigious vehicle as she approached along the pavement, Dodo and Fran had been hardly recognisable. Their heads had acquired the unequivocal shape of the Marcel Wave. The morning had been spent at Lamport and George's prestigious, and inordinately expensive, Hairdressing Salon. The results were wildly, but somewhat inappropriately, glamorous. The aunts, whose ambitious project it had been, were a breed unto their own, Stella decided. They were also worth their weight in gold; a considerable tonnage of dependable interest between them. The church dances became the highlights of the year as the elderly ladies, via their nieces, competed mercilessly to establish supremacy over their rivals, providing enormous entertainment for Stella and Fran as they did so.

But, the dances did not hold the same fascination for the boys. Every move they made was open to public scrutiny and more particularly to their elders. Neville Reynolds had a much more appealing plan. He got involved with the founding of a local tennis club. The sister of his partner in this project was the object of his increasingly obsessive attention and he did not want his mother to know about it, let alone interfere. There was little likelihood of the aunts turning up there and passing on tales as the existing facilities were far too primitive. Even though he had the money to set about improvements, he chose not to immediately. He set too much store on his privacy.

Neville now worked for his father and apart from the setback of the Wall Street Crash, the business was thriving. That time had been the most threatening. That time the house had not been full of the noise of boisterous youngsters set on enjoying themselves. That time it had had a density of silence that was the stuff of nightmares. Being young he could push it to the back of his mind. Not so Fran.

Fa, she recalled with constant gratitude, had pulled them through. His foresight and Izzie's determination had pulled them through. But it had been a bad time.

When Fa had come back from the war and set about rebuilding the business which he had inherited from his father, he had made a promise to himself. He would employ all ex-servicemen. He even bought old war horses to pull the waggons and used ex-cavalry men in the stables. The other thing he promised himself when outside influences made it hard, like the time of the General Strike, he would not sack a man. And he didn't. He didn't then and he didn't when The Crash came. It had not been easy. There was no work. Men idle. Wages to be paid. Horses to be fed.

He had been so desperate that he had toyed with the idea of accepting an approach from the local undertakers to go into partnership with them. But when he had been requested to go and measure up a man in Blucher Street and found him not yet dead he had protested. He made his protest by pulling out of the prospective deal. He would not stoop that low.

It had been Izzie who had sorted it. She had sent Fran, still a small child, to her mother with a note. Could she loan them the money for the wages? Granny Mitchell, née Mackenzie, had obliged.

The requisite amount had been sewn into the lining of Fran's coat and she had hurried home, her knees shaking with the responsibility of it all; her heart in her mouth in case it had disappeared by the time she reached the house. Fallen out! Perhaps down a drain? But it hadn't and the wages had been paid, that time.

As the Depression deepened and the next crisis inevitably came, it brought with it the deathly silence that hushed even baby Charlie. Izzie could not ask her mother for a second loan.

Fran was sitting at the big table in the kitchen, her hands clasped in front of her, hardly daring to breathe. The only sound was the hissing of the fire; an intrusive, positively insolent sound. Then she heard Fa move from the front room where the office was, to the stairs, his heavy footfall ascending the treads. It was as if every step he took was magnified. Next came the creak of the big wardrobe door in her parents' room and, after what seemed to be an interminable time, Fa's footsteps coming back.

He sat down heavily in his Windsor chair next to Fran. His face was severe. It did not suit him. He was a jolly man, a big, jolly man. Somehow the creases on his face seemed all wrong when he frowned.

He brought his hands up to the table. He was holding a leather money bag which he proceeded to empty on to its surface. Out spilled golden sovereigns, lots of them, tumbling on to the smoothness of the white cloth, clattering and chinking as if the room had been invaded by noisy birds.

Fran could hear Izzie sigh. A long sigh. The rainy day had come for which the sovereigns had been put by, hidden at the back of the wardrobe. Fa had not trusted the Bank to have everything, not ever, but particularly not since '29. Now these would be gone too. The next rainy day would be their last.

But Fa had made it all good. He had held on and his men were safe and they repaid him by working harder for him than they had ever worked in their lives. Because, quite simply, without any reservations, they loved him.

Now that was all in the past and the daughters of the house were having the time of their lives. It was Neville who was protesting. He wanted his freedom. He wanted to make choices on his own without his mother determining the outcome. Using the Tennis Club as an excuse, he was never at home. He was round with Bill Myers and Bill Myers' sister.

* * *

Stella too wanted her independence. It was her stepfather who organized her articles with a firm of accountants in Hope Street. He had not made the anticipated objections to her proposal. He had not sneered at her determination to break into a man's world.

He had telephoned a golfing friend, a Mr Booth, and that was it. She was to start the following autumn.

The idea had originally come from Aunt Maddy. Each summer Stella organised her annual escape. She would go back to Hampshire to see her old friends and, once she became old enough, she helped out at the Foundation. It provided a chance for Liddie, particularly, to have a break. Liddie was having to accept that she was getting on in years and she welcomed the time off which Stella provided. She, for her part, saw her former home as a safe refuge and was eternally grateful for it.

Recently, however, things had not been good. The Crash had resulted in Aunt Maddy's solid stocks and shares losing a substantial part of their value and the Foundation was struggling to survive.

It was a strange hybrid sort of place, neither orphanage in the strictest sense of the word, nor boarding school. It was a bit of both. Stella knew as little about the man in whose name it had been founded as she knew about her own father. Grown-ups tended not to talk about what had happened in the war. All she knew was that her mother and Aunt Maddy had worked at a hospital in Yorkshire almost up to the end. Then, once the Foundation opened, she had gone there as a baby so that her mother could become a proper nurse. At Southampton. That was where the Bug Man had first made his appearance.

Stella did not reveal to Aunt Maddy what horror she felt in her heart about that. The Bug Man might be a genius at what he did in his Bug House but he was the source of such misery in his own home. She did not reveal to anybody why she was afraid of him. Why she avoided him at all costs. She avoided her mother too. She felt that Lou was somehow responsible and yet she knew that she wasn't. Not really. She was making her mother desperately unhappy and there was unhappiness enough, God alone knew, in that household. But there was not a soul that Stella felt she could confide in to find a way out. Especially not anyone at The Green. She could not, would not, spoil what was there, for all of them, not just herself. It was a haven of warmth and goodness and trust. It was a unique little sanctuary of untainted innocence.

And now Aunt Maddy was in difficulties.

The main anxiety was for the young ones. These were children of men who had died in the aftermath of the war. They had come to Maddy because their widowed mothers lacked family of their own to take the children in. She had given them the same chance as she had done many others, over a decade ago: the opportunity to earn a living, to rebuild their lives. All those who had been there with Stella were now grown up and out in the world, apart from Dee who had won a scholarship to the local grammar school and was still living nearby with his father in the village. But now, if Maddy's funds ran out, the current intake would have nowhere to go. Nowhere that would compare with what they were used to, in the house on The Green. Their mothers, visiting at weekends, had no suspicion of the threat of closure.

During the long summer evenings, as they sat together in the room that led out on to the long garden, the light fading and they too absorbed to bother to switch on the lamps, Aunt Maddy confided to Stella that Liddie and Miss Sefton, the senior teacher, were working for no wages at present, just their keep. She was determined to ride the crisis but she was all too aware that she would have to adjust the whole ethos of the place. She would have to think about taking fee-paying day pupils and begin the inevitable metamorphosis into a school proper. The Foundation's original function would soon become obsolete. It would have to change if it was to continue.

Stella sensed a great sadness about that. She felt it on the air, in the pauses when Aunt Maddy chose not to speak. It was in the humming of the insects as they hovered above the lawn, waiting for a lamp to be lit. It was the sorrow that the one who had been lost might be forgotten. The Stanhope Foundation would cease to exist.

But as always, and whatever her own preoccupations, Maddy was somehow in tune with Stella. The girl was ill-at-ease. She had become so guileful in her evasiveness. There had been innumerable occasions when Maddy was well aware that deception had been practised on the parents, not in any serious way, but in little lies; what seemed to her to be unnecessary prevarications. So Maddy made her own assumptions. She thought that it might be that Stella was recoiling from her financial dependence on the less-than-popular stepfather. That she needed to be free of him. There was also an underlying understanding that somehow Lou would be relieved of a constraint too, if this situation were to be resolved. That all was not well with the Bundenells became more and more obvious. Maddy thought up all kinds of alternatives for Stella's future which they discussed at length.

But not a word passed between them about the real state of things between Lou and her husband and Stella's increasingly untenable position. All that remained untold.

Instead, Maddy was encouraged to repeat the stories from the Kelsay days: of the tearaway her mother had been, probably the first woman in England to ride a motor-bike. Too young to be accepted as a nurse, Lou had turned her hand to everything during her time at the hospital. She had run one of the ambulances and learned how to maintain it, by trial and error from a handbook, after which she became the mechanic for all three. She had dug up gardens and helped to feed the whole community, virtually single handed. She had bullied the able-bodied patients, and some who were rather less than that, into chopping mountains of logs to keep the fires going. Kelsay could not have functioned without Lou, yet she had broken all the rules. Stella learnt more about her mother on those summer evenings than she had learnt in seven years of being with her in the house on the Esplanade. Her mother had obviously closed doors too. She was unrecognizable from the girl she had been. Stella wished that she could have known her then.

A wave of sadness enveloped her as it did when she deliberately refrained from asking about her lost father. Aunt Maddy would know it all. Whether it had been at that hospital that her mother had met him. Had he been a patient, or, like Aunt Maddy's Captain, had he been away in the trenches until he had been killed? What had he been like? She could not ask. The spectre of the Bug Man consumed her; too threatening and too large. She wanted to hang on to her daydreams about her real father and she must return to her own immediate future, she reminded herself. Attempting to construct a myth to parallel that of Captain Stanhope was not going to offer any solutions.

It was Maddy's influence which guided her towards wanting to work with figures. It was the record of her mother doing the jobs of two men as well as her own; of Aunt Maddy, as a mere slip of a girl, being the administrator of whole hospital. Stella wanted to prove that she could do that too.

She decided to apply for articles with a firm of accountants. On her return, Edward Bundenell had helped her gain an opening. She had not protested. She had, in fact, manipulated him into doing it. She had squandered rather less than a minute on arguing with her conscience.

* * *

Back in Merseyside, across the water, Jack and Pinny were on their way into town. There was a certain swagger in their gait as befitted those in their final year at St. Aidan's. Their hands were in their pockets as they sauntered along Conway Street. They were aiming for Birkenhead Park. As men-of-the-world they felt that they ought to know what was going on in it. And plenty was. Speakers' Corner was their destination and, in recent months, listening to the various harangues had become a habit rather than an occasional diversion. Since the protest marches and deputations had increased throughout the summer, the demands for better relief for the unemployed were becoming more desperately vociferous. It was imperative that they witness the outcome.

Jack's imagination had been fired by the passion of it all. He had an ingrained aversion to what he saw as injustice. Pinny loved to heckle, even when he tended to agree with the sentiments of the speaker in question. He felt it a matter of principle not to allow anyone to become complacent. Besides, he informed Jack as they got nearer, an old woman had recently appeared on the scene since Leo McGree had made his address. The 'Red Flag' had been sung, did Jack not remember? Jack most certainly did remember. He had not been there but he had heard about it with a mixture of exhilaration and terror. Exhilaration that such a thing could happen; awe at the sense of history being made by the hour and blind terror that Communists, the arch enemies of the priests whose dogma dictated his waking thoughts, whose teaching was that they were agents of the devil, should be virtually on his doorstep. And now, according to Pinny, an old woman was holding forth with an energy that belied her years. It made a change from the usual, alright.

The usual were nearly all from the Workers' Unions protesting against the Means Test, demanding that more concessions should be made available for the unemployed. Some of them were obviously Communists. There was a thrilling sense of danger about them. The Sally Army lot were always there but they did not thrill in the slightest and only served for Pinny to exercise his wit if he became bored by the others. Then there was The Atheist. He was the maddest of them all, his cadaverous frame enveloped in a long, buff-coloured mackintosh, high up on a cart so that he could be seen in his entirety whilst his surprisingly cultured voice urged them to cast away the superstitious nonsense that had held them in thrall to their masters for centuries. It was their bounden duty to think for themselves, he roared, otherwise they were less than asses, beasts of burden. He would always finish by recommending to his audience to come again the next day, 'Weather Permitting' and the caveat, 'God will have nothing to do with it!'

The Atheist had been there for years, saying the same things, always ending with the same blasphemy. When Jack had been younger he had invariably looked up to the heavens, convinced that a bolt of thunder would come down and strike The Atheist dead but in all that time no such phenomenon had occurred; it had singularly failed to appear. Even so, Jack still occasionally found himself casting a surreptitious glance skywards. Also, if any of the Fathers had known that he and Pinny had been listening to this man since they had been in short trousers, it would not have needed a bolt from the heavens to exact retribution. Not in Jack and Pinny's case. It always made his pulse go faster, the hazardous threat of it.

Whatever the priests might surmise, had they been aware of the boys' presence on the notorious corner, Jack's faith remained intact. He did not actually question it, ever. It was as natural as breathing. He was not a devout boy; not overtly devout in the way that his mother was, who went to Mass every day without fail and stacked up Novenas and Plenary Indulgences as if she was putting them in the bank for when the Final Reckoning eventually came. Jack could not think why. She never did anything wrong that he was aware of. She took the Lord's name in vain on the frequent occasions when one or other of her children got on the wrong side of her and she had a tongue on her alright when his father got in her way, but he did not think that that would add up to much when it came to it. As for himself, he always *tried* to do what was right. If he failed, he always went to Confession. He could not envisage a time coming when the rituals of the Catholic Church were not forming part of the fabric of his life. And his beliefs were impregnable however long

The Atheist might spend in attempting to undermine them. The priests had nothing to fear. They would waste a beating if Jack was ever caught.

This particular evening, as the boys approached, Jack's pulse was racing even before they got there. They were accosted by a policeman. There seemed to be be more than the usual number about.

'And where do you think you two are off to?'

Pinny answered, as quick as a flash.

'Into town. The covered market. We've been sent to get some mackerel from Mrs Flynn.'

'Well you can just shove off! This is no place for lads such as you. Get along with you now and don't let me catch sight of you again.'

Pinny muttered, 'Miserable bugger,' under his breath as they moved away. 'There's something going on!'

Jack turned him into a back entry and then through a labyrinth of side streets until they emerged, breathless, on Park Road East. The sight that met their eyes was confusing, demented, frightful. There were hundreds of men milling around, going at the railings with stripping hammers, obviously intending to form arrow heads to throw at the police, many of whom were already grappling with those on the outer limits of the mass.

There was no shouting from the crowd. Instead a sepulchral voicelessness marked them out, accompanied by the efficient banging of the hammers and a grunting exhalation of breath as the railings were ripped from their footings. And the shuffling sound of hundreds of pairs of heavy boots; workmen's heavy-soled boots grinding out a purposeful rhythm against which the bawling screech of police whistles and the flaying of their batons seemed like the buzzing of tiny, whirling insects.

It was as if they were all deranged, all of them.

Jack and Pinny turned tail and raced towards the town centre, dodging through the back alleys. There was plenty of noise there obviously, a riot of noise in fact, but somehow it seemed less menacing. It was the more familiar expression of anger: discordant shouting, obscenities flying through the air, the occasional crash as something was thrown. They came out opposite a big showroom window, full of glossy new cars. As they did so a fat policeman was rammed through the plateglass. A roar surged up from the crowd.

The boys danced like boxers on the edge of the action, requesting repeatedly to be told what was going on. An oldish man in clean work clothes pushed them into the safety of a shop doorway. He was holding in his hand a home-made placard, 'INCREASE RELIEF NOW!' was painted across it.

'You lads bugger off, do you hear me? It's turning ugly. You don't want to be involved in this. There'll be a killing before long, if not one already, the bastards!'

His voice was raw with shouting.

The boys looked with alarm in the direction of the showroom window but it was impossible to ascertain the fate of the fat policeman. The whole area was dense with scuffling bodies. The man had his hands in the small of their backs and was pushing them out into the street.

'Slip away now, and don't run. You'll be under suspicion if you run. Remember!'

He nodded his head at them grimly and made shooing gestures with his hands.

The boys did as they were told and slid off whilst attention was still focused on the opposite side of the street.

They avoided the back alleys. They could be trapped there. The walls of the yards were too high to scale in a panic. They had not the faintest idea where they were aiming for, they just slid quietly along, putting as much distance as they could between them and the noise and the screaming of the police whistles which filtered through the deafening boom of heartbeats in their ears.

They eventually found themselves at the ferry quay.

'Let's cross,' Jack suggested. 'Let's see what's happening on the Pier Head.'

But they did not get the chance. As the ferry boat drew in to its moorings, hordes of policemen poured off it at the trot. Row upon row of them, gleaming batons at the ready, their faces totally impassive. Set blank.

Another ferry was coming across the water at full speed. It too was crammed to the gunnels with police. They learned later that by the end of the week horses were being shipped across as well. By night. Under cover of darkness. Big, fearless horses, trained to charge at crowds.

'Let's go.' said Pinny. 'I hope that old woman did not turn up tonight. I wouldn't like to think of her in the middle of all this. I'm sorry you missed her though. She talks a treat!'

They walked home in silence, each thinking his own thoughts, each wondering at the combination of excitement and fear inside himself, each determined not to miss whatever might come next.

As they were about to part at the end of Pinny's road, a tram came rattling along the rails. They watched as it passed. Crammed inside, silhouetted by the lights, were scores of policemen. The ones standing in the aisle seemed to be laughing. Or perhaps it was a grimace?

The boys followed it with troubled eyes until it had lurched round the corner on its way to the dockside.

'See you tomorrow,' said Jack as he turned to go. He was conscious of a muscle twitching at the side of his eye.

'See you tomorrow,' echoed Pinny over his shoulder as he walked away.

The darkness had intensified. Faint sounds came from the direction of the river and nearer to him, from one of the houses, a child cried, followed immediately by the scolding tones of adults. Jack caught in his breath. He could not go home yet. He could not just walk in to the same sort of scene; his little brother most likely fretting, Molly fluttering about intent on supremacy in the domestic scene, keeping the younger girls in order. It was all too humdrum, too ordinary. He needed to settle himself down, to put things in perspective, before he could pretend that things were normal. He did not want his family to sense the agitation inside himself that kept the muscle fluttering above his eye.

He deliberately turned off before he reached the house and headed for the church. He could see a glimmer of light from the windows long before he got there. He knew that it would be open. He hoped that it would be deserted.

The door clanged shut behind him as he entered, the sound echoing away, high up into the spaces of the roof. It only did that if the church was empty. Jack genuflected automatically and made his way to the far side of one of the back pews. Here he was in darkness. Here he could kneel and restore the equilibrium he needed; here where nothing ever changed, nothing *could* ever change, no matter what human beings chose to do to each other. Here, he felt, God listened. His presence was palpable. It was in the air around him, which seemed warm even though it wasn't. It was in the scent of burning wax, the persistent hints that incense had been wafted some time before, leaving a slight mist which always clung round the altar. The whole atmosphere breathed, as though someone was *living* there. Waiting to hear.

But Jack did not pray. Still kneeling, he rested his arms along the top of the pew in front of him and leaned his chin on his folded hands. From this position he contemplated the familiar length of the church and waited for the drumming in his ears to stop. He waited for the confusion in his mind to settle. He waited for the calm which came with certainty. Then he could pray.

The only light was the glow from the red sacristy lamp and a full set of candles burning before the statue of Our Lady further down the left-hand wall, near the altar. Sturdy little flames, they reflected the brass of the tiered stand which held them. In turn, they caught the gold leaf in the paint on the Stations of the Cross nearest to themselves and they too flickered and shone. It was as if they were the source of warmth, all on their own, these brave little candles.

It was unusual to have the whole rack lit at once except on Feast Days. Jack guessed that the wives and mothers had been creeping in to say a "Hail Mary" and to appeal for the safe return of their menfolk. The news of the armada of police must have spread quickly.

He too appealed, although he did not light a candle. Jack prayed to Our Lady to keep those men from harm. Those men whom he had seen in the park, who did not know what else to do but to use the tools of their trade to tear down railings and transform them into weapons. How much anger did it need to do that? And it was a terrifying anger; it was quiet, fiercely deliberate, savage almost. He had never seen anything like it. It unnerved him in its intensity. He waited again for the calm to come.

Jack often sat quietly in the church when it was empty, especially when he was troubled by anything. He had never been troubled by anything as serious as this before. Usually it was after a row at home when he had been accused of not looking after his sisters well enough or some such domestic injustice. Molly, particularly, made it quite plain that she could look after the girls on her own and any interference from him was unwelcome, thank you very much. His mother on the other hand...the responsibilities of being the eldest often weighed heavily on his shoulders. He adored his sisters, particularly Molly, but he could not resist teasing her and he had suffered the effects of his mother's sharp tongue more often than he would like. That did not worry him. The fact that his mother made so much of the girls did not worry him either. What did worry him was when he plainly was not at fault and was blamed. He would take up the challenge and say things that he did not mean, be guilty of injustice himself. That was when he needed these quiet moments, to reflect on how silly it all was. It all seemed especially trivial now.

He was brought out of his reverie by sounds coming from the sacristy. Fr. Welland emerged, walked across the space in front of the altar rails, bobbed before the altar and then turned to walk up the central aisle. He was carrying the sheafs of weekly notices.

Jack thought that he had better resume his praying if he was not to be kept there all night. Fr. Welland was not at all bad, as priests went, but he could talk *all* the legs off a donkey, not just the hind one, if he had a mind to. He put his head down, hoping not to be seen.

'Is that you, Jack?'

'Yes, Father.' Jack's heart sank. It was late enough as it was, now he would probably miss his tea and he was starving. He smiled at the priest all the same. It was usually the best policy.

'What are you doing in here at this hour?'

Jack refrained from stating the obvious.

'Are you in any kind of trouble?'

'No, not at all, that is...'

Fr. Welland had deposited the sheets of notices on the table near the entrance door and come back to sit next to Jack. He was blocking his way out. Jack cursed him under his breath. The priest's face was questioning. Then, without meaning to, without any inner warning, Jack found himself blurting out what he had seen. He sat up and in a whisper, as though fearful of being overheard, he said,

'Oh, Father, there are terrible things going on in the park. There must be thousands of men there and they... someone will be killed as sure as anything.'

'Where did you say?'

Jack explained, described, what had happened.

'Dear God!' the priest crossed himself. 'And you saw all this?'

'Yes, Father.'

'God help them!'

He was staring at the altar with a look of profound sadness on his face. He was silent for a long time. Then he turned to Jack.

'What were you doing there in the first place, Jack Jamieson? Were you with that holy terror, McLaughlin? You weren't down there amongst the heathens were you? In the Haymarket! Surely not you?'

Jack panicked.

'No, of course not, there was no-one there today.'

The priest's eyebrows shot into his hairline. He tilted his head to one side, his mouth expressing a sort of exasperated hopelessness at the ways of boys.

'I'm surprised at you Jack. I would have thought that you had more sense.'

'We don't go very often, Father.'

It was useless to lie to priests. Jack wished it unsaid.

'Now look,' Fr. Welland stared down at his feet, 'I know that you don't mean any harm and that it is all very *...very interesting* but you are putting yourself in moral danger, you know that Jack?'

'Yes, Father.' This was much milder than the response Jack had anticipated. If it had been Father Coogan he would not have got off so lightly. 'I'm sorry, Father.'

But the priest had not finished.

'I'm sure you are, but listen to me Jack, it is not just the threat of these people preaching sedition. You do know what sedition is, do you?'

Jack nodded.

'And God knows, there's reason enough, but that is not the way. It is not the way, do you understand that?'

Jack nodded again but he was certain that Fr. Welland did not know the way any more than anybody else.

'They are putting their immortal souls in danger, these people, by denying God and His teachings and so are you Jack, so are you and that McLaughlin fellow, by listening to them.'

'We don't listen. We laugh at them!'

'Ah! You do now ...but poison filters.' He paused and then repeated, 'Poison filters!'

'Yes, Father.'

'And that McLaughlin will be after the girls, is he? Is that why he is down there so often?'

Jack was not going to give anything away this time. Pinny *was* on the look-out for lasses. He was always on the look-out for lasses in town but it had nothing to do with this issue.

'I'm sure not, Father. He just likes a laugh, that's all.'

'Well, you watch your step. We have great hopes for you Jack, great hopes. Get along with you now and think about what I've said.'

Jack made his exit as decently as possible and hurried home. The phrase, 'great hopes' agitated him almost as much as the reasons that had guided him into the church in the first place. It could not possibly be that Fr. Welland and the others had the idea that he might be in line to become one of them. Could it?

His head whirled with images of desperate men, police, priests and preachers and, for some reason, Pinny's old woman being apprehended for a breach of the peace.

* * *

The 'old woman' referred to in the arrogance of Pinny's youth and who featured so graphically in Jack's imagination as grey-haired, wrinkled and walking with a stick, was Lou Bundenell. She was far from being apprehended by anybody. That particular evening she had spent writing letters to *The Times*, *The Telegraph* and *The Liverpool Echo* expressing her concern at the inflexibility of the local councils and pointing out that to use the Communist element as the scapegoat was not an answer. In impassioned terms she accused them of using evasive tactics to stave off an admittance of the truth. The country was not 'Fit For Heroes' and how was it that the heroes in question were now regarded as a needless excrescence of embarrassingly large proportions which they wished could be wiped out?

When she read in the same papers the following morning about the extent of the disturbances in Birkenhead, she was furious with herself for not being there. It had not been her day to go across the water. She had missed all the action.

Lou had become involved in politics quite by accident. She had started out by doing voluntary work in the dockland area. The conditions she witnessed appalled her. Some families were burning their furniture for fuel. They were left with nothing. That way they could claim the miserable benefit available through the Means Test. She could not see an answer. The whole world seemed to be caught up in this cycle. Most just accepted it. Got on with it. Made the best of things. Others were as feckless as they had always been and went under, living from hand to mouth. Lou tried not to make a distinction. She tried hard not to judge.

One afternoon, some months prior to the current disturbances, she had become caught up in a heated exchange on the waterfront as she made her way to the train. The hecklers were out in force against the Member of Parliament who was attempting to preach patience and restraint. He was not a good speaker. In a way, he was eminently bulliable and she found herself bullying him, arguing furiously, not with what he was saying but with the way he was saying it. The frustration and impotence that had been pent up for so long in all areas of her life were suddenly released in a furious outburst against this pouter-pigeon of a man and what he represented. Before she knew it she was hoisted on to a crate, along with all her shopping bags, and was addressing the crowd.

It was intoxicating. All those faces tilted upwards, wrapt by the passion which drove her on. It was not necessarily the significence of the words. She hardly knew what she was saying herself, she was so light-headed. But she knew beyond any doubt that she had every single member of the audience completely in her hand; mesmerised, captive, infinitely malleable.

Next time she went prepared. Next time she had facts and figures. By then she had read Kier Hardy and Karl Marx.

PART TWO

COMING TOGETHER

4. Unpredictable Currents 1934

THE LINER FROM New York was held up at the bar. There was a rumour among the passengers that the pilot had been taken ill and the pilot boat had returned to port. The replacement was taking its time to arrive if that was the case.

Timothy Dundonald was up on deck leaning over the rail, smoking a cigarette. He looked with fondness on the elongated smudge which was all he could see of the western coastline. He had not been in England for years, not since the end of the war. He wondered how much had changed. Not much, he suspected, and it would be more than primitive after the high life in New York. He did not expect it to be other than it had always been. Muddle-headed and class-ridden.

He threw his half-finished cigarette over the side and watched it descend into the darkness of the water. He smiled as he toyed with the idea of a possible visit to Yorkshire. He might go and see what what was happening up at Kelsay. It would no longer be a hospital, of course, it might even have changed hands, but he would like to see it again. And the cottage in the Wolds where he had convalesced. He would like to see that again. He might even track down some of the girls. They had been wonderful girls, those nurses at Kelsay, full of fun. Full of spirit. There had been one in particular, the one who had organized the cottage for him, she had been....

Whilst he was searching for the word which would describe her exactly, with limited success, (there had been so many girls in his life, especially then), the bustling pilot boat drew alongside and instructions were roared to and fro. They would be docking soon. He must get ready. And then he would have to go home. For the funeral.

He lit another cigarette awkwardly as he made his way to the cabins. He decided against looking up the girls. It was nearly twenty years ago, all said and done. They would no doubt be married off to fat gentleman farmers, most of them, surrounded by broods of braying children. He would rather think of them as they were. He had to get through this family business first in any event.

Tim Dundonald had been summoned back to Ireland when it was obvious that his father was hardly likely to last the week. He was arriving just in time to bury him. He had not been back to Ireland for decades. He disliked it. He disliked it intensely. But he needed to know what the situation might be regarding his inheritance. He was in dire need of more funds. And it was impossible for him to return to New York. He owed too many people too much money.

He had always been reckless in this respect. He had been brought up in a household where it was not considered necessary to think about it. When the money began to run out just before the war, and particularly during it, it did not register on his consciousness that there was no-one else to pay the bills except himself. So he ran up debts and then invariably managed to find someone else to pay them for him as he continued to live as he had always done. It wasn't that he was mean; quite the reverse, most of what he had he gave away in one form or another. His greatest flaw was indiscriminate generosity.

And he had enormous courage and endurance. During the war he had been involved in the exodus from Serbia into Albania over the mountains. It had almost killed him as it had thousands of others but he managed to get back to England by sheer willpower and the outstanding audacity which was as natural to him as breathing. It had been Lou who had found him wandering off the wrong hospital train in the middle of the night, as good as dead and effectively a vagrant. It had been *her* audacity which had saved him. She had insisted on taking him under her wing and installing him at Kelsay against all opposition. Her propensity for taking on lame dogs had saved his life.

But he was as feckless with women as he was with money and because they invariably succumbed to his more than fair share of Irish charm he scattered them to the winds like so many fragments in a paper chase. His whole life was like that, a paper chase:

ephemeral, inconsequential, but full of whirling heights of frantic euphoria and excitement. When they passed, he would move on.

On disembarking, he made the decision to stay at The Royal rather than one of the big hotels in the city. He had done so because it was the first half-decent place along the coast beyond the bustle of the docks. As he remembered it, that part of the coast had the atmosphere of a quiet seaside residential area, the hotel overlooking the bay at the beginning of a marine drive. He had learned from his fellow travellers that its reputation for good service was still intact, so despite the expense, The Royal was the one he chose. He had not the first idea that he had a daughter within three hundred yards of where he was to spend the night before catching the Dublin ferry the following morning.

He settled in full of reminiscences. Selective reminiscences, full of nostalgia. The cunning, the callous usage, the cynical betrayal which filled the troughs between the ecstatic heights of his existence, even as he approached middle age, he conveniently forgot. It was as if that part of his nature did not exist. His head, comfortably nestling into the luxurious pillow, was basking in blameless dreams, his dark red hair forming damp curls along his forehead in the warmth of the summer night.

* * *

Further along the front, in her room overlooking the sea, Stella was awake. She was sitting at her window with the curtains drawn back contemplating the tide coming in; it had almost completed its imperceptible crossing over the miles of flat sand from the deeper hollows of the channel.

The surface of the black water was glittering silver, as smooth as the proverbial mill-pond, broken only by the frothy lines at the edge where the sequence of little waves murmured with hardly a sound. An idyllic scene.

She stared at it grimly. How could it change so quickly? Who would have thought that such a perfect-looking stretch of water could be so treacherous? The treachery lay in the fact that it all looked so innocuous, so inviting now. Three days ago it had claimed the life of the sister of one of her colleagues. A dear young man. A dependable young man. And he was devastated. She could hardly bear it for him. The water had not been shimmering with reflected light then, it had been rough, dark, with hidden currents that were lethal. Casually it had taken to itself, like so much flotsam, Molly Jamieson and her friend, Tess. They had both been fourteen years old.

Stella could not remove from her inner eye the picture of Jack when he had arrived in the office the morning after the drowning. He was an attractive young man, with a lick of dark hair falling across his eyes; intelligent, china-blue eyes which were usually so full of merriment. He was immensely amusing in the ordinary run of things, always ready with a joke and always ready to put himself out to help. He worked so hard, could always be depended upon. And he was an innocent. There was nothing underhand or scheming in Jack Jamieson. His flirting with the girls was totally inoffensive. It was not quite artless, he did it to flatter them. Having four younger sisters, he knew what to say to make them feel rather better when he went out than they had done when he came in. They all warmed to him.

But his recent appearance in the office, ashen-faced, his eyes registering the agony of bewilderment and loss, was haunting Stella. He had tried to behave as if nothing was wrong but they all knew that he was in a bad way. In fact, Molly had been closest to him, the one who shared his secrets, the one nearest to him in character. He felt as he might if he had lost a limb: debilitated, crippled. During the previous couple of days he had spent more time than he cared to think just staring into space.

Stella could not understand how it had happened, the accident. They were fanatical about physical fitness those two. He was always at the Athletic Club when he wasn't on the golf course or running or in the gym, as were most of the young men she knew these days. It was like an addiction. Molly had been interested too, but she did not go to the gym. She was a swimmer, a good swimmer; Jack had often boasted of it. So when she and her friend had gone off down to the beach with their towels, no-one had been unduly alarmed even though the sea had certainly been a bit rough that day. She had been warned to be careful. She was a sensible girl. And there were two of them.

And then the police had come to the house and it had been Jack who had answered the door.

The funeral was in the morning, if it wasn't morning already.

A tearful wave of sympathy for Jack threatened to overcome Stella. Her eyes blurred and she had to move to find a handkerchief. As she did so she became aware of raised voices from downstairs. Another row! She peered at the alarm clock on her bedside table but could not make out the figures. Quietly she switched on the lamp. It was just gone two. She had assumed that her parents had been in bed for hours. Obviously they had not.

She sat down on the crumpled eiderdown with her head in her hands. She really could not stand the fights that had become an increasing occurrence in the relationship between Lou and her husband. They had started when Lou had defied him and continued with her political activities. Edward had been violent in his opposition to her 'soapboxing'. He had accused her of shaming them all (that was rich!) and betraying everything he stood for. He could not walk from the University without being aware that she was making a spectacle of herself on the pier head. His friends were abandoning him. It was scandalous. Lou had not given an inch. She had continued to battle with him and on behalf of those who could not help themselves. He told her that that was poppycock. They could all help themselves. She was a dangerous idealist working on a crusade which was entirely emotional; a crusade which was as naive as it was specious. He would not have it. But he had had to 'have it' ! Lou refused to divert her energies in any other direction and Stella loved her for it. But she feared for her too. Mightily.

Even when things looked as though they were improving on Merseyside with the definite increase in demand in the shipyards and the opening of several new factories on both sides of the river, Lou would not give up her principles and continued to insist that her work was still important. And she fought against him bitterly. In her opinion Edward never got his head above his microscope long enough to see what was really going on in the world. He thought more of his work than he did of people. His ambition was the thing that drove him on, nothing else, unless it was his pride. That insufferable pride which demanded the sacrifice of all the things which she considered to be of primary importance. Demanded that she subscribed to his values. His judgements. She could not do it. They were lacking in humanity, his judgements; cold, reptilian almost. Except perhaps, where Stella was concerned. She supposed that she ought to be grateful for that, that he could be kind to Stella.

Lou was incapable of envisaging what might have led her husband to make this exception. She failed to piece together the clues. She failed because it was beyond her imagining. In that respect she was naive and her naivety rendered her culpable.

Stella, for her part, feared for her mother. More than anyone, she knew to what lengths Edward Bundenell would go and that particular night the voices, loud enough to be heard upstairs, sounded violent. Out of a sense of her own preservation, she invariably crept away when these quarrels erupted and she never let it be known that she took sides but that night she felt that she had to risk it.

She put on her dressing-gown and slipped downstairs. The sitting-room door was ajar, the chink of light coming from it made the panelled hall, Gothic in its atmosphere at the best of times, shadowy and unfamiliar. Stella jerked with an involuntary shiver. There was silence, the voices had stopped. She pulled the door open as wide as it would go and stood framed in the darkness behind her.

What she had interrupted was not pleasant. Her stepfather had obviously just pushed her mother down into a chair and he was standing over her with his clenched fist raised, his face contorted with anger.

Lou had her head turned away, her arm up to fend off the blow. It was her husband who first saw Stella standing in the doorway, motionless with dread. He unbent slowly and attempted to pull Lou's arm down from her face. When she turned, she too froze.

She did not even begin to get up. Wearily she said,

'It's alright darling, you go back to bed.'

Stella did not move.

'Really, it's alright.'

It was plainly far from 'alright' and Stella had not planned what she might say, what she might do. She remained standing there, helplessly, watching them both.

Her mother struggled out of the chair and joined her at the door,

‘Go on up now, I’m coming too, very soon.’

Stella backed away and crept slowly up the stairs, pausing to listen at each step. There was only a murmur of voices coming from behind the closed door.

She arrived back at her window, staring gloomily at the water as it sighed over the sand. The tide had come in so far it had almost reached the garden gate. It still looked beautiful, the water. But it was not beautiful, she decided. It was an insidious monster. All deception. All guileful depths and lethal, hidden cruelties. Untrustworthy. All its power lurking under the smoothness of its oil-like surface. It was hateful to her, as was everything else. Eventually she fell into a miserable half-sleep in the chair.

It was little wonder that by the end of the following afternoon she was almost as dark-eyed and frayed as her friend Jack. He had been keeping his head down, attempting to avoid eye contact with his colleagues. He had come in late, once the funeral was over. He had hardly been seen by anyone other than those in the adjacent desks. And people tended to keep their distance. It was very difficult to know what to say to someone who had been involved in such a tragedy, they convinced themselves. What *could* one say? ‘I’m sorry your sister died!’ What good was that? And where did you go from there? ‘Are you alright?’ As if anyone could be alright under such circumstances. So they decided to avoid the platitudes and ended up transformed into the established cliché....the buttoned-up Englishman. Poor Jack! But he was glad not to be disturbed. That way he could keep himself under control. If he concentrated very hard on the tasks in front of him he might not even have to think. So he hid behind a pile of papers and worked like a demon the whole afternoon.

Stella was determined to see him as they were collecting their bikes to go home. She waited until she heard the mass exit from the clerk’s office and then she picked up her things and made her way to the bicycle store. She saw Jack hanging back to let everyone get away first. She pushed her bike against the wall and waited until he hesitated as he drew alongside her. She did not give him time to say anything. She just took hold of his arm and held it very close to her side for a minute.

‘Do you want to talk about it?’ she asked.

‘No.’

‘Let’s walk then. I don’t want to go home either.’

He made no answer but he pushed his bike along behind hers. They both knew that they would head for the first strip of sand.

The bicycles parked against the sea-wall, they walked in silence, side by side. Jack was grateful for her company and even though she did not utter a word he knew that she understood exactly how things were. He felt comforted; Stella too, in her turn. Here was someone who had the weight of the world on his shoulders, as she had, and neither of them had to describe what it felt like, even admit to it. They had no need to make excuses to each other for how they were. They continued to trudge along through the sand until they reached the point where they had to turn.

On the way back Jack told her that he could be leaving Harcourt & Booth’s. One of the senior managers, Mr Mifflin in fact, had made arrangements to set up on his own. He was going to specialise in Hire Purchase and had acquired some offices on Lower Bridge Street. He had asked Jack to go with him.

Stella was horrified.

‘You are not going to risk it, are you? I thought that you were happy with us.’

‘I am. I have been. It’s just that this offer is pretty exciting and it looks as though I’ll get promotion quicker if I take it and now, with Molly gone it ....well, it seems the best thing to do.’

‘Of course.’

Stella found that she could not say anything further. She liked Jack Jamieson. Their friendship had developed, rather uneasily at first, when she had made the discovery that Mr Booth, her stepfather’s golfing friend, had also been responsible for Jack’s presence in the firm. Leasowe Golf Club had brought good fortune to both of them. She was not in love with Jack, she was certainly not that, but she had come to depend on him as a soul-mate and she could not bear to think of him suddenly disappearing. Her enjoyment of the office would be diminished without him and she did enjoy it. That aspect had proved to be an unexpected bonus.

‘I wish you didn’t have to go, that’s all. I’ll miss you.’

Jack nodded, but he did not add that he would miss her.

‘Does Mr Booth know?’

‘Oh, yes. He says that it would be a great opportunity. He cannot promise to find good places for all the trainees with H. &. B., there just isn’t the scope. He says that Mifflin is absolutely on the ball. Getting into this Hire Purchase thing, you know. It could be quite interesting to be in at the beginning of that.’

It was obvious that Jack would make the move.

‘When would you start?’

‘At the beginning of next month.’

The bicycles were in sight, still leaning against the harbour wall, one behind the other.

‘I wish you luck, Jack Jamieson.’

To her astonishment he bent towards her and kissed her on the cheek. She did not flinch. That fact astonished her too.

‘I’ll still be around. Mr Booth says that he might look into this new payment scheme. There could be quite a lot of communication between them and us if he is really serious about it.’

‘That’ll be fine then.’

She looked at him and smiled and he actually could not quite believe that he smiled back.

When they cycled off in their different directions, he to cross the water back to Birkenhead and she to pedal down the Dock Road, they both felt more able to face what might be waiting for them at the other end.

* * *

Some months after this, it came to Stella’s notice that a vacancy was coming up at Booth’s for a replacement in the typing pool in the New Year. She had a wild hope that Fran might apply but Fran was just finishing the first term of her course at the Secretarial School so there was no hope of her being able to even think about it. Stella resisted the urge to tell her about the vacancy.

They were still great friends, she and Fran. They went to dancing lessons at Fletcher’s Dancing Academy once a week, Dodo too. They had to travel to Formby but Fletcher’s was considered to be the best of its kind, Fran reliably informed her, when she had grumbled at the distance. The dance hall was behind the house, taking up most of the garden. It was like a massive conservatory and did actually have potted palms and other exotic plants adorning the narrow raised balcony which went round the inner edge. But the main thing was the floor. It was parquet and polished to glassy perfection. It was intimidating at first, the hugeness of it, but the girls soon got the hang of its danger areas, as they became more proficient with their dance steps.

Fran could not go unless Dodo went with her and vice-versa. They were both convinced that their mother was turning very odd these days. There was such a tussle every time they wanted to go anywhere. Such a fuss. When they went to the actual dance, at the Queen's Hall on a Saturday night, Neville had to go with them.

He refused to sit anywhere near them on the tram journey into town. He kept well away from the three girls. In his opinion they looked absolute idiots with the long skirts of their dresses carefully folded across their knees. This was the inevitable result of their thorough and vociferous commentary on the condition of the floor of the tram. 'It's always the same, every week! What a bloody fuss over a few fag-ends and a bit of spittle!' he would say, with genuine acidity. 'You should be in Formby anyway. If Ma knew what goes on at the Queen's she would have something to say about it, I can tell you!' To cap it all, they perched their shoe boxes, containing their dancing shoes, on top of their already encumbered knees. He considered them alien species and a real pain in the neck. And he hated having to go with them.

He was feeling particularly bitter as his plans regarding Jilly Myers had backfired. The Tennis Club was thriving but Jilly had shown no interest in him. She had recently become engaged to an extremely glamorous young man, David Castledine, who had joined the Club the previous summer. The Castledines owned the Royal Hotel. Neville knew that he could not compete. In any case, she did not love him, that was plain. It had all come about because he and Bill could not get a licence for the Clubhouse. They could only offer tea or lemonade. The Castledines, David and his brother, persuaded everyone to meet up at the hotel after the evening games. That was how it had all started, Jilly being bowled over by him. It was all so desperately unfair.

He nursed his grievances, looked upon every girl who was not Jilly as a personal affront and did no service to his sisters and their friend other than provide them with an escort, albeit with such bad grace.

It was at one of these Saturday dances that Fran learned of the vacancy at Harcourt & Booth's from one of her dancing partners. Her immediate instinct was to rush across to Stella and ask her about it but she couldn't. She was stuck with this particular young man until the end of the dance. He was a pretty uninspiring creature, she decided, somewhat dumpy and inelegant about the feet. However, he had his uses. By the time they parted company Fran had decided not to talk to her friend about the prospective job. It might be wrongly construed; not by Stella, but by others if they knew about it. As she had traversed the dance floor, nimbly avoiding having her toes crushed, and even more importantly, her satin shoes scuffed, she had made up her mind. She would secretly apply for this job, even though she was only a third of the way through her course. Her mother would be furious but she need not tell her unless she was actually offered the position. Her mother would be furious anyway once she learnt about Dodo's conquest. Her sister was at that moment clasped firmly in the arms of a rather dashing young man by the name of Neville Kennedy. She had been dancing with him all night and he looked decidedly smitten.

This fact, and the excitement she felt about her own plans, added an extra sparkle to her eyes. Her smile, as she accepted the young man's thanks for the dance, could equally be described as radiant. It all tended to give him the wrong impression. On his return to his corner and his pals, he assured them with no small degree of pride that he had made a hit with that stunning girl in the silvery blue dress. He was somewhat bemused, and not a little hurt, by the fact that for the rest of the night he might have actually gone home for all the notice she took of him.

In due course Fran turned up at Harcourt & Booth's for an interview and a shorthand and typing test, along with several other girls who had been shortlisted. It was quite by accident that Stella knew that she had been there at all. Towards late afternoon she had an urgent query downstairs in the typing pool and decided to go down herself. Miss Wilkinson, who was up to her eyes with the normal pressure before the post was due to go, had hardly time to deal with the tests from the day's applicants. She asked Stella if she could possibly give her a hand.

‘Will it wait until I’ve solved this particular problem? I don’t mind staying on for a bit if that will help.’

Miss Wilkinson beamed at her.

‘Oh, would you Miss Bundenell? That is so kind.’

‘I’ll come down after five then, shall I?’

Miss Wilkinson beamed again.

This was how Stella came to discover that her friend had applied for the job. When she was discussing with Miss Wilkinson which of the applicants had fared best in the interviews, Frances Reynolds and a young woman called Cecily Jackson had made the most favourable impression. By sheer chance, Miss Wilkinson had passed Fran’s test piece to Stella and taken Miss Jackson’s to examine for herself. Fran’s paper revealed how hopelessly inexperienced she was and what a ghastly mess she had made of the test. There was no way she could be accepted. Unless...Stella worked out that if she substituted the body of the test done by someone else who had done reasonably well, for the one done by Fran, all might be resolved.

She fussed about with the papers for a little while. Miss Wilkinson was also looking at some of the others. Stella made her move.

‘How did Miss Jean Allen strike you?’

Miss Wilkinson referred to her notes.

‘Awful. A brash little baggage. Couldn’t be doing with her at all!’

That clinched it for Stella. The unfortunate Miss Jean Allen had Fran’s flaws attributed to her in an inkling and her more than competent paper was slipped behind the frontispiece of that purported to have been done by Miss Reynolds.

Stella did not suffer a qualm about it, just a thrill of triumph when it was announced that Frances Reynolds was due to start at Harcourt & Booth’s on January 1st.

⋆ ⋆ ⋆

Jack Jamieson did not go dancing as a regular thing. He much preferred to be involved with the Athletic Club activities on a Saturday night. No more was he interested in girls as such, unlike his friend Pinny who took every opportunity to enlighten Jack as to the nature of the joys he, Jack, was eschewing. Fond as he was of Pinny, he vaguely disapproved. It was not that Jack was prudish, or used his Catholic upbringing to judge Pinny harshly on these occasions. Pinny was almost a grown man, it was not up to Jack to remind him of the Church's teaching on these matters, even if it had entered his head to do so, which it hadn't. As long as Pinny did not develop an interest in Jack's two sisters, who were at an age when they would be more than willing to show an interest in *him*, Jack would refuse to criticize. It was partly this, coupled with the genuine protectiveness that he felt for the said Monica and Clare, that prevented Jack from joining Pinny on his various exploits.

This did not mean to say that Jack ignored the opposite sex altogether, far from it. Stella was not the only girl from H. & B. who had walked along the beach with him. He had taken out almost all of them at some stage during the two years he had spent there. Now, even though he was at Mifflin's, he still appeared from time to time and offered an evening out at the cinema to the latest recruit.

He was a bit of a flirt in his own way. He could not help but know that he looked good. He was extremely fit for one thing, and the girls were obviously interested in him despite the rapid fire of insults which came his way when he teased them. But he wasn't vain and he wasn't interested in having a steady girl friend. He was far too busy with everything else.

Nevertheless, he made his regular appearances in the doorway of the typing pool, his hat nonchalantly pushed to the back of his head in blatant imitation of the latest Hollywood hero, and always ready with a joke for anyone who would listen. Then he would disappear having broken the concentration of everyone except Miss Wilkinson who muttered veiled threats along the lines of having him banned from the premises. Secretly, she was very fond of him. He could be extremely chivalrous to her when the occasion demanded; an experience which was becoming more and more welcome as her spinsterhood entrenched itself.

Fran was not impressed. She thought him cocky and too full of himself. Even when she became aware that Stella was a particular friend of his she did not alter her opinion, nor did she believe it when Stella claimed that his flirting was just as much of an act as the stance in the doorway. She chose, therefore, to dismiss Jack Jamieson.

One lunchtime however, when he made his usual visit, after the requisite amount of banter, he said that he was going down to the Kardomah. He offered to bring back cream cakes for anyone who wanted them. Alternatively, he was prepared to treat anyone who would care to join him. The other girls just laughed and told him to get lost but Fran was starving. The thought of lunch at the Kardomah was extremely tempting. She said that she would go.

It wasn't just the other girls who were surprised that she had responded. Jack was nonplussed. He had not expected to be taken seriously. The fact that she had shown no interest in him so far, had ignored him in fact, made it all the more intriguing. But he was pleased. She was an extremely pretty girl and it flattered him to have her walking by his side, even more so when he became increasingly aware that she turned all heads as they progressed. When complete strangers looked at her, their faces lit up. More often than not, they smiled. Jack suddenly felt proud to have her at his side. He began to listen to what she was telling him about her friendship with Stella and how they had known each other since they were children. A small hope that the reason she was with him might be that she had liked him all along insinuated itself into Jack's mind.

Little did he know that the only thing on Fran's mind was lunch. She had overslept that morning and had not only missed her breakfast but realised too late that Abby had gone off with the sandwiches which were rightfully Fran's. She was ready to eat a horse if it was offered. If the provider had been Quasimodo she would not have cared.

Once she had enjoyed her coffee and egg on toast, she became a little more circumspect. He was asking her if they could meet after she had finished work. Perhaps she might like to go to the pictures?

A flicker of panic seemed to go right down to her toes. Her mother would kill her if she knew that she was out with a young man on her own. She stalled for time. She explained that she would have to be home by ten at the latest so, as it was impossible to see a film to the end, there wasn't really much point. But he *would* persist. They could go over the water to the Wirral. There was a lovely beach-walk there. He would be sure to have her home by ten, safe and sound.

It was difficult. She regretted having accepted the offer of lunch. She could not just turn him down now. Her mind was busily working out if she could risk telling them at home that she had to work late at the office. What was more, she would have to risk using the office telephone to do so.

Another earnest plea came her way.

'Alright,' she said, more than certain that once they had met after their respective offices had closed at six, gone across on the ferry and walked to the beach, it would be almost time to come back again.

She was right. And her previous worries about what they could possibly have to say to each other proved unnecessary. Jack, in his nervousness and his anxiety to impress, rather overdid his developing passion for Socialism and did not give her the chance to utter more than a monosyllable all evening.

It was just as well. Fran, who came from a household where politics were something that one read about in the paper, and had no place in the general conversation at home, did not actually know what he was talking about. But she did feel that here was an extremely well-read young man. He certainly knew a great deal. And he was interesting. Dangerously interesting. Not the usual flirt at all. And she had never been *taken* to the Kardomah before, except by her mother for tea. And then she had had to keep her hat on and her mouth shut. Izzie Reynolds liked to have her girls silent when they were on show. Lunch with Jack Jamieson had been very different.

She cast a sideways glance at his profile as they walked along.

He must be clever if she did not understand a word of what he was saying. He was not bad looking either!

Jack got her back to Oakshot Road by ten but then had to travel the eight miles back into town. He only just caught the last ferry and had to walk home the rest of the way. He hardly noticed. He was working out how long it might be before he could decently ask Fran Reynolds to go out with him again.

Fran, in her turn, was not giving him another thought. She had rounded on her sister Abigail the minute she got in and castigated her severely for stealing the packed lunch she had so carefully prepared the night before.

5. Invitations
1935

FURTHER ACROSS the water, in Dublin, Tim Dundonald was in a serious state of frustration. He had not been able to escape from Ireland. His father had obviously had the measure of his son and there was no direct inheritance coming his way. What there was was left in trust for any children he might have, or failing that, the money was to go to his cousin Gerald.

Tim was furious. On top of all, his mother insisted that he remain with her indefinitely. She claimed that she could not possibly cope without him. Not now. Not now that she was widowed, and he had returned after being away for such an interminable length of time. She needed him. She had wept.

He was trapped.

The allowance that she received was far from being adequate to support them both and there were few openings in Dublin for anyone with his strange Curriculum Vitae. Somehow though, he had to find a job.

It was his cousin, in the end, who provided a form of rescue. Gerry ran the farm which was all that was left of the family estate. He was wanting to increase his export of beef cattle and pigs to England. As part of his strategy, he suggested to Tim that they set up a bacon factory on the Lancashire coast and the curing and marketing could all be done from there. There would be little problem transporting live pigs to Liverpool. The beef export was already in the capable hands of a manager based on Merseyside. Tim did not need to concern himself with that side of it but he could be useful if he was prepared to run the bacon factory and there were developments going up in the Maghull area, a huge new complex. If they could get hold of one of those sites the prospects looked very good. Tim would be required to manage the factory with the help of a first class accountant. Gerry was not going to risk his cousin getting his hands on an open cheque book. He, also, was well-versed in the saga of the debts. Tim could live on that side of the water and come over regularly to check on his mother.

He agreed. It was the only way out. Within the year he was installed at the Royal as a permanent resident. That had become part of the deal.

⋆ ⋆ ⋆

Months later, on a sunny March morning, Lou and Stella decided to risk sitting outside with their coffee. They generally had coffee together on a Sunday. Stella would purport to chatter on about the week's events at the office and what her friends were up to. Lou would only half listen. There was an accustomed brittleness to this ritual which she found distressing.

This particular morning Lou was bending down over the side of her chair in order to extract a weed from between the paving of the terrace, her face averted. She was really pondering on the likelihood of the cellar flooding again with the next spring tide. Stella was regaling her with the latest news from the Reynolds. Dodo had acquired a regular 'young man'. He was actually rather nice and Dodo was in a constant flutter about him. But as ever, she fussed through what she saw as crisis upon crisis. The most recent episode was typical. They had been invited to meet the brother of his boss, he was an importer of some kind, and she had been so nervous that she had insisted that Fran and Jack went with them. They did, of course; Fran always helped Dodo out. They had had an absolutely splendid dinner at the Royal and now they had to return Mr Dundonald's hospitality and they were planning to take him to the Adelphi the following week-end and had asked Stella to join them to make up the numbers. What did Lou think? Should she go?

Lou straightened up, the weed clutched in her fingers which suddenly seemed to be paralysed. Stella was looking out to sea, her hand shading her eyes, following the stately progress of the Isle of Man boat as it made its way towards the bar.

'Who did you say he was?' she asked. Alarm bludgeoned away inside her chest.

'Neville? He's an importer; cattle from Ireland. We call him Neville K. because of his having the same name as Neville Reynolds. He is rather special, I can tell you, terribly handsome. His proper name is Kennedy.'

'No, I meant ...' Lou felt her tongue dry out inside her mouth. She could not bring herself to repeat the name. She knew with a shocking clarity to whom it would belong.

'Sorry?' Stella said.

'The other man, the one who took them to the Royal?' The reply was firm this time.

Stella shifted round on her chair to get closer to her mother, her eyes bright with amusement, not untinged by a certain cynicism.

'He didn't take them. He lives there. Fran is frightfully impressed, would you believe? She says that he is the most glamorous man that she has ever met. He has been all over the world. Well, America actually, but he has been all over Europe too. Fran says that he is absolutely *fascinating* and so charming. He's old, of course, and has a gammy hand, but she says that you would hardly notice. Do you think I should go?'

Lou was staring at her as if she had not heard.

'Mum! You're not listening. Should I go?'

'Go? Where?'

Stella had to restrain her urge to shout, as if her mother had suddenly gone deaf. Instead she spoke slowly and carefully, her patience stretched to the limit as if, in fact, Lou had already deteriorated into senility.

'To the Adelphi. Next Friday. To meet Mr Dundonald!'

Lou felt as though all the blood in her veins had somehow contracted at the same moment. To her horror it then seemed that it would all rush to her head. She would possibly faint.

She leaned down to tug at another weed, to keep her face away from Stella's puzzled scrutiny.

'Mum?'

When Lou sat up again she was as pale as death.

'You must do what you want to do. You usually do.'

Stella clicked her tongue in exasperation.

'You always say that! What I want to know is, is it right? You don't think that it would look fast do you, to go rushing off to have dinner with a man I've never met? I mean there is no question that it is anything other than an idle curiosity, and to help out Dodo and Fran. But I should die if anyone thought that I was being fast!'

'If you want my honest answer, that is what it is. It *would* look fast and you could get hurt. Very hurt. But it's up to you.'

Lou made to go back into the house. As she passed, she paused to kiss the top of Stella's head. She hoped that the girl was unaware of the involuntary shaking of her limbs as she stood behind her. If she was, she prayed that she would put it down to the sudden gust of wind which came off the sea.

'I must go in,' she said. 'It's getting cold.'

Stella nodded but did not turn her head. She concentrated on the promise of blossom, just hinted at on the sturdy little apple trees in the orchard, and beyond there, the endless stretches of sand waiting for the tide. It was a view which would normally have given her great pleasure but she was not, at that moment, registering it at all. A troubled frown formed twin creases between her eyes. Was her mother ill? Her face had suddenly gone ashen, all the colour drained out of it. That was not like her at all; neither was the muddle-headedness. She would wait half an hour or so, she decided, and then go and see if there was any improvement. And she would decline Dodo and Neville's dinner invitation. She suspected that it had come about through Fran's machinations anyway. Fran would be wanting to show off their sophisticated new acquaintance. Stella toyed with the idea of loaning her the new green dress she had just acquired. It might offset her friend's disappointment when the invitation was refused. She would not go. She did not want to be anyone's partner. Besides, Stella felt more and more like a spare part when she was in the company of Fran and Jack. They did not mean to be selfish but it was obvious that they were only interested in each other, as were Dodo and Neville. It would be left to her to entertain a perfect stranger. She couldn't do it.

Meanwhile, Lou had gone upstairs. When she reached the gallery landing, she listened at the door which led up to the old nurseries. Edward had his study up there and she could hear the steady thrumming of the typewriter keys. He was working on his book. He would be there till lunchtime. She had time to think.

She found herself creeping along to her bedroom as if there was an urgent need for secrecy. She hated the immediate realization that she was skulking. Furtively...! She pulled herself together and strode into her room. Once inside, she shut the door firmly behind her and lay down on the bed.

There was no doubt in her mind as to who this Mr Dundonald was. The arm had been smashed during a landslide in the Albanian mountains during the war. Tim had been an interpreter seconded to the Serbian army and had been involved in the mass exodus out of Sarejevo. He had been a vagrant when she had first come across him. He had not fitted anywhere and had been shuffled from pillar to post despite his appalling physical condition. She had picked him up from a hospital train one miserable, wet, winter's night and had bundled him into the ambulance bound for Kelsay with the other official patients which she had been sent to collect. She could not help but smile as she remembered the ferocity of the whispered row she had had with the duty nurse that night. Whatever-her-name was had not known how to cope with what she had termed Lou's anarchy. It had been strictly against the rules to take a patient without all the requisite papers from the Red Cross. It had also been strictly against the rules to share a cottage with a patient when he was a convalescent. But that had come later.

Lou had never been one for rules. She had considered herself to be fearless in those days; now she looked back on her actions and judged them as reckless. She had also thought that she was brave until the day that she had discovered him making love to someone else. She hadn't been brave at all then. The vehemence of her reaction had almost scared her out of her wits, particularly the propensity for violence which had previously gone unrecognised.

It was that, really, that she had run away from. The consequences of being out of control. She had run away. From Kelsay. From Maddy. Without a word. Her pregnancy had been confirmed only days later. And now, here he was, after almost twenty years, virtually on her doorstep, posing a threat, a decided threat, to Stella.

She had never told her daughter about her father. She had always allowed her to assume that he had died in the war. Another instance of her loathsome cowardice, she recollected bitterly. Maddy had not given her away either and there were so many orphans at The Green it had just been accepted that that was what had happened.

She had always had moments of unquiet about it. She knew that it was an evasion. Stella did not deserve evasions. Not from her.

She had always tried to think of her daughter as an individual rather than an extension of herself. It had been difficult because in many ways Stella was an extension of herself. The things that she recognized as coming from Tim, Lou pushed to the back of her mind. Stella was *her* child. Only Maddy had any form of claim on her otherwise. And what tortured Lou was that she felt that she had failed Stella somewhere along the line. There was an underlying unhappiness there that seemed beyond repair. And Lou had failed her. She had not confronted it and if Maddy had done so at any time in the recent past she had kept her findings to herself.

Maddy! She would ask her what she should do. She would go downstairs right away and telephone her. Maddy would know the best thing to do.

As she was running down to the hall to the telephone, Stella was coming through from the garden. Lou stopped in her tracks, confused for a moment. She felt herself flush. Stella was also taken aback. Here was her mother, no longer languid and ashen, but pink-cheeked and animated.

'I've decided not to go. You were right. I'll tell Fran,' Stella said, anxiously scrutinizing the face that bent to kiss her.

'Good,' Lou whispered as she hugged her. 'Good!'

* * *

That same morning Fran was crossing the water on the ferry in response to an invitation from Jack. The intention was to cycle to the Wirral together with some of his friends.

She liked Jack. He was fun. The more she got to know him the more she realized that he was the kindest person she had ever met. The 'man of the-world' exterior was a total facade. He might have seemed like a flirt when she had first caught sight of him but he had not so much as kissed her so far and they had been courting for months. It wasn't that he wasn't affectionate, he was, and immensely concerned for her welfare; he always saw her home even though he often risked missing the last ferry when he did so. She decided that he was just a good man through and through.

She peered over the stern of the squat little boat, attempting to make out Stella's house on the far shore, pushing her hair out of her eyes as the breeze picked up on the water in spite of the lovely day.

Yes, Jack was alright. He might be a bit too serious sometimes which was the other side to his sense of fun and his love of a good joke. His politics got on her nerves a bit but she now understood more clearly the reasons why he should feel so strongly about it. Mrs Bundenell, Stella's mother, was just the same, but it did rather take them over on occasions. Both of them. And they would become angry and start to shout and pace the floor. They behaved in exactly the same way although they had never set eyes on each other to her knowledge. It must be part and parcel of being a committed Socialist, she concluded, all this furious gesticulating. She knew that her mother, and even the easy-going Fa, would disapprove. They certainly disapproved of what Mrs Bundenell got up to. And then there was the huge obstacle of his being a Catholic. They would disapprove of that too, she knew they would. In their opinion, Catholics did not get on in the world. There was too much set against them. And the Reynolds had always got on in the world, or had done up until now.

As the boat bumped alongside the landing-stage, she could see Jack standing with his bicycle waiting to meet her on the quayside. She pushed such apprehensions from her mind and hurried along to the gangway even though, with her bike, she was supposed to wait until the other passengers had disembarked first.

'Fran, I would like you to meet Pinny,' he said as she approached. 'And this is his friend, Megan. She comes from Flintshire.'

Fran was delighted to meet them, especially Megan who, as it transpired, knew Babyll, the village where the Reynolds had had their farmhouse when they were children. The girls cycled along together, two abreast, talking non-stop. Jack and Pinny kept a few yards behind them. They rode in silence. Pinny occasionally caught

Jack's eye and pulled a rueful face. He had not bargained for such a rival turning up. Jack was amused. He should have warned his friend that Fran had a gift for talking. It was hard to stop her once she was well underway.

They were still at it when they all arrived at the seafront at Meols and set out their picnic. Pinny was sulking but Jack had not heard about this part of Fran's life, he had had no occasion to, and he was fascinated. He sat on the sand with his back to the sea wall and allowed his imagination to conjure up the long stone farmhouse she was describing. He heard about her cousins and how they had taken it in turns to bring up buckets of water from the spring next to the old house because there had been no running water inside. And they would help to clean the paraffin lamps which they used in the evenings and cough in the smoky glow if they had failed to do it properly and the two aunts would scold them mightily then. Megan laughed; a throaty, sympathetic laugh and then her eyes lit up and she became animated as she hugged her knees into her chest as she asked Fran if she remembered the village shop which smelt of new bread and sugary sweets all mingled together with the fumes from the paraffin and the huge sacks which held meal for the sheep-dogs. It was a wonderful shop. It was an Aladdin's Cave!

Would she ever forget it, Fran said. She and her cousins would find an excuse to go every day and on the way home they would pick the wild strawberries which grew all over the hedgerows and Neville and her cousin Oliver would cram fistfuls of them into their mouths like the little pigs they were. She and Dodo, and her cousin Grace were only marginally more delicate in their greed. When they got back, they would be scolded again because they had not had the sense to collect the fruit and bring it home to be washed. The aunts had threatened them with the details of all kinds of dreadful diseases if they were so careless, but they never caught anything. Well, not quite; Fran had developed scarlet fever but that had been in the winter when they were back at Oakshot Road and the aunts could not possibly blame her for that. The epidemic had raged through the whole of Liverpool.

Fran was laughing with pleasure at being reminded of it all and then told them how, on the journeys there at Easter time, in the old Bentley, there was always such a struggle to get the car up Peny Boor and they would invariably all have to get out and push, but on the way back, at the end of the summer, it would sail down the mountainside with the children cheering for all they were worth as the scenery flashed by and the sheep scattered in every direction.

As Jack listened, he began to understand the extent of her bemusement at his outrage at the state of the world. She did not know the state of the world. She had never known how it was. Not directly. She must have thought him deranged. Her attempts to go along with his way of thinking, her efforts to understand the plight of the shipyard men and his concern at what he saw as the injustice against them were all the more admirable as the picture of that part of her childhood unfolded; spontaneously, joyously.

He looked at her, happy and smiling, making Megan smile too, and both of them totally at ease with each other as if they had been friends for years. It wasn't only a gift for talking she had. Her nature was warm and generous. She had a gift with people. Even now she was drawing Pinny into the conversation, his sulk forgotten as she made him sparkle.

Later, the two couples parted company for a while. They decided that they needed a walk. Pinny drew Megan off in one direction and Jack and Fran tactfully chose the other. They talked about the proposed dinner at the Adelphi Hotel and Jack revealed how embarrassed he was that Neville K. was adamant that he bore the cost of it. Jack found that unacceptable. He must pay his share. They had a heated argument about it as Fran insisted that it was part of Neville's business expenses and there was no need, no need at all, but Jack persisted. He would offer to at least, particularly if Stella was to join them. But secretly he was worried almost to death about it. He could not possibly afford dinner at the Adelphi, not even for himself alone and there would be three of them if Stella came. Right from the days of the precious caddy fees he had handed over to his mother everything he had earned and she would give him his pocket money. It would take him months and months of scraping to pay back the loan that he was certain Pinny would provide to cover it; months and months it would be, but he could not possibly allow Neville K. to stand treat for the whole lot. Through no fault of his own he had got himself into an awkward situation and he hated having to ask Pinny to help him out. Pinny, the erstwhile 'scruffy bugger,' was now well on the way to becoming a successful businessman. He dealt in second-hand cars and seemed to be making a small fortune. Jack was sharp with Fran when she seemed so dismissive of the problem.

'You don't know the first thing about it. How could you? You are a girl! You haven't the first idea how it is.'

Fran rounded on him,

'There's no need to snap at me like that just because you are in a temper! And how can you be so arrogant? Don't contradict me. You are arrogant to say such things, and obstinate, and what's more, you must be *deaf* if you haven't heard what I have been saying all this time.'

She stood still and faced him squarely, then proceeded to shout at him very slowly and deliberately as if he really was deaf, and a foreigner to boot.

'It —is —part— of —Neville's —expenses! '

And followed that with,

'IDIOT!'

Jack stomped purposefully onwards to the top of the hill they were climbing, muttering furiously to himself. He did not care if she followed him or not.

They made up by a stile at the summit. Fran was breathless from the climb and flushed from their quarrel. She looked so pretty that Jack could not help himself. He had to kiss her. 'I'm sorry,' was in his head to say, but he did not say it. He kissed her again instead.

Then they ran back down the hill almost as fast as the old Bentley had swept down Peny Boor all that time ago, Jack singing, his lungs fit to burst. They could also have cheered, as the children had in the time of Fran's childhood, cheered with the unexpected exhilaration of it all.

Jack was still singing when Pinny and Megan eventually made a somewhat dishevelled reappearance. It was obvious that both couples had had a most satisfactory afternoon in their respective ways. The ride back was marked by an increasing silence as they pedalled wearily home. Crossing the water, Fran decided that at the next opportunity she would invite Jack to one of the Saturday parties at home. Nobody could object to Jack. How could they? He was lovely. Just lovely! But the business of the Adelphi dinner was obviously worrying him. She would call in on Stella, it was only a small diversion from her route back, and she would find out what her friend had decided. Then she would settle it with Dodo. She knew that they would not hear of Jack contributing, it had been made clear from the start, but Jack *would* fuss so. He really was stubborn and obstinate; she had seen it in him before today. Still, it was worth it for the kiss; NO, two kisses in actual fact!

She pedalled on with some degree of smugness which increased as she turned off the main road and cycled towards the beach and the Esplanade.

The road to the shore was deserted, as it usually was at this time of the evening. On one side was the field, the main function of which was to host the Annual Show as it was a good, large space. Sometimes the travelling circus came, or the fairground. It wasn't much use for anything else. It had never had anything growing in it to Fran's knowledge. At the far end it became just sand dunes fringing the beach. A row of large houses ran along the right of it, until the road ended at the turn into the one where Stella lived.

The song that Jack had been singing would not leave her head as Fran cycled along. It was, *Stay as Sweet as You Are.* She would buy the sheet music at the first opportunity, she decided; she would play it when he came to the next party. All her earlier apprehensions about his reception at home were for the moment forgotten, as was the quarrel. She was completely lost in happy thoughts.

The man coming towards her had come from the beach. He was also on a bicycle. His head, presumably, was also full of thoughts but of not such a sanguine kind. His trousers were still unbuttoned after the solitary occupation he had been pursuing among the sand dunes. It was called Indecent Exposure, the offence he was committing. As the two cycles approached each other from opposite ends of the road, and he saw Fran with her skirts blowing about her knees, her face radiant, almost abstracted with thoughts of Jack, it turned into something else.

She had seen these men before. They lurked among the sand dunes. Sometimes they would spy on children playing. Fran had not been frightened of them, she knew that they were harmless enough, just a source of bemused merriment and giggles, an experience not to be talked about at home. Otherwise they knew, somehow, though not really understanding why, the beach would be designated Out of Bounds. Because she was no longer a child, and because she had almost forgotten those beach-playing days, this man seemed different.

He was looking steadily at her, one hand coming off the handlebars and moving down to the opening in his trousers, the bicycle veering off its course.

Fran pedalled faster, her heart beating with the effort. And now she was afraid. 'He's nasty,' she thought, 'ugly and nasty; not funny at all.'

By the time she had parked her bicycle near the gate and run up the path to Stella's door, she was breathless and considerably unnerved. But the man had not turned his bicycle round; he had not followed her.

Once inside, to her immense relief, she found that they were alone. Mrs Bundenell had decided, on the spur of the moment, to go off to Hampshire and had left immediately after lunch. Stella had seen her off at the station and spent the rest of the afternoon at the Art Gallery. She had only just returned. Fran wondered how on earth she could have spent all that time looking at an exhibition until Stella explained that Dr. Bundenell was working on a very important book and she had wanted to leave him in peace so she had made herself scarce.

They were up in Stella's room. Fran had remembered that Stella was her alibi for being absent from home for the day and so she had to give some sort of credible account and Stella had suggested that they would be better upstairs. But up there the thump, thump of the typewriter keys seemed to thud right through the ceiling. She wondered how Stella could stand it. It was physically irritating, it assaulted the ears. It went on and on.

Stella, realizing that Fran was registering distress, said, 'He's nearly at the end. It's taking him over somewhat.' Shrugging her shoulders, as if the whole thing bored her, she went on, 'It could mean that he gets his chair if it's a success. The old professor is retiring. He could get the chair in his place. It's important to him.'

Fran did not care less if he got the chair or not. Dr. Bundenell left a lot to be desired as far as she was concerned. Compared with Fa, he was a washout as parents go. He was a pale shadow of a thing, hardly ever seen, pursuing his ambition relentlessly. Stella's mother might not exist for all the notice he seemed to take of her. Fran disliked him. She considered him a cold fish. But neither could she escape from his overriding presence. The drumming of the typewriter saw to that.

It did not exactly dispel the intention to share her news but it postponed it. The sounds coming from the attic disoriented her, as had the sight of the man on the bike. The wondrousness of that first kiss had inexplicably been turned into something grubby. The feeling was exacerbated by being in Stella's impeccably clean room. It was always so, as was Stella herself. Her friend invariably looked newly scrubbed, her skin emanating the perfume of Parma Violets, as though she had just come straight from a bath. Strangely, some how, it made Fran feel ashamed. She was aware of a guilty flush rising up from her neck and to cover it she pretended that she had just come to confirm that Stella would be making up the six at the Adelphi.

Her disappointment at Stella's refusal aggravated her sense that the wonderful day at Meols was rapidly becoming tarnished. She scoffed at Stella's reasons for turning down the invitation. It was perfectly understandable that Dodo's Neville should want to make up the numbers, she said. Mrs Bundenell was being a pain by objecting to it and whenever had Stella taken any notice of her mother before? She was just being silly. However, the offer of the loan of the green dress was accepted with alacrity. She knew that she would look stunning in it.

By the time she left, any apprehension she might have anticipated about cycling on alone was replaced by the working out of a scheme by which, just for once, she might be allowed to borrow Grandma Mackenzie's fur cape instead of her cousin Jardine who always had the monopoly of it. Cousin Jardine was courting a solicitor and was consequently in great favour. It incensed Fran that this particular cousin had first claim on the furs.

In the space it took her to get as far as Oakshot Road she discovered that she was in a real fury about such partiality, which was extremely fortuitous on several counts. Her uneasiness about the strange atmosphere in the house on the Esplanade that evening (which in fact was to haunt her for months to come), had been redirected. The flush on her face when she tackled Izzie on the subject of the furs, which she did as soon as she had crossed the threshold, seemed as if she and Stella had spent the whole day innocently making plans for the great event at the Adelphi. Izzie was completely ignorant of her daughter's real movements on that day and did not dream that her rosy cheeks were the result of a clandestine trip to the Wirral, her first kiss and a bizarre confrontation with indecent exposure committed whilst riding a bicycle. She put it down to Fran's indignation at the favouritism shown to cousin Jardine. And Izzie grew just as indignant herself by the end of it. So it was that Fran was promised her grandmother's cape to complement Stella's green silk dress.

As she curled up in bed that night she congratulated herself on most counts, but her smiling was tempered with no small degree of accountable anxiety until she ultimately fell asleep, the thud of the typewriter keys still in her ears and the vision of the sad old cyclist with his busy hand, flickering in and out of her dreams.

Stella, no longer alone in her room, was living her particular nightmare.

6. Hampshire

MADDY AND LOU had the sitting room to themselves. Lonsdale was away with the school rugby team at an end-of-term tournament. Lou, with some degree of guilt, was glad of it. She loved Lonsdale, and it wasn't as if he did not know the circumstances which had pertained at Kelsay when Tim Dundonald had been there; he had been there himself, but she wanted to be alone with Maddy.

It was a comfortable room, warm and cosy, cluttered with books and photographs, its untidiness radiating a certain contentment with itself and its occupants. Lou was curled up in Lonsdale's chair by the fire, her friend in the other, looking relaxed at last in spite of their total pre-occupation with Lou's astonishing news.

Sitting there, a glass of whisky in her hand, in this haven of normality, Lou was momentarily prepared to convince herself that the re-appearance of Timothy Dundonald had been a product of her imagination. Maddy was not so encouraging.

She urged her friend to use this chance to tell Stella the truth. Even if this man was not who they thought he was, it was a God-given opportunity; such a one might not come again. And if it was he, and Stella learned the facts from somebody else, it could prove disastrous, especially for Lou. In any case, Maddy pointed out, she could never understand why silence had been kept on the subject. It was against everything else in her character. It wasn't as if Lou was averse to disapprobation.

'She's mine. She's always been mine. He has had nothing to do with it. He does not even know that she exists. Why should he know now? Why should he come muscling in now?' Lou drained her glass in one gulp, 'Stella is mine!'

Maddy pointed out, as gently as she could, that Lou was in blatant contradiction of her own principles by making such a statement. Stella was Stella. She was her own person; she did not belong to anyone. Lou had always claimed that. She had vilified parents who claimed otherwise, in the past. What was so different in this instance?

Lou refused to answer.

'You are in the wrong if you deny her knowledge of her father forever, irrespective of the turning up of this proverbial bad penny, if that is who this person is. You are in the wrong, Lou. And could you ever forgive yourself if she discovered the truth over a dinner table in the company of her friends? Think about it.'

Lou stared blankly into the fire as if she was incapable of thinking about anything at all. When she looked up, her face was grey with exhaustion.

'I told you, he doesn't know. Nobody knows except you, down here. She couldn't find out from him!'

It was a feeble answer.

Maddy got up to replenish Lou's glass, frowning with concentrated effort which had little to do with the act of pouring the whisky.

Lou took hold of her free hand to keep her friend close to the chair.

'I don't want her to know about him, Maddy. And there is something else. I've screwed everything up for her, I really have, one way or another. I've ruined her life.'

'Nonsense! You are devoted to her. She is a very lucky young woman. But I'll tell you one thing, Lou, you really will do a damage if you can't bring yourself to treat her as the adult she is.'

'I've always treated her as an adult!'

Maddy stood looking at her, the decanter poised in her hand,

'To own? To make the most important decision in her life on her behalf. Is that what you're telling me? You have never subscribed to such a stance and you know it!'

A flash of defiance sparked in Maddy's direction but she held her ground until it had subsided and Lou put her head down, biting her lip.

'What am I to do?'

'You are to tell her the truth. You have no option.'

In the glowering silence which followed, Maddy moved back to replace the decanter on the table beside her chair. Then she sat down.

'Tell me the rest?'

'The rest?'

'Yes. What you have screwed up, as you so delicately put it. Is it to do with Edward?'

'Everything's to bloody do with Edward!'

Another uncomfortable silence followed. Maddy waited until she could bear it no longer.

'Is it that he doesn't care for Stella?'

'He is affectionate with Stella. Charming, in fact, as he is with his colleagues, particularly those he is trying to impress and he does seem to want to impress her. But she doesn't reciprocate. She keeps a courteous distance. I don't think that she has ever felt easy with him, right from the start. She is as nervous as the proverbial kitten in his presence and her excuses for avoiding him are legion. They would be amusing if things weren't so dire. And she is evasive with me too, of course, and I cannot begin to tell you how painful that is. I think that we disgust her, Edward and I. What passes for a marriage between us disgusts her and I feel totally responsible. I should have been better at hiding the problems. And now, how am I ever going to find the strength to confess to the disaster that Tim and I were, as well as everything else?'

'You were not to blame for what happened with him.'

'It doesn't matter. It doesn't matter who was to blame or who was not to blame. I failed there and I've failed again and in the process she has become extremely wary about relationships. She has never had a boyfriend, never. Her friends have, but not Stella. She seems afraid to commit somehow. The damage is done, whoever was originally at fault, the damage is done and this is going to make it worse.'

Maddy felt that she had to interrupt:

'That's nonsense, Lou. She is still so young, there is plenty of time yet. And if you'd seen her with Dee Mason when she was down last summer you couldn't say that. They were as thick as thieves, those two, and it was a delight to watch them. They saw a lot of each other, you know. Didn't she tell you?'

'Dee Mason does not count. She's known him from her cradle, for God's sake. He's on exactly the same par as Fran Reynolds. He's *safe*. What I mean is, that she will not commit to an emotional involvement. She will not allow anyone to get near her in that way. I had great hopes of one of the young men she met at the office. That seemed to be coming along really well and then he suddenly falls in love with Fran and Stella does not turn a hair, in fact she is over the moon about it. There is something wrong with her, something profoundly worrying and I feel that a lot of it has to do with me.'

Maddy had her own thoughts on the subject of Stella's increasing detachment, despite the validity of her reference to the obvious friendship with the Mason boy. That summer, in her own dealings with the girl, she had found herself becoming anxious and disturbed. She hated herself for even allowing such suspicions to come into her head and they were such that she did not dare hint at them under the present circumstances unless Lou gave her a more positive opening. Lou, for her part, was obviously innocent of these particular imaginings; she had quite enough to deal with as it was. Maddy felt that it was the wrong moment to risk revealing what she had come to suspect. Instead she said, as kindly as she could,

'Maybe she is just not ready yet.'

But Lou would not have it. She shook her head vehemently and stared miserably into the fire again. Too much reality was invading the sanctuary she thought that she had found.

'You can have no idea, Maddy, how it is, living with Edward. He behaves as if I am a rather tiresome visitor in the house whom he is being forced to tolerate. There is a meanness of spirit there which appals me: the closeting away behind closed doors, the icy politeness, as if to a total stranger and an inconvenient one at that.

He can hardly bring himself to say a civil word. Stella witnesses all this of course and it has got much worse since I crossed him and demanded that my work for the Workers' Party went on. He loathes it. He says that I disgrace him. I probably do, but I cannot change myself any more than I already have.'

She had changed, Maddy thought as she contemplated the jaded, but still beautiful face, the rosiness of the firelight giving the lie to its underlying pallor. Whatever she had experienced with the passage of the years, Lou had lost the fierce independence of her spirit and her thirst for adventure. There was a deep sadness in her actions now. It showed in the set of her eyes and the way she held her head. It was an unbearable contrast for her friend to make.

'Have you ever thought of leaving him?' she asked, tentatively.

'I should have done, at the beginning, when he got rid of the dog.'

Maddy leaned forward in alarm. She thought that maybe Lou was going a little mad.

'But Lou, it was your decision to leave Puff here. Edward did not get rid of him.'

There must have been something in her tone which made Lou look up sharply. Maddy flushed. She was being patronizing, to Lou of all people. Before she could redeem herself, Lou was explaining:

'I'm not talking about Puff. He belonged here with the children. I could not have dragged him away from where he was so happy. Besides, he was old. It would have been too cruel. You know that. We went through all that.'

Puff had been with them at Kelsay. He was an abandoned stray and Lou had rescued him, a great white Husky, and they had adored each other, but he had come to The Green with Stella, when she was a baby, and he had stayed there until old age had taken its toll long after Lou and Stella had gone. They *had* been through all that.

'I don't mean Puff. I mean the spaniel I bought when we first went to Liverpool. He got rid of it. He couldn't stand it. He does not like dogs. Don't you think that there is something terribly wrong with someone who cannot love a dog?'

Maddy did not answer. She was attempting to absorb all of this. She was attempting to find a solution.

'I do!' continued Lou, 'I think that there is something wrong with Edward under any circumstance.'

Lou was smiling grimly as she went on,

'Stella was inseparable from the spaniel, of course. That was another contributary factor to its demise, I suppose. Besides, he was afraid of it. It would go for him when he hit me. Once he had got rid of it there was no question of us having another one.'

The shock of what Lou had said, so nonchalantly, almost casually, left Maddy breathless. She was horrified at what was unfolding.

'So you see, Stella has not exactly been party to the best of unions. It is no surprise to me that she does not want to risk making the same mistake as her mother. And she is not going to know that I've done it twice, not if I can help it.'

'You cannot blame yourself!'

'I can and I do. And now there is this hideous dilemma to face with the re-appearance of Tim. I don't know what to do Maddy, and I'm too tired to cope with it. Tell me what to do.'

They both stared into the embers of the dying fire until Maddy pulled herself together enough to throw another log on it. She leaned forward with the brass poker in her hand and stirred up the smouldering ashes.

'I think that you must think seriously about leaving Edward. I do not suggest this lightly; your situation is virtually impossible. It is insupportable. More urgently you must see this man as soon as you get back. You said that he was only down the road. Well go and call on him. Make any excuse and find out if it really is Tim.'

'I don't want to.'

Maddy sat back in her chair abruptly.

'Whether you want to or not is not the issue. You must go. If it is Tim then you have to tell him about the existence of Stella. You must do that at least, even if you can't face telling her. You have to do it. Do you understand me Lou?'

Lou was looking at her strangely.

'And what if he takes her away?'

'Don't be ridiculous! How could he do that? She is a grown woman, she has a mind of her own and a very good one from what I can tell!'

Lou had an expression of extreme bitterness on her face.

'Precisely!' she said. 'There is no reason for her to value what she has with me, there never has been. The last time that she was really happy was when she was here with you. I did to her what I wouldn't do to the poor old dog. I took her with me and she hates me for it. Why shouldn't she choose to go off with her intriguing, fascinating, miraculously- returned father?'

'Because she loves you.'

Maddy nervously bit her lip in the telling silence which followed and then she said,

'Cross your bridges when you come to them, Lou. And I know that it is not my place to say this, but for God's sake be careful that it is not you he takes away. Don't fall into the trap yourself.'

Lou laughed; a genuinely amused laugh.

'There is absolutely no fear of that, my dear, no fear of that at all.'

She gulped the last of her whisky too quickly and coughed.

'But I shall do as you say, I will see him.'

'If it is he.'

'If it is indeed, he.' The sardonic note in her voice was against herself, not Maddy.

'I think that you should get some rest now; sleep on it. We'll talk again in the morning.'

They went upstairs together and Maddy saw her friend settled in to her room. Then she returned to her chair by the fireside. There was a lot to think about. Lou's situation was well and truly in crisis and she was not convinced that her advice had been the best she could give. But she knew in her bones that both Lou and Stella should get as far away as possible from Edward Bundenell. Even if her suspicions were outrageously far-fetched, she was certain that there was something radically wrong with Edward. They had to get away!

She wished that Lonsdale was back. She needed to hold him. She needed to curl up beside him. She needed to tell him, just by touching him, that she knew how lucky she was to have him and she did not care that he was bound to have got himself into some scrape or other. On his return, he would shamefacedly ask for her forgiveness as always, but with Lonsdale there was nothing to forgive. There never had been.

7. Confrontations

LOU AND STELLA spent the evening of her return ostensibly catching up on the Hampshire news. News of everyone, it seemed, and Stella did not regret for one minute that she was not at the Adelphi with the others. And Lou, refreshed by the few days with Maddy, found it less difficult than she had thought to be animated and gossipy about the doings of old friends. Stella, greatly relieved to find her mother more like her old self, delighted in it. But she had something of importance to impart too. She could hardly wait to tell Lou of the momentous step which Fran had taken and which was to occur the following weekend. Fran had asked Jack to the Saturday party at the Reynolds'. It was a big decision. It was a highly significant decision, to her mind. Lou was genuinely interested and concerned. She was also rapidly making crucial plans of her own.

What Stella had not told Lou was that Fran had asked her to bring Jack along as *her* friend. She had willingly agreed to comply with this little deception. It would mean that Jack would be assessed on his merits, without bias, if he was thought to be Stella's beau. She was not averse to deception of any kind. The practice of it had become as normal to her as breathing. Fran's initial scruples she had considered to be charmingly guileless. Between them they arranged that Jack should call for Stella at the Esplanade and they would go along to the Reynolds' together.

At the appointed time then, the following Saturday, Jack approached the row of imposing-looking houses where Stella lived. He felt more than usually nervous, conscious indeed of the auspiciousness of the occasion.

He used his hands to smooth down his hair and wished that there had been a shop front in which to inspect his reflection in the window. He was sure that he ought to check his collar, but when he touched it it was reassuringly rigid with the starch that Clare had used according to his detailed instructions. He had been forced to bribe her for this sisterly service and she had grumbled at his interference and called him a fussy beggar and told him to kindly get lost. Nor had he liked the way in which she had gone into a huddle with his other sisters as he had been leaving the house and they had all been laughing and exchanging significant glances, even the occasional wink. He had held his tongue however. It would not do to arrive in a fluster. Now, he was certain that he had marked the collar with his fingers and would be on edge until he could make sure that he hadn't. He began to wish that he had not agreed to come. But when he was ushered into the magnificent hall with the oak staircase winding its way upwards and Mrs Bundenell came down those very stairs to welcome him, he got the shock of his life. She was Pinny's 'old lady'! She was the woman on the hustings. She really was the woman he had heard speak so passionately and so eloquently at Labour Party meetings. He could not believe it for a minute and then he felt so much at home that he talked nineteen to the dozen and Stella had almost to force him out of the door as it was time to go.

All the way along the maze of streets to Fran's he asked Stella over and over again why she had not said who her mother was. It was extraordinary. He had known of her for years, he had seen her more than once on Speakers' Corner, and he had never connected the two of them. Yet when he looked more closely at Stella, he could see the resemblance. Apart from the hair, which invariably reminded him of copper beech trees, and the smooth, unlined face, Stella was very like her mother. But why had she not mentioned it? She had been in no doubt about his political involvement. She must have known that he would have come across her and why had he not connected the names? Then he recalled that Mrs Bundenell was not referred to as Bundenell at all, but by another name when she spoke at meetings. Probably her maiden name. The whole thing was strange. Furthermore, he simply could not think what reasons Stella had for keeping so quiet about it. He ultimately put it down the secretiveness which was part of the unfathomable nature of women.

By the time that they were ringing the bell on Fran's door the collar, smudged or unsmudged, was totally forgotten and his every nerve-end was tingling with the delight of his unexpected discovery. Their first sight of him, as he was introduced to Mr and Mrs Reynolds, was that of an extremely personable young man, his more than handsome face alert and bright-eyed. They were impressed. They were even further impressed after supper when he sang to Fran's accompaniment on the piano and they realized how good his voice was. Someone,(they had forgotten who, probably Fran), had also told them that he was a splendid golfer. He would be a welcome addition to the Saturday parties, Izzie decided, and it was so nice for Stella to have someone of her own at last.

As Fran gave up playing and handed over at the piano to Stella for a while, she whispered her thanks to her friend.

'I think that he has made a hit, don't you?' Her face was shiny with happiness.

Stella laughed, 'It isn't the only hit he will have made tonight either. *My* mother is quite bowled over by him. I could hardly drag him away from her!' She laughed again. 'You could have a rival there.'

Fran leaned down to be closer to her ear, 'Well, you shall have your reward, just you see. We have asked Mr Dundonald to come. He will pop in later, he said, as he has to see some other people first. Fancy, you will get to meet him after all.'

They both kept an eye on the door throughout the evening whenever they remembered to do so but they were disappointed. The intriguing Mr Dundonald did not turn up.

He was, in fact, walking along the sea-front with Lou, all other arrangements he had been committed to long thrown to the wind.

* * *

As soon as her daughter had left with Jack, Lou had grasped her opportunity. Stella would be safely involved at the Reynolds' house until midnight at least. She could get this ghastly thing over with and be back and in bed before Stella returned. By morning, Lou reckoned, she should have been able to pull herself together enough to deflect any curious questions, should Stella notice her distress. That she would be distressed went without saying.

There was to be no thinking about it, no argument with herself. If she did not go as soon as the two young ones were out of sight then she would be wasting her effort. Tim, if it was really he, would have left the hotel for the evening.

Her coat was on as soon as the door was shut behind them. She then let herself out through the garden and hurried along the dunes which ran behind the length of the Esplanade. Once she reached the point where the Marine Drive started, she emptied her shoes of sand and flitted across the road. There was no sign of Jack and Stella further along the right angle which the junction formed.

She reached reception and asked if Mr Dundonald had left for the evening. The receptionist knew her, of course, and Lou wondered if she could sense the agitation under the deadly calm with which she requested that his room number should be rung. There was no reply. He must have gone out already. Lou swore violently under her breath but smiled and said that it was of no consequence, she would try to contact him later.

Just at that moment she heard the ping of the lift bell. She panicked for a second. If Tim emerged from the lift and recognized her in front of the receptionist there would be no knowing what might follow. She thanked the girl and asked her to tell him, on his return, that an old friend had called.

'Shall I give your name, Mrs Bundenell?'

'Of course.'

'How's Dr. Bundenell?'

Dear Christ! Was the woman going to go on all night? 'Very well, never better,' called Lou as she made for the exit. 'Thank you for asking.'

'And Stella?'

But Lou was in the revolving door, waving and nodding to her by then. She might as well have saved herself the effort. The receptionist had already dismissed her from her mind. Mr Dundonald was at the desk handing in his key and the telephone was ringing. She mouthed the message to him coquettishly and pointed to the exit as she dealt with the enquiry. He did not hurry to the door. He had never heard of a Mrs Bundenell and he certainly did not want to be held up by a stranger. He had a client to see before he joined his charming new friends at their party. He had never had a friend called Bundenell, old or otherwise, and he had little curiosity about the matter that particular evening.

Lou had sat down on the bench which was placed to one side of the door. It was there for the clientele to enjoy the view. Now it was dark and not particularly warm but Lou was unaware that she was shivering. The pain in her chest was threatening to force her to cry out. She thought that she would die of suspense, sitting there, waiting for the occupant of the lift to emerge.

He went straight past her and paused on the top step before descending. Although he had his back to her, she recognized him immediately. The set of one shoulder was slightly higher than the other since his useless arm had had to be compensated for. He had not gained weight despite the passing of the years. As he stood there, awkwardly lighting his cigarette, he could have been the young man she had known almost two decades ago. The trench-coat that he was wearing contributed to the uncanny feeling Lou had, which increased as he awkwardly returned his left hand to his pocket. She could have been back at Kelsay!

'Tim?' She uttered his name softly, her voice coming huskily out of the darkness. Her throat was as dry as dust. 'Tim, it's Lou. I need to speak with you.'

She had stood up to face him as he turned. Now that she was confronting him, her fear had left her. In its place was a cold determination. There was nothing cold about him. He seemed overjoyed to hear her. She had her back to the light which spilled out from the hotel foyer; a tall, vaguely familiar silhouette was all that he could see.

'Lou! Good God! Where have you sprung from?' He moved towards her as if he was going to embrace her. She took a step backwards.

'I live here.'

'At the hotel? I don't believe it!'

'No. Further along the front.' She waved in the vague direction of the Esplanade. 'My husband works at the University.'

He was open-mouthed with pleasant, unsuspecting surprise. Then he said,

'How did you know I was here?'

She took a deep breath. 'I found out by accident,' her voice was no longer soft and querulous, 'and I need to talk to you. Tonight!'

Tim looked at her steadily. He had picked up the urgency in her tone. It was some sort of warning, he felt sure.

'Well, let's go back in. Let's have a drink.' He paused for a moment and when he next spoke his voice did not lack irony, 'For old times' sake'

She moved to the edge of the steps.

'No. They know me in there. It's a fine night. I'd prefer a walk.'

She was already half-way down, making for the gateway. He followed her, instinctively knowing what she was going to tell him.

He caught up with her and they walked for some distance in silence until she said,

'I'm not here for old times' sake Tim, nor for catching up on your news, however adventurous it might be. I'm here to tell you that you have a seventeen-year-old daughter and that she avoided meeting you last week by the narrowest of chances. I cannot risk that happening again.'

She expected him to halt in his tracks but he didn't, he continued walking. Lou became slightly unnerved.

'I'm not going to make any demands on you,' she said, 'financially or otherwise. I just want you to be prepared, that's all. I don't care about you but I do care about her. She must not be hurt. Do you understand? On no account must she be hurt. If she is, believe me, I will kill you with my bare hands. I have nothing whatsoever to lose.'

She meant it. He knew she did. He stopped then.

They had reached the part of the front where the road ended and where a small wicket gate led out to a lane and the streets beyond. Below them, some water-marked steps led down from the sea-wall and the hulk of a massive breakwater stretched out along the beach. He signalled to her to go down and they sat, side by side, on the blackened and barnacled buttress which propped up the walkway. They both stared back at the route along which they had come, the lights from the greatly self-important houses of Beach Lawn reflecting on the water as the tide pushed in, swishing in little waves. Out to sea, the buoy-lights twinkled and a ship slid silently, as if through a density of oil, towards the bar. It was the Irish Ferry.

'What is she like?'

It was his turn to have trouble with his voice. Lou felt a stir of sympathy for him which she immediately suppressed. She wanted to say, 'What is that to you?' She wanted to wound him, but she didn't. She thought for a while, then she said,

'She is very beautiful.'

Tim had picked up a bit of flotsam from the sand and was examining it in the gloom, keeping his eyes fixed on it as if there might be some secret, outlandish creature lurking in the seaweed which clung to it.

'To look at. She is very beautiful.' Lou also fixed her eyes on the piece of mishapen wood in Tim's hand, mesmerized by the movement of his fingers. It was nervous, almost obsessive, his constant turning of the thing. She had to force her eyes away. She had to wipe out any consciousness of what he might be feeling; she must say what she had to say and then go. 'She is articled to a firm of accountants. She is very good with figures.' The words sounded clipped and rather sanctimonious. She was finding the situation, and her position in it, almost intolerable.

Tim laughed, breaking the tension. 'She doesn't take after me then?'

'Not in that, no. She is like you in other ways though.'

'What ways? Feckless? Faithless? Is that it?'

He at last turned to look at her. Harshness had replaced the momentary amusement in his tone. Now he was challenging her to accuse him.

'No,' she said, 'none of those things.'

'What else is there then?'

Lou was gazing straight ahead, following the rows of winking lights which traced the shoreline, with unblinking eyes.

'She is not strictly honest, I suspect. I certainly know that she is capable of deceit, of evasion. And she does not seem able to commit to any emotional entanglement whatsoever. Maybe she is right. Maybe you were right.'

There was yet another prolonged silence but there was no blame reverberating through it. Lou surprised herself by being genuinely interested in the ways in which Stella resembled her father. Previously she had always automatically discounted him. Put him firmly out of mind. With him there beside her she suddenly had a vivid recollection of things which Stella had done which fitted so perfectly with her recollection of Tim. The only difference was that Stella was not promiscuous, or at least, she did not think she was. Quite the reverse in fact.

'But she is deceitful.'

She found herself unnerved once more but not enough to suspend her judgement. She was waiting for him to ask her to elucidate. She remembered that Tim already knew Fran. She was not about to tell him how Stella had gleefully detailed how she had got her into H. & B.s, unqualified though Fran was. Stella had been lucky. Her friend had not given the game away and after bemusing Miss Wilkinson for a week over the discrepancy between her mediocre performance at her desk and her glowing test papers, Fran had suddenly come into her own and astonished Stella by becoming super-efficient, seemingly overnight.

Lou decided that her daughter had also inherited her father's propensity for good luck. Had the substitution of the test papers been discovered, Fran would not have been the only one without a job.

'She knows what she wants,' Lou continued, 'and she makes sure that she gets it.' There was a pause. 'Just like you. In my opinion though, she wants better things. Should that excuse her methods?'

Tim did not answer. He could not resent Lou's assessment of himself, in fact he was thankful that she did not seem to be more vengeful. It was not the first time that he had had to confront this situation. Guilt was not a part of his make-up, but he was genuinely sorry that Lou had been landed. That was his word for it, in his head, 'landed.' He had been fond of her, he recalled. He would not have wished it upon her. However, here she was, married, evidently prosperous. She could not have suffered all that much as a result of their wartime liaison. If she had, she would be attacking him instead of sitting there so mildly. He failed to recall that mildness was the last characteristic he would have attributed to her twenty years ago. Nonetheless, something, some echo in his memory, some atavistic gift for self-preservation perhaps, hinted that there might be danger in her stillness.

'I will do whatever *you* want now,' he said. 'Just tell me what it is.'

'I suppose you want to meet her?'

'I would like to. Yes, I would, if it can be arranged.'

'Anything can be *arranged* !'

Lou's cynicism was raw. She felt as though her tongue was swelling to twice its normal size, that it would choke her. 'This is what real fear is like,' she thought. 'This is it. Only my fear is selfish. For me. I do not want him to take her away.' But a terrible, chilling truth which had haunted her since she had first heard of Tim's arrival was that her daughter, whom she loved more than her own life, might in fact be better off if she did go. She drove back the rising panic which was starving her mouth of saliva.

'She does not know about you. I allowed her to think that her father had been killed, like Maddy's brother and her fiancé. Shot to pieces in some God-forsaken trench. She was used to those sort of stories.'

Tim's brow furrowed as a picture of Maddy's younger brother came into his mind. The last time he had seen him had been at Kelsay. He had come up to visit. He was making a splendid catch on a cricket pitch, knee high in vegetation because they could not afford to waste the hay. He was eighteen years old and about to go to France. As he caught the ball he fell and disappeared for a moment, only to emerge, laughing, his trophy held high above the waving, blue-tinged grasses. The red ball gleaming in his hand. It was brilliant sunlight...

'I'm sorry,' he said, 'I had no idea.'

'No,' she said, 'how could you? I had left Kelsay when the news came through.' It had not occurred to her to say that she had also left him.

But Lou had no intention of being diverted by nostalgia. She wanted to get this meeting over with as soon as possible; as soon as she had forced him to some sort of agreement. She reminded him of his request.

'You are bound to come across her without any help from me, actually. There is no need for any special arrangement. She is very friendly with the Reynolds.'

'Reynolds?'

Lou became impatient. The connection was so etched on her brain that it did not occur to her that he had to be totally ignorant of it.

'Your business associate, Neville Kennedy! He is very friendly with Dodo I believe.'

Tim was staring at her, his eyes wide with astonishment.

'Neville knows my daughter?'

Lou snapped at him sharply. 'He invited her to the Adelphi last weekend. I persuaded her not to go.'

'Good God!'

The piece of wood dropped to the sand with a dull thud as he looked at his watch, 'And I'm supposed to be calling in on them within the hour.'

'Well, I suggest that we agree a plan. I am asking you not to tell her who you really are!'

Tim leaned forward, his elbow on his knee, his right hand covering his eyes.

'I don't even know her name!'

Lou was not a hard person. In fact, compassion had been her downfall more times than she could count, particularly so with Tim, but she resisted the temptation to offer him comfort.

'It is Bundenell. She took my husband's name.'

Somehow, she could not bring herself to form the word 'Stella'. It had nothing to do with him, nothing at all. And yet, she supposed, he did have a right. He must have some rights. And she found that thought appalling. She sighed, involuntarily, as her innate sense of justice told her that now that he had reappeared she had to play fair. 'Her first name is Stella.'

Tim did not respond. He was pushing sand about with his foot, forming a miniature entrenchment, unconsciously. His head was bowed. Lou pressed on.

'I would much rather that you did not reveal your relationship to her. You *must* not do that. Of course you will see her, that's unavoidable, but I'm afraid that I will need rather more than your dubious promise that you will do as I ask.'

Why was she being apologetic? she asked herself. Why was she behaving as though it was some enormous favour that she was demanding of him? An hour ago he did not have an inkling that Stella existed. And what could there possibly be that would mean more than a promise between them, even if he should give it? Nothing. No guarantee at all. And his word was hollow, meaningless. She had no faith in it. All it represented was months, possibly years, of anguish living with the knowledge that he would break any undertaking that he had agreed to, on a whim. And she would not know when he might have done it. She would live in torment. She would find herself spying on Stella, to see if she knew. Forever watching her, fearing for her. The future then, was hateful. She was busily convincing herself of this when he broke in:

'I should like to meet her with you. I don't want to come across her in the company of others. I might...Oh, I don't know what I might do, really. Could you bear that? Could you? You can say that we are old friends. We are old friends, aren't we?'

Lou did not respond. She was confused because he had not offered to promise. She did not know whether that was a good sign or a form of evasion.

'And how do you propose I engineer such a meeting?'

Tim lifted himself up from the breakwater and offered his hand to her. She rejected it and stood up unaided. He pretended not to notice the rebuff.

'Come on,' he said, 'let's go back and have a drink now. We need it. It's getting very cold. We'll talk about it on the way.'

Lou nodded, curtly, and walked on ahead of him up the steps.

They had a very limited range of options available to them in their agreement to deceive Stella. The only one which sounded in any way plausible was to say that her mother had, by sheer chance, met an old patient from her days in Yorkshire. They had recently come across each other when returning home via the overhead railway. They were overjoyed to see each other, they would say, and Tim had insisted on being introduced to Stella.

Lou did not like it. She did not like any of it. She felt worn out by the time they reached Marine Drive once again.

'Ah,' tinkled the receptionist as they entered the foyer of the hotel, 'you found each other!' She took in Lou's appearance from head to toe in one self-satisfied glance, her white-toothed smile remaining fixed in place all the while. The doctor's wife was showing her age tonight, was the thought in her mind as she smiled on; Mrs Bundenell's usual elegance was slipping. The darling Mr Dundonald was still her property.

She cast him a warmly sympathetic glance as the couple passed by her desk, a glance which indicated that she knew that he would much rather be spending the evening with her. But he did not acknowledge it; instead he walked straight on, ushering his companion towards the double doors which led to the bar.

Once she had established that they were safely inside, she shrugged her shoulders and turned to admire herself in the large ornate mirror behind her and pushed her hair into deeper waves with fastidious care. Then she ran a finger along the line of her lips but before she could continue congratulating herself on the conquest of Mr Dundonald she was interrupted by the insistent ringing of the telephone. As she answered it, she flicked on to a new page of the booking register barely suppressing a sigh. She would be off-duty soon and surely he would not be lumbered with Mrs Bundenell all night?

* * *

The following Monday morning, first thing, one of the office boys thrust a note on to Fran's desk with a peremptory, 'From upstairs!' as he swanned off on his rounds. He obviously was of the gratifying opinion that it was some sort of summons to penal servitude. Fran glared at his back as he disappeared into the far reaches of the great office. He was a cocky little devil at the best of times. Short of stature but big of swagger! He irritated her.

When she had expended her disapproval for long enough, she remembered the note and opened it, not without a small degree of trepidation. She flushed as she attempted to recall what possible misdemeanours she could have committed the previous week and was aware that there were several enquiring eyes upon her. To her relief it was only a message from Stella asking her if she could get out at lunchtime. She had some news which would not wait until they could meet up that evening.

Fran was intrigued. She wrote a hasty reply to the effect that she would see her at the Kardomah as soon after 1.00 as she could make it. Then she hailed the office boy, once he was en-route for his return, with a haughtiness which put her in mind of one of her aunts. She did not care, the little beast was far too big for his boots in her opinion. However, she did not risk a further put-down. This particular creature had an unerring habit of getting the better of his adversaries, as she knew to her cost.

'Urgent reply to Miss Bundenell,' she said, utilizing her best voice, 'as quick as you can.'

He treated her to a patronizing look as he twitched the envelope from her fingers,

'Oi, Lah-di-Dah, it will get there when I'm ready!' And then as a precautionary afterthought when he saw Miss Wilkinson raise her head from her papers, ' Soon as maybe, *Miss*.'

Fran felt an urgent desire to wipe the smirk off his face. He was no bigger than her little brother Charlie. She certainly would have doled out a slap to him for half the cheek. However, she treated the boy to a dignified nod and sent him on his way.

As she ploughed through her morning's work, she wondered what it might be that Stella felt was so urgent. The Saturday party had gone well. She hoped that it was nothing to do with Jack. Could it be a warning that her parents had divined that he was not Stella's boy friend at all? She would be in trouble if that were the case, especially if someone had revealed that he was a Catholic. A sudden sinking feeling in her stomach caused her to make an error. She ripped the paper out of the typewriter with uncharacteristic violence. Miss Wilkinson looked up again. Fran smiled at her and raised her eyes to the ceiling in mock exasperation. Miss Wilkinson smiled back.

Fran turned over in her mind the significance of what she had done in inviting Jack to Oakshot Road. It was a big step. It was a sort of signal to him that she was serious. Was she serious? She might be, in a year or two. She certainly loved him. As soon as she had thought this, she corrected herself. She was absolutely *in* love with him, there was no doubt about it. He was the most interesting young man that she had ever met.

He was never without a book in his hand and it was always, without exception, something *weighty*, something serious. He read Darwin in secret, he told her, as it was on the list of books banned by the Church. Her brother Neville had hardly heard of Darwin, let alone felt a driving need to read him.

At first Fran had thought that it was a form of affectation, that Jack had wanted to be seen as an intellectual, but she had soon come to realize that this was not the case. Jack's father, apparently, although she had yet to meet him, was the same. They would spend hours together discussing literature and politics and people like Lytton Strachey! It seemed inbred in them, this passion for books. Jack had told her that his father's family had only been able to afford to send one of their sons to University and it had been the eldest, naturally, but Jack's father had been determined that he would not be outdone. Nor would any son of his. Since Jack had been old enough to listen he had talked to him, just as he did now, when he was fully grown. Far from being a pretence, this love of learning was second nature to him.

Perhaps it was because he read so much that Jack never tried to take advantage of her, unlike the other boys who had previously asked her out. She had never had to wriggle away from any pawing by Jack as she had had to do with Neville's friends at the tennis club. She had been going out with him for months and they had only just got round to their first kiss. He was infinitely more sensitive, more respectful than any of the others. There was obviously a connection.

The explanation could simply be that he was a Catholic, of course. A good Catholic, not given to insisting that she responded to uninvited, and in the main, sickening attentions. She admired Jack for his restraint. But she knew that being considerate wasn't all that being a Catholic meant by any manner of means. That particular virtue had not featured at all in what *she* had learned from *her* parents.

As children, Izzie had forbidden them to mix with R.C.s. R.C.s were looked upon by her family as the most lamentable blot on the landscape of Liverpool. Fran and her sisters had been warned that the Catholics were a dirty, scavenging lot of Irish immigrants who lived in squalor and were averse to work. Associating with their children was not to be contemplated. Fran had not needed much persuasion. They all had impetigo, she had been told, and that was tantamount to having the plague. And their fathers were either out of work or dock labourers. She was to keep away from them.

But this had not tallied with what she had seen on her way to school. The girls from the convent and the boys from St. Mary's had all looked very respectable. They walked on the opposite side of the road, of course, and they did keep to their side of the pavement, even when the two groups had shouted insults to each other through the gaps in the traffic. 'Catty Cats! 'Catty Cats!' followed by jeers and a general jumping up and down on their side and then the inevitable 'Proddy Dogs! Proddy Dogs!' accompanied by gales of laughter to the irritation of the more adult among the passers-by. It had all been in fun, she thought.

She had never questioned any of this till now. Had it really just been in fun? All Catholics stemmed from Bootle and the notorious Scotland Road and that, as the Reynolds and the MacKenzies had instilled into her, was an origin of unspeakable stigma. That was why, from being a babe on her mother's knee, she had been forbidden to talk to them. The family had a position to keep up.

But Jack did not fit this scheme of things. Jack was nothing like what she had been warned against. Were her parents bigots then? Was she a bigot herself? Or was it that Jack originally came from Glasgow as opposed to being Irish and had always lived over the water, well away from the downtrodden area her parents were so averse to.

It was Izzie, rather than Fa, who laboured the point. Fa just got on with the job of providing for his ever-increasing family, loving them all and escaping to the Burlington Club on a Sunday morning whilst his wife had her hour's peace in Church. He looked after his men as well as he could and he never questioned them as to their religious affiliations when he took them on, unlike many of his fellow businessmen who would have no truck with Catholics. Their stance was that Catholics were a feckless, idle lot. They drank themselves into a stupor whenever they got the chance, they bred like rabbits and they lived in decadence, fighting and brawling more often than not. They would refuse to employ them.

Although Fa knew that all of this could be said to be true, he also knew that it was not the whole story. One of his best friends in his younger days had been a Catholic, Joe Hoolihan, and he had told him many tales of how things really were, especially in Belfast. Besides, Fa employed men on their merits, not because of their religious affiliations. He considered it none of his business as long as his men were loyal, trustworthy and gave him value for money by their effort. But he would turn white if he thought that one of his daughters might marry into such a persuasion. And Izzie, quite simply, would not countenance such a thing. It would be right out of the question.

Fran was so taken up with all these thoughts that she had to type out several of her letters twice as she made so many mistakes, and, by the time she got to the Kardomah she had convinced herself that either Dodo or, more likely Abigail who was far from being the sweet thing that her parents thought she was, had snitched on her. She was in a state of acute anxiety by the time she joined up with Stella. Jack's religion was something that she had to think about much more carefully.

Her reaction to her friend's news that she had had tea with Mr Dundonald the previous day was initially one of anti-climax. She was so relieved that she hardly heard all that Stella was telling her and had to ask her to repeat it.

She had felt very let down that Tim had failed to appear at the party on the Saturday night. Now, it seemed, he had been with Stella's mother all the time and that they had known each other for years, ever since the war. It was such a coincidence that they had met on the train, or at the station or wherever it was. Stella had been so astounded that she had laughed outright, she said, and she was laughing still.

'Did you have tea at the Royal?' Fran, unaccountably, felt a twinge of jealousy. Mr Dundonald had been her 'find', or so she had persuaded herself. She had wanted to be the one to introduce him to her friend, not Mrs Bundenell. Since the dinner at the Adelphi, when the chair next to their guest had been empty, she had entertained secret hopes of Stella falling in love, at long last, and with the exotic Mr Dundonald, and she, Fran, the one who had brought them together.

'No, no. We went to Southport. We went to the fair and everything first. It was fun, except for when they kept on for hours about the people they had both known; you know how they do? When *I'm* old, I am not going to indulge in that sort of thing in front of people who haven't got the faintest clue what I'm talking about!'

Fran's matchmaking schemes seemed doomed before they began.

'Mr Dundonald isn't old, Stella. Well, if he is, he is still stunningly attractive, don't you think? And you'd hardly notice his hand, if you did not know about it.'

Stella halted the progress of her fork to her mouth and laughed so much that the other diners shot disapproving looks at them across the room and huddled their heads together, making tutting noises in their direction.

'Well, would you Stella?'

'You are not serious, Fran?' She leaned forward in order to scrutinize her friend's face more closely, 'I do believe you are!'

She laughed again, but this time into her napkin, her eyes streaming with merriment at the pricelessness of the joke.

'You are incorrigible! Believe me, if I were to fall in love, which I have not the slightest intention of ever doing, by the way, it would NOT be with Mr Dundonald. He is older than my mother, for Heaven's sake!'

Fran was forced to agree that this was the case but she felt bound to add that it did seem a pity to waste such a romantic opportunity. And then, he was so very, very appealing. This last was uttered with genuine regret.

'Fran,' said Stella, 'I want to tell you something.' Suddenly serious, her voice had softened, as if she were dealing with a small child. 'I want you to curb this fantasy of yours. I am not going to get married, not now, not ever. I put too much emphasis on self-preservation perhaps, but don't take that as a criticism of you and Jack. You are one of the lucky ones, Fran.'

'Oh! I'm not going to marry Jack Jamieson.'

Stella looked astonished.

'Why ever not?'

'I *can't* marry Jack.' To her embarrassment, tears had sprung to her eyes and threatened to make her nose run. She rummaged up her sleeve for her handkerchief, attempting to pull herself together.

'I cannot marry Jack because he is a Catholic,' she said, with firm conviction.

For one second the look in Stella's eyes was hostile.

'That's not a valid reason. Besides, he loves you. He loves you more than anything.'

Stella was angry. Since the death of his sister she had become quite the confidante of Jack Jamieson. Now she had to hold back her knowledge that Jack had been on the brink of entering the priesthood when he met Fran. He had gone through, was still going through, agonies about the decision. It was obvious that Fran had no idea, however, and she decided that the present moment was unpropitious for such a revelation. Fran was manifestly upset and her own self-control was not exactly dependable, so instead of saying anything, she watched her friend miserably push away her plate to the other side of the table.

'My parents would kill me, they really would! And it's not just his religion. There's his politics as well. It's all so complicated.' She blew her nose loudly. 'It's alright for you! Your mother thinks that he is the bee's knees. Well mine wouldn't. She would not allow him in the house if she knew the half of it!'

She looked as if she was about to cry in earnest and Stella softened. Fran was right with regard to Lou. Jack could have come from the moon and she would not have cared as long as he was his own man and was prepared to stand up for himself. The fact that he was in tune with the things closest to her own heart was just a delightful bonus as far as Lou was concerned.

'Well, you can depend on me to cover for you as long as you want,' Stella said, 'I quite enjoy it actually.'

Fran smiled. 'He's lovely, isn't he? But I cannot think about marrying him, Stella, I really can't; it's far too early anyway, irrespective of anything else. I hardly know him if one is to be truthful about it.'

Stella bowed her head. In her bitter recollection it took about thirty seconds to know if someone was good or not. And Jack was good and he was absolutely certain about his feelings for Fran. He loved her more with every minute that passed. Stella could not bear to think of him rejected and hurt. Particularly for the reasons Fran had set out.

She sighed and then looked up, pretending to smile.

'We must get back. It's nearly time.'

Fran stood up rather shakily, collecting her things from the adjoining chair. She looked as though she had the weight of the world on her shoulders. Stella stopped herself from giving her hand a sympathetic squeeze. Fran had to get her priorities right all by herself.

* * *

As the following months turned spring into summer, Stella had no need to sustain the pretence regarding Jack when they were at Oakshot Road, as they were hardly ever there. The weekends were taken up cycling to the open-air swimming pools at Southport or New Brighton, dancing in the evenings, racing each other through the new tunnel under the Mersey and exploring as much of the coastline as their wheels would take them. All their friends had come to think of Jack and Fran as a permanent couple.

Gradually it became acknowledged by the Reynolds that Jack had 'transferred' his affections from Stella to Fran. Not a word was said, but Izzie pursed her lips more than was usual with her, and the two youngest boys sensed that they must not cross her these days. Fa just pretended that the situation did not exist. His favourite daughter was still his 'baby', despite the presence of the four noisy siblings who had come after her. According to him, Fran was far too young to be involved with anybody. He could not understand what his wife was getting all steamed up about. He found it very wearing, all this suppressed agitation and headed for the Burlington and the safety of his male cronies as often as he could.

The subject of Izzie's fermenting ire, Jack himself, was far too busy to notice anything. When he was not with Fran and all their friends, or at work, he was at meetings with Mrs Bundenell. They became firm allies and he began to look upon her as some sort of oracle. She loaned him books and pamphlets. She encouraged him to question everything, something which he had tentatively begun to do himself, coincidental with his discovery of her, something which, initially, had excited him. It brought with it, however, no small degree of alarm.

His blind faith in the veracity of the printed word had paralleled his blind faith in the dogma of his church. It was unthinkable to challenge either. But, one night, as he was lying on his bed engrossed in an article, the content of which he no longer recalled, he found himself suddenly sitting bolt upright and thinking, 'Not only do I not agree with this, I don't *believe* it. It's untrue!'

Whatever it was that he had refused to believe had already, by the time he met Lou, become a blur in his memory. What was of much more significance was the recognition of an overwhelming feeling of liberation. He *need* not accept what other people put in print. He need not believe what other people *told* him. It was up to him to decide what was fact rather than opinion; superstition rather than logic. All this time he had felt deterred from questioning anything, knowing that it would incur disapprobation from the priests. But long before this he had been secreting away banned books and reading them voraciously, his guilty heart beating wildly in his ears. The difference was that now he was encouraged to discuss them all, right out in the open, and being with Lou Bundenell was like having a microscope applied to all his former certainties. She was the hardest task-master he had ever come across. It was demanded that he accept nothing at face-value or he need not waste her time by bringing up the issue. He must challenge and explore. It was she who convinced him, beyond any doubt, that the sacrifice of her generation had been in vain. Another war was not only inevitable, but pending. And it was she who first took Jack and Pinny to visit the internees from Spain.

With all these prescriptions, the dilemma regarding his leanings towards the priesthood intensified. At one stage he had persuaded himself that it was through the church that he might do most good. Then the idea was cast aside. He would have to serve years of training and then he would have no control over where he was ultimately sent. He could end up in Africa and that would be a *great* help to the immediate community. Besides which, he had become too much of a radical to be able to stomach the narrow-mindedness and blinkered vision of the Church as it stood. He doubted now that blind faith was justifiable at any level. And then, towering over all of this, there was what he felt for Fran. He was in no position to commit himself to a life of celibacy, feeling as he did about her. He was not like Pinny; he was not given to arbitrarily sowing wild oats, he genuinely loved Fran, wanted her, ached for her to the point of torment. He should break with her that very moment if he was even vaguely serious about the other, he told himself. Break with her at once!

But he couldn't do it. He loved her too much and yet he had so little to offer her except trouble. He was not unaware of the stance the Reynolds took where he was concerned. His anxieties intensified all the more as the battleground which Spain had become seemed to look ominously like the precursor of a greater struggle. He could not escape from it. What could he do for her if he had to go to war?

8. Catalysts
1937

JACK WAS NOT alone in suffering sleepless, anxious nights. Lou was in the same position but with added reason. She felt that the continuous proximity of Tim Dundonald would turn her already greying hair to white.

He had, so far, kept his promise regarding Stella, but she could not trust him. A curious arrangement had evolved because of *his* inability to trust himself.

From the first sight of his daughter, he had adored her with a protective tenderness he would not have believed possible. The intensity of his feelings for her took him by surprise. It was not that she was exquisite, which she undoubtedly was, with her mother's looks and her mane of chestnut hair, it was the recognition of himself in her that reduced him to tears in the privacy of his hotel room. She had inherited the few good things in his nature, whatever Lou might think to the contrary. Her eyes, dancing with good humour and love of fun, did not quite disguise from her father, who was seeing her for the first time, the vulnerability which lay beneath. And he sensed that she did battle with that. That there was courage there and a fierce longing for independence. She was as he might have been. He must ensure that she never turned into what he actually was!

He insisted that he would only see her in the presence of Lou. That way she could be confident that the secret was safe. Lou found it an enormous strain.

The practicalities of it were difficult enough. She was extremely busy with her own projects which had to be manoeuvred around Edward's requirements and it was not easy to find time to spend with Tim. She had to invent excuses to Stella for their meeting at all and she was in the bizarre position of appearing to be, in the eyes of the world, in need of a chaperone; that it was she who Tim was so desperate to be with.

Stella thought it a great joke, but she complied. She enjoyed Tim Dundonald's company; she felt that she had a sort of affinity with him somehow, middle aged though he was. But she could not resist telling Fran that her mother was having a fling with their glamorous friend. She felt that it was an excellent way in which to deflect Fran's match-making propensities. And it was such fun to embellish the details of their trips across to Wales or up into the Pennines, which is what they always did except for the appalling day when he had insisted on showing them round the bacon factory. That had been tediousness stretched into infinity. When she had been complaining to Fran about this, and felt the need to lighten it up a bit, she had gone too far. The imagined scenario took over and she hinted that it would not be long before Tim would be whisking her mother away. The temptation on Fran's part to tell Dodo proved irresistible. Dodo was not the only one she told. And neither of them could keep the secret.

It was only a matter of time before whisperings reached the ears of Edward Bundenell, and once alerted, he began to watch.

* * *

The office from where Lou organized fund-raising for the victims of the Spanish Civil War was above a small shop in the streets behind the University area. Above that were the offices of the N.U.W.M. She spent most of her time there and enlisted help from all and sundry to advertise her campaign. When the occupants of the shop could no longer afford the lease and moved out, she snapped it up and filled the windows with photographs of the bombing and pictures of war scenes painted by the soldiers, smuggled out via Santander. Jack and Pinny needed no coercion to keep the window up-to-date.

Stella did. She pretended that she hated her mother's political activity and distanced herself from it as well as she could. The increasing hostility between Lou and her husband made Stella's situation increasingly tortuous. But in this instance her mother took a strong line. It was imperative, for humanitarian reasons if for no other, that help was given.

Lou's motives however were not entirely altruistic. The office was a good place for Tim to call in, as if he had just been passing, and it gave Lou the chance to get on with her administrative work whilst Tim, ostensibly helping out with the young ones, was effectively getting to know his daughter. The week-end outings which had put such a great strain on Lou, had become a thing of the past. In their place, food parcels were packed for transport, blankets were folded, medicines sorted and Tim even helped Stella with the clothing for evacuated children. As far as she was concerned, the fact that Jack was often there, working alongside them, made it a bit easier. He wasn't always there of course but when he wasn't able to come one of the young men from upstairs would take his place. This particular one was a student at the University and greatly given to prolixity in the expression of his views on the evils of Fascism. He was an earnest young soul, made to appear even more so by the horn-rimmed glasses he always wore. Stella found that she quite liked him, even so.

Eventually, despite her self-preservatory instincts, she became totally involved with the Spanish situation.

The turning point came when Lou took her, along with Pinny, to Nazareth House one Sunday morning. Pinny could only help then as Saturday was his busiest day at the garage. He would get to as many evening meetings as he could but that was not often. As a result, she did not know Jack's friend all that well but his reputation had gone before him and she invariably kept her distance. She was pleasantly surprised on that Sunday morning, however.

They were delivering clothing and toys for the Spanish children, orphaned in the war, and sent to the nuns in England. It was still Lent, but just this once it was thought expedient to forget that and let them have just a little treat. Stella had in her hand a large basket filled to the brim with fluffy toy chickens, made for them by the wives of the local Working Men's Club. Her mother and Pinny were manhandling several boxes of clothing with some difficulty when the children were ushered in by a round-faced nun. It was into the best parlour, smelling of polish and last week's stew, its bulky furniture dispelling a dim glow which deepened, rather than lightened the gloom.

Stella would never forget the haunted little faces attempting to hide behind each other as they were invited to greet them. Confronted by strangers, jabbering at them in a language they did not understand, these children were plainly terrified.

The voluminous skirts of the nun's habit were clutched on all sides and pulled up as far as their noses so that the countless pairs of dark, frightened little eyes looked like so many exotic, pendant gemstones cascading down the folds of Sister Zaviour's apron. Those in the forefront were urged towards Stella's basket which she had put down on the floor. But they would have none of it. It was if they could not recognize that what was in it was a gift specially for them; that the chickens, looking like a heap of iodine-stained cotton wool, were things to play with, not something to be alarmed by.

It was Pinny who came to the rescue. He realized very quickly that communication was imperative and that sign-language was the only way. Holding a chicken between his thumb and forefinger, he thrust his neck forward, bent his knees and stretched his arms behind him like wings and then proceeded to hop round the room squeaking 'cluck-cluck'. At first it seemed that this quite passable impersonation would only succeed in frightening the children out of their wits entirely but soon one little boy allowed part of himself to emerge from his share of the all-enveloping skirt, and then another peeped further out until Stella could balance a chicken on the flat of each hand and get them to take one.

Soon the room was filled with the sound of triumphant cheeping and clucking as they all grasped their tiny, unanticipated little gifts, hopping and skipping with great glee around the ugly furniture, in imitation of the redoubtable Pinny.

Stella's heart was captured. From then on she showed no reluctance at all to man the shop on Saturday afternoons, work as many nights as she could manage in the office and tie up parcels until her fingers blistered. She did it with a good will.

To her astonishment, however, one night when Jack was working alongside her, he asked her not to make a big thing of his presence there to Fran. He sensed that his social conscience was almost as great an impediment to her peace of mind as was his religion, he told her, and it worried him. It would be better if Fran didn't know the true extent of his involvement. He trusted Stella to be tactful about it, after all, she knew the Reynolds well enough to sympathise with his predicament. They already thought of him as a Radical; it would be better to keep quiet about this latest call on his time, he suggested. They would be thinking that he was a Communist next and Fran would get upset.

What Jack referred to as his 'social conscience' was leading him into areas that no-one, apart from Pinny who went with him, knew about at all. His instinct was correct. If Fran had got to know what he was up to she would have been distracted out of her wits.

They made regular visits to the camp in Maghull where the soldiers who had escaped from Spain were interned. They were boys, these soldiers, unable to speak a word of English, and both homesick and confused. That they were labelled, probably registered as, 'rebels' when they had been fighting to support a legally elected government made Jack rage with fury. He and Pinny took them cigarettes and sweets which they provided from their own money. They played cards with the sweets as stakes and Pinny taught them swear words to shout out when they lost. He always returned their stakes to them though, at the end of the evening. The boys had nothing other than the shirts on their backs. Nothing. Their homes and families were as ethereal as a dissolving dream in their memories.

Jack and Pinny decided to find out what it might be like to be homeless. They knew that it could only be an experiment, that they would not really be able to experience what destitution actually felt like, but they were ready to give it a try. It was one thing to have a dog-eared copy of the latest Yellow Book under one's arm, but it meant nothing unless they could get some first-hand experience themselves. The plight of the Spanish boys generated the notion that they might spend a night at the Salvation Army hostel to see what living in such conditions might mean.

The hostel was on Norton Street, conveniently along the street from the N.U.W.M office and Lou's shop. They went along one night after putting in their usual stint for the Spanish War effort and paid their 9d. at the door and were given a bowl of soup and a ticket with the numbers of their respective cubicles on it.

They put off the evil moment of discovery where that was concerned, however; they were none too keen on the thought of the beds they were to sleep in. They had reached a compromise, even so, by paying for a cubicle. If they had not, they would have been in a communal dormitory. That, they felt, would have been taking the experiment to extremes.

For as long as possible they hung around in the grimy hall talking to the old fellows who were the regulars. These, in fact, were not old men at all, they were not much over thirty, but they had been unemployed for years and it had taken its toll. They looked as if their days on this earth were strictly numbered. This seemed to be confirmed when the bell went and they all had to go up to the sleeping quarters before 'Lights Out'.

The thin-walled cubicles might just as well not have been there. They did not reach to the ceiling and the front was just a bit of rag. They gave a little privacy, it had to be admitted, but Jack took one look at the dirty straw-filled mattress and decided to keep his clothes on. The ticking pillow was in an even worse state. It made him feel queasy. He gritted his teeth, wrapped his jacket round his head and crawled under the blanket, wondering what else might be crawling around in that bed with him. He could hear Pinny sucking in his breath, with similar expression of distaste, next door.

He lay on his back staring up at the stains on the ceiling and the patterns of peeling paint curling away from the walls. He had enough light to see. The curtains on the windows were so meagre and thin with wear (it had to be wear, they had not been washed for centuries, Jack reckoned) that the street lamp virtually lit the room. He resisted the urge to scratch and tear at his skin. It would be his imagination more than anything else, he tried to persuade himself. He tried to concentrate on other things. Then the noises started.

There must have been eighteen or twenty cubicles, all occupied and all reverberating with sound of one kind or another. The snoring was bad enough but it didn't alarm him. It was just infuriating. The moans did alarm him; deeply harrowing sounds suggestive of torment, they were. Purgatorial. But the coughing was the worst. He had expected some coughing but nothing like this. He had never heard a death rattle but he felt certain that this must be as near as one could get. There was a terrible gurgling behind those coughs which, once started, went on and on until the phlegm was spat out, God knew where.

He thought the night would never end.

The next morning as he and Pinny rushed home for a good wash and a change of clothes, there was not even the hint of a suggestion that the experiment should be repeated. Once had been more than enough to satisfy their curiosity and, in part, to assuage their guilt that they were not, as they both secretly wished to be, fighting in Spain.

* * *

That same night it had been the student who had worked with Lou. It was a slack time and Stella had decided to go to a film with Fran. As Lou was locking up, Tim appeared, apologising for not being able to get there earlier. When he discovered that Stella was not there anyway, he invited Lou and the young man for a drink. The boy refused, he had to catch up on some work, he said. The other two bade him goodnight and went along to the pub at the corner of the street.

Lou felt much more at ease with Tim these days. She did not believe that a leopard could change its spots but he had impressed her with his commitment, not only to her project, but for the first time it seemed, to his job. And then there was his undeniable devotion to his daughter. The two seemed to go together. He had to stay put if he was to see Stella. Whatever he might feel about the constrictions his cousin had put upon him and the mundanity of running the factory, he could not go flying off to try his luck elsewhere if he wanted to stay close to her. And he had kept his word. Lou was certain that he would not do anything which might upset the present arrangements. She felt secure.

They had sat down with their drink and were talking about Lonsdale, in fact. Tim had known Lonsdale from the Kelsay days and was familiar with his propensity for disaster. They reminded each other of some of the more preposterous happenings which had beset him there. Even though Lou had stressed the calming effect his marriage to Maddy had brought about, they were still laughing, their heads leant together, Lou with her elbows on the table.

Tim paused in his laughter. He looked up enquiringly. There was someone standing behind Lou. He offered him a smile.

Lou swivelled in her seat to see who it was. It was her husband.

'Hello, Edward, come and join us. This is Tim Dundonald, he is an old friend...'

'I know who he is. Now get into the car. It's outside. I am taking you home!'

He took her by the arm and virtually dragged her to the door. Tim had stood up, as if he was going to follow. Lou looked over her shoulder, her glance telling him to stay where he was. The crowd at the bar turned to watch this highly interesting scene, winking at each other and murmuring what were obvious obscenities, from behind cupped hands. Tim downed his Scotch and left.

When he got outside there was no sign of Lou, or her husband. He went to find a taxi, hurrying towards the main road, anxious and perplexed. He had not liked the look of Edward Bundenell at all.

He had good reason, but he did not know what to do about it.

Edward drove the car in silence. He did not speed. He was coldly angry and he knew that he had to drive with precision. Lou sat beside him, seething with indignation, but she knew better than to confront him in such a confined space.

When they arrived at the house, he once again took her by the arm and half-dragged her up the path. His fingers were digging into her elbow, even through the fabric of her coat. As they got to the door, she tried to shake herself free whilst he was in the process of unlocking it.

'Let me go, Edward, you are being ridiculous!'

He took no notice but pushed her through and on into the drawing room. It was cold in there, there was no fire. He switched on the light and at last let go of her arm.

She shot to the far side of the room.

'What is all this about, Edward?'

'You know perfectly well what this is about. It is about you and your... paramour!'

Lou laughed.

'Oh, for God's sake, don't be so *pompous*. He's not my paramour as you call it. He isn't my lover either. You have got it all wrong this time Edward. He is not anything so exotic, he's just someone I knew from years back.'

‘*Is* he now?’

‘Yes. Is that all you’re worried about?’

His narrow, pointed face was contorted. He did not take his eyes off her as he moved across towards the drinks’ tray. It was the face of some slippery, gliding creature of prey, working by night, never getting caught... Lou’s indignation turned to fear. He was ready to hit her. She knew it.

‘Edward, please. You are totally mistaken. Tim Dundonald is nothing to me. There is nothing going on between us. Nothing at all.’

‘Is that why he is hanging around night after night in that squalid hole you insist on frequenting? Is he one of your half-baked anarchists that you think so much of? What is he there for if he is not after a bitch on heat? Where do you copulate? In the back of his car?’

Lou stared at him, stunned, almost paralysed with shock. She heard herself saying,

‘He does not drive a car. He is disabled. He cannot use his left arm.’

‘Really?’

Ice had already crept through Lou’s veins.

‘Yes, really! And he has no interest in me. None whatsoever. It is Stella he comes to see.’

A malicious sneer formed itself on Edward’s lips,

‘I see,’ he said, ‘so that’s it!’ But before he could deliver whatever vicious remark he was obviously intending to make, she cut him short.

‘He is her father.’

They stood, each hating the other, at opposite ends of the room, her heartbeat drumming, hammering into the silence which followed.

There was menace in the set of his mouth. There was defiance in hers.

‘I see it all now.’

‘I’m glad you do.’

‘Oh, yes! I see it all. You have deceived me right from the start. You have lied to me from the very beginning. Lied! You told me that he was dead; killed in France.’

‘I told you no such thing, Edward, and you know it. I never spoke about him at all, except to say that Stella did not have a father, which...’

‘You led me to believe...’

‘I led you to believe nothing! I told you that I was unmarried and that I had a child. You accepted that, or so I thought.’

‘Oh, I never accepted it. I tolerated it.’

Anger rose up into her throat. Her breath came in spurts.

‘Then who has deceived whom?’

He ignored her.

‘So, he has come to claim what he left behind, has he? Well, well. That will please you! And should I take it that you have been included too, in this reclamation?’

His face pinched up as he moved towards her.

‘How long have you been sleeping with him? Months? Years? And are you going to tell me that you do it to protect Stella? That was the only reason that you slept with me, wasn’t it? To give your bastard a name! And do you imagine that I didn’t know it? But I would like to enlighten you. You have have not protected Stella at all.’

Lou took a further step backwards. He was totally repulsive in his sense of triumph. Repugnant. She could not bear to be breathing the same air.

‘You are being unjust, Edward; it belittles you.’

‘I’m not the one who is belittled, my dear, except by you and your dependence on the gutter. You are nothing but a slut; a scandal to your class, to your background and to me. And so is that daughter of yours. What’s more, you have dragged my name down with you. Not once, but time and time again. You have *stained* my reputation. The pair of you!’

He at last took his eyes off her and turned his attention to the tray of decanters on the table alongside the dead fire and poured himself a whisky.

'Now I suggest that you go and live with your lover who has so conveniently re-appeared. Or your derelicts, your down-and-outs, as I suspect that he has since moved on to *fresher* pastures. Let's see how you really get on with them, shall we, your unemployables; your dirty, feckless layabouts?'

He tipped the glass towards his mouth, looking at her steadily, through narrowed eyes, like slits. He took one fastidious sip and swallowed it soundlessly.

'And you can take your brat with you!'

Lou forced herself to walk the length of the room composedly but she was rigid with loathing. She kept her eyes away from the lamps, the heavy vases. They were too much like blunt instruments. She could smash any one of them across his head. Again. And again. And again. Until there was no more strength left in her arms to attack him.

She closed the door with quiet, deliberate care as she left the room. She did not dare to provoke any further either of the monsters which threatened her: the one on the other side of the door, and the one inside her head.

She went upstairs to wait for Stella to return. There was a great deal to say to her and she must be in control of herself in order to say it.

★ ★ ★

The bombing of Guernica was already taking place as Stella made her laborious way to Spain. It was wanton destruction of innocents. It was a cynical testing out of new weapons dropped on the people of a country town during market day. Stella heard the news as she stepped off the boat at Santander. She felt that the world, and everything that she held dear in it, everything in which she had trusted, had come to an end.

Her flight had been not been an involuntary action even if it had been precipitated by the devastating news her mother had just imparted. She had needed to run and run she had. She had been planning it for weeks. She had no idea what she might do but if she could get to Barcelona perhaps the Republicans could find a use for her. The harder the work, the better it would be; she wanted no time to sit and think. The train was hours late and the inside of the carriage filthy. She was so exhausted she hardly noticed.

★ ★ ★

As usual, Fran and Jack met after leaving the office at the end of the day. They made their way down to the Pier Head, from where Jack would go over the water back home, as this particular evening they had not arranged to go out together later on. But he always spent a little time with her before he went for the ferry when this was the case.

She had been very subdued all the way, offering nothing in the way of conversation and answering in monosyllables when he tried to draw her out. It was as if she was refusing to speak to him for some reason.

They were leaning with their backs to the railings, the India Buildings across the cobbled square in front of them. Tramlines criss-crossed like a giant page of puzzles. Fran was wearing a trench-coat and the wind was blowing the skirts out in front of her but she was too busy dealing with the strands of hair being whipped across her mouth to do anything about it. Jack, standing beside her, was hardly aware that the legs of his trousers were shuddering and flapping round his calves. He was going over and over in his mind what he could have done to offend her. More to the point, what she might have found him out in! He was certain that it was something which he had done which was upsetting her. At last she spoke, but he could hardly hear her over the wind.

'Why didn't she tell me? Why didn't she warn me? I'll not forgive her, Jack!'

He had no idea what she was talking about.

'What? I can't hear you very well.'

'Why did she do it? How could she do it?' Fran's usually strong voice was querulous, making matters worse. 'Without telling anyone. Without giving in her notice at the office.'

'What are you saying?'

'Stella's gone. She's run off to Spain! Nobody knew the first thing about it. You didn't know anything, did you Jack?' She suddenly turned on him accusingly. 'I'll be really furious with you if you did and you didn't say anything!'

'Why should she tell me?'

He was being evasive. Stella could have told him but she hadn't. And how much did Fran know about his involvement with her over this Spanish thing? Jack suddenly felt a little querulous himself.

'We must get out of this wind. Let's go over there, in the porch.'

He took her hand and they ran across the square and up the steps of the India Building and took shelter in the entrance.

'Now tell me again.'

Fran's anger had dissipated. She looked tearful.

'Stella's gone, Jack!'

He took her in his arms, letting her head rest on his shoulder.

'She just took off. I thought that she was my friend and she has taken off without so much as a word. I can't believe that she would do anything like that.'

'And she has gone to Spain?'

'Yes. And she could get herself killed. What's more, she *hates* politics, you know she does! I simply don't understand it.'

Jack could, but he wasn't going to say so.

'How did you find out?'

'Her mother came into the office this morning and saw Mr Booth. She said that Stella has gone off to Spain. You don't think that she might be making it up, do you? Mrs Bundenell? She is very odd sometimes.'

'No, I don't think that she is making it up.'

'But why didn't she tell me? She should have told me! She had to get a passport didn't she, she couldn't do that overnight? She must have been keeping it to herself for months.'

He pulled her closer to him. She could hear his heart beating fast, even through his jacket. She wondered if it was the shock.

'I don't know, Fran.'

But he thought that he might.

Until a few days ago, he would never have thought it possible that she, who walked away from anyone who so much as picked up papers such as 'The Manchester Guardian', would have taken this step. Stella, whose habit it was to refer to her Socialist mother as a hopeless case, who would believe it? But now he did and he suspected that he knew the reason.

His heart skipped a painful beat. If Fran had the least inkling of what they had been up to, he would lose her. She would sever all connection with him. He would never see her again.

Guilt at keeping her in ignorance swept over him like a fever; that and the dichotomy within. How could he reconcile his recent, irrevocable action with everything that had been his life before; that still was his life, in fact? He was in a constant state of turmoil inside. He could not lose Fran now. She was his anchor. She was the one sane, lovely, unswerving thing in his life and he depended on her. She must never know how far he had gone in his passion to reverse what the future unequivocally held. Spain was only the precursor, the beginning.

The previous week they had all been to a lecture to be brought up-to-date on what was happening via the International Brigade. The bespectacled student had arranged it and he had invited Stella, Jack and Pinny to go up to the offices upstairs to meet the speaker afterwards. This office was in the next room to the N.W.U.M and they had not investigated it before. They just knew that it belonged to another group, all working towards the same end.

The young man, the one who had given the lecture, had come from Oxford. He was extremely persuasive. He had talked at length. Now, in the privacy of the little room, he expounded further and what he was saying appealed to Jack. It appealed to his sense of justice and fairness; to his insistence on equality and the right to human dignity whatever the circumstances. When he had left that erstwhile unexplored little office, he was not just an anti-Fascist; he was a fully paid-up member of the Communist Party.

Stella must have responded in the same way. Only she had had the guts to act upon it whilst he was still battling with torn allegiances: conscience, his duty to contribute to the support of his family, his religion!

He felt unaccountably put to shame. Confusion threatened to knot his insides into a spasm of intolerable agony. It did so more and more these days. He needed Fran.

'Fran?'

'What?'

She was still bristling with a sense of exclusion. Stella had kept secrets from her and she, Fran, would never have done the same to her. Never. And she was sure that Jack knew more than he was admitting to, which added to the hurt. It made her feel isolated; shut out from both of them.

'What?'

'I love you, you know. I can't be without you.'

The wind had suddenly taken a rest and his words rang out across the heads of a queue of people recently collected at the bottom of the steps. A tram was due. All the heads turned, as one.

'Sh-sh-sh!'

Fran was embarrassed and cross. What on earth was Jack thinking of?

'Sh-sh-sh-!' She pulled away from him, trying to disappear into the wall behind her. 'You idiot, everyone can hear!'

The tram queue had pricked up its ears even more sharply. Significant looks were being exchanged, and several smiles, but most of the heads were turned towards the quayside, studiously intent on the gulls noisily circling the incoming ferry. Even so, he moved closer to her, into the corner of the lobby. His voice had dropped to a whisper,

'Fran, let's get engaged.'

'What for?'

Jack was somewhat taken aback. He had expected her to fall into his arms and weep with joy or something, like it was on the films. Instead she was leaning past him to see what the queue was up to. Her face registered exasperation.

'Because I love you, that's what for, and...' he was almost shouting, 'I thought that you loved me.'

She darted back instantly, '*Will* you be quiet?' She had blushed scarlet. 'Just be quiet!'

Some relief was offered by the arrival of the tram. At last the space below them was empty, the smirking eavesdroppers borne away. He tried again.

'Fran?'

She turned her head away from him, concentrating on the set of the steps below them. She watched a discarded ticket flutter upwards only to fall back and try again, like some frantic little bird.

'There is too much against it. Too much coming between us. Don't force me to think about it.'

Jack stood as if stunned. He put his hand out to touch her and she pushed it away.

'What is there to come between us, if we love each other?' There was hurt in his voice, confusion. 'We do love each other, don't we?'

She stood and faced him squarely. The worries that had been eating at her just came out, without introduction, as if she had taken it for granted that Jack's mind would be occupied by the same anxieties.

'Would you give up your faith for me? Would you? That's what it means, doesn't it? One of us has got to do it. And you won't. I know you won't, so don't even answer. It will have to be me and I can't do it.'

'Fran!'

He knew she was right. There could be no 'mixed' marriage. His mother would not agree to that. His mother would die rather than agree to that. And he, tortured by doubts for months. That would kill her even quicker if she thought that his faith was wavering. It was a bitter irony. He could not even reveal to Fran what he had on his conscience.

'I know a good priest. He will explain things better than I can. Will you give us this chance? Will you go to see him? Will you Fran?'

He looked so anxious, so forlorn. She could hardly bear it.

'I have to go for my train,' she said. ' Maybe I'll think about it.'

He took her in his arms and swung her round.

'I only said maybe, remember!'

But she was laughing and he wanted to kiss her.

As invariably happens, a second tram trundled up almost at once, the previous one having taken what seemed like an age to arrive. People were getting off. Before they could be observed again, they dashed down the steps and away towards the overhead railway. They were doubled up to face the wind and could not even straighten themselves when they were on the platform.

'I *will* think about it,' she mouthed through the window as the train moved away.

As Jack crossed the water on the ferry the thought of Stella, still probably at sea, set him into a form of panic. The gale would be even worse where she was. She might not even arrive in Spain at all. That, and the host of other problems whirling round in his head, aggravated the nagging pain in his stomach. Or perhaps it was just the rolling of the boat? That would be it. Just the rolling of the boat. It would be better if only he could be sick. But he knew that it wouldn't be. It never was.

PART THREE

RUNNERS

9. Aftermath

THE LITTLE OFFICE in Norton Street was full of cardboard boxes. They in turn were full of broken biscuits from the biscuit factory. Lou was in the habit of buying up as many as she could and then selling them in the shop to raise funds for her various projects. Usually she welcomed their arrival but today she wished them at the bottom of the Mersey.

She would have to make room in the shop itself if she wished to use the office as living quarters which was exactly what she had in mind. With Stella gone, there was no reason why she should not camp out in the back room. She had no energy to think of a better plan.

She had no energy to think of anything except the practicalities of lugging box after box from one space to another when every bone in her body refused to function as it should. Tim arrived, unannounced, whilst she was still in the throes of the worst of it, hemmed in on all sides by cardboard towers haphazardly piled up wherever they would stand.

She sent him on his way. She had no patience with herself and even less to spare for his histrionics when told of the probable reason for Stella's flight. To have him weeping tears of self-pity and self-castigation when her own grief at Stella's abrupt departure was blindingly unabated was more than she could bear.

He had threatened to go after her, to bring her back. Lou told him to do as he liked just so long as he buggered off, and fast.

Once he had gone, stooped, suddenly shuffling like an old man, she felt immeasurably weary. More sympathy might have been in order, she supposed. He had had a shock. Well, he would have to get over it as she would have to do. And if he really loved Stella as much as he claimed, he would leave her alone.

Lou had every confidence that her daughter would cope with the conditions in Spain. She did not consider her to be in mortal danger. Not from the guns. She was much more worried about her emotional state. Lou's own state was hardly better. There was a nagging suspicion, now persistently in her mind, that the revelation about her natural father had not been the only catalyst that night. There was something else and try as she might, that other something remained elusive.

She forced herself to work on until she was too tired to worry any more and the shop was reasonably ship-shape. Switching out the lights, she then went in to face the bleakness of the back room. If she stacked the rest of the boxes at one end of the table which she used as a desk, she could improvise a bed. Wrapping herself in her coat, she stretched herself out and fell into an exhausted sleep. It was Edward's laboratory bugs in their tanks which monopolised her dreams. Continuously hurling themselves at the sides in a futile effort to get out, they formed a heaving, scummy swarm over the glass. It was exactly as she had seen it on her occasional visits there. It was exactly as she had heard it. A muffled buzzing. The glass reduced the sound of frenzy. Eventually they would fall to rest on the bottom. But they would try again.

In her sleep she knew that she was dreaming, she knew that what was disturbing her could not actually be in that dingy room with her. She still found herself pondering on the question of their survival if they ever did escape. Surely the cold outside the tank would kill them? The question acquired a disproportionate importance until she awoke, wearily unrefreshed, and discarded it altogether. Ensuring her own survival, and that of her daughter, was of more immediate relevance.

Edward had not seemed to be affected by Stella's disappearance at all. He behaved as though she had never existed and he certainly had no consolation to offer Lou. He then told her that he wanted a divorce. It was his intention to cite Tim Dundonald, he said. He had already seen his lawyer. She had laughed in disbelief. There were no grounds, she had said, no grounds at all. Desertion was what she had in mind. That was when he had hit her, even though she was on her guard. He knocked her to the ground then turned his back contemptuously as she crawled away. She had left after that.

* * *

That night, Jack too was unsettled. He decided to go and talk to Fr. Welland. He had known the parish priest since he had been a boy and he trusted him. Fr. Welland was not a bigot. He would not hold it against him that he had fallen in love with a non-Catholic and he would give him sound advice on Fran's instruction and also how to break the news to his mother. Mrs Jamieson would need even more careful handling than Mrs Reynolds. He felt confident that Fr. Welland was his man. Even so he found himself ringing at the doorbell with a thudding heart.

He was totally unprepared for what came next; a revelation which removed every other consideration from his head and left him reeling.

To his initial astonishment, the priest was almost perfunctory in his dismissal of Jack's anxieties about the step Fran might be taking. It was as if he could not be bothered with it. What Fr. Welland was more interested in making clear was that he had a very good idea of the happenings at Norton Street and Jack's involvement with the student from Oxford and he had heard about it from Pinny McLaughlin.

To say that Jack was disconcerted was to underestimate the case. He felt as though he had been in receipt of a physical blow. His discomfort was further exacerbated by the shock of learning that his friend was to enter the Seminary within weeks. Pinny was going to be a priest.

Jack could not believe what he was hearing. Pinny of all people. It was an impossible joke. It must be. But it wasn't a joke that he had betrayed Jack's partisanship with the Spanish cause. A surge of anger rose in his throat. He got up as if to leave but Fr. Welland suggested that he return to his chair. There was more to say.

Obedience was automatic in a presbytery. It always had been. To Jack's further fury, he found himself sitting down again, on the edge of the hard seat, waiting for the lecture, just as he had done as a small boy.

He had the greatest difficulty in concentrating on what Fr. Welland was haranguing him about. It was an harangue despite the soft, almost whispered tones this priest habitually used, just as if he was always in the confessional and in danger of being overheard by the queues of kneeling penitents outside. The inadvisability of

Jack continuing his association with Mrs Bundenell was the main theme of the reprimand. She was tantamount to a moral danger with her political leanings and was most unfeminine in her execution of them. Jack must stay away from Norton Street and that wicked woman. His immortal soul was in jeopardy should he not heed this warning.

It was obvious that the true extent of Jack's commitment had not been revealed. It would be based on conjecture anyway; the only other person who actually knew what he had done was the Oxford man who had enrolled him.

The curious position that he was in was pushed to the background of Jack's consciousness. To have a covert member of the Communist Party, in a priest's back parlour, seeking advice on the procedure involved with a mixed marriage was bizarre to say the least. Jack did not think it absurd, however. He hardly thought about it at all. His head was full of images of Pinny creeping off behind bushes with a sequence of pretty girls; Pinny, up to mischief as his second nature; Pinny, pursuing experience as if it was his life-blood. And then Pinny bending down to kiss the altar. In vestments. For some reason, in Jack's mind's eye, they were green, the gold cross down the back shimmering in the glow of the sacristy lamp. His head was cropped close, impossibly smooth and neat. He would never again even verge on being a scruffy bugger.

The dreary, cluttered room closed in on Jack. The chipped brown paint, the wallpaper of indeterminate age and pattern, every joint of which seemed stained, only the doleful pictures of the Sacred Heart, the stoning of St. Sebastian, St. John the Baptist, seemed to hold it all together. The items of lumpy, ill-matched furniture crouched like dead beasts on lino the colour of mud. Fr. Welland himself, his clothes crumpled, his vision myopic, now applying his attention to what Jack had come for, lessons of instruction to Fran, talking slowly in his low, hushed monotone; he, too, was suddenly sinister.

Jack had been familiar with this room for as long as he could remember. He had, at one time, expected to end up in a replica of it. Now he was seeing it with new eyes; annihilatingly critical eyes. There was a terrible negation in the way that the priests lived, it seemed to him. It was debilitating. It threatened to drain his anger and turn it into hopelessness. They had no answers because they asked no questions. They were fixed in their intransigence; fixed in ritual. What Fr. Welland was reciting at that very moment was a sequence of well-rehearsed platitudes; he had not given a thought for Fran, he had not expressed even the vaguest interest in what she might be like, this girl whom Jack had chosen. And Pinny's choice was made too, it seemed.

He had chosen them.

It became imperative that Jack should escape from the Presbytery as soon as he could and get himself down the road to the McLaughlin household. His friend must be brought to his senses.

At last he managed to get away, but Pinny wasn't at home. Jack was told that he was still at the garage, working late on the 'books'. Jack ran back the two streets to collect his bike and pedalled furiously all the way to the yard where Pinny kept his vehicles. He arrived breathless and red-faced. He could see Pinny at his desk in the office, a wooden shed with glass windows along the front of it, the only place in the immediate area with the lights on. Jack skidded round the collection of cars and motor-bikes which loomed through the constricted space, coming to a halt with a screech of tyres and then he burst in.

Pinny looked up unconcernedly. His expression changed however, when Jack's fist hit the surface of the desk and sent half the papers flying.

'How can you do this, Pinny, without telling me? What the bloody hell are you playing at?'

Pinny leaned down to the floor in an attempt to pick up the scattered bills. But he too was flushed when he straightened up.

'What are you talking about?'

'You know damned well what I'm talking about, you going for a priest. It's just about the craziest thing I've ever heard.'

'Is it?'

Pinny was infuriatingly calm. 'Jack, just do me a favour. Take your face out of mine will you? And there's no need to yell like that.'

But it was as if Jack hadn't heard; he continued to shout, leaning right across the desk, his fingers gripping the edge in order to prevent himself from thumping the surface yet again.

'First Stella disappears and now you. She I can understand, but this is beyond me. This is sheer lunacy!'

He stood up straight, a further thought having struck him.

'You didn't have anything to do with her going off did you? You didn't encourage her? Damn you Pinny! How is she to manage, a girl on her own?'

'I knew nothing about it. The last I saw of her was at the meeting and she certainly had no such intentions then.'

'And that's another thing. You told Fr. Welland that I was there. You had no right to Pinny, no right at all, I don't care what excuse you might think you have. It's nothing to do with them how I go about my business, nor what causes I support. I turn up at Mass each Sunday; they don't need to know any more.'

'They may not need to but they do. He already knew that you had been there. I only confirmed it.'

Jack looked murderous, a muscle twitching above his eye.

'Then you are one of them already. And a liar! How else could they have known unless you told them?'

Pinny looked down at his feet and squinted at the paper-heading which was half-obscured by his right shoe.

'They have spies.'

'I'll bet they bloody do! And you are one of them.'

'No. I'm not.'

For the first time Pinny sounded rattled but Jack was not going to relent.

'Well, at the very least you subscribe to it.'

'No. That's not true. I'm telling you, they already knew. They are not daft, Jack. They've had tabs on that office for months. They know exactly who goes there and what for. They have reasoned it out.'

'Reason, my arse! Is it reason to damn Lou the way they do? Is it reason to call what she does wicked? And they really believe that, you know, that she is wicked. Not Franco! Oh, no! Not that precious upholder of the Church, not a word of criticism in that quarter, but Lou they go for! When did they ever do a fraction of what she does for those down on their luck? Never! They are too busy taking money off the likes of my mother and for what? I'll tell you for what. To convert the bloody Africans, that's for what! They don't want to know about what is going on under their noses because the poor buggers who are struggling here are already in the fold, or most of them are. All they can do is to rant on to the likes of me for trying to do something about it. Don't talk to me about reason, Pinny, not in this case.'

But his rage was giving way to bewilderment. He knew that he had been out of control and that his accusations were in some measure unjust. He needed a diversion. Pinny was offering nothing. He threw a pile of ancient motoring magazines off the chair where they had been gathering dust and placed the rickety thing in front of the desk and sat down. His hands dropped on to his knees. He and Pinny together had been searching for a kind of solution, forever it seemed, and just when he thought that they had come up with the right one, Pinny apparently loses his wits.

'Why you, of all people? What made you do this?'

'You. You made me do it.'

Jack looked at him, registering astonished disbelief.

'What?'

'It's true, Jack. Right from first knowing you I thought that it would be you who would be the priest. Everybody did. There was just something about you that was different. It had nothing to do with piety or even goodness particularly; you just had that aura of being singled out.'

Jack's mouth had fallen open. His head was reeling with the shock of it. It was the last thing that he had expected Pinny to say and his disquiet increased as Pinny continued.

'I thought about that quite a lot. I admired it in you, even envied it, I suppose. And then I thought that maybe I could be like that too and before I knew it it was the only thing I wanted. I couldn't get out of it then. It became a certainty.'

'Well, you did a bloody good job of hiding it. The only thing you seemed certain about was leading half the female population of Merseyside astray, Megan Hughes for instance and scores of others like her. You are not suggesting that you got that from me?'

Pinny grimaced,

'She knew what she was at.'

'And you? Did you know what you were at?'

'Oh, yes.' Pinny grimaced again. 'I needed to know what I would be missing. Saints and sinners, Jack. And rest assured; I confessed it.'

Shame and anger rose in Jack's throat. When he at last spoke, his voice was constricted.

'You won't do it Pin. You won't manage. You have to be kidding. Tell me that you are just kidding me.'

In answer, Pinny shrugged his shoulders. The gesture said it all. His mind was made up but Jack could not leave it at that.

'And what about your involvement down at Norton Street? What was all that about? Were you just playing games there as well? Just stringing us all along? Just making sure that you did not miss that either? Or is it the war that you want to miss? Is that it? Did they convince you that we will be at war before the year is out, and you have decided to bolt? To do a runner?'

Pinny stretched forward to look more closely at Jack.

'You are more confused about that than I am, Jack. I was not playing games. I was learning, just as you are still learning, the best way to make a decent attempt to bring about a more decent life for decent people. In the end I shall work for my parishioners in the way that I think it ought to be done and fear not, if a war comes in between, then I shall go off to that as well. But you don't know where you are yet. You don't know how to reconcile the tuggings going on inside you, do you? You want to be all things to all men. You are an idealist, Jack, and you have, for the moment, found Karl Marx, but you cannot quite break from what you really believe in. However justifiable your criticisms are, you are unable to totally reject your Church. Reject your faith. And the two are enemies. And neither has the actual answer, not for you, not in the present circumstances. That is what makes you angry. My decision has very little to do with it.'

Jack chose not to reply. He was self-consciously aware of Pinny's relentless gaze. He knew that Pinny was right.

'That's it, isn't it?'

Jack still chose not to respond.

'It was not the answer to join the Party, you know. You did not have to go that far.'

'How do you know that I did?'

Pinny half-smiled at the defensive, involuntary retort.

'Come off it Jack. You're just being evasive. I've seen it coming for a long time.'

'And I suppose you now think the same as Fr. Welland, that my immortal soul is lost forever?'

'Your soul, Jack? You could not even mislay it, let alone lose it. You are all soul, that's your biggest problem.'

Pinny went back to sorting the papers. Jack felt duty-bound to help him, having been responsible for the mess they were in. They worked on quietly, the constraint between them making them awkward. Jack offered to take over the account book which was instantly passed across, and he set about organising it. Pinny's brother was to take over when the time came. Jack hoped that he would keep things a bit more ship-shape but he made a mental note not to make it his business to find out. Not for a while at any rate.

They had been working for a good hour before things were complete. It was Jack who first spoke,

'I think I ought to tell you, I've asked Fran to marry me.'

Pinny was filing receipts into a drawer. He did not look up.

'I knew you would.'

Jack was vaguely irritated by this claim to omniscience. It was rather too early on in Pinny's new career for that.

'How did you know it?'

'Because Fran is not a Megan Hughes.'

Pinny's head was still bowed over his task. His hair was more unkempt than ever with the constant, exasperated pulling at it with his fingers which had gone on all night. Pinny hated paperwork.

'And no matter how far forward you think you are in your new ideology, you would have run a mile if she had been. And perhaps she will be the one to sort you out. In the end.'

Jack leaned back in his chair to ease the stiffness which had come from sitting too long. But he locked his hands behind his head with an unaccustomed ferocity.

'Maybe. If she says 'yes'. She hasn't yet.'

The air of relaxed nonchalance was false. His hands gripped the back of his head even more fiercely.

'She's not going to your friend Fr. Welland for instruction, I'll tell you that. *If* she agrees to it, and that's not certain.'

Pinny looked at him curiously. Jack had got up and was gathering his things together during Pinny's reply.

'Why should she come right across here? She would need someone on her side of the water. Try one of the Benedictines at Little Crosby. They'll make a good job of it.' He hesitated. 'To see you married, Jack, that would be something!'

Jack knew only too well that Pinny would not be around to see. Nor would he hear, except from others. Once he became a novice he would be inaccessible for years, and if he, Jack, with all that was known about his activities, was to insist on contact with him, Pinny most likely would be summarily ejected from the seminary forthwith.

'And that would be the greatest irony of all,' Jack thought to himself as he mournfully let himself out, 'the greatest bloody irony of all!'

* * *

Pinny's generosity before he left overwhelmed Jack. He gave him his motor bike. He refused to listen to Jack's protestations that it was too expensive just to be given away. Pinny insisted that it was nothing at all. He had rather Jack had it than one of his greedy brothers who were all getting good pickings anyway. But his greatest parting gift was a less tangible one. It was the recommendation of the Benedictines. Fran agreed to go and hear what they had to say but she insisted that the final decision was to be hers. She did not want any undue pressure and she would brook no discussion with Jack about it.

A lovely old monk, Fr. Christian, was made responsible for her and Christian he undoubtedly was. The depth of his sincerity was a revelation to Fran. Her own church had featured largely in her childhood and, from being a tiny tot at Sunday School to her attendance at the most recent of the regular dances, it had structured her social life, most of her friendships and the way of her thinking. But it had had nothing to compare with the genuine radiance of spirit that this old man communicated. He came across as the very essence of goodness, selflessness and humility. Fran was swayed.

Nevertheless her anxieties remained. They were not for herself. She wanted a life with Jack, she knew that now, and it would be a good life if this old man truly represented what was in store. It did not matter if it turned out to be hard. She could stand on her own two feet, she could parry ignorant jibes, but she worried about children. She did not want any children she might have to carry a stigma, as she felt sure they would. She could not contemplate them being disadvantaged in a society which turned its back on them. But Fr. Christian's inspiration was difficult to resist and the problem of children would not be for years yet. Not too many months later Jack had his answer.

The weekend immediately following Fran's acceptance, Jack turned up at Oakshot Road in his best suit in order to formalize his engagement. He was extremely nervous. Before he rang the bell, he stood on the top step, flanked by a pair of particularly virulent laurel bushes. They were a variegated variety and the shiny green leaves were spotted with a bilious yellow as if they were subject to a curious blight of some kind. Abstactedly, he considered their distinct lack of appeal. Maybe they were what Mrs Reynolds took to be the fashionable adornments for a front entrance, the mark of a person of quality. They certainly were not having that effect on him, if that really was her intention. But then, he did not consider himself a person of quality, nor a sophisticated follower of fashion, especially as he stood there gawping at them instead of taking stock of his position.

His position was not totally unpropitious. The Reynolds held strange views about Catholics on principle, but they liked him. He knew that they liked him. They had welcomed him with open arms when he had first gone there with Stella. Admittedly there had been a few sour glances from Mrs Reynolds when it became clear that he was Fran's beau, not her friend's. However, no-one had actually expressed disapproval, not even the elder brother. Neville always had a face like a wet Sunday anyway, so it was difficult to tell, but he did not think that there was any real hostility there. Her father might object to the lowly position he presently held at Mifflin's but that was in relative terms. He had good prospects; he certainly had good prospects, and it wasn't as if they were intending to get married immediately. It would be years before they had saved enough for that.

He still didn't ring the doorbell. He had not rehearsed enough. He had to go over again what he was going to say. The thought then occurred to him that he had come empty-handed. It might be a good idea to arrive with some flowers or something for Mrs Reynolds.

He abandoned the pretentious sentinels at the door and ran down the steps and on towards South Road. If he was lucky there might be a florists still open. He knew that by indulging this whim he was only manufacturing an excuse to put off the evil moment but it might bring its rewards at that. He was unlucky. The florists was closing up and they refused to alter the total on their cash register at that late hour on a Saturday even though Jack gave the girls one of his best smiles.

He was near to panic. He had convinced himself by this time that it was imperative that he arrive bearing a gift. It was impossible to envisage not doing so. The fact that the idea had only just occurred to him, that it had been of no significance whatsoever ten minutes earlier was forgotten. He would have to cancel the whole thing if he could not find something appropriate and it was already gone half-past five.

He dashed down the street in a lather of anxiety, peering at all the shops to see if they might be still open, even the one which only sold large items of furniture. That wouldn't do. He ran across the road in desperation and found himself outside Satterthwaites. This was a cake shop of some renown. The girls were clearing the window. Despite the CLOSED sign on the door he banged on the glass and caught the attention of one of the assistants.

'We're shut. Go away!'

Not to be dissuaded, Jack mimed a mock prayer and went down on one knee in supplication. The girl laughed and opened the door.

'What do you want? We're closed.'

He explained his predicament, looking as helpless and lovelorn as he could. He was going to his girl friend's to ask permission to become engaged and he wondered if they might have a large cake which would be a suitable bribe for the mother? They shook their heads, but eventually took pity on him and he left with half-a-dozen jap cakes and a few iced affairs, boxed and beribboned, with their compliments.

Armed with his trophies, he returned to the house, marched straight up the steps ignoring the laurels and pushed the doorbell. He could hear its confident ring inside the house as he stood there clutching the box to his chest. Fran had the door open within seconds. She must have been behind it all the time.

To the immense relief of both of them, no immediate opposition came their way. There was just a rather glum acceptance of the situation. This ungraciousness extended itself to the tea. Izzie was very competitive when it came to hospitality. Normally she was generous to a fault and what she provided for her table was the envy of the neighbourhood, as well as that of her sisters which was her ultimate aim in the first place. The nature of the 'celebratory' tea for Jack and Fran should, in retrospect, have set alarm bells ringing in both their heads. Initially, innocent and unsuspecting as they were, it did not.

Fran, bubbling with pride and excitement, was instructed to round up her siblings from the various parts of the house. Jack was invited to sit in one of the armchairs in front of the fire to talk to Fa. He found this a bit daunting and was relieved when he could turn his attention to the two youngest boys who came clattering down the stairs into the big room which had once been the kitchen before the more modern set up was created to the rear of it. It was always referred to as the kitchen but in effect it was where the family tended to congregate unless visitors were being entertained in the front room. It was invariably warm and cosy and the big dining table, which had been known to seat up to fifteen in its time, usually groaned with goodies at meal times.

The butler's pantry, opposite the entrance to the very grand front room, was where Izzie kept most of her stores. It had not been used by a butler since she became mistress of the house but she found it extremely useful, especially as it had a key and surprises could be hidden in there at Christmas and for birthdays. Treats of all kinds.

She chose not to provide a treat that day. She emerged with a tin of pilchards which she ultimately put into Fran's hands with instructions to use for sandwiches and then went off to set the table with the every-day crockery from the dresser. The occasion obviously did not warrant the Minton. The gift of the cakes had already disappeared into the said pantry. They would grace her bridge party the following evening.

Fran hated pilchards, especially the ones in tomato sauce which these were. She was also hurt and not a little angry that her mother should snub Jack in such a way. It was so cunning of Izzie. No-one could say that she was not making him welcome, she was giving him tea after all, but it was blatantly obvious to all the family that they were on short rations. The injustice of it, and the pungent taste of the spicy fish in equal measure, threatened to choke Fran. Her inner fury increased until, come the time of Jack's departure, she had to rush upstairs to the bathroom to be sick.

Izzie was waiting for her at the bottom of the stairs when she came down. For one second Fran was grateful that her mother seemed so concerned but she soon realized her mistake when she was pushed into the front room and the door firmly closed after them. Izzie had convinced herself that Fran was pregnant and accused her roundly of being so.

'You stupid little fool! So that's what all this engagement nonsense is about? You might have known what would happen, associating with the likes of him. It will be a baby every year for you from now on, if you have to marry him. That's what their church makes them do, or didn't you know that? Well it serves you right. You'll be old before your time and God help you! You'll not get any help from me. That you can count on!'

Fran was rendered utterly speechless. That her mother should think her capable of such a thing was horror enough but to malign Jack was adding insult to injury. Jack, who was the most perfect gentleman in that respect, Jack whose emphasis on chastity was almost priestly in its constancy. It was monstrous. She told her mother so and received a sharp slap for her pains.

Once she was allowed to leave that hateful room, she raced upstairs to be sick again.

The whole day was spoiled by this episode, as was the next when they went to look for a ring. Their joy had been tainted. Izzie had given vent to spiteful behaviour and unfounded accusations. Fa, by his non-intervention, had condoned both. Less distressing but just as hurtful was Abigail's dismissive shrug when she heard the news of their engagement. The only one who had kissed Fran with genuine pleasure and happiness for them was Dodo. And it was she who had hugged Fran close when their mother's malicious reaction was tearfully discussed between them as they sat up in bed late into the night.

On two points, they were in total agreement: that it was fear of the drubbing she would get at the hands of the Mackenzie clan that had caused their mother to say such extreme things and secondly it would be wiser not to tell Jack. It would be too insulting, and he did not deserve such treatment, such calumny. For calumny it undoubtedly was.

The modest little ring that Fran ultimately chose had a row of three tiny diamonds in a dainty gold setting. It was charming and as far as she was concerned it was as good as the most valuable ring in the world. Even though she knew that it would be viewed with a lack of enthusiasm at home she still could not prevent herself from showing it off.

But the raw recollection of that shameful scene with her mother diminished Fran's delight in it and fuelled her anger at the wrong done to Jack whenever she caught sight of it on her finger.

10. News from Spain

THAT SUMMER, THE Reynolds decided that Fran would join the aunts in Wales for her annual holiday. They were not going to risk any prolonged contact with Jack if they could possibly prevent it. Of course, it was Izzie who was the prime motivator of this edict. Fa went along with her to keep the peace; at least that was how it was at the beginning. He just wanted a bit of peace. Izzie's confirmed belief was that the relationship with Jack would lose its attraction when Fran had wider horizons. How she imagined that the farmhouse in Wales was to achieve this desired aim was a fancy known only to herself.

Fran was bitterly disappointed. The children who were spending the summer there that year were all under ten, and all boys: her two younger brothers and two cousins. The excuse that they were too much of a handful for the ageing aunts on their own was only partly true. The old ladies might have become a little forgetful and a little less mobile but their tongues had not lost the familiar waspish sting when called for. Besides, Abigail was going. But Abigail had cleverly cultivated a reputation for incompetence long before this. It was Dodo and Fran who were relied upon for help whenever and wherever it was required, whilst Abigail smirked at her sisters from behind her mother's back with no small modicum of triumph.

Fran, who had been so looking forward to her week off was forced to accept the inevitable; she would have to go to Babyll. Jack had naturally arranged his holiday for the same week and the fact that he would be left high and dry whilst she was stuck with that unruly crew of boys enraged her beyond measure. That Jack would be understanding, that he would be sympathetic in his acknowledgement that such was the way of things, did not relieve her frustration.

The more she thought about it, the more unfair it became. Dodo had had her holiday. There had been no objection raised to her spending time with Neville K., when her parents had been allowed to know about it. Fran had to admit that Dodo had been very economical with the truth when she had made her plans. Neville had hardly featured in the reports coming back to Izzie and Fa of the lovely days spent at the Lido in New Brighton or the tennis matches played away at Hightown and Ainsdale. Dodo had got away with it.

Jack took the news philosophically. He was still depressed about Pinny's departure. Even the remarkable gift of the motor-bike did not make things easier. The wretched thing reminded him of the loss of his friend every time he rode it. However, he did come up with the positive suggestion that now that he was lucky enough to have it he could easily ride over to Flintshire on one of the days whilst she was there. They could surely arrange to meet far enough away from the farm to avoid any comment from the aunts. Fran felt that something might be salvaged from the disaster, but it was small compensation at that.

Just before she was due to leave, she received a letter from Stella. It had taken months to arrive. Izzie pounced on it immediately; warily suspicious. The Bundenells' affairs were still the main focus of the local gossip. Lou was inexorably, mercilessly condemned for abandoning her husband. It was considered to be scandalous; *she* was considered to be scandalous and the daughter fared no better during the exchanges over the bridge tables.

Izzie demanded that Fran destroy the letter unopened. When Fran demurred, she tore it up and threw it on the fire. It was not to be read. But Fran held out against all her mother's threats and got down on her hands and knees and snatched what she could from amongst the embers. She was desperate to know what was happening to her friend and she would not be bullied, not this time. Izzie capitulated and gave in to her tears, but the scorched pages had to be handed over for her to read first. Fran writhed at the indignity and high-handedness of it but it did her not the slightest good. She had to wait until her mother had pieced it back together and scrutinized every decipherable line before she was allowed to have it.

If Izzie had been expecting to find sedition, or even worse that which she termed, 'moral laxness', in Stella's communication she was doomed to disappointment, as were her gossips over the bridge table later on in the week when the account of the incident circulated. The letter contained neither. It was a simple chronicle of events; very ordinary events at that.

From what they could make out, Stella had been befriended on the passage out by one of the nuns who was on her way to collect yet another group of refugee children. Through her she had been given a contact in Barcelona who might be able to let her a room. This had proved an inspired suggestion as she was on the outskirts of the city which was less dangerous and the family had proved to be very kind. She had managed to find work alongside other international volunteers at one of the many relief centres and she was learning Spanish much faster than she ever could have imagined. But the political situation was immensely confusing. The various anti-Fascist groups seemed to working against each other and it was difficult to sort out exactly who was who, especially as there was so much street fighting. She had arrived in Barcelona at the worst possible time, it seemed. She apologised for her sudden disappearance but no explanation for it could be found in what remained of the letter. If originally there had been an attempt to clarify the causes of her hasty departure not a scrap had survived. Fran was still as unenlightened as ever.

The letter contained nothing that Izzie, in conscience, could object to and Fran was grudgingly allowed to keep it. The first thing she did when she met Jack at the end of the day was to give him an agitated account of the confrontation with her mother and they pored over the scraps of scorched paper, heads close together, as they sheltered from the wind behind the single storey building which graced the pierhead. Stella seemed safe, that was the main thing and it was exciting to be able to think that she was there, making a stand for all of them in her way. It did not sound quite as romantic as they had anticipated and in Fran's case that element tended to become embellished and polished the more frequently she retold the story. Jack's father and Lou were the only people in receipt of Jack's version and her response was typical: 'Sounds like the usual bugger's muddle to me!'

Jack had gone straight to Norton Street once he had seen Fran ride off, rather than catch the ferry. He felt that he ought to establish whether Lou had also received any news. To his certain knowledge, Lou hadn't had so much as a word so far, but then if the post had taken so long for Fran's letter to reach them, maybe one for Lou would also be on its way. Because he played down the extent of his contact with Lou where Fran was concerned, he had chosen not to confide his anxiety about her condition during their brief meeting on the pierhead. Lou was unhappy. He also suspected that she might be ill.

He was as bemused as anybody as to why she was living in her former office. Surely she could live anywhere she wanted even if she had done a bunk from her husband? He had never asked questions about the crisis which had resulted in both she and Stella leaving the house on the Esplanade. There had obviously been a crisis, and a big one at that, but he felt that it was none of his business. Nevertheless, he worried about her a great deal and racked his brains for ways in which he could help without being obvious about it. He loved her and it upset him that she was in trouble. He went to visit her as often as he could but that was not easy. He was desperate for promotion and he really was having to work late in the evenings, instead of claiming that he was when he needed an excuse to cover the fact that he was at a political meeting. Whatever the pressure, he was determined to see her that night.

Since Pinny had told him about Norton Street being watched, he had been using the back entry instead of going through the shop. It was awkward with his motor-bike as the alleyway was narrow but he hated the thought of being spied on so much that he put up with it. He negotiated his way into the yard and parked the bike where he could. Lou did, from necessity, use up a great deal of space and there was very little room left.

There was no answer to his knock and the door was locked. Lou was obviously out. He felt sure that there was no meeting of any kind scheduled for that evening, so he assumed that she would be down at the Heatons'. He perched himself against the seat of his bike and settled down to wait.

Lou had 'adopted' the Heaton family during the Depression and it had not occurred to her that it should be a temporary measure that would come to an end once the port had regained its economic importance and things had begun to improve. She no longer contributed to their support on a regular basis but if the husband was laid-off and out of work she would make sure that food and fuel came their way; always from her own pocket, depleting her private resources in the process. She never used the allowance Edward gave her and neither did she dip into the funds she worked so hard to build up for other purposes.

From the outset, she had made it a principle never to give money; she knew too well what smacked of charity, and she had resisted that, even when the children had been sick. She would do the nursing herself; only rarely did she have to pay a doctor. She never made a fuss about anything, she was never critical and she was never condescending. She had looked upon Annie Heaton as her friend right from the beginning and Annie, once she had got over her defensiveness, ultimately came to feel the same way about her. These days she never thought to bring out the best tablecloth for tea and the Apostle spoons now stayed in hock when Lou was due to visit. This was taken as irrefutable evidence of acceptance and Lou felt able to turn up unannounced whenever she needed to. She never went empty-handed, especially when the deplorable hiring system at the docks meant that money was tight. There was always a little something for the children; something chosen with thought, that would make their faces light up with pleasure, but never anything so grand that it would cause embarrassment.

The thought of expecting anything in return had not occurred to her, but what she actually got was real friendship. Since the time with Maddy Lonsdale when they had been together during the war she had not experienced such an easeful, relaxed relationsip with any other person.

She missed Maddy more than she cared to admit. They had been comfortable with each other, confident that no strictures applied, certain that support would be forthcoming whatever the circumstances. If things were hard they had just got on with it and made the best of it, gifted with the ability to see a funny side to every setback, even if, in extremity, they had had to invent one. Consolation had come with uninhibited laughter. She had been able to be totally herself with Maddy and she loved her for it. She loved her for her indomitable courage and her loyalty. Now she loved Annie Heaton too, for exactly the same reasons, despite the differences in their character and the huge discrepancy in their social backgrounds.

It could have been very different. She could have been allocated one of the many feckless families which blighted the area. 'Bad buggers' Annie called them and kept her children away. When she and Lou were alone, she would regale her with hair-raising stories of their doings with a turn of phrase and natural wit that had Lou helpless with mirth. Annie was a born entertainer and it was she who, unwittingly, had kept at bay the despair which had been threatening to cripple Lou since the loss of Stella. The true nature of this loss Lou kept to herself. She turned her grief inward.

She felt that she was in mourning for what would never come again. She had been forced to reveal the existence of Stella's father and the circumstances under which she had been born. Stella's response to this news had been devastating. Hysteria, an extreme hysteria had ensued and her adamantine refusal to forgive had almost destroyed her mother. Everything that Stella meant to her Lou knew to be in jeopardy.

She had always loved her with a fierce intensity. She looked upon the birth of Stella as the greatest achievement of her life; nothing else she might aspire to could be compared with it, and she had done it entirely alone. She had welcomed the child as a gift. Her coming was not seen as punishment, nor a reason for shame, but as a kind of forgiveness, a compensation for her rashness in loving Tim so passionately, for her naivety in taking for granted that he had seen commitment as she had seen it. She had never suspected that, for him, she was one of many ships that passed in the night. His need was to grasp experience and then move on and her failure was in not recognising it. The damage on the way, least of all that which was inflicted on himself, Tim Dundonald discounted.

It was the physical damage he had sustained that had brought them together in the winter of 1916, by sheer chance. Lou drove the ambulance for the hospital at Kelsay. The collection point was Leeds. Under normal circumstances she would remain in the cab on the forecourt of the station, along with all the others, waiting for their allocation of patients. In those days the ambulances did not possess side doors and the relentless, bitter rain had driven her to seek shelter inside, although she hated the nightmarish gloom of that cavernous, benighted place. The platforms seethed with the disgorgement from the trains. Lines of stretchers went on into the infinity of swirling, acrid smoke, the startling white of the nurses' caps busily flitting in and out amongst them had reminded Lou of trapped moths, frantic in the murky shadows. Trails of walking wounded shuffled wearily towards the exit, bandaged, stumbling along on crutches, cigarettes dangling limply from lips that lacked the strength to remove them. It was a far cry from the garrison town where the regiments from the barracks entrained, sent on their way as heroes, to cheers and band-playing. They did not return that way. The ambulances had to rumble all the way to Leeds in the dead of night to collect the survivors. The boys going out were not allowed to witness the scenes that would tell them their fate.

Lou had been leaning against a pillar, her oilskins dripping water into a pool on the floor, when her attention was caught by a heated exchange going on within a yard of her. An emaciated creature in a threadbare trench coat, one arm in a dirty sling and feet enclosed in seeping bandages, was gesticulating furiously to the officer on Transport Duty. It seemed that he should not have been there. The officer claimed that there was no record of his name on any of the hospital lists. He would have to go back and sort out the mistake. He had been put on the wrong train.

It was obvious to Lou, observing this acrimonious scene as she waited for the Kelsay contingent, that the soldier was in no condition to go anywhere, especially not back to London. She stepped in and took over.

It was the combination of his extreme vulnerability and his uncowed spirit which had acted like a magnet. She was hopelessly in love with him before she had completed the job of smuggling him into her own hospital at Kelsay and making sure that he was permitted to stay there. She was not the only one to find him irresistible. Despite his mutilated state, every nurse on the campus was vying for his attentions within hours of his arrival, but it had been she whom he had chosen.

When it was time for him to convalesce, she had rented a cottage in the Wolds where he could live. Before that she had risked infection from his tubercular lung by refusing all advice to stay well clear of him. She had found it impossible to do that. She would die too if it came to it, rather than do that.

But he had recovered and ultimately she had moved in with him. From her meagre resources she had provided for them both. In the greenness of her youth and the complacent confidence in the strength of their love, she had not anticipated faithlessness. When the blow came, she savagely punished herself for her folly and like Stella, in her turn, she had run away, not knowing where the violence of her reaction would take her, but with the conviction that the damage she had done to her face would keep her safe from any further attentions. Her attractiveness, she clearly saw, was her enemy. It was an enticement. That was all it was. It encouraged casual attention which was an anathema to her. So she took action against it. She hacked off her sheet of beautiful golden hair.

And then she had learned that the child was coming and with the child came healing. Tim Dundonald became a distant memory, attributed to the experience of war; closed off as shutters are closed, putting that part of her life in permanent darkness, as the rooms of those who would not return were closed; the doors sealed. And then he had sailed home across the Atlantic; the shutters had been opened, shedding light so catastrophically on that which, for two decades, had been hidden behind them. Her relationship with Stella, flawed as it undoubtedly was but nevertheless her life blood, could never be the same again. It was a kind of death and for that, inwardly, she wept.

She did not blame Tim; she blamed the cowardice within herself which had led her to be dishonest with her daughter and dishonest with her husband. She who would not tolerate deception in others was guilty of it herself, on the one hand because she loved too much and on the other because she did not love at all. And she did not love Edward. In the early days, when she had been bowled over by his attentiveness and flattered by his courtship, she thought that she had loved him for his dependability, for his apparent commitment to her. But she had failed to see the inner man in exactly the same way that she had failed with her first love. She had only discovered her error after she had given everything of herself; generously, openly, brimming over with misguided trust. What had she received in return? Nothing but blows of one order or another.

She had given much reflection to this subject and concluded that she was not suited to marriage. She was not cut out for such emotional subordination. Her union with Tim she had looked upon as sacred, however badly it had turned out. What she had had with him still made her senses reel, made her stagger with the intensity of it, when she allowed herself to think about it at all. But her expectations had obviously been unrealistic in respect to him. Other women, scores of other women, had felt the same. She had not been special. She had ended up with the same distaste clogging her throat, the same anger at her disillusionment, the same despair and the same conviction that it must be some lack in *her*, not him. Because she had married his opposite and fared even worse.

In order to escape from such circumspection, she spent more and more time with the Heatons who had now become her neighbours. She had learned to depend on them when she needed confirmation that she was loved. But even with them she felt that she could not totally reciprocate. She could not be open with them as they were with her. She could not admit that she was a failure. She was driven to invent excuses as to why it had become so often necessary for her to sleep over in town. She knew that Annie had guessed that her marriage was in ruins, but she did not give so much as a hint that that was the case. She disguised the constant underlying misery she felt at not having news of her daughter by means of pretence. She had no perception that her laughter was brittle and her brightness transparently false, nor that Annie recognised it for what it was and was troubled by it. Lou felt incapable of sharing with anybody the extent of her grief.

It was always as she was returning to Norton Streeet that she would ponder on the reasons for her reticence. She had a sneaking suspicion that it was pride that prevented her from speaking out; a residue from her background which had always discouraged the exchange of confidences. As a child, she had been conditioned to look upon the need for such as a contemptible weakness. One must remain aloof and therefore inviolate. This was one of the rare occasions when she had heeded such advice and it made her wonder whether her soldier father, long ago buried in India, had also crept away, to lick his wounds in secret like a stray dog, as she now did. But still she kept her silence.

She had not expected to find Jack sitting in her back yard on this particular evening and she had been so absorbed by her thoughts that she had started with surprise on first seeing him there. He had jumped to his feet, eager to know if she had had a letter but anxious to be diplomatic if she had not. He had had plenty of time to work out what his approach would be but she did not give him the opportunity to put it into practice. She took one look at him and knew what he had come to tell her.

'You've heard from Stella?'

He gave her an exultant smile.

'Fran has.'

She fumbled with the key in her agitation. She could not make it turn in the lock. She was in fear that if she took her eyes from Jack's face he would somehow disappear, the communication from Stella disappearing with him. She was unable to concentrate on the task.

Jack gently took over and opened the door for her to enter and as he did so he told her that he had read the letter to Fran; he could recite to her everything that was in it, he said, word for word. It was plain that she had had no news herself and he sensed the urgency of her need for reassurance. He tried to imagine the state his own mother would be in if either of his sisters had done a bolt into the middle of a messy civil war and there had been no word for months. Lou must be desperate.

'You'll hear any day now. It was ages ago when she wrote. There must be a problem with the shipping.'

Lou looked decidedly ill in Jack's opinion. She had a strange look on her face; a closed, set look which was so contrary to her usual animation. It seemed that it took an almighty effort for her to speak.

'She's safe then?'

'She is! And you'll hear tomorrow, believe me. I'm not always right, but I'm never wrong.'

She smiled at his attempt at a joke but shook her head at the same time. She had every reason not to believe him.

'Sit down, Jack. I'll get us something to eat. Will bacon and eggs do?'

He had intended to go without supper; he often did when he met Fran after work, before he went back to do another stint in the evening. He had thought that he wasn't hungry but when Lou suggested bacon and eggs, he suddenly felt famished and accepted her offer with alacrity.

As she bustled about in the tiny kitchen created from the lobby by the back door, Jack marvelled at the transformation she had wrought on the erstwhile dingy little office. It was now a comfortable living room graced with few, but very good, pieces of furniture. A leather-topped desk stood under the window with her piles of correspondence neatly stacked on its surface, the solid brass handles on its numerous drawers below waiting for the lamp to be lit in order to show off their propensity to gleam. In the centre of the room was a small circular table of very fine wood and against the back wall was a divan bed serving as a sofa and draped with a richly embroidered cover in greens of various hues, turquoise and gold. It looked decidedly exotic, Indian possibly, an impression which was substantiated by the abundance of cushions competing for places along its length. She had improvised bookcases at either end of the divan which were overflowing with books, as were the upright chairs which filled every other available space. A heavy velvet curtain covered the alcove at the side of the fireplace, and a matching one hung over the door to the shop. There was no carpet on the floor. She had painted the wide boards in a sort of dark ochre and together with the pale yellow walls and the yellow velvet of the curtaining it gave the room a sunny feel which it did not naturally have.

Jack was intrigued by its novelty. He had never seen such a room. He did not usually take much notice; his appraisal of people had little or nothing to do with their possessions, but he was arrested by this one. It had nothing of the calculated 'good taste' of the house on the Esplanade. Lou, on her own, had created something altogether different, something mysterious and enigmatic. Just like herself.

As they shared the meal, Lou contemplated the young man across the table with a great deal of fondness. It was the inherent kindness in his nature that drew her to him. Underneath the fiery anger with which he ignited many a political meeting, and the uncompromising stand he took when required, there was a great deal of sensitivity and no small amount of compassion. Jack was striving to better himself, to better the world he lived in, but he would never do it on the back of anyone else.

She appreciated Jack's dogged efforts to reassure her about Stella's situation, his insistence that her errant daughter would soon be home. He did not know any more than any of them. He was just saying that to make her feel happier. He was telling her what he thought she wanted to hear. The extent of his concern touched her profoundly but he had no real idea of the complexities of the situation and they were both aware that he was out of his depth.

'Stella is as unlikely to come back as Pinny is. They've both grown out of us, Jack. Pinny will be safe when the war comes, Stella won't be unless she decides to return to England. I doubt that she will do that. There is nothing I can do about it, except pray that she sees the danger and overcomes her aversion to me.'

Jack put down his knife and fork with a clatter,

'Why on earth should she have an aversion to you?'

Lou told him. Calmly, and with an increasing sense of a burden lifting, she related to Jack all that she had deliberately kept from those who loved her most: from Maddy, from Annie Heaton. It was as if his very nature invited confession. She knew that he would not pity her. Neither would he judge. He would just listen.

11. Motherly Love

FRAN DID NOT enjoy her holiday at Babyll. She returned to the office heartily thankful to be released from the clucking presence of the elderly aunts. She had also missed Jack and was inordinately impatient for the end of that first day when they would meet as usual.

He seemed different. Quieter.

'What's the matter with you?' She found herself testily accosting him instead of running into his arms as she had meant to do. 'Are you in one of your moods?'

'I don't have moods,' he replied.

'Yes, you do. You are a gloomy devil at times, and this is one of them. You might at least have the grace to tell me what is the matter.'

'There is nothing the matter. I am not in a mood!'

But he was. He needed to talk about their future and he had to hedge round the aspect of it that made him sick at the thought of himself. Circumstances were forcing him to become devious with her. Expediency was becoming a necessity. It was a situation which he found untenable.

He had made a decision to move out from home and take a room on the Liverpool side of the water, he told her. He was having to work late such a lot and it made sense to cut out the ferry journey. One of his friends had offered him a room in his house near Sefton park. He would be moving the next week.

Fran was delighted. She considered that that was good news. She did not see any reason for getting into a mood about that. 'Men are such babies,' she thought to herself. 'Any change and they're knocked for six, poor things.' And she kissed him lightly on the cheek. 'I think that that is wonderful, Jack. Really wonderful,' she said. 'Good for you!'

But it had not been like that at all. His father had been laid off again and if Jack's wages were coming into the house there would be no benefits paid. The family would have to depend on Jack's wage packet and it was not nearly enough to feed seven. It had been made clear to him that it would be better if he left.

There was also the added dilemma brought on by his mother, in the heat of the argument, demanding to know what was happening about Fran. Where was she receiving instruction? With whom? When was she to be received into the church?

Fran was still postponing the issue of conversion. When they discussed the topic it was with no sense of urgency. They did not want to get married immediately, quite the reverse in fact, and Jack was happy that she seemed to be getting on so well with Fr. Christian. He had been content to let things be. Now Jack felt pressured to bring up the subject again. It would certainly calm things down at home if he could provide evidence of honourable intentions, so to speak.

But there was something not altogether right about this request to Fran. He was doing it for all the wrong reasons in his opinion. He was asking her to take on a commitment which was even more demanding than a marriage and that, by recent accounts, was bad enough. What was more, he was not one hundred percent certain that he wanted her to do it. It was not that his own innate faith was shaken but the peripherals were certainly undergoing a rigorous scrutiny.

But he asked her if she would be prepared to do it, even so. Fran, reluctantly, agreed and her preparation for entry into the Church began.

It appeased his family temporarily but the Reynolds' hostility could no longer be described as covert. Prohibitions of all kinds became the norm. Fran could no longer cycle into work, nor was she allowed to go by train. She was fetched and carried by car. Fa drove and Neville went along for good measure. If Jack appeared she was hustled off without ceremony.

One allowance was made. She could go to the pictures on a Saturday night but she had to be back home by ten o' clock, or she could go to the dance but only if she was accompanied by Dodo and a strict curfew was enforced. On every other night she was banished to the billiard room. 'In you go!' her mother would say and turn the key in the lock.

Fran dealt with this with her usual pragmatism. Thoughts of rebellion did not cross her mind. 'I'll just bide my time,' she thought, 'I'll just bide my time. One of these days I'll be free of this.' Simultaneously, she thanked her lucky stars that it had not been the cellars which had been the place Izzie had decided upon. She hated the cellars. They had been the kitchens in the old days and were now full of discarded furniture, old toys cocooned in cobwebs, heaps of dusty coal dumped in corners. She was sure that the whole place was infested with mice. Being mortally afraid of vermin, she would have gone wild if she had been locked in there. Instead she taught herself to play a natty game of billiards, her only regret being that it had not been the front room she had been banished to. She would have played the piano in there till bedtime and not thought another thing about it. She would almost have been happy in the front room.

Her situation also provided opportunity for a great deal of thought. Nothing on earth would make her give up Jack now, whatever punishment Izzie might inflict upon her. Izzie's prejudice was rebounding upon itself. Fran had also discovered that the preposterous notion that the Catholic Church demanded an annual pregnancy from its married women was an ignorant falsehood. She had accosted Fr. Christian on the subject and received a predictable lecture on purity in marriage followed by the excruciatingly embarrassing, but extremely enlightening, details of the rhythm method of contraception. Her mother had been wrong. But there was no way that she could tell her of the fact even if, God forbid, she had wanted to. Her visits to Little Crosby and the reason for them, were still ostensibly covert. They were an act of defiance which compensated, in some part, for the treatment she was in receipt of.

The puzzling thing was that not a word was said as to *why* she was being incarcerated. She was not verbally forbidden to see Jack. No-one demanded that the engagement be broken off. The Saturday visits to the pictures had not been further curtailed. She was just locked in six nights of every seven and she did not display one sign of protest.

The outward signs of passivity belied her actual intentions. She could not accept that they would win. She would hold out until she was old enough to marry Jack, whatever they did or did not do. If it took all those years then that was the way it had to be. She would just hold out and she knew that Jack would too, even though they could only manage to see each other in stolen moments at lunch time and once a week for a few hours at the weekend.

Whilst she was perfecting her skills with the cue, Fran also had leisure to work out her accounts. She was earning good wages and after she had given her mother her share she put the rest in the bank. Her savings account was beginning to look decidedly healthy as a result. The fact that she was virtually under house-arrest also contributed in an ironical sort of way. There had not been any new dresses for dances for a long while. As the weeks went by it gave her great satisfaction to see the total grow.

The crisis which followed could have been motivated by various factors. Izzie could have come across the books of instruction which Fran had not hidden despite her knowledge that her mother checked out the bedroom she shared with Dodo. It could have been that Fran actually looked smugly complacent on occasions when in unguarded moments she cast a thought in the direction of her bank book and her mother immediately interpreted that as, 'dumb insolence.' Much more seriously, it could have been that Fa had been informed that his future son-in-law was a committed Communist.

Jack and Lou had recently attended a big meeting at the Rotunda Theatre in Kirkdale. The speakers were a delegation from another section of the Party, the Anarcho-Syndicalists who were, in the main, Trotskyites. They were intent on subverting the support Jack's group was giving to the war in Spain. What they were proposing was tantamount to world revolution. Jack was not inclined to this at all and had noisily told them to get lost. He then walked out of the meeting in disgust. Unbeknown to him, an acquaintance of Neville Reynolds, a plain-clothes policeman, was lurking along with several other colleagues amongst the audience. Jack had undoubtedly made himself conspicuous. In retrospect, it was quite conceivable that Neville had been slipped a warning. If this had been the case he would have lost little time in making it known to Fa that Jack Jamieson was a Red, a Revolutionary.

Whatever the reason, Jack and Fran suffered further indignities at the hands of Izzie Reynolds.

Fran, shielded by her ignorance of Jack's political activities and their graver ramifications, chose to believe that her mother's behaviour could be directly attributed to snobbery and as such should be pitied rather than resented.

Dodo and Neville K.'s engagement was the first clue that hostility was on the increase. Izzie arranged a dinner party to celebrate and Jack was grudgingly invited. As Fran helped with the elaborate preparations, she could not but remember the miserable offerings which had been produced on a previous occasion. This time there was to be a feast. It did not alleviate matters that the massive piece of beef had been provided by Neville himself and that it was his mother, not hers, who had made the magnificently decorated cake. Even so, Fran could not be other than distressed.

Izzie fussed over Neville K. all evening. She went pink with pleasure when he mentioned how well his business was doing. He and Dodo would soon be able to have a house. They had been to see one near Hightown.

Dodo giggled nervously. She had a little girl's giggle which suddenly irritated Fran beyond measure. She examined her sister's face for signs of treachery; had she revealed that Fran went to see the priest at the Presbytery near there? Fran could not be convinced that she had. Dodo had a little girl's face to match her giggle. She was still a little girl despite being four years senior to Fran. She was incapable of duplicity. But Fran was uneasy.

The inevitable snub came when Izzie was serving the food. They were all round the dinner table, Jack having been placed on a corner. He and the younger children had to contend with the table legs between their knees. Fran was in the middle but she was fully aware of what her mother was doing. Fa, the two Nevilles and the aged aunts were given the choicest slices in abundance. Jack was served last. His plate was full enough, but he had been served the scraps.

He did not seem to notice anything amiss but Fran could feel tears pricking at her eyes in mortification on his behalf. It was shameful of her mother to discriminate in such a petty way. It was inexcusable. Small-minded and inexcusable.

She could not eat her portion. She pushed it around her plate and only accepted a piece of cake because Abigail caught her eye with a look that suggested that Fran's lack of appetite she attributed to jealousy.

The rest of the evening was a disaster as far as Fran was concerned. She was not even allowed to go to the door to see Jack out when he left early. Her brother Neville went.

If she had not been stuck at the piano, entertaining everybody, she would have taken herself off to bed.

It was the following Saturday night that provided the catalyst. Fran and Jack had been to the cinema on South Road. They still had to leave before the end of the picture in order to get Fran back by ten, even though they were so near to her home. They thought it wise for Jack to go straight to the train rather than take Fran to her door. They would part at the end of Oakshot Road which happened to be on the way to the station anyway.

Fran was particularly happy that evening. She had got a new job to go to. She would be, by the beginning of the following week, personal secretary to the director of a company based in Aintree at a considerably better salary than she had earned so far. She had not mentioned it at home. For one thing she wished to avoid the derisive snort Abigail was sure to give had she been unsuccessful at the interview and secondly, she would let Neville find out for himself where she was in future, if he and Fa pursued their body-guard act as she knew they would.

Another reason for her good spirits was that her cousin Grace had passed on to her a couple of very attractive evening dresses. She was looking forward to inspecting them when she got up to her room. She would try them on and admire herself in the long mirror which she and Dodo had just acquired between them. She would enjoy that.

She was humming under her breath as she ascended the steps to the front porch. She should have been more alert to the fact that all the lights were off. The big door was usually left open until Fa locked up when everyone had gone to bed. As she passed through to switch the light on and open the vestibule door, Izzie leapt out from behind it and laid about her with a leather strap.

The shock was so great that Fran did not know who it was who was attacking her. She had put her arms up to defend herself from the fierce blows which were raining on to her head and shoulders and they were lashed in their turn. She thought that she had disturbed a burglar for a second or two and she cried out. Then she knew that it was Izzie. She could not see who was beating her but she knew. The homely smells which clung around Izzie's clothing: Lavender water, fire-smoke, children, were in extreme contrast to the violence she was perpetrating. The impact of it took Fran's breath away. Izzie's breath too was coming in short gasps with the unaccustomed effort and the vehemence of her anger.

Once Fran had been pushed inside she wriggled free and rushed upstairs to her room, banging the door after her. Dodo was not yet back, she had the mirror to herself.

She inspected her face and arms. There were great weals rising already over her skin, great red weals which would turn black and blue by morning. She tried to remove her blouse, it was painful as she had caught several blows across her knuckles and her fingers were stiffening. At last she could gingerly slide a sleeve down her arm and let the blouse fall to the floor. It would be a long time before she could be seen in any evening dress, or in much else for that matter.

She crept along to the bathroom and pressed wet facecloths to her bruises wherever she could reach. When she heard Dodo come in she scuttled back to their room and crawled into bed. She pretended to be asleep. She did not want to be seen.

She was up and out before anyone else the following morning. It being Sunday she had the whole day to sort out what she was going to do. She went to one of her colleagues whose mother, she knew, kept a respectable lodging house. There was not a vacancy there but another friend of hers knew of a place in Venmoor Street and she had more luck with them. She immediately rented a room, wrote a note to Jack and left it at Mifflins on her way back and then got the train home. She was fascinated by the weirdness of coincidence. It was in Venmoor Street that her mother had been born. She toyed with the idea that it might be some sort of a sign, but she did not allow that to alter her plans.

On reaching Oakshot Road, she went straight upstairs making as little noise as possible. Lunch was in progress and she could hear the clatter of cutlery and the murmur of voices. Her absence was probably being discussed but she did not let that concern her. Fifteen minutes later she had her bags packed. No-one heard her leave through the front door. She caught a taxi at the station.

⋆ ⋆ ⋆

Whatever ructions followed Fran's disappearance, she and Jack could only guess at. Jack was appalled when he saw the effects of the beating the following Monday night. Her note had told him where to meet her in Sefton Park. He was not allowed to visit her in her room in any event, and the park was the nearest place. It was raining and they huddled together under the band-stand whilst she related all that had happened. She was neither tearful nor vengeful, just icily rational. She was determined that she was not going to suffer any more of her mother's unreasonable behaviour. Locking a daughter up was one thing; beating her up was another. Izzie had gone too far.

It was Jack's turn to be mortified. He saw it as all his fault. She had had to suffer this because of him. He did not know how to forgive himself. What had possessed the mother to behave in such an extreme fashion that particular night he could not comprehend. They had not broken any of the rules. Nothing unusual had occurred to instigate such lack of control. It was unfathomable. However, the deed was done and Fran was adamant that wild horses would not drag her back again.

They were very cautious about revealing to anyone their whereabouts. Fran did not consciously go into hiding but she was certain that the Reynolds would be searching for her and she was not going to make it easy for them.

She had not returned to Harcourt and Booth's. She had gone to see Miss Wilkinson to explain why she could not work out her notice. She said that she had had an accident on her bicycle. Miss Wilkinson might or might not have believed this tale but she was in total sympathy even though she could not pay Fran her week's wages in lieu. However, it was significant that when a strange man came to make enquiries as to where Fran Reynolds was presently employed, Miss Wilkinson, for reasons known only to herself, refused to give him the information.

The man in question was a private detective hired by Izzie to track down her errant daughter. Miss Wilkinson's instincts, if that is what they were, were correct. Simultaneously, Jack's antennae seemed to be working overtime too. He was so used to looking over his shoulder since he had been warned by Pinny that he could be being watched that he cottoned on very quickly that there was someone tailing him. It did not take him long to work out who it was. It took him no time at all to work out who was responsible for him being fired from his job.

Izzie had gone to see Mr Mifflin. She had told him that Jack Jamieson had behaved shamelessly regarding her daughter Frances, that he had got her pregnant and had as much as abducted her. She hinted that the police could quite possibly become involved if the detective she had hired proved unsuccessful. Mr.Mifflin, fearful of unfavourable publicity and in total agreement with Izzie that Jack was a disgrace, took immediate action. Jack was summarily dismissed.

He was devastated. What Izzie had told his employer was blatantly untrue. He considered it vicious defamation, the aftermath of which was alarming to contemplate. Jobs were like gold dust and to find another one without a reference was almost an impossibility.

He dare not tell his parents what had happened. However unpleasant the circumstances of his having to move over the water had been, they now proved fortuitous. His parents were not witness to the extent of his distress and had no suspicion that he was in such dire trouble. He was determined to keep them in ignorance and prayed that gossip would not reach them until he had sorted himself out.

Day after day he trailed round, searching for employment, any sort of employment; the rent had to be paid and he had to eat. He did not eat much; when he did he always seemed to get indigestion. He decided that he suffered from chronic indigestion and put it down to the worry of it all. All the plans he and Fran had made were in tatters. It upset him beyond measure.

On the surface, Fran appeared not to be so affected. She had faith in Jack. She did not see the loss of his job as the calamity he made it out to be. She felt certain that he would soon be back on his feet again. The mischief her mother had caused made her profoundly angry but she wisely decided that she could not waste good energy on that. Anger was destructive and she needed all her wits about her if she was to make an impression with her new boss. It was important that one of them was able to put savings in the bank. As far as Fran was concerned there were no changes to their plans. She and Jack were still on course.

She was not quite so sanguine when it became clear that the only job that Jack could get was selling vacuum cleaners from door -to-door. She was almost destroyed by that. He had worked so hard at Mifflin's; he had had such prospects; he was so good at what he did. Her mother had, in her unfounded attack on him, wiped away his future in a few moments of neurotic outburst. As a Christian, as a potential Catholic, Fran was reminded that she was expected to forgive the harm that others did to oneself. She had forgiven Izzie for beating her black and blue but she could never forgive her for taking away Jack's self respect. She did indulge in anger then, and in caustic recriminations. She vowed that she would never speak to her mother again, not as long as she lived. Not ever.

But she underestimated Jack. Far from spending time in regret for what had been taken away from him, he now had a target. He was paid on commission; the more of these new-fangled appliances he sold, the more he earned. He would make his circuit the envy of every other salesman in the company. He would be out there day and night. He would work till he dropped to make it up to Fran for what she had suffered because of him. Whenever he closed his eyes, the vision of her battered face appeared. He could only imagine what the rest of her had been like. His utter contempt for the Reynolds spurred him on. He considered them to be bad buggers, all.

Apart from selling a vacuum cleaner to Lou, he hardly saw her for weeks on end. He gave up going to meetings, even the anti-Fascist ones; he gave up driving golf balls along the beach, he even gave up reading. He had no time for any of these things. Everything was geared to acquiring an impeccable reference and, subsequently, a permanent job.

Inevitably he did so. He was appointed to the accounts department of a prestigious furniture company. This store was about to embark on Hire-Purchase sales. Jack's previous knowledge from his time at Mifflin's had fortuitous results. He dazzled his interviewers with his innovative ideas, so much so that they considered him far too good for the advertised position of clerk and asked him if he felt able to consider another post they had to offer. At the beginning of the following week he was installed as assistant manager in the Credit Department at almost double the salary he had been earning at Mifflin's. Izzie Reynolds had been well and truly thwarted if her intention had been to bring Jack down. As a direct result of her malice he had gained a promotion that would have taken him at least another year or so had he remained in his previous post. He would have liked her to know.

Eventually she did, but what she might have thought about such an ironic turn of events was obscured by her immediate aim which was to get Fran back home. The detective, after presenting a great bill for expenses, had ultimately been able to inform her of the whereabouts of her errant daughter. She sent Neville with the car to lie in wait at the factory gates in Aintree. Fa had refused to go. He had become more and more disgusted by the methods his wife employed over the issue of Fran. He washed his hands of it after Izzie had refused to let him go to her lodgings and attempt to reason with her. In his opinion, Izzie was behaving like a mad woman and he had grave reservations about the use of the detective. He considered it unseemly. It was also apparent, from what the odious man had reported, that Fran's pregnancy was a figment of Izzie's imagination; an imagination he was increasingly aware, which gave cause for anxiety. Izzie should see a doctor in his considered judgement. But she dismissed his objections and Neville was despatched in the Rover.

For his part, Neville was uncomfortable about this particular assignment. It was one thing picking his sister up from work when she was living at home under the jurisdiction of their parents, he had supported Fa in that, but it was quite another when she had made it clear that she wanted nothing to do with them. He hated this cloak and dagger stuff and he was not sure who to blame for his involvement in it. His mother was off her head, he decided, as he drove along, muttering under his breath. And as for Fran, she had always been wilful in his opinion and he was sick of her shenanigans. Why couldn't she just give in as they all had to do. It was easier in the long run. He couldn't understand what she saw in Jack Jamieson anyway. He wasn't anything so bloody special, not as far as he could see.

The new factory had a car park but he decided to remain on the road. He took care not to be too conspicuous. He got out and lurked behind the Rover until he saw his sister walking towards the gates. He was a lanky young man and, big as the vehicle was, he had to crouch down beside it. When she was near enough he leapt out and attempted to drag her into the car. His general exasperation led him to use more force than he had intended. Fran screamed for help. She had recognized Neville instantly but she knew that the considerable number of onlookers would think that he was a stranger. ' Let me go! I'm not going with you.' And she screamed all the louder. 'Help me!'

'For God's sake Fran, get in the sodding car!' Neville was panting hard and red-faced with fury at his own predicament and her intransigence. 'Just get into the sodding car!'

Her colleagues understandably made the erroneous assumption that the boss's secretary was being kidnapped for the White Slave Trade, a not unlikely event in Liverpool, but one not usually perpetrated in broad daylight in the precincts of a busy factory. They were incensed. Outraged. 'Hold on, Miss. We'll get him!' and they raced forward to the rescue, noisily excited by the drama of it.

Fran was dragged back into the crowd and Neville had to make a precipitate and undignified scramble back into the car to get away before someone knocked him on the head. The attempted retrieval of Fran had turned into a farce worthy of the silent movies. It was a complete fiasco and as he roared away he swore that he would get even with someone if the Police turned up on the doorstep later that night.

Jack and Fran roared with delight as she regaled him with the story over supper, but Fran's laughter hid the alarm she felt at the steps that were obviously being taken to bring her back into the family fold. She would not go, she said. Whatever they did to her, she would refuse to go.

What they did eventually decide to do was to write to her parents requesting permission to marry. There was a war coming, they pleaded; they wanted to be married before it began.

It was the only way that they could see to provide a way out of the dilemma. It was not what either of them wanted. They had planned to start off properly with enough money for a little house of their own and no worries when Fran would have to give up work. If they married now they would have to rent somewhere to live and Fran would have to keep very quiet about her new status. She would have to leave her job if it was discovered that she had become a married woman. However, they agreed to risk it if it would bring to an end the harassment from the Reynolds.

They were not at all confident of the success of this plan despite the fact that they had been allowed to become engaged and, had Fran actually been pregnant then as Izzie had believed, the issue of consent would not have been an obstacle. No apology for her mother's aberrant conclusion had, of course, been forthcoming.

In the light of recent events they did not trust Izzie any further than they could have thrown her and Izzie had developed into a formidably stout woman. Their worst fears were realised. The reply came by return of post to the address which they had given, Jack's lodgings. In it came a prohibition on marriage under any circumstances and they were reminded that Fran was under-age. The Reynolds would go to court to stop her if any attempt was made to marry without permission.

To marry without permission was immediately transposed into a feasible possibility. Both of them had been too highly principled to consider it an option before. Now they were being threatened as well as being tormented and harassed. The agreement made at the time of their engagement had been reneged upon by the Reynolds, it seemed. Well then, they would elope to Gretna Green on the motor bike.

They laid their plans carefully. They would drive through the night on the following Friday and arrive early enough on Saturday morning to locate the minister and organize the practicalities. They booked a room at a small hotel in Carlisle for the Saturday night and they would spend the Sunday driving back through the Lake District.

The weather did not look very promising. It had been a wet autumn and was now turning bitterly cold. Fran was intending to travel in a pair of Jack's trousers, her best skirt safely in the rucksack she would have on her back. They prepared for every contingency:

rain, snow, ice, fog. The bike was taken over to Pinny's brother to be thoroughly serviced and then kept under wraps until it was required. It was exciting. They felt a great deal of empathy with that other pair of star-crossed lovers who had made their stand the previous year. It was not quite on the scale of Edward and Mrs Simpson but it was just as momentous for them. Their own little drama seemed to be equally romantic and almost as awe-inspiring in relative terms.

In the early hours of Saturday morning on a miserable October night, Jack collected Fran from the back gate of her lodgings. They wound their way through the maze of back-alleys, pushing the bike in case there was still a watch on Fran's house. Once clear of the immediate area they roared off towards the Preston road and the way to the Borders. They had told no-one of their plans; not a soul knew what they were up to.

It was freezing cold. They had not gone very far when Fran came to the conclusion that she would be locked in position, clutching Jack's back forever. She felt that she would never be able to straighten out her legs again. Her face was not so bad, she was able to shelter against the warmth of his thick coat. Jack was not so lucky. Apart from his goggles, he was unprotected.

They made good headway and were beyond Lancaster when they first stopped. They had to refuel from the tin Jack had strapped to the back of the bike. There would be no garages open at that hour. His hands were so rigid that he could hardly open the cap. Fran had brought a flask of hot tea and they stood by the bike, warming themselves up once the petrol was safely in the tank. She dreaded getting back on the pillion. It was not quite so romantic as she had anticipated, this flight into the wilds. And the thought of the comic figure she must cut, bundled up in her weird assortment of clothing made her snappy. It was a far cry from the weddings her Mackenzie cousins had enjoyed. But it was the thought of the surprise they would all get when she returned, brandishing the gold ring which Jack had safely stowed in his jacket pocket, which kept her going. And the thought of breakfast at Penrith.

They did not make Penrith for breakfast. The bike broke down well before that and they had to walk miles before they found a garage, pushing the clumsy machine in front of them and balancing precariously on it to free-wheel down the hills. The situation became desperate when the mechanic claimed that he did not have the right part to repair it. It would take the best part of the day to get it. His man could give them a lift to Penrith, he said, where they could get a hot meal, but they would have to make their own way back to pick up the bike. He suggested that they were there before six o'clock. He would be shut after that.

Jack attempted to take issue with him about the length of time it would take but the man shrugged his shoulders as if to say that they could take it or leave it. Jack offered to pay his assistant to take them and the bike into Penrith where they might fare better but was told, in a more than peremptory fashion, that that was out of the question.There was only the one small car available. The bike would not fit on it and he reminded them that it was not a taxi service that he was running. Did they want to leave the bike or not?

There was no alternative but to do as he suggested.

Once they had found a cafe and warmed themselves up, Jack left Fran at the table and went off to establish how and when they could get transport back to Langdale in the afternoon. There was a bus which left at 3 o'clock. He worked out that if he could persuade the surly garage man to hurry himself up, they might make the Borders in time. He was determined to tell Fran that anyway. She had looked so utterly miserable when he had parted from her.

Luck was not with them. They hung around the garage for over an hour whilst the man huffed and puffed around the bike, casting aspersions on Jack's choice and spending time lecturing him on which machine he should have bought instead of landing himself with this heap of tin. Jack's patience was sorely tried. Fran's gave out. She told him to mind his own business and get on with the job they were paying him for. A heated altercation ensued and she was called an impudent baggage who needed a strap taking to her. Fran's retort almost got them both thrown out on the spot, the pieces of the bike with them.

They eventually got on their way at half past five. Jack drove like a maniac but they were doomed to arrive at Gretna Green to find everywhere shut up until Monday. It was heartbreaking.

The big decision then was whether they should wait and miss a day's work or make their way back home, their mission unaccomplished. They decided to go back to Carlisle for the night as planned and attempt to resolve the problem when they had had some rest. It seemed to take them forever to get there and then, in order to keep up appearances, they changed into their best clothes in a public lavatory and made for the hotel. They were tired out, half-frozen, sniping at each other over the incompetence of Pinny's brother as a mechanic and, more than anything, desperate for some sleep.

Jack did not get much of that. Their hotel room was hardly big enough for the bed. There was only space for a tiny hard-backed chair and a dresser with a wash-bowl. Jack slept on the floor jammed up against the clammily cold wall on one side and the legs of the bed on the other. It had not gone as they had hoped.

There was a further cross to bear at breakfast time in the hotel dining room. The proprietress came out to see them and fussed around their table for a while. Fran was glad that Jack had persuaded her to wear the ill-fated ring, but they were both anxious that questions were not asked. Luck was not with them in that either.

'Are you on your honeymoon, you two?'

They were silent, looking at each other in embarrassment.

'Yes,' said Jack. 'Yes, we are.' He gave her a weak smile.

'I knew you were,' said the woman, beaming at them.

Jack looked blank.

'My husband commented on it when he brought your suitcase in last night. 'They're on their honeymoon those two,' he said. 'Right as ninepence.' He's never wrong you know.'

'How amazing,' said Jack. 'What gave us away?' He refrained from looking at her. He signalled to Fran to pour him some tea in what he hoped was the suitably proprietorial manner of a married man.

'New shoes. When he followed you upstairs. The soles of your shoes looked as if they'd never set foot on the ground. Not a mark on them. You can aways tell the honeymooners!'

He looked at her then and the tea cup was held in mid-air.

'Well, I'll remember that next time.' And he smiled again.

‘Get along with you,’ she laughed. ‘What a thing to say! Don’t take any notice of him dear.’ This was directed at Fran. ‘Is he always such a joker?’

‘I’m used to it.’ Fran’s reply was hardly audible. ‘But if you’ll excuse us, we have to be on our way.’

‘Of course.’

The woman bustled off, laughing to herself as she turned towards the kitchen.

It was mostly despair which prompted them to return to Merseyside after that, as well as the fear that an unscheduled day off work would be too big a risk to take. It was a wretched couple who crept back to their respective lodgings that Sunday night, exhausted and unhappy but not daunted. Fran had decided, after the dreadful business of having to take off the wedding ring once they were away from the garrulous landlady, that she was going to be married, come what may. She determined to apply to the court herself. If her mother was using the threat of a magistrate to intimidate them, then she would spike her guns and get there first.

It was Lou who helped them to fix it up and she offered to give a character reference if necessary. She had known Fran since she had been a child and she certainly had no hesitation in putting forward a good word for Jack. Her only reservation was that her own reputation might work against them.

That did not turn out to be the case. The magistrate refused to look at the testimonial once he knew of the circumstances. He was obviously unsympathetic to mixed marriages and gave the impression that her intention to marry a Catholic was an act of folly which could only be accounted for by her immaturity. He refused permission. His advice was that she return home for twelve months and, should she still feel the same after that, then she should apply to the court for the case to be re-considered.

Fran’s little group was sent packing and he turned his attention to the next case.

It was not just the disappointment which caused Fran’s uncontrollable desire to sob, it was the sight of Fa looking ill-at-ease and decidedly despondent. He had hated having to come to court. He was hating being there now, even if he had gained a victory of sorts. But she had to hold firm. She had to tell him that she could not go back.

'I know,' he said.

'I just can't.'

'I know.'

Fran plucked up the courage to look at him.

'You'll tell mother.'

There was an awkward silence. Fa rolled his fingers round the edge of the bowler hat which he held in his hands. Then he said quietly, 'What am I to tell her, Fran? That you are going to defy the court? That you hate your home? Is that what I am to say?'

'Tell her that you might just as well sign the consent forms now, Fa, because you'll have to do it in the end. Tell her that I will not come back, that she is wasting her time if she tries to force me. I want to get married. We can't afford to keep two separate places going. It's taking everything we have. We need to be together.'

He went to move down the steps.

'Fa! Will you do it, will you sign?'

He moved back up and impulsively caught her in his arms pressing her face into the lapels of his best coat so hard that when she came away she had the mark of the buttonhole on her cheek.

'I cannot do that to your mother. She would never forgive me.'

He fumbled in his pocket and pulled out two white five pound notes which he pushed into her gloved hand.

The next moment he was gone, down the steps and away down the road.

Fran stood looking after him. Disappointed, angry, her urge to run after him and plead again having to be curbed, she wept leaning up against the stone. It was the power that the mothers wielded that enraged her. She could never really be angry with Fa. But he would not go against his wife in this. It was as if he was afraid of her. In the same way, Jack would move mountains rather than offend Mrs Jamieson. 'I will not be afraid!' she said to herself. 'I damned well won't be afraid. They'll see!' But it was boastfulness rather than conviction. On the question of religion it was her future mother-in-law who was indomitable and Fran was helpless in the face of that. She knew it, but such thoughts she kept to herself.

They all met up that evening at Lou's. Fran expressed the view that Fa would have given in, she felt sure, if it was not for her mother. Her suspicion was that things could only get worse in that quarter from now on. Izzie would feel that she had the magistrate on her side after what he had said. Lou warned them that Fran could be made a Ward of Court. It was conceivable that that might even be extended for longer than her official coming-of-age. Fran was seventeen. There was a long time to go until she was twenty one. Beyond that was eternity as far as she was concerned. Whether or not the war which was bound to come sooner rather than later would make any difference to the attitude of the parents, Lou could not tell. Fran considered that it would have no effect at all. They were set against Jack and that was that. Something else would have to be done.

Fran was already germinating an idea as to what that something else might be but she was intent on keeping it to herself for the present. What she intended to do was to get hold of a consent form and forge Fa's signature. She had signed things for him in the past when she had been helping out at home. She had been answering the phone to take orders for him since she had been able to write down the messages in the order book. She had signed receipts for him when he had been busy more times than she could remember. She would have no difficulty in reproducing his signature now. But she would not tell Jack. Not for the time being. Jack had scruples which she was wary of. It would take very careful preparation before he could be in on it.

She made more of the bigotry of the magistrate than was actually there. Her usual pragmatism had deserted her. 'I'll bet he was a bloody Orangeman!' she thought to herself and by the end of the evening she had persuaded herself that that was just what he was. It made her determined to make arrangements to be accepted into the Church without delay. Jack would have scruples about a registry office wedding as well.

But when Jack saw the forms and extracted from her what she had done, he tore them up. 'Get another set,' he said grimly. 'If anyone's going to do this it will be me.' And he did.

Lou could not be their witness. Maddy had insisted that she spend Christmas in Hampshire and she would not be back in time. There was no one else whom they could trust.

The Registry Office ceremony was a desolate affair with a po-faced registrar singularly lacking in any hint of bonhomie, or a flicker of interest. The Church wedding could be considered to have been even more forlorn.

They had gone to the local priest to have the bans put up. They would have to wait three weeks before they were legally married in the eyes of the Catholic Church. The priest would marry them in the evening but he gave them, particularly Jack, dreadful warnings about submitting to carnal instincts before that, civil wedding or no. They must not on any account live as man and wife until the ceremony had been performed.

Jack took a room in the same lodgings as Fran and lived on the floor below her. She had not told anyone at work that she was married for fear of losing her job so she wore the infamous wedding ring on a chain around her neck.

Jack and Fran were still without a witness of any kind when they went along to St. Joseph's to have the Church's seal put upon their union. The priest called in two strangers from the street to attend that particular nuptial mass. After that they never saw either of them again. It was not a wedding that would inspire the celebration of anniversaries in the years to come. It was best forgotten. But the reasons that such measures had to be endured were not forgotten. Jack had been born with a kind and generous heart but there was one corner of it which was permanently hardened on that night. It had always been hardened against injustice but to that he added maltreatment. Izzie Reynolds could never be forgiven for driving her daughter to such extremes by the abuse to which she had subjected her.

12. Happy Families 1937-1938

AN UNEASINESS about Stella was troubling Maddy Lonsdale's nights, far away in Hampshire. It was to Maddy that Stella had run in the first instance, her passport and ticket from Portsmouth to Santander already in her possession. That Lou had been forced to reveal not only the existence but the identity of her real father had precipitated her departure by a short time only.

It had been a very confused and distressed Stella who had arrived on the Lonsdales' doorstep that spring and as Maddy had painstakingly attempted to ascertain the reasons for the deep unhappiness which had motivated the decision to run to Spain, Stella had given Maddy cause for even deeper alarm regarding Edward Bundenell's relationship with his stepdaughter.

There was nothing that Maddy could do or say which would alter Stella's decision to go. Nor was there anything she could do to invalidate the increasing conviction that Stella *must* go. She had much rather that the girl had not chosen to expose herself to yet another danger. The situation in Spain was frighteningly serious and what it might lead to was more frightening still. The only thing she could think of, in her panic, was to put her in touch with Dee Mason who was already there. He was not in a position to protect Stella but he had always been a trusted friend and, at the very least, she might not feel so alone.

Her instinct had proved sound. They had met up on several occasions when he had returned to Barcelona from whatever front he had been fighting on with the International Brigade. They had both repeatedly expressed their gratitude to Maddy via the erratic post which dropped on to her doorstep in the succeeding months. She was pathetically grateful for these scraps of information. Her overriding thought, that if a bigger conflict came, they could help each other, dominated her days.

Yet, Maddy had been not been able to rid herself of her misgivings about Lou's husband. Worrying about a hypothetical world war was one thing. What she suspected Stella had suffered at the hands of Edward Bundenell was another.

When Lou came for Christmas she felt strained and anxious. This was something she had never had occasion to feel when she was with Lou. Maddy felt that she was being dishonest by not broaching the subject but if Lou had been in ignorance all this time then the outcome could be more than either of them could handle. And Maddy had no proof; only suspicions. Stella's disturbed behaviour was all that she had to go on and even that could have been triggered by the drama of learning about the existence of her real father. She dare not risk it.

Lou herself was edgy. She was painfully aware that Maddy had regular news of Stella and she did not. That she only had herself to blame did not ease the situation at all. Also, although the divorce proceedings were going ahead, the dilemma was that Edward's grounds were false. He refused to sue on the grounds of desertion. It was adultery or nothing. And there *had* been no adultery and unless there was undeniable proof of it Lou would most likely remain married to him. That prospect she would not contemplate. Neither could Maddy. In desperation she came up with a most uncharacteristic proposal.

'Give him grounds then', she said. 'Get Tim to take you to a hotel and make sure that everybody knows about it. Keep the receipts, everything. Forge others if you have to.'

Lou was dumbfounded. That Maddy should propose such a solution; Maddy, the respectable principal of a thriving school; Maddy the wife of a much decorated war hero and a pillar of the community, that it was she who should suggest that collusion be contemplated was quite unbelievable, shocking even. But Maddy calmly went on:

'I am absolutely certain that Tim would not be worried about his reputation being further tarnished. He ought to be used to it by now.'

Lou would not hear of it.

'I will not spend the night cooped up with Tim Dundonald under any circumstances. It is unthinkable. To say that I am not very fond of him would be a gross understatement, Maddy. I only suffered contact with him in the first place because of the complication over Stella. And it is an insane suggestion that we fabricate evidence. Insane! Whatever has got into you?'

Maddy remained firm,

'It is the only way out. You have got to do it. You have got to.'

The intensity of her tone startled Lou.

'You made a mistake Lou, and it didn't only affect you, I might add. Stella has suffered for it too, you cannot deny it.'

'I know.'

The way that she voiced her agreement, despite the anguish underlying it, convinced Maddy that Lou had no idea of just how Stella might have been affected. Secrets must surely have been well kept, she told herself, her heart thudding at the very thought of it.

'Well, it's time both of you were free of him. Now, I am going to invite Tim for the New Year. You are going to spend the night together in a hotel and I'm prepared to go to court to say that it has been going on for years. I am willing to be a witness.'

"Good God!' was Lou's only response.

'It did go on for years. I'm not telling a total untruth.'

'You do realise that it is illegal, Maddy, what you are suggesting?'

'I do.' Maddy's confidence in the rightness of such an action had little to do with legality. Whether or not her suspicions were founded on fact, Stella must never be under the same roof as Edward Bundenell again. Of that she was totally convinced.

'I'll go and write to Tim now. Where did you say he lived?'

* * *

Jack and Fran managed to find a furnished flat to rent in Orrell Park. It was snowing when they moved in late in January. Fran was in her element. She had soon made it into a rosy, welcoming, well-run little home despite the fact that she was still working full time. She had not informed her employers of her change in status but someone had informed the Reynolds of it.

It was Dodo who told her that Izzie had discovered that Fran was married. Fran immediately suspected that her sister had blabbed. Once she had felt inviolate as the new Mrs Jamieson, she had not been able to resist telling Dodo. She had impressed upon her the need for strict secrecy, of course, and invited her and Neville K. to visit the flat. She missed her favourite sister; she missed all the things that they used to do together, particularly the week-end dances. She loved dancing. She loved going out in evening dress and all the preparation it took that she and Dodo would spend hours over. Now she cursed herself for her rashness in trusting her dizzy sister to keep her mouth shut. She ought to have overcome the temptation to show off. It had been a mistake.

But her suspicions did Dodo a disservice. She had not revealed that she knew where Fran and Jack were living. It had been the detective who had tracked them down and immediately informed the Reynolds of the current state of affairs.

Dodo and Neville K. got over to Orrell Park as soon as they could. They needed to warn Fran that Izzie was making plans to have the marriage annulled. She was threatening to expose what they had done, to inform both their employers that they had broken the law and have them sacked from their jobs. She would make sure that they had no means of support. She would break Jack Jamieson if it was the last thing she did.

It had not taken her long to work out that Fa's signature could not possibly have been genuine. The resulting scenes made it virtually impossible for anyone at Oakshot Road to trust in her sanity. Fa had taken her to see a doctor and she had been put on pills for what she would describe as 'her nerves'. Even Dodo, famous as she was for her lack of astuteness, could substitute bigotry and thwarted will for those alleged 'nerves'. Dodo was frightened by the ferocity of it all; she did not know where it was all going to end.

Jack and Fran had grave fears too, as to where it was all going to end, and not just on the domestic front. There was a war coming with ominous inevitability. It was only a question of when.

Once Dodo and Neville had gone, they sat down together to judge the seriousness of their immediate situation. It was plain that if Izzie was prepared to expose the forgery, she could have the marriage annulled. That was the least of it. They could possibly go to prison. They would be apart. They might be apart forever.

The whole thing was unspeakably desperate.

Fran wept bitter tears. She did not understand her mother. As a child, she had been idyllically happy. There had been troubles but Fa had always managed to make things right. She adored Fa. From an infant he had taken her with him on the waggons, sitting beside him behind the heavy horses which clomped along, their harness making music to the steady rhythm of their massive hooves, shining blue-black with oil. She had gone everywhere with him, even across the water on the ferry. All the things associated with Fa spelt dependability; timeless, unchanging dependability. He was as solid as the great posts which towered above the waggons as the horses were driven down the ramps to the loading bay on the quayside; great lichen-covered piles around which the water lapped. They still gave her confidence, those huge supports. They would always be there, uncomplicated in their structure, impervious to the temper of the tides. She had thought of Fa like that. But now her mother seemed to have destroyed his will. He was standing by when she seemed intent on destroying him, on destroying them all. Her wisdom, her genuine love for her children had become distorted, mangled, cankered by her blind prejudice, her inability to tolerate the defiance of her daughter.

Jack understood it more clearly, although this was the first time that he had come face-to-face with such open, obdurate ill will. He was beyond anger. Sadness was his overriding emotion. Prejudice could not be combated, it seemed. Ancient hostility founded on ignorance was what it was. Centuries of it.

He felt that he had put Fran into a totally impossible position.

'Do you want to pack it all in and go back? Would that be the best thing?'

He dreaded her answer. He did not know what he would do if she left. He was very near to tears himself. The Reynolds had been so alarmingly extreme over this. What would happen to her if she did return, and he powerless to help, he being the cause of it all?

But Fran did not hesitate.

'Never!' she said emphatically. 'I shall never go back. How could you think that I should even consider it? I'm your wife now, Jack. We're in this together.'

'What can we do Fran?'

‘I’ll tell you what we shall do. I really will get pregnant this time. She was ready to accept that we would get married last year when she *imagined* I was up to no good. She wouldn’t attempt an annulment if there was a child involved now. She couldn’t? Could she, Jack?’

Jack looked as if he was completely nonplussed as to what Izzie Reynolds might do. He had never come across such bullying tactics in his own family, especially where the girls were concerned. His sisters were cherished, whatever their failings. *They* were not beaten with a leather strap. And there were all kinds of other objections to Fran’s proposal. They had no savings to talk of, to fall back upon. The war would come any time now. He would be away, for years maybe. What would become of Fran then?

‘Jack, think about it. It’s the only way to spike her guns, I’m sure of it. Don’t worry about the money. We’ll manage somehow. I’ll go on working for as long as possible. We will manage, we’ll have to. And it will put an end to all this. Mother will have to give in, leave things as they are. Now come on Jack, see sense.’

He eventually went along with her.

But it was not as easy as they thought it would be and when, after months of trying, Fran knew that she was pregnant it was because she became very, very ill. There was no question of her continuing with her job. She was in and out of Walton Hospital from the start. There was little chance of her enjoying the haven they had made for themselves in the flat in Orrell Park.

Jack was existing from day-to-day on Boots No.1, or if they were unavailable, Boots No.2. Nothing else seemed to ease the pain in his stomach. Nothing at all.

There was not a single word from the Reynolds. Fran was ostentatiously ignored. Her tactic had worked it seemed; Izzie had not carried out her threats but she would leave her daughter to suffer alone.

Jack was working day and night in order to keep on the flat. The only time he had a chance to sit down was when he went to visit Fran in the hospital. He did not avail himself of it. He paced the floor instead. He had read up about Fran’s condition, he knew what toxaemia could do. He could lose both Fran and the baby. Izzie Reynolds would have a lot to answer for if he did, he promised himself. He had neither time nor energy to work out what he might do if the worst happened, but he knew that he would do something terrible.

It was his mother's idea that they went to live with them. They could have the front room to themselves, she said, and Fran would have some help in the early days, when the baby was born. She was very persuasive, there was no point in paying out good money in rent all this time when neither of them was ever there. They should think about it.

So Fran found herself living with the Jamiesons on the other side of the water. If she was disappointed at the loss of the flat she did not let on to Jack. Nor did she feel able to tell him that she had an insurmountable problem with his parents. She could hardly understand a word either of them said. Both spoke with a heavy Glaswegian accent and despite her own ancestry on her mother's side, she was more often than not having to ask them to repeat themselves. But she was compensated for her consciousness of how much of an irritation she must be to her mother-in-law by the fuss made of her by his sisters. They were cheerful, good-natured girls who felt that she was the most important person in the world as she was about to make them both into aunts. They welcomed her as a sister with affecting sincerity.

In spite of her own reservations, she had to admit that it was a happy place, the Jamiesons' house. There was always a good fire with a pan of Scotch broth bubbling away on the hob. This was for emergencies. The Jamiesons believed in good wholesome food and when the wages were coming in Jack's mother provided it. They all sang well and many an evening meal turned into an impromptu party. The whisky would come out, the pianola would be started up and the girls would partner each other in the space around the big table, treating their audience to a preposterously exaggerated version of the tango or the foxtrot, their faces deadly serious until they collapsed in a heap of merriment on the floor. They believed in enjoying themselves, the Jamieson girls.

Fran was only seven months pregnant when she was rushed in to Queen Alexandra's. Jack arrived home from work to find her gone and the whole household in a state of turmoil.

At first he thought that the fuss was about the postponement of the Munich talks and the mobilization of the Czechs on the

Sudetenland border. His head was full of it. He was ready to joke with them about the telephone girls at the Liverpool Exchange having to practise talking through gas masks. The reports in the paper had put the most inappropriate visions into his head regarding that contingency. He was ready to share them with his sisters and Fran. He had reached the conclusion that the only way to cope with the current crisis was to be flippant. But any irreverence in that direction disappeared at the news that Fran had gone into premature labour.

Jack was prepared to rush off immediately but he found that he had to remain at home and fume. Hospital regulations stipulated that he had to wait until he was called for. He was awake when the voluntary driver arrived in the middle of the night to take him to Tranmere.

He was a huge man, squashed into the driving seat, and his breath came in wheezes; a hollow monotone that seemed to issue from somewhere else, as if he had got an injured animal trapped in the back of the car.

'That Chamberlain seems to have a job on his hands, d'yer think?'

'Bugger Chamberlain!' said Jack.

The wheeze turned into rolls of laughter. The sound seemed to be full of fluid.

'As yer like!'

Jack willed the journey to be over. He did not want to talk. He did not want to listen, especially not to the fat man. Under normal circumstances he would have indulged in pleasantries, found a joke to put the crisis in Munich in its place, made the man feel at ease. Not tonight. He wanted to be where he was going. He wanted to be with Fran.

But he was prevented from racing straight up to the ward when he at last arrived. His wife was being looked after. That was all he was told. He must wait.

He hovered around in acute anxiety. There was nowhere proper to sit. He was not told where he should go. The place was deadly quiet and only half-lit. Passing nurses clucked at him as if he was an alien. He felt like an alien. He had expected activity; he had expected to be passing the time of night with other distraught fathers-to-be. He had not anticipated this nothingness.

Eventually he was thrown out by an impatient midwife.

'What are you doing hanging about at the bottom of the stairs at this hour, getting in everybody's way?' Her uniform was bristling with starch. Indignation made it shiver.

Jack looked round for 'everybody'. The place was deserted.

'I need to know about my wife.' There was an urgent plea underlying his tone. 'My wife... Mrs Jamieson?'

'You'll have to go now. Nothing's happened yet. Maybe tomorrow. Think yourself lucky, Saturday is visiting day. You might get to see her. *If* baby has arrived by then, that is.'

'But my wife! Is she alright?'

'She never was 'alright', was she?'

This last came as an accusation; as if Jack had committed a criminal act in putting Fran in such a condition in the first place. She bustled off up the stairs without a backwards glance and he turned to go, shoulders drooping with the weight of it.

His imagination ran riot as he set off to walk the miserable miles home. There was no voluntary driver provided to take him back. The doubt that had rippled around that word 'if' with reference to the baby had turned his feet to clay. He was beyond hurrying. He did not want to go home anyway. He wanted to be near Fran. What was the use in going home?

He had, quite literally, been walking for hours when he decided to stop at a telephone box. He could stand it no longer. He had to know the worst. He fumbled in his pocket for the coins, his fingers clumsy with dread. He studied the concrete on the floor of the kiosk as the ringing tone sounded in his ears. Once he was through to reception and made his request for information there was no sound at all, just a painful blankness. That went on so long that he convinced himself that they had cut him off. He was just about to put down the receiver and try again, when the midwife came on. It was the same one who had sent him packing.

'You have a daughter, Mr Jamieson,' she said, 'weighing just under four pounds. I must warn you that she is very fragile.'

'My wife?' said Jack. 'My wife? Is she alright?'

‘Come in at two o’ clock this afternoon. You can see her then.’

The phone was put down.

He stepped outside the phone box into the night, looking up to thank the God he had been systematically and guiltily rejecting for so many long months. For the first time he noticed that it was an incredibly clear sky; stars winked at him from the infinity of blackness which was almost tactile in its density. It was as if for the length of that night, he had been walking along with his eyes, and his mind, closed. Trapped in his own darkness, his senses had benumbed themselves.

‘I have a daughter,’ he shouted to the sleeping houses. ‘I have a daughter!’

And then he ran with mercurial speed to deliver the news to his family.

‘Awa’ w’ yer bletherin’ about the stars,’ his father said. ‘ It’ll be bombers ye’ll be seein’, noo stars. The skies will be thick wi’ em afore ye can blink? A wouldna be waxin’ lyrical in your position!’

Jack hung his head, his joy temporarily diminished.

‘We’ll stop them.’ His head was up now. ‘I’m going to volunteer for the Air Force and we’ll stop them.’

‘Will ye noo?’ was all he got in reply. ‘Y’d better get on wi’ it then.’

He shoved his newspaper in the direction of his son.

‘The Germans are a step awa’ from Sudetenland, I’m tellin’ ye, and the French are mannin’ their borders already. It’s a bad business.’

Jack turned on his heel and left the room. Clare followed him.

‘Congratulations, Jack,’ she said. ‘Congratulations! Don’t take too much notice of Dad. He was never one for handing out any bouquets. Not even at the best of times.’

‘I don’t need bouquets,’ he said. ‘I need to know that Fran’s alright.’

* * *

The courtroom was oppressively dingy with its preponderance of dark wood, high painted walls of an indeterminate green and tall, unfamiliar structures around which the dusty lawyers stood in conference. Maddy, not required as a witness as it happened, but who had come to give moral support to Lou, was somewhat ambivilent about her relief that it was only a matrimonial case they were about to be involved in and nothing worse. Her distress was not only on Lou's behalf. Her greatest fear was that, even though the case was to go through undefended, there should be a hitch in the proceedings.

Lou had insisted on being there. It was a kind of masochism, Maddy concluded to herself, as they found a bench at the back and seated themselves at last having been waiting about outside for an age, it seemed. There was no need for Lou to punish herself, if that was what she was about; the case would go through whether she attended or not. And she had made the bizarre request that they took with them an unlimited supply of tomato sandwiches. She had been working her way through them half the morning, her right hand disappearing surreptitiously into a brown paper bag and emerging with a morsel of soggy, pink bread between her fingers. She had, in all seriousness, informed Maddy that tomato sandwiches were the best thing to alleviate tension. It was at this point that Maddy cast aspersions on her sanity and then promptly turned to the matter which had brought them there.

Apart from the lawyers, there were the usual court officials seated in front of the judge's bench, languid in their perennial boredom and some press people shuffling along the front of the gallery. She could hardly bear to look at Edward who was standing with his barrister at the far end of the room. She had allowed her eyes to slide over him, once she had registered that he was there, only to avert her gaze immediately.

The judge, when he entered, caused Maddy's heart to sink. He was small and pinched, his face as grey as his wig in the inadequate electric light which struggled to supplement what the grimy glass dome above his head had always failed to do; light the place. She calculated that if this man suspected that the evidence of adultery had been fixed, he would show no mercy to those who had had any part in it. And Lou would be worse off than ever. She wished that she had with her a more effective panacea than tomato sandwiches.

She was not to be delivered from her initial fear of this particular representative of the judicial system, however. He had immediately established that the errant wife was present in court. He had carefully adjusted his glasses and had ostentatiously pinpointed where they were before the clerk had even instructed them all to be seated. He had no way of knowing which of the two standing at the back was Mrs Bundenell so he regarded both women with equal repugnance. His mouth curled down in an expression of utter contempt. Maddy was convinced that the whole court could hear her nervous swallowing. Lou seemed oblivious to everything.

The hearing was mercifully short. Edward's lawyer read out his client's affidavit. It was a catalogue of disloyalty, wilful waywardness and finally, adultery. Then Edward went into the witness box.

Maddy almost laughed with relief that the 'evidence' of adultery, substantiated by the written statements from the hotel in Lyndhurst and the testimony of the receptionist at the Royal, was accepted without question as being true. It was the rest of what Edward had to say that horrified her. She became increasingly aware that Lou had kept from her the fact that Edward was pressing for a charge of mental cruelty against his wife and, what was more to the point, he believed that he was in the right. To Maddy's eyes, it seemed that a ghastly dance of death was being played out in that court room. In order to put an end to this ill-fated marriage, Lou was to be pilloried.

The decree nisi was granted without hesitation but Lou's defiance of her husband with regard to her political activities, her persistent disregard of his wishes in this respect, her withdrawal of conjugal rights and her blatant adultery were listed mercilessly.

The newspaper men in the gallery flamboyantly flicked over the pages of their notebooks as they scribbled with amazing rapidity in their greed to get it all down. The judge had given them a good story. Stella's illegitimacy had been made much of; the location of the adulterous liaison, *in the vicinity of two major ports* sent all kinds of frissons fluttering amongst the vultures up above. They were reminded that she had been seen at the infamous meeting-place of agitators and anarchists, the Rotunda Theatre, and that at a time of national crisis. Maddy thought that she could hear them smacking their lips in malicious glee.

It was poisonous. Lou's selfless social conscience, her commitment to her adoptive family, her unstinting efforts to relieve the lot of the needy as her primary objective had become distorted, contorted one might even say, into an alleged obsession with foulness and subversion. It was grotesque.

And all the while, Edward Bundenell was playing the injured party. He looked immaculate, the perfect gentleman, grieving for what he had lost, dignified and controlled as he tilted his head towards the judge during the summing up. The wounded partner demonstrating to the whole court what it took to be courageous in the face of such perfidy. And the court was with him. Maddy felt that she might be ill.

She gathered all her strength to look at Lou. She was motionless and expressionless beside her. She did not seem to be breathing. It was as if her senses were shut off, suspended, waiting with infinite patience for the whole thing to be over. An empty brown paper bag was scrunched in her fist.

It was only possible to leave once the judge had vacated the court but they could get no further than the lobby. The litigants in the next case were milling around in the narrow space and these were soon joined by the newspaper men scurrying down the stairs from the gallery. Lou and Maddy could not get out. There was a fluted pillar to their right. They were beyond noticing that the ancient yellow paint was pock-marked and grease-stained from the thousands of shoulders which had huddled against it over the years, in varying degrees of despair. Maddy guided Lou towards its lee side in an attempt to get her out of the crowd.

Edward Bundenell was emerging from the court, paired with his barrister as they came through the double doors. They could not do other but pass by the pillar. An officious, rotund little man had made his way to the front of them and was demanding that a way was made. No doubt that he was the solicitor, Maddy decided; no-one could possibly look like that and not be a solicitor. She reckoned that he probably had changed very little from the age of twelve, or thereabouts. Possibly he had been born like that. On any other occasion she would have been amused, but not today. Today, her soft, pretty smile was not in evidence. She was white-faced and thin-lipped with anger and frustration at the indignities her friend had been forced to endure and the damage done to her, still being done to her, in fact. If she had been in possession of proof that Edward Bundenell had committed the crime she suspected him of, she would have blurted it out there and then. That Lou would be even more damaged by that revelation failed to cross her mind.

Maddy was conscious of the Press men jostling with each other to get to the exit. To her everlasting surprise, as Edward passed by she found that she had an almost irresistible urge to spit in his face. Saliva was collecting on her tongue, rolling round in her mouth.

'You evil man!' she whispered as he came alongside her, 'You evil...bloody...monster!'

He stopped and looked unflinchingly at her with his ice-cold eyes. She returned his gaze, her chin up, ready to spit at him in earnest if he so much as uttered a word. He chose not to. Instead, he took the handkerchief from his breast pocket and patted his upper lip with one slow, deliberate movement, almost as if she really had spat at him. She was waiting for him to strike her but he walked on without a backward glance, out of the front door and out of their lives.

Lou had suddenly re-animated.

'What did you say that for?'

'Because he is despicable. Thoroughly despicable!'

'A bit extreme for you though, wasn't it?'

'I don't care! If I could repeat it to that judge, I would.'

Lou smiled and took her by the arm. She was squeezing it tightly. The hallway was almost clear. She leaned down and whispered in Maddy's ear.

'And I'm free. That's all that matters. I'm free. The rest was par for the course.'

Then she was out through the door and running down the steps.

'Come on, Maddy, or you'll be telling me that you've got to get back to Lonsdale and we're going for lunch at the Exchange before you catch your train.'

Lunch was the farthest thing from Maddy's mind. She felt that she would have difficulty in eating anything ever again. However, she joined Lou at the kerb where she was hailing a taxi.

The ever-present screaming of sea gulls took Maddy's attention momentarily. She looked up instinctively, hoping to see them whirling. But she could not locate the ones in flight; they were down near the pier head in anticipation of tit-bits from the ferry boats. She glanced instead at the roof-top to the left of them. It appeared to have an interesting architectural feature along its highest ridge;

an ornamentation of some kind, like a series of squat little urns or tessellations. Suddenly she realized, with secret amusement at her mistake, that they were the very gulls she was seeking. An exact line of them, the length of the ridge, as if rooted to the tiles. Motionless replicas of each other, they witnessed with detached superiority the human activity below them.

Maddy's glance fell away. Even further along to the left, sitting on a bench in an area of small park, was Edward. His elbows were on his knees, his hands covering the whole of his face, but she knew that it was Edward. A solitary gull was pecking round his feet, its neck thrusting to and fro in the self-important way they had. There was no longer anything self-important about the human figure on the iron bench. It registered a forlorn, irredeemable despair.

Maddy immediately repressed an involuntary pang of sorrow for him. Where had his good points been? she wondered. What side of him had attracted Lou to him in the first place? What had made him do the thing that she was sure he had done? Then she turned her head away and regretted the second's thought she had given him.

'In you get, we're meeting Tim. The Royal Exchange Hotel please, fast as you can.'

A taxi had drawn up and as they clambered in it was as if Lou had been out for a morning's shopping rather than the ordeal they had both been through.

Edward was still in sight until they had turned the corner. Lou had not seemed to notice him. A terrible anger swept through every part of Maddy's body. She allowed it to exhale in one long sigh, although she was sure that she was holding her breath. And then, pushing itself into her consciousness, came the mention of Tim.

She sighed again. It was more of a groan, in effect.

'Lou, no. Not Tim!'

'Don't be stuffy. He's just treating us for lunch. A celebration, that's all'

But that wasn't all. The minute Tim jumped up from his chair where he had been waiting for them in the foyer, Maddy knew that whatever he might, or might not, have felt for Lou in the past, it did not compare with what he felt for her now.

He did not kiss her, instead he pulled her close to him and buried his face in the collar of her coat. Lou, her eyes shut, leant her head against his. She was smiling.

Maddy turned to go. She felt that she was entirely superfluous under the circumstances. She gave a self-deprecatory grimace as she recalled her recent anxieties about false evidence. It looked as though there was nothing false about it. And in law, it was still adultery whether Lou had been living apart from her husband or not. And there was a bitter irony in the recollection that her own part in it, by interfering last Christmas, had most probably been the instigating factor. A lot had obviously happened in the months since. She had done Lou no favours. She walked away.

'Maddy?'

Lou had come after her and caught her by the elbow.

'Come on. They'll be ready for us in the dining room.' She looked at her quizzically, as if she could not understand why her friend was making for the door.

'No. No, I won't join you. I really must get back.'

Tim was alongside her as well, by this time.

'Maddy please stay. There is something I want Lou to address and she refuses to see sense. I wish you'd talk to her. I want her to go to Dublin for a while, till things settle down.'

'With you?' Maddy registered the definite censure in her tone and wondered if he had too.

'No, I have to stay here but I'm worried that there might be some sort of backlash. It could turn nasty if the press make the most of that summing up.'

'You were there?'

'Until that point. Help me to persuade her that she must go away.'

There was genuine concern, dismay even, in his plea. She looked at him steadily. She had never trusted him and with good reason she felt. She did not know what to make of him now.

'She could come back to Hampshire with me,' she said.

He nodded, relieved, and guided her towards the dining room.

Lou, however, was resistant to persuasion. She did not see why it was necessary to be anxious. Over lunch she argued it out. Why should anyone be interested in her insignificent political activities, she demanded. She had never done anyone any harm. Try as they might they could not get her to see that she had been branded as a Communist, and a dangerous one at that, and in public with the press there.

'So what?' she said. 'People are far more concerned about the mobilization of the fleet, for instance. I know I am. There are much bigger issues to worry about at the moment. A grubby little divorce case will hardly attract any attention at all.'

Maddy caught her train alone. But when Lou and Tim reached Norton Street at the end of the afternoon, after having seen her off, all the front windows had been smashed in and the shop was in tatters. What they discovered when they eventually got to the back room through the rubble, was that everything had been daubed with red paint: the walls, the furniture, the floor. All her correspondence had been gone through; the drawers of her desk gaped open. The pretty gift for Baby Jamieson had been torn from its wrapping and thrown carelessly into the dead ashes in the fireplace.

Despite her protests, Tim had her on the Dublin ferry that night.

* * *

Jack, meanwhile, had been nowhere near Norton Street and was in total ignorance of the drama. He spent the week in which he had to wait before he could go back to Queen Alexandra's trying to prepare their room for the arrival of the baby. It was all the fathers were allowed, to be present during visiting times on a Saturday and he was somewhat peeved about it. He was rather banking on Fran being discharged soon after that, hence the urgency about creating a bit more space at home. He refused to see Queen Alexandra's as a hospital, it was more like a prison to his way of thinking and he looked upon her return as a release from a six month stretch. That was how long she had been in and out of one hospital or another and he having to face up to the mercy of the nursing profession, who harboured some decidedly intimidating females in his experience. Strangely enough, Fran did not seem to have come across the harridans who dealt with him. She assured him that all the nurses and midwives were candidates for canonization, if not saints already and she accused Jack of provoking them when he complained to her about their caustic attitude towards him.

'You must have rubbed them up the wrong way,' she said, as she busied herself with straightening the top sheet which he had inadvertently dented when he had bent to kiss her. 'Don't be so aggressive, Jack, it's a very bad fault.'

There was little use in contradicting her. This baby business seemed to be surrounded by all kinds of mysteries, the shrewish pedantry of the women who dealt with the new fathers being the most unfathomable.

Fran was in a side ward on her own. She was going to be incarcerated for a long time, he had been told, as he was led down the corridor. The word 'incarcerated' was not actually used, but whatever term it was, Jack had immediately interpreted it as such. The reasoning behind the decision to take her out of the main ward was that it was not only the baby who was frail, Fran needed total peace and quiet if she was to recover properly. On no account was Jack to upset her, he was warned, in trenchant terms. There was also a decided assumption in the particular tone of voice, that his sole intention was to do so and that such a trait must be nipped in the bud immediately. 'Absolutely no newspapers. Do you understand me? No newspapers.' The command was as impregnable as the starch in the formidable apron.

Jack felt that the weeks ahead would be decidedly onerous, irritating and interminable.

Fran was, in fact, lonely once her strength began to return. On her bad days, she agreed with him that it was tantamount to being put on punishment in an isolation block. Generally though, she was grateful for her privacy even if she missed the bustle and companionship of the other young mothers. The nursing staff basked in their inviolate status of Oracle. Jack gave them a wide berth when he turned up each Saturday, clutching his box of chocolates and sometimes he would succesfully smuggle in a magazine donated by one or other of his sisters, who tended to acquire them from their friends at work.

One memorable visiting day, he was overjoyed to discover that his enemies had got their come-uppance. Fran was complaining bitterly about the hospital; she was convinced that the nurses had not the least idea of what they were doing and, in a state of extreme agitation, threatened to discharge herself and the baby.

It transpired that, during his week-long absence, an episode had occurred which had modified his wife's opinion of the exclusive sainthood that Jack was still waiting to be introduced to.

The babies were kept in the nursery until feeding time when they were distributed like so many parcels, with unerring and speedy efficiency. On the occasion in question, Fran had had rudely dumped on to her lap a great, bawling, red-headed boy and the offending nurse had immediately disappeared on her clicking heels, well beyond hearing distance of Fran's horrified screams. It had taken what seemed like hours to sort out the mistake. It had in fact only been minutes, but to Fran and the mother of the giant of a boy, it had seemed an interminable time. They had both been near to apoplexy. The whole ward had been in pandemonium. Fran was incensed with fury. She and the other unfortunate mother had been blamed for causing such a fuss.

In Jack's opinion, she had good reason to be angry. He leaned over to view his miniscule offspring, now safely retrieved, recovered and sleeping peacefully under the straighter-than-straight coverlet in the canvas cot, wheeled in for visiting time. Her head was smaller than his fist, with a down of soft fair hair which grew in a perfect circle in the middle, where her parting would ultimately be. It was stupifying to imagine how such an error could have been made. His baby was the size of a toy.

'Stupid woman,' he thought to himself. 'She must be the idiot of all time, as well as being blind to boot.' But he did not risk expressing his opinion. Discretion was the better part of valour. And he was getting to know Fran very well. It was one thing for her to malign the culprit but it could turn out to be another thing altogether if he joined in. So he kissed Fran sympathetically and murmured suitable platitudes, erring on the side of caution.

Fran leaned across her pillows and pulled the cot nearer to the bed. She looked towards the door to make sure that she was not in danger of being observed and then she gently released the baby's feet from the sacrosanct strictures of the bedding.

‘I’ve made doubly sure that it won’t happen again,’ she said complacently. ‘Look.’

Tied around the tiny ankle was a rubberised name bracelet. It had ‘Baby Jamieson’ printed on it. Fran had put a line through ‘Baby’ and in letters as large as there was space for, she had written ‘Alexandra.’

‘There! That should scotch any further nonsense they could be about. You do believe me, don’t you Jack. We could have lost her forever. How I did not have a heart attack on top of everything else, I really don’t know. And you should have heard her screaming. It was pitiful! You will have a word with Matron, won’t you, on your way out? Give her one of your dressing-downs? You’re good at that.’

‘Of course,’ Jack said, weighing up who might come out best if he did attempt the sort of dressing-down that Fran was depending on. But he would have to register some sort of complaint.

He was still at a loss regarding Fran’s wish to name the child after this particular hospital when they had all three been made to suffer in it. And it was not over yet, apparently. But Alexandra’s birth had been registered; her name could not be changed now. He toyed facetiously with the idea of asking Fran what she would have called her if the birth had been in Walton as originally scheduled, but he thought better of it. He would rather gaze adoringly at the way his daughter’s tiny little legs took advantage of such unexpected freedom and kicked randomly in the air.

‘I can’t wait for you to come home,’ he said.

‘Neither can I,’ said Fran. And she promptly burst into a flood of tears.

13. Dark Days
1938-1939

IT WAS WELL into November when Fran was finally discharged. She had almost become institutionalized, she had spent so much time in hospital during the past year. She took a while to settle.

Jack had done his best. He had redecorated their room in his parents' house and made it as welcoming as he could. It looked rather grand, in fact; the wallpaper having been donated by Pinny's other brother, as opposed to the one who was so bloody useless as a motorbike mechanic. Jack had his suspicions about the legality of the origins of this particular wall paper. It was the quality of the velvet flock which inhibited him from asking any pertinent questions as to how the young McLaughlin had acquired it. He did not really want to know the answer, especially as the boy had just started work on the docks. He was also dubious about Fran's response. The room looked as if it was part of a very exclusive doll's house where the owner had lined the walls with the remnants of what had been chosen for the grandest room of the real house. The pattern seemed to overwhelm everything else. He had spent hours trying to re-arrange the furniture in order to tone it down a bit, apart from the original intention which was to give them more space, but there were now extra things to be accomodated: the cot, the pram, all the appurtenances that went with babies. It could not be other than crowded and the wretched wallpaper seemed to have made it more claustrophobic than ever.

It was not just the cramped conditions that posed the problem. Things were different from when Fran had first agreed to live there, she soon discovered. For one thing, Jack had returned to how things were before he was married. On Friday he handed over his wage packet and his mother gave back ten shillings for his fares and lunches. It had become established that that was how it was to be. The re-appearance of Fran did not alter the arrangement.

Then, she was alone with her mother-in-law for almost all of the day, the elder girls being at work and the two younger children at school. The baby's schedule was interfered with. All the things she had learned in the hospital were dismissed as new-fangled nonsense. The special baby formula was discarded and replaced by tins of Nestlés milk.

'This bairn needs feeding up,' Fran was told, in response to her objections. 'She's like a wee skinned rabbit.'

There was no way out of it. Fran had not the wherewithal to buy the formula herself even if she had felt strong enough to contest the unalterable right which her mother-in-law considered was hers; to know best. Fran was not strong enough. Mrs Jamieson was.

The evenings were worst. The house seemed to be overflowing with people and noise. There was no space to sit quietly or to put Alexandra's things down without Jack's younger brother and his horde of friends throwing themselves down on chairs without first making sure there was nothing to squash. Even if they did, they then appropriated whatever item it might be for microscopic examination with their grubby little fingers before the inevitable, and offensively dismissive, tossing aside. And Fran could not complain. If she took herself off to the cold front room to curl up with Alexandra under the big eiderdown on their bed, she was accused of being anti-social, and even more unjustly, lazy. She felt that she was about to burst with indignation and suppressed fury.

Jack was no help. He did not arrive back until late most nights. He worked long hours and then he had to wait for a ferry crossing, not to mention the considerable walk after that. When he was at home he tended to talk to his father rather than to her and it was always, always about the inevitable outcome of Germany's obsession with power and greed. Poetry and books had given way to politics with a vengeance.

Heads close together in an exclusive huddle, they recalled all the warning signs which they had gleaned from years of reading the *Manchester Guardian*. They went over and over it all: how they had known about the concentration camps for gypsies and other undesirables as long ago as 1933. The same would happen here if Hitler should invade, and everyone who opposed him would become an undesirable, and what then? It all became a refrain, a sort of litany it seemed to Fran...Mussolini had done away with the

Italian Mafia alright, but what had he done then? He'd immediately outstripped their capacity for brutality by employing machine-guns against spears in Ethiopia...he was as greedy as the Germans...he was clamouring for other people's land...just like the other one...huge chunks of Czechoslovakia ceded to *him* by that sham of an agreement in Munich and the bastard was helping himself to more in defiance of the worthless scrap of paper brandished as a trophy at the bottom of aeroplane steps.

'Bletherin' fool! Bletherin' bloody fool tha' Chamberlain!' He turned the other cheek alright, all four of his cheeks, if ye ask me!'

But although he was looking straight at Fran as he said it, she had no intention of asking him, as he well knew. She did not want to ask him about anything. She could not bear to listen to her father-in-law being vulgar, as a matter of fact, irrespective of the context, and she hated what that wretched context did to Jack. It changed him into someone she didn't know. Someone aggressive and raw and fanatical. She thought that if she heard the words 'War,' 'Re-armament,' 'Appeasement' or 'Fascist' ever again she would scream until she was hoarse. All she wanted was for her child to be safe, her husband to be safe, and most, most of all, she wanted to be back in her own little flat in Orrell Park. Her heart broke each time she thought of it and she thought of it every other moment of every day. She found it hard to forgive Jack for letting it go.

Consequently, her misgivings about the current domestic situation increased in intensity; neither could she foresee an escape unless the much talked-of plans to evacuate children away from the danger areas came to fruition. She and Alexandra must be allowed to do that, if it really was to happen. She indulged in daydreams about getting herself back to the farmhouse in Wales with the baby and Jack's little brother and sister. She would take them with her and she would tell them all about the planes Jack was learning to fly and what a hero he was. When the war came, and Jack was in the R.A.F., that was what she would do. She would go back to where she had spent her childhood, where, in the edited version of her imaginings, it was perpetual summer and nothing bad happened, nothing bad at all.

She edited other recollections too. She forgot how she had cursed her little brothers on a regular hourly basis and longed to be free of their pestering. Now that she was, she missed them. In compensation, she was very kind to the two younger children. She began to love them both, despite Robbie's propensity for noise and sudden, precipitate action. He intrigued her. Like Jack, he had inherited his mother's beautiful singing voice and was the Head Chorister in the church choir. He looked like an angel then. His hair was so blonde that it was almost white. Usually it was an unruly thatch but when he was to sing in the choir at eleven o'clock Mass, it was wetted down and brushed vigorously into a disciplined cap clinging to the lines of his head. He hated it and protested and wriggled until the hairbrush was used as an instrument of discipline and his legs received a good, sharp smack. It made no difference that his protests were sustained without interruption. He was marched off to the Presbytery and handed over personally to the priests, in a state of cleanliness supervised by his mother until that point. Then, he transformed into a celestial being, fooling everyone in the congregation with the exception of his immediate family and Fran. Underneath, he was a mischievous little devil with a latent potential for becoming the plague of the neighbourhood. Jack often swore that he would disown him.

Beth, the youngest of all, lacked his buoyant character. She was timid and shy and grasped at every opportunity to lose herself in dark corners out of the way. But she listened. She took everything in with an expression of extreme anxiety which was decidedly at odds with the plump roundness of her childish face. The high spirits of her elder siblings tended to trigger her retreat from them but she was also badly frightened by the talk around the fire. She only half-understood it and did not know that it was other people's wickedness in places far away that caused her father to swear and her big brother to shout in outrage. She somehow thought that it was something *she* might have done which made them both so cross. Fran saw it and she recognised it.

The child was actually waiting for the Armageddon which her father talked so much about and, if it really meant the end of the world, what it would be like and how much would she have had to do with it? And the perception of this fear ignited Fran's simmering anger at the stupid insensitivity of the grown men in the house, as she saw it. It was only a matter of time before she would explode.

The coming of Christmas was a most welcome diversion. All talk of the war was suspended. There was far too much to do and the fireside philosophy had to be put on hold whilst the annual preparations went on. Inroads were made into this oasis of normality however, which forced Jack and his father into the scullery when they felt the desperate need to discuss the most recent turn of events. The activities of the Irish Republican Army had spread to England and telephone boxes were being blown up, time-bombs were being put in suitcases and distributed at random around major railway stations. Shop windows, particularly of the plate-glass variety, seemed to cause insufferable offence if they remained *in-situ*, and were summarily smashed in. Mrs Jamieson refused to have any of these alarming developments mentioned in the house, hence the whispered exchanges over the scullery sink. It was not until after Christmas that Fran discovered precisely why the subject was forbidden. She also discovered, in a way that she could not possibly have foreseen, the reason for her mother-in-law's unprecedented insistence that a visit to Glasgow had suddenly become imperative.

Mrs Jamieson disappeared to Scotland, allegedly for Hogmanay, and Fran was left to look after the family single-handed and with no small degree of strain.

The New Year brought back politics with a vengeance. Barcelona had fallen. It looked as though the Republicans were to be routed and Jack was inconsolable. Apart from his worry about where Stella might be in all this, the Germans could count on yet another ally and Fascism was rampant. The world was going crazy. The rest of Czechoslovakia was sure to be sacrificed and everyone else would just stand by. So much for pledges. So much for honourable agreements.

He was so bound up in his fury about the drama on the world stage that it escaped his notice that honourable agreements were being broken under his very nose.

When Jack arrived home, cold and tired, that first Friday evening in January he discovered that his mother had returned. But she had not come alone.

There was no room to sit down. The whole family was congregated in the living room, nine of them; eleven if you counted the babies, for his young Auntie B. had come down from Glasgow, bringing with her her son, not much more than a year old.

The Friday fish was stinking the place out. It was simmering away to flaky bits of nothing in a pan of milk on the stove. If he had been able to get near enough he would have noticed that the pan was boiling dry and a toffee-coloured scum was beginning to form on the bottom. Even though he was unable to see this for himself, he said goodbye to his supper, sensing that more important things were afoot.

Sighing audibly, he went into the scullery to wash his hands and to deposit his wage-packet in the tin on the shelf where it was kept, along with those from his sisters, next to the tea caddy. He fished out a ten-shilling note and, stuffing it into his pocket, self-pityingly surmised that it did not seem that there would be a cup of tea on the go either. He made do with a mug of water, after running the tap for a long time to give himself a chance to pull himself together. He really was very tired.

On his return, he made his way over to where Fran was standing, near the door to the hall. She had Alexandra, half-asleep, against her shoulder. He could not quite see her face but he knew by the set of her body that she was ready to become incensed, a state of affairs not entirely unfamiliar to him during the past few weeks.

'What's going on?' he whispered to her, as he retrieved the baby for himself.

'Auntie B. is in some sort of trouble in Glasgow. Your mother has brought her back and expects her to stay here. With us. God knows where she'll find room!'

There was a mixture of disbelief and impatience in Fran's tone. But there was also a hint of apprehension. The whole situation surrounding this unexpected invasion had unnerved her, thrown her off-balance. One minute she had been preparing the supper with the girls and the next, the house had become chaos.

'So what's happening?'

'How the hell do I know, Jack? Nobody tells me anything around here. I had no idea that they were coming back. Not a word. And now there won't be enough food to go round.'

Before Jack could respond, there was an almighty wail from Clare who had just discovered the state of the pans on the stove. There was a hiatus whilst the two older girls attempted to make something of the mush that the potatoes had become, and the brown-edged flakes of fish. The peas had escaped damage. They were the only edible things which eventually arrived at the table, Jack having chivvied Robbie and Beth into action and forced them to make it presentable.

Fran went into the front room to bring in an extra chair, and then changed her mind. She sat down on the bed and buried her face in her hands. Auntie B. could have her chair. She could have her supper too; she didn't want it. She would go without rather than be caught up in that maelstrom next door. She preferred to sit quietly on the bed she and Jack shared and imagine that it was in their own house, their own place, away from all of this.

She was totally unprepared for the entry of her mother-in-law.

Fran never did reveal what was said between them that night, which resulted in immediate eviction. The first Jack knew of it was when Fran re-appeared, one side of her face turning rapidly crimson from the recent slap it had received.

'Come on, Jack. We're going,' she said as she wrenched the baby from his knee. 'Now, this minute!'

Alexandra had begun to howl, but Fran took no notice as she went into the scullery and took a tin of Nestlé's milk from the shelves and snatched a feeding bottle from the basin of boiled water where they were kept on the draining board. It was still dripping wet as she came back into the room, her skirt acquiring a pattern of dark stains where the droplets had spattered. Everyone had suddenly become silent; every head was turned towards her, gazing at her in amazement. Alexandra's protests had turned into screams.

She swept by into the hall and dumped the baby firmly in the pram, pausing only to go back into the bedroom to collect some nappies and to put on her coat.

Jack, bewildered, followed her. His coat was still on the back of the scullery door. He would have to go without. Fran was already manoeuvring the pram out of the front door.

He could not bear the baby's yells, so he picked her up as they walked along, Fran hardly pausing to allow him to lift Alexandra out of the pram. He had to almost run to keep up with her. And he knew she was crying.

'What is all this about? What's happened, Fran?'

She did not answer. He had to wait until she slowed her pace. In fact, she was searching her pocket for a handkerchief whilst she held on to the pram with one hand. He gave her his.

Alexandra had fallen asleep. Worn out with wailing, she had succumbed to the warmth of being enclosed inside her father's jacket, clutched tightly to his chest as they hurried along. Jack put her down gently, tucking in the blankets with immense care so as not to wake her. He put the hood up for good measure, to keep the cold out.

'Now, what's going on?'

He had put his arm round Fran and even through the thick fabric of her coat he could feel how thin her shoulders were. She should not be walking through the dark like this. In midwinter. None of them should. It did not make sense to him.

'Come on, let's go back.'

She pulled away from him. 'We can't go back,' she said. 'Your mother has made that quite clear. We cannot go back, even if I wanted to, which I don't.'

For the first time, Jack became aware of the seriousness of their predicament. Prior to this he had thought that the two women had just had a tiff and that Fran had flounced out in a temper, intending to walk around for a while until she cooled down. But it was not that at all.

'Besides,' she said, 'I will not be hit. My own mother did not get away with hitting me and yours certainly shan't.' She was crying again.

'But where are we going to go? Where are we going to sleep?'

'I don't know. We will have to find a hotel or something. There's nothing else for it.'

Jack felt in his pockets and pulled out the ten-shilling note, a couple of sixpences and a few coppers. It was all he had until the next Friday when he was paid again. It would hardly get him to work, let alone pay for a room somewhere for the three of them. He did not know how to tell Fran that his wage packet was already in the kitty, but she had guessed.

'You'll have to think of something. I'm not going back. She was going to make us move in with the girls. Auntie B. insisted that she have our room, and the cot for Joe, or whatever his name is, and your mother gave in to her. It is absolutely scandalous, Jack. And now you have handed over your wages! Whatever are we to do?'

Jack did not know. If Lou had been around he knew that she would have helped them out, but she was still in Dublin. Pinny was lost to the land of the living, or as good as. Who else was there?

Fran was walking on more quickly, in the direction of the ferries, but there was no real point to it. They would be as badly off over the water as they were where they were. It looked as though they would be wandering about all night. And she was refusing to speak to him. Her whole body stiff with outrage, her vision blurred by tears, determined to outpace him, she pushed on obdurately.

Suddenly, they had to come to a halt. A policeman had appeared in front of them, silhouetted in the light of the street lamp under which they had stopped. He was not hostile, he just wanted to know what they thought they were doing walking a baby at that hour of the night.

It was Fran who told him. They had nowhere to go, she said. And they had no money, the person who had thrown them out had got it. There was nothing till next week. She was at her wit's end to know what to do.

It was he who suggested that they try the Workhouse. He thought that he was being kind.

He began to give them minutely detailed directions as to how to get there but he was talking to the air. Jack and Fran were in such a state of shock that neither of them took in a word of what he was saying. The Workhouse. It was the end then, if they had to go there. The man was trying to be helpful. It was not really his fault that his words might just as well have been blows.

However, they ultimately set off along the way that he had advised. They did not look back. If they had, they would have been touched by the fact that the policeman still stood under the lamp post. He shook his head sorrowfully until the shape of the little family had moved in and out of the light from the street lamps enough times to finally become just darkness. That was all he could see, although he knew that there must be a deeper shadow in there somewhere. Then he turned to resume his beat.

‘It’s a real bugger, this world,’ he thought to himself, ‘and they hardly more than children themselves, never mind the pram. It’s very hard. Very hard. And the war coming and all.’

But he was due to come off duty at midnight and he spent the rest of his uneventful walk along his uneventful route thinking mostly about the prospect of his warm bed, himself and his plump wife cosily tucked up in it.

Jack and Fran, meanwhile, traipsed along in dispirited silence, neither of them caring if they were on the right road or not. Their half-hearted attempts to follow what little they had taken in of the policeman’s directions were a token only.

They were walking parallel to the river in relatively unfamiliar territory. Carried on the chilly night air came the just-audible sounds of the ferry coming in to port a mile or so away: the shouts of the ferrymen as they heaved the heavy ropes shorewards, the great swish of churning water as the boat turned about to come alongside, the muffled thud as it bumped up against its moorings, then the faintest clank of metal. That would be the gates opening up for disembarkation. There would not be many passengers at ten o’clock at night. There would be ferrymen coming off shift though.

‘Telephone!’ said Jack, suddenly urgent with a flicker of hope, ‘Look out for a telephone box, Fran. I may have got the answer. Make for the ferry landing.’

She did not ask any questions, just did as he said. They were out of breath and warm by the time they reached the first telephone box which Jack had rightly suspected, would be near the ferry. He had remembered an old acquaintance from the past. Teddy Marwood. This excellent young man, from Jack’s caddying days, was now a captain on the ferries and a fully paid up member at Leasowe. Occasionally, he had invited Jack for a round or two as his guest, an act of generosity much appreciated at the time, but Jack had not seen him for over a year, not since he had married, in fact. Teddy and his new wife now lived at Bebington, just down the coast. They might be able to help them out. It was worth a shot. It was an emergency after all.

He had the coins in his hand well before they reached the telephone box; they could see it lit up from quite a distance away. Then, to his fury, he realised that he would have to look up the number. He wrenched open the stiffly resistant door and hurled himself inside, pulling the directory from its shelf as he did so. Fran was rocking the pram backwards and forwards outside, in the hope that Alexandra would remain asleep. It was beyond her feeding time and Fran did not dare to tell Jack that when she had thrust the can of milk into the bottom of the pram, she had failed to see that it was an open one. Most of the sticky contents had, by that time, managed to seep all over the blankets and the nappies. There would be no way she could make up a bottle if the baby started to grizzle.

Jack was struggling to push the door back open. He poked his head out; the set of his eyes revealed the depth of his panic.

'The coin won't go in the slot!' he said, frustration pitching his voice high. The force of his despairing breath fluttered the pages of the directory still hugged to his chest.

'What?'

'I'm trying to get through to Teddy. He's there, he's answered and I can't get the bloody money in!'

Fran had not the slightest idea of what he was trying to do. He had not shared with her the idea he had come up with and she was preoccupied with the ghastly stickiness invading the whole of the interior of the pram.

'What are you on about? Teddy who?' She was looking murderously inclined, but her right hand still went forwards and back with a studied gentleness entirely at odds with her mood. She stared at her husband as if he had taken leave of his senses, 'It had better be good, Jack,' she snapped, sharply, 'and for Heaven's sake, what's the matter with you? *Make* the blasted penny go in. It can't be stuck!'

Jack was losing patience to the point of complete exasperation and he wasn't helped by the door being intent on crushing his shoulder in its determination to close on him.

'Teddy Marwood. You know. Lives in Bebington. Big flat. Flashy wife. Golfer. And it's not stuck, I think the box needs emptying.'

Enlightenment flooded across Fran's face. 'Oh,' she said, 'you think that they may be able to put us up? Oh, yes, I know who you mean, Teddy....'

She stopped rocking the pram and made to change places with Jack. 'Here, let me have a go. Give me the number.' The long anticipated cry immediately issued forth from under the hood as she tried to get into the kiosk.

'Oh, damn it! You take her, Jack.'

Jack was disconcerted by the hungry yells of his daughter reverberating through the night air. He half-expected windows to be thrown open and angry, threatening fists to be waved in their direction; possibly missiles to follow if she did not quieten down soon. He picked her up, soaked blankets and all and swaddled her round in an effort to keep out the bitter cold. Fran meanwhile was dialling Teddy's number. He could see her listening to the ring tone and then she tried to get the coin in the slot.

If it had not been stuck when Jack had attempted it, it well and truly became so with the force with which Fran had pushed it in. The Button B refused to press. That call too was abortive.

To give Jack his due, he did not make a fuss.

'We'll just have to walk and risk it,' he said. 'At least we know he's there.'

But it was at least three miles to Bebington and the baby would have to wait until they got there before she could be fed. Even if his friends were not able take them in, they could not refuse to let them feed the baby there surely? And get her cleaned up? It did not cross his mind that he had had little or no food himself, nor had Fran.

Mercifully, the lights were still on when they eventually arrived at the Marwoods'. Jack's knock was tentative. It had seemed such a good idea when he had first thought of it, to go to Teddy's. Now it had transformed itself into the most monstrous presumption on his part.

It was Carol Marwood who answered the door and welcomed them as if they were long-lost family, once she had heard their story. She insisted that it was no trouble at all to have them; they could stay as long as they liked. Teddy was just as pleased that they had turned up and he re-affirmed his wife's welcome. He was delighted that he could help them out, he said. He loved other people's adventures, their own lives being so humdrum. Except that they had got a bit alarmed when the phone kept ringing off. They had been worried that it might have been burglars. They all laughed at that, although it was a reasonable supposition under the circumstances. Carol, seemingly delighted to have a baby around, was already on her way to put the kettle on for Alexandra's bottle.

Fran was not so sure about the set-up. The flat was beautifully furnished and immaculately kept. There had been no children in it, nor were any likely to appear. Carol was considerably older than Fran, older in fact than Teddy if she remembered correctly, and being childless had not been a deliberate choice. She wondered how Carol would feel about the invasion of Alexandra into such a little palace, for little palace it was.

The guest-room was very comfortable when they were eventually established in it, fed and warmed by tots of whisky and hot-water bottles. It made her think of home, somehow, all this abundance of good things. And thinking of home made her overwhelmingly sad.

She could not sleep in spite of her exhaustion. Neither could Jack. They lay there in the dark, whispering so as not to wake the baby in her now pristine-clean pram alongside their bed, towels serving, temporarily, for blankets.

'I'll start looking for somewhere tomorrow,' Jack said. 'Where we can go after next week. Can you manage till then on what we've got? I'll only take out what I need to get to work.'

'I'll make sure I do,' Fran whispered, 'but we'll have to reimburse Carol for what she spends on housekeeping if we do stay, so don't look for anywhere too grand.'

There was no point in attempting to plan any further than that and neither was there point in dwelling on the precariousness of the situation they had found themselves in. Teddy had referred to it as an adventure; rotten bad luck would be nearer the truth. But whatever it was, it was not conducive to sleep.

'Tell me about Auntie B. Why did she suddenly descend like that, with your mother? Without warning or anything. What the hell's been going on in Glasgow, Jack?'

He turned over to lie on his back whilst he tried to make sense of the events of the evening. He couldn't really come up with any answers. He had been more wounded than he cared to admit that his mother had behaved as she did. He could not understand what had possessed her enough to throw them out. He knew that Fran would undoubtedly have defended her own position rather more aggressively than perhaps his mother was used to, which would explain the slapped face, but the rest of it it was a conundrum.

'I don't know what's been going on up there, and that's a fact. It's not unusual for us spend the New Year with the Scottish lot, but it has never been my mother just on her own before. Come to think of it, she went up fairly recently, when you were in hospital. I'd forgotten that. I think you're right Fran, something must be up! For B. to come rushing down now is very strange.'

'And push us out of our room. Don't forget that! Actually, it's unforgivable. Outrageously unforgivable!'

Fran had tensed up and was all ready to launch into invective once again. Jack pulled her closer to him and held her tight in an attempt to calm her down.

'Auntie B. is much younger than my mother. I suppose she has always had her own way, being the baby of the family, and her husband spoilt her a bit, I think. She would never be content with second best. She's not badly off now as far as I know. He had a good job.'

'And he left her the house. Why on earth should she abandon all that to come rushing down here to live in one room at her sister's?'

'God knows.'

'Well, that was what she was about. Your mother told me straight out.'

Things were gradually beginning to take shape in Jack's mind. Old stories, family legends, which had been muttered about in corners throughout his childhood reasserted themselves in his consciousness. He shifted position awkwardly. This was going to be difficult.

'It could be something to do with the recent bombings. He was connected with the Irish Republican Army at one time.'

Fran struggled away from him in order to sit up. He squeezed his eyes together waiting for the explosion which would surely come from her. 'What?' she almost shouted, 'The I.R.A.!' and then she allowed herself to relax and fall back down, 'That was not a very good joke, you know, Jack, it really wasn't.'

She pulled the covers back over them, almost companionably.

'You shouldn't joke about things like that.'

'Shshsh. I'm serious. He truly was a member of the I.R.A. We all knew about it, all us kids, although we shouldn't have. As a boy he was involved in the Easter Rising. That was the first time he went into hiding, after that. He was sixteen then, I think. I don't know if he was one of the Michael Collins' lot, but I do know that he fought against the Black and Tans. It was when there was that first debacle over Home Rule which started the Civil War. That was how he came to have consumption, after he had gone into hiding in the mountains. He lived in ditches in the bogs, he and his friend, and he developed pneumonia or pleurisy or something and he never really recovered. They were about my age then, about twenty one, or two, perhaps. I'm pretty sure that his friend was shot.'

Fran could not find anything to say.

The darkness seemed suddenly to press in on them. Instead of being hospitable and sheltering, the room had instantly acquired susceptibility to what lay outside. Of such dramatic import, the story Jack had to tell, related as legend so many times, had for him become matter-of-fact. In Fran, it let loose a host of imaginings. Black and Tans, Black Marias, *Blackshirts,* all seemed to be massing up outside in that bleak January night, ready to sully their own generation and themselves. And there was not a thing that they could do about it.

She suddenly realised that Jack was still speaking and that she hadn't heard. She had to ask him to tell her again.

'I said, that it could be that B. was in some sort of danger. The I.R.A. might be about to exact revenge in some way, now that they are operating on the mainland. Her husband had defected to all intents and purposes; run to Scotland and turned his back on them. And, you see, it was B. who enticed him away from Ireland in the first place and we don't know how important he had become in the meantime, or how much he knew. *Who* he knew! And names will be a very valuable commodity at the moment. B. could possibly be in possession of them and she owes no loyalty to the Republicans. What could be easier for them than to settle an old score and ensure her silence at the same time? While they are doing the whole country a favour by diverting attention away from Hitler and his rather more ambitious programme of pyrotechnics, they could easily do away with her. No, I think that Auntie B. is doing a runner herself and hopes to become anonymous by hiding out with big sister. We just happened to be in the way. That's what I think, Fran. I mean, it's all guesswork, all hypothesis, but it would explain the panic Mother was in and why she was prepared to oust us because we crossed her....'

'I crossed her, you mean.'

'Well, yes, I suppose so. But if I'm right, then it really was an emergency. She just had not told us about it, that's all.'

'That still does not explain why they had to have our room! Why couldn't she have put B. in with the girls rather than us being shoved up there? How *were* we supposed to manage?'

But Fran was so tired that she could not summom up the energy to be angry any more. Then, a further thought occurred to her.

'There is no knowing who could turn up on that doorstep, if you are right, Jack. We are much better off out of it, funnily enough.'

He yawned widely with the effort of thinking,

'And the irony is that we are now the anonymous ones. Again! We are virtually in hiding for the second time in a year. But I don't think that my mother will set a detective on us somehow. I don't see her doing that.'

He was almost asleep but Fran needed to know still more.

'I don't understand how B. came to be married to that man in the first place. She lived in Scotland. How on earth did she get to be involved with him?'

'She had gone to stay with her grandfather, my great-grandfather that is, who lived in Londonderry. That was where my mother's family originated from. She met him there, when she was on a visit. When they got married, he went back with her to Glasgow. I suppose he was doing a runner too, at the time.'

He did not hear her say, 'I see.' He was sound asleep and, within minutes, so was she, but her dreams were uneasy and featured mountains and soldiers and she and Jack riding like fury on a motorbike and getting nowhere, achieving nothing; except exhaustion.

* * *

The following morning Jack went off to work in the company of Teddy and spent the ferry journey scouring the local papers in search of rooms to let. In his lunch hour he went to see a house just round the corner from where he worked. It was a large, rather jaded Georgian building, double-fronted and obviously substantial. There were two rooms available, unfurnished, on the top floor. Jack said that he would take them from the following Saturday and would pay in advance from then, if the landlord, a Captain O'Hara, could wait that long. He explained that he had a young baby and that things were a little difficult.

The O'Hara household was full of children, one more crying in the night would make little difference. They had no objections to the baby at all and they were prepared to wait. Jack liked them. He liked them a lot and he could not wait to get back to Bebington to tell Fran the good news. He had not quite worked out how they would manage without any furniture, but he had great faith in the maxim that something would turn up.

They stayed with the Marwoods for that week, very happily. Carol and Fran became good friends, partly because Fran was a responsible guest and shared the chores with a will and made sure that their intrusion into that immaculate flat was minimal. Even when Jack had gone back to collect their belongings from his mother's house, Fran made sure that they were neatly packed and stored away, especially the baby's things which had a habit of spreading as if of their own accord if they were not kept severely in check.

Alexandra herself came in for a lot of attention. Teddy spoilt her, Carol adored her and kept appearing with gifts: a pretty little dress, a beautiful knitted coat and bonnet, fluffy toys. Fran, protesting loudly at such indulgence, was browbeaten into accepting them in spite of her embarrassment. Carol was a stranger. She had only known her a matter of days and such excessive generosity seemed inappropriate to Fran, especially as she was not in a position to reciprocate. She could not even get Carol a bunch of flowers in her present predicament. It was a bitter pill to swallow that her mother-in-law had not seen fit to refund Jack his week's wages when he had gone to retrieve their tiny collection of worldly goods. She supposed that it was a punishment for the things she had said. Things which could not be forgiven. On both sides.

She knew that she ought not to think about it. What was done was done. What had been said could not be unsaid. Yet it kept on nudging at her conscience, the knowledge that she had made herself an alien in the Jamieson household, or so it seemed. Another door closed in their faces, on the three of them.

She must look forward. It was a negative thing, to dwell on mistakes. One must go forward. Avoid making the same mistakes again. And she tried to follow this simple advice to herself by clinging on to what Jack had told her about the O'Hara's and the new place that would be theirs by the end of the week.

It sounded hopeful. They would manage. Despite the fact that they hardly had two halfpennies to rub together, they were managing. She began to count off the days until the weekend when Jack would be paid and they could move.

On their last night there, their hosts seemed most regretful that they were going. Carol cooked a special meal and wept into the pudding when she was thanked for all her kindness to them. Fran had their two cases packed and ready for an early start the following morning.

When she went up to change Alexandra after breakfast early on that memorable Saturday, she checked everything over once again. When she came to her purse she discovered that it had been denuded of all the pound notes which Jack had carefully handed over to her the previous night. He had given her all he had except for the loose change in his pockets. The precious wages were missing. She thought that maybe she had put the notes somewhere else, for safety.

She emptied everything out of their suitcases and searched through them with an increasing sense of dismay. She searched everywhere: in every pocket, right through her bag, through the baby's things. She could not believe that she had lost the money. She remembered putting it into her purse; she clearly remembered doing it. Then it had gone into her bag which she had found exactly as she had left it, on the dressing table.

When Jack came up to find her, to ask what was taking her so long, he discovered her sitting in the middle of what seemed like total disorder, her face pinched-in and pale.

'The money's gone.' Her voice was thick, as if she had an obstruction in the back of her throat. 'I can't find it anywhere.'

The baby was lying in the middle of the bed amongst the scatterings of clothes and shoes, hairbrushes, nappies, Fran's bits of make-up. She began to whimper. Why did babies always have to start crying when the utmost concentration was not only essential, but imperative?

'It can't have. When did you last have it?'

Without waiting for her answer, Jack began to search through everything again, fruitlessly, Fran looking more grim by the minute as she picked up the baby and patted her back with unprecedented vigour.

'Change her again,' suggested Jack. 'It may have got tucked in between the rubber pants if it had been left on the bed.'

Predictably, that proved not to be the case and Alexandra's infuriated screams at being put back down almost drove them both to distraction.

He went to the bathroom and stared glumly down at the lavatory bowl. Had it got mixed up with the baby things and been flushed away? This was where Fran emptied the nappy bucket after she had rinsed them out. It seemed to be the only rational explanation.

He swore under his breath and returned to give Fran his verdict. She was attempting to re-pack their things one-handedly, moving with unaccustomed awkwardness. She had the baby on the other arm.

'Will you finish off here?' she said, 'I'm going to ring my father.'

'Don't Fran. Don't do that. Not after all they've done to you.'

'There's nothing else for it. I've lost the money, haven't I? What else is there to do? And don't say a word to Teddy or Carol. That would be the end, if they got to know about this.'

She struggled to assume a cheery face and then went into the kitchen to ask if she could use the telephone.

14. Helping Hand

THAT SATURDAY morning, Izzie Reynolds was indulging in a second breakfast. She had had the first one at five when Neville had to be got off early. It was a removal job, out into the country somewhere. Fa had not lost any time in acquiring a big van, especially equipped for the purpose, to add to his new fleet of motorised haulage vehicles. People were moving out of the town in increasing numbers. It was all the talk of war that was in the newspapers and coming over the wireless. It had added a lucrative extension to his business. Neville dealt with most of it and Charlie was under him, in his team.

Izzie wished that her sons got on better with each other. Neville could not be persuaded to show any patience with his next brother down, but he was Job himself with the two younger ones. She supposed it was jealousy, but what Neville had to be jealous of in Charlie, she could not imagine. He was no threat to him. He lacked his brother's business brain and competition with Neville was not on his agenda. He preferred to spend his time with the horses. They were his passion. That was where his brilliance lay. But he was lackadaisical in everything else and Neville bullied him mercilessly; intolerance keeping him short-tempered and surly. Charlie took not the slightest notice. His nature was too generous to offer challenge or to bear resentment. He chose to ignore Neville's barbs which had the unfortunate result of provoking his brother even further. There was no peace when those two were around.

She could handle the two girls more readily. Dodo was silly and did not have an independent thought in her head. She was also impractical and depended on others to carry her. She welcomed the fact that her mother made all the decisions, told her what to do. She was agreeably malleable in that respect. Abby liked her easy, comfortable life far too much to do anything to jeopardise it. She would acquiesce to anything without demur. Izzie had driven away the one with the spirit, the one who could turn her hand to anything and make a success of it.

She sighed, a long dissatisfied sigh. It distressed her to think of Fran. It distressed her to be reminded of her own behaviour regarding her. But what else could she have done, she asked herself. As a child, Fran had always been troublesome. Izzie had never known where she was with her. She had been a wanderer, her curiosity leading her into all sorts of fixes, giving her mother nightmares of anxiety. And then she had not always been under Izzie's dominant wing. She had spent months in the Fever Hospital, away from them, when she had gone down with scarlet fever. She would have been about ten then. And Fa had ruined her, especially after that. He had always ruined her. It was wrong to have favourites. Plain wrong. And he had got nowhere with her. She had run off in spite of him. And she, Izzie, had had to bear the blame.

Resentment at what she considered to be injury against her in that respect made her purse her mouth into a straight line. She had only been trying to protect Fran. Fa himself had said that there was danger in the Jamieson boy's politics. More than once. What had he expected her to do? Just what had he expected her to do?

She did not want to dwell on it any more. She must put her mind to practical things.

'I've been thinking about turning the cellar into our own private air-raid shelter,' she said to the newspaper held up between her and her husband and the coffee pot. 'I don't want to be mixing with every Tom, Dick and Harry down the road the way we are being told to do. I'm not having that. What do you say?'

The double spread of newspaper did not stir, neither did the two sets of fingers, to each side of it, holding it up. She could not see his head.

'Fa, I said what do you think...?'

'I heard you.' The paper remained motionless. 'Do what you want.'

'I want you to tell me what you think about it. Will it be safe enough? What will your councillor friends have to say about it at the Burlington? Will we be breaking the law...? Fa!'

The newsaper came down slowly, as if it was the entity demonstrating infinite patience, rather than himself. Fa folded it resignedly and put it to one side. He knew better than to allow it to stray near the marmalade jars.

'Well now, I don't know if it will be safe, and I don't give a jot for what Eddie Bolton and his ilk might have to say about it, seeing as you asked. If you want to do that, then do it. The law will not affect us much if we are bombed in any event, and we will be as safe there as anywhere else, I reckon. As the case may be.'

'We could repair the old kitchen stove and put some stores down there. There's the old copper too, still intact. The other two rooms could have proper beds in. We would be much better off than in those brick hut things that they are putting up all over the place. You don't know who you might be forced to be crammed in with, in there. It could be anybody.'

Fa restrained his smiles.

'Oh, indeed. It could be anybody.'

Privately, having had a great deal of experience of being under fire, he thought that, come the bombers through the clouds, she would not find herself being all that fussy about who she took shelter with, but he might have anticipated that she would not be prepared to die amongst the likes of those who might have originated from the Dock Road, if she could plan otherwise. That really would spell ignominy.

'You want me to go and have a look down there, is that it?'

'When you're ready,' and after a slight pause she repeated herself.

'When you're ready.'

'Alright then.' He lifted himself heavily out of his chair. 'We might as well do it now.'

The stairs down to the cellars were through a yellow varnished door in the small lobby outside the living room, where the coats were hung. Another few steps led up to the main hall, on the right, and on to the billiard room and the drawing room. It was a small space. Fa thought that any large furniture she had in mind to go down there would have to be put through the area windows. It would be impossible to negotiate the lobby.

‘Maybe I could have the ceiling reinforced? I’ll think about that,’ he said to himself as they descended the stone steps. The project, as a project, had begun to interest him. ‘That would be a good idea.’

Fa was measuring the available spaces in the larger of the two main rooms down there by pacing it out, one foot in front of the other, and assuring her that bunk beds were the only solution, when the telephone went.

He was nearest to the door, so he went to answer it. In relative terms, she was the more sprightly, and would normally have gone, but she was busy inspecting the neglected stove and chose to ignore the insistent ringing. Fa laboured his way back up the stairs.

‘Hang on. Hang on. I’m coming, whoever you are!’ he said out loud, knowing that he would be out of breath when he picked up the receiver, which irked him. He liked to sound dignified on the telephone, especially if it was a customer.

Izzie went on with the measuring. It was a good space, she decided. It could be made very habitable once they had got rid of all the junk which was cluttering it up at present. The boys would have to help. It was about time those two youngest earned their keep. And it needed a good clean; perhaps a fresh coat of whitewash.

Fa had come back down the stairs very meditatively. When she turned to glance at him she stood up from what she was doing. Even in the dim light from the one, fly-spotted bulb hanging gloomily from the centre of the ceiling, she could see the pallor of his face.

‘Are you alright? Were the stairs too much for you?’

She felt guilty about letting him go. His chest had been bad for years, ever since he had come back from the war.

‘Who was it?’

‘Oh, just an enquiry for an estimate for some people in Bebington. I’ll have to go over. I’ll go now. Get it over with.’

The colour was returning to his cheeks.

‘It was a good idea of yours, Izzie, to use the cellar. While I’m out, get hold of a builder and see what can be done about strengthening the ceiling. We’ll get on with it straight away.’

Izzie flushed with pleasure. It was not often that she came in for praise these days. There had been a gradual withdrawal of Fa's affections since Fran had gone.

But she consistently refused to acknowledge any blame.

* * *

When he arrived at the Marwoods, Fran was alone with Carol. The men had gone on to work. Fa was relieved. It would be easier with the husbands out of the way, he thought, easier to persuade her to come home.

He had driven the Rover through the tunnel at a stately pace; a big, solid man in a big solid car. He knew the sort of figure he cut; prosperous, comfortable, emanating nothing but well-being. The truth was, at this particular point, solid was the last thing he felt. It was certain that 'well' would not describe him and he knew that his prosperity would probably add to his discomfort. His daughter was in trouble and whilst he might solve her immediate problems by putting his hand in his pocket, that would not solve the fundamental issue. Not to his satisfaction. It could never be to that. Not now.

He had deliberately shut out all thoughts of Izzie. He did blame her for the plight they were in over Fran. It was his confirmed opinion that she had handled the whole situation badly. She had bungled it. One minute she was smothering her children with over-indulgence, the next she was putting a detective on one of them, behaving like a mad woman to boot. It was no surprise that she was in such a nervous state that she spent half her time in the doctor's surgery demanding pills. Pills for her 'nerves.' As if they would provide answers. As if all the pills in the world could possibly heal the breach with Fran which she, Izzie, had single-handedly brought about. He had no patience with it. And now the girl was in trouble.

He would keep from his wife the nature of this visit to Bebington.

'We need help,' his daughter had said. 'Otherwise I would not be ringing.'

She had not said what sort of help. He had not given her the chance. He had never given her the chance to have her say, he realised. He should have insisted upon it this time.

'Tell me where you are,' he had said, 'I'll be right over.'

He suspected that they were short of money.

Fran was there waiting for him on the doorstep when he arrived. And she had with her a baby, fast asleep on her shoulder. It was his grandchild, his first grandchild who, up till this moment, had only been rumoured to exist.

'This is Alexandra,' Fran said stiffly. She was embarrassed by not knowing how to behave.

Fa held out his arms to take the baby. He looked down into the tiny face, spreading the shawl as gently as he could with his big man's fingers so that he could get a better look at the roundness of her cheek, the length of the lashes as they fluttered open to reveal a steady gaze directed straight into his own eyes. His heart lurched with the intensity of it. Then the perfect little mouth puckered; a cry was coming.

'She's soaking wet,' he said and looked up at Fran helplessly.

'Oh, Fa! Is that all you have to say? She's just been fed. What do you expect? We'll go in and I'll change her.'

But Carol insisted on taking the child when they entered the flat.

'I'll do it,' she said, 'you talk to your father.'

Fran produced an edited version of the disaster. She said that all their money had disappeared and that they were desperate. She did not tell him how they came to be so dependent on that one pay packet. If Fa could just loan them the week's rent for the new lodgings they would be alright, but he refused.

'No, Fran. I want you back home, you and the baby. You will be much better off at home. I'll make it right with your mother.'

'And Jack?'

'I can't speak for your mother as far as Jack is concerned.'

'You mean that he is not welcome?'

Fa hesitated. When he did speak he sounded apologetic, shamed almost.

'I mean that I cannot guarantee that she will take Jack in.'

'I see!'

The obstinate chin tilted upwards. Fran was ready to hold out. She was adamant.

'I will not come home, not now, not any time. I am a married woman. You don't own me any more. I have a husband and I must be with him. And he must be with his baby. You cannot take his baby away from him Fa. All we need is one week's rent. We'll pay you back, you can depend on it, we'll pay you back.'

For once in her life, Fran found herself pleading.

'Just the rent,' she repeated again and again. 'Just the rent, nothing more.'

Fa knew he was beaten. He would be returning without her.

He put his hand inside his jacket and brought out his wallet. Pound notes were placed on the table. Fran took what they needed and gently pushed the remainder back in his direction.

'Is that all?' he said.

'That's all. Nothing more. And thank you.'

She had taken the money and was folding the notes into the smallest square they would make. She then put them into the pocket of her skirt. She looked more vulnerable than he had ever seen her, her eyes studying the carpet rather than have to meet his. She suddenly looked tired, worn out.

He put his hand into his trouser pocket and emptied out the pile of change.

'Have that for yourself and the baby,' he insisted. 'At least do that. For me.'

It was a jumble of shillings, silver sixpences, threepenny bits and coppers. He pressed it into both her hands, closing her fingers over it.

'And Fran. Go to see your Aunt Hannah. Will you do that please?'

Aunt Hannah was Fa's sister. Fran knew that he was suggesting a safe line of communication.

'I will,' she said, 'as soon as we're over the water.'

'Good. Now let me take you there. I'll take you to Stanley Road in the car.'

But she denied Fa the pleasure of taking her to her new home. She had things to do first, she said. She would much rather make her own way and Stanley Road was not far from the ferry landing.

So she hugged him hard and pressed her cheek against the scratchy tweed of his jacket, the smell of tobacco and leather and saddle soap as familiar as her own childhood.

'Thank you, Fa,' she said.

He left without saying goodbye.

The truth was that Fran knew that the battle would be lost for ever if her father had seen that she was taking the baby to two empty rooms. She would be forced to accept that Oakshot Road had to be the most sensible place to go. She did not know herself how she would actually cope, but she was absolute in her certainty that she would rather exist on bare boards than be under the same roof as a mother or a mother-in-law, no matter how comfortable the accomodation.

She would make her own way, she had said. She could manage quite easily with the cases on the end of the pram.

She would make sure that she managed. And then she could tell Jack that all was well, once she was over the water. Fa's change added up to fifteen shillings. It was tantamount to freedom.

That fifteen shillings bought food for Fran's little family for the week and Jack had already seen to it that essential bits of furniture had appeared, bought in Paddy's Market for a few pence: an old iron bedstead and a rickety table. He had made little cupboards from empty orange boxes which he had also scrounged from the stallholders, for nothing. They doubled up as chairs for the time being, even when Fran had made little curtains for the fronts.

It was a far cry from the prettily furnished place in Orrell Park which had haunted Fran's thoughts for almost a year, but it was a fresh start and she was grateful for it.

* * *

Captain O'Hara's household proved to be a happy place, where low spirits were a thing of the past. Within weeks they had even reimbursed the Marwood couple for their stay with them despite the fact that by that time they knew where the money had gone.

It was Teddy's brother who told Jack. They had met by chance on the street and Jack had movingly expressed his appreciation for the exceptional hospitality Teddy had extended. The Marwoods had saved their lives, he said. He could not begin to imagine what might have happened if they had not come to the rescue.

To his utter amazement, the response came in the form of a joke. 'Well, I hope you held on to all your things!'

Jack blushed, 'Whatever do you mean?' He was confused. No-one knew about what had happened, no-one at all.

'That Carol! She's an absolute kleptomaniac. Bloody magpie. Teddy has a hell of a job with her. Breaks his heart. She nicks from shops and everything. Don't tell me you didn't know? I thought everybody did. It's been in the papers.'

Jack did not reveal that the warning had come too late. 'We had nothing worth taking,' he laughed, 'but we should have given it to her with pleasure if we had!'

Fran was not quite so sanguine when she received the news.

'Bloody Hell, Jack! The deceitful, scheming little minx! And she looked as though butter wouldn't melt in her mouth. It is no wonder then, that she dresses so well and there was I thinking that Teddy must be making a fortune!'

She was scrubbing up a pair of erstwhile elegant chairs that she and Mrs. O'Hara had found on the junk stall at Paddy's indispensible treasure of a market.

'Whoever would have thought it?'

'She does not know that she is doing it, apparently. It's a kind of illness. She can't help it,' Jack offered.

'Can't help it, my foot!' said Fran. 'The trouble with you, Jack, is that you refuse to see ill in anyone close to you and nothing but evil in the rest of the world! Where do the two meet? That's what I would like to know. Where do the two meet?'

But she did not pursue it. She was too busy. Philosophy would have to wait. She sent him downstairs to empty the bucket. The vigorous assault on the chairback increased in intensity. Carol Marwood would have known all the time the reason for the urgent telephone call to Fa. She had not so much as blinked an eye. How she must have laughed when they'd gone! Fran was inwardly raging with fury at being tricked so easily. And all the time she had blamed herself for being careless and irresponsible.

Conflicting judgements on the Marwoods occupied her thoughts for the rest of the day. Further insult was added to injury, as she saw it, when that night, as she was putting the baby to bed in the beautiful new cot provided by Aunt Hannah and sorting out the child's clothing for the morning, it suddenly dawned on her that Alexandra was most likely in receipt of stolen goods. The little woollen dress and the matinee jacket which she had just set out had come from Carol Marwood.

She hastily collected together all the other items: two more dresses, the coat and bonnet, innumerable toys. She screwed them up and pushed them to the back of the shelf in one of the orange boxes and then stood staring at the makeshift cupboard as if it would suddenly ignite and set the place on fire.

'I'll think about that later,' she said to herself. But she never did. The little garments would have stayed there till this day if she and Jack hadn't moved house yet again, by which time Alexandra had well and truly outgrown all the items of dubious origin.

* * *

Fran was not the only one who was setting up in a new home that January but Stella was able to effect it with less adversity. She simply moved out of her lodgings on the outskirts of the city and took a room in a hotel nearer the centre.

She had several reasons for choosing to abandon the relative safety of her previous arrangements. It was not that she did not get on with the family who had taken her in, she did, and she was more than grateful to them for the generous way in which they had helped her. She could not have learned the language so quickly without the chattering sisters and their determination to include her in their gossip. Once fluent, she immediately became more useful and could move around from job to job as the need arose.

Much more significant was a personal development which could only be attributed to her stay with them. Enfolded in their midst, accepted as an honorary daughter, she progressively shed the wary cautiousness with which she had invariably approached any new relationship in the past. They were entirely honest in their dealings with one another. Openly candid about their loves and hates, they would quarrel and argue passionately but make up the next instant with just as much fervour. This volatility had alarmed her at first until she realised that there was not a hint of bad feeling in it. They could say what they felt without the least fear of the insidious retribution which had been the invariable result of plain speaking in her experience. It took her quite a while to adjust to it but she gradually came to realize that, however perilous the conditions outside, inside that house no-one dreaded the arrival of another, no-one cowered at the sound of a voice raised in anger, no-one wept through interminable nights. As she had done. Hating herself for her cowardice.

Ironically, surrounded as they were by the inevitable atrocities and turmoil of civil war, it was through their example that she learnt what a normal, loving family could be like. It was with genuine regret that she had to move.

The most pressing reason for her decision was that she was now working at a supply depot on the other side of the city. Making that journey each day would, at the best of times, have been difficult. Under the present circumstances, it was proving to be impossible. Her concern for Dee Mason was the other reason.

She could not bear to think of him returning, near-to-insensible with fatigue and half-frozen into the bargain, with the bleakness of the military barracks as his only option for respite. When his stint at the front was done, she made herself responsible for the provision of warmth and comfort. Such as it was.

Barcelona was in chaos. The Government forces were fighting for their lives; amongst each other on grounds of ideology and against the increasingly successful Franco in the field. On the latter count Stella knew, more than most, how desperate the situation had become. It was one thing being good at logistics; it was another thing entirely when what there was to move up to the front lines was heartbreakingly, glaringly inadequate.

When Dee came back each time, they would huddle together in the preposterously ornate brass bed which dominated the rest of the crumbling, erstwhile self-important, hotel room and, almost hidden beneath a mountain of quilts, work out what they should do. For defeat was imminent and plans had to be made. That they would no longer ever be apart was tacitly understood.

15. Blitz
September 1940

THE VOLUNTARY ambulance station was housed in a school. The vehicles were parked in the playground, in a line, ready for action alongside the air-raid shelter, the first one meticulously placed between what remained of the pillars which had once held gates.

This particular night, the crews were not up on the first floor where they usually waited, they were already in the shelter, the attack was so bad. They knew that their call would come any minute. One man only was left up there, waiting to relay the signal for the alarm.

Inside the shelter, they were calmly waiting for their night to start, even though bombs were falling like bloated black hailstones and the noise of explosions almost drowned out their own contribution.

They were singing a decidedly ribald version of the tune, 'Two Lovely Black Eyes,' as they played cards for threepenny stakes. One or two of them were deep in the *Liverpool Echo.* It was as they were dinning out, "OH,WHAT A SURPRISE! ' that the bomb exploded near the shelter. It was no surprise at all to find themselves bounced up in the air, coming down like so many pieces of old rag, the playing cards fluttering aloft, competing with flakes of lime-washed brick to cling to their clothing.

The alarm came just as they were pulling themselves together, inspecting personal damage, searching for the coins which seemed to have fused themselves into the debris. As they emerged from the shelter, it was raining tracer bullets; lines and lines of them up in the air, glinting with startling speed. They dodged them, weaving their way to the vehicles.

'Hang on to your tin hats, lads!'

Engines turned; doors hanging open as the vehicles began to move.

'Same area as Monday,' called out Jack to the leading driver, 'but this time Walton Gaol. There's a wing gone.'

'You're bloody lucky there isn't a wing gone on this, an' all!' The driver was smashing a hole through the shattered glass in the windscreen with his gloved fist. 'There will be by the time we get there, I reckon.'

Jack did not hear the rest. The ambulance moved out and he was hauled up into the back, the door pulled to behind him.

His driver led the convoy out into the streets, peering through the hole in front of him in order to avoid craters. There was no problem with visibility. The whole city was alight.

The electricity supply for the prison had been severed as soon as the bombs had begun to explode. A sub-human sound mingled with the roaring of the flames and the crashing down of masonry as the wing disintegrated. It was an unholy descant to the persistent bells of the fire engines as they arrived from all quarters. The ambulances followed close behind, their bells ringing a different, deeper note, and still the high-pitched sound wailing above it all.

It was the screaming of the men in the main block. They were still locked in their cells. Only the frantic criss-crossing of the searchlights stabbing the sky illuminated their plight and the recurrent explosions as the bombers completed their unloading before returning to base. More would surely hit, or the fire would spread, before long.

Below, the jets from the firehoses paralleled the pattern of the lights in grotesque imitation, their lines crossing with the same demented, scouring energy. The ambulances ceased their wild clanging as the vehicles slowed down to crawl their way through the mass of fallen masonry and the fog of acrid smoke which formed a blanket up to man-height over the ground. Jack and his fellow crew members leapt out of the rear of their vehicle, following orders to support the firemen who were about to attempt rescue from the demolished wing.

A line of firemen, ambulance men and police was quickly assembled, crowbars distributed and they began to pull at the smouldering rubble.

The wail all round them as they worked had gone beyond the tolerable. It had become articulate. 'Let us out! For Christ's sake! Let us out!'

But nobody could. Nobody did. The men in the main block would have to take their chances along with everyone else. Evacuating prisoners was not on the agenda.

The rescue team levered away for what seemed like hours, grunting with the effort of shifting blocks of misshapen, awkward stone and smouldering wood jutting out at impossible angles. Worse even than this were the iron girders which had twisted themselves into a grotesque mimicry of arborescent shapes, but from under which, to the immense relief of the exhausted workers, men at last began to crawl, black-faced and vocal.

The inventiveness of their improvised obscenities was lost on the ambulance men who were calmly intent on getting on with the job. Warders and prisoners alike were summarily lifted and carried across, between, amongst, the treacherous debris. The waiting vehicles stood patiently, the red crosses on their roofs obscured by blackened ash. The violence of the sound around them negated the need for any response from the rescuers to the colourful expletives which, in any other circumstances, would have entertained them.

It was difficult getting back, much more so than during the previous heavy raid at the beginning of the week. Many more craters had appeared along the road and some had acquired barricades of rubble strewn across them from houses recently bombed. Jack's driver had to turn back and they only just escaped with their lives when a gas main fractured in one street just as they had turned the corner out of it.

It was worse at the hospital. Queues of ambulances were waiting to get into Casualty. Jack knew when they were getting near their turn. The light from under the entrance canopy suffused itself through the bluish windows of the back of the ambulance. That was his signal to open the rear doors.

Everything happened quickly then. Their patients were handed on to the nursing staff, stretchers and blankets replaced and they were off again, struggling through the continuous raid, back to the prison.

Jack's companion, erstwhile garage owner, ex-novice priest and by now notorious fornicator, was none other than Pinny and he was complaining about his foot. He was attempting to sit on one of the stretchers as they bumped and swerved along. He was trying to get his boot off.

'You'd be better on the floor,' shouted Jack. 'It will be a bit more stable. What's the matter with it anyway?'

Pinny groaned as the boot eventually gave way and fell off his foot of its own accord.

'That bastard of a policeman. The one that claimed that he played rugby for Wigan. Feet like tug boats. He weighed about four tons, I'm bloody telling you.'

'What about him?'

Jack was hanging on to the top bunks in an attitude of crucifixion as he tried to keep his balance and peer down in the direction of Pinny's socks at the same time. There wasn't really room for both of them on the floor, not with Pinny with one leg stretched out and the other bent over his knee. He was gingerly attempting to flex his toes.

'Arrrrrrrh! Christ!' was the only reply.

'What about the policeman?'

Jack had risked squatting down to get a better look. Pinny was obviously in some difficulty.

'Did he play for Wigan?'

'Holy Mother of God, Jack! What does it matter? He's broken my bloody foot, that's what.'

Jack had got a purchase with his backside by this time. He was wedged on the floor, his parted knees each side of Pinny's outstretched foot.

'Let's have it. Let's have a look at it.'

Pinny, with some difficulty, edged his other leg down to Jack as the ambulance lurched round a corner.

'I wish they'd hush that perishing bell!'

Jack was feeling along Pinny's toes as gently as he could. They felt fat. Like unpricked sausages about to burst.

'This is probably broken. Did he stand on it then?'

'Stand on it! Pinny was gasping out his indignation.'The dozy bugger was using it as a buffer for his heel as he dragged that big warder out, the one that had bitten the end off his tongue, face looked as if he'd fallen into a vat of jam. Did you see it?'

'Why didn't you say something? Make him move off?'

'Like what? 'Excuse me, constable, but would you mind not grinding my effing foot against this brickwork, it's a trifle uncomfortable.' In those circumstances? Don't be so bloody gormless, Jack!'

The sock was off. Pinny's foot was swollen and black, up to and beyond his ankle.

'It's broken. Bloody Hellfire! Get your boot back on or else you never will. We'll finish here tonight and then get someone to look at it.'

The ambulance suddenly screeched to a stop. Jack struggled to his feet and opened the door. They were not back at the prison. They were still on the road. The other ambulance man who had been sitting with the driver, was running round to the rear door.

'Watchpost's just been hit, up ahead. Alf says we'd better see what we can do. We can't get through in any case, there's bleedin' sandbags all over the road. He's bleedin' furious, is Alf. He's behind his schedule. So move yer bleedin' selves, right sharp!'

He was a diminutive man, quite ordinary-looking normally, with a narrow nose and a small mouth which he was now licking compulsively, like some sort of exotic lizard. By day, he was employed as a clerk with the Mersey Docks and Harbour Board and, to Jack's certain knowledge, would never consider saying boo to a goose. Not even to a gosling. The situation had to be more than serious if he had resorted to swearing!

Jack helped Pinny out down the steps and held on to his arm as he hobbled towards what had been the A.F.S. post. There were at least six men crumpled in the mess of exploded sandbags from which the building was made. There were sandbags everywhere, strewn across the street, hanging from window ledges, wrapped round bent and leaning lamp posts. A great gaping hole was where the roof had been.

‘Quick. Round the back. There are more round the back.’ Alf, the driver, looked decidedly demonic. It *could* have been the flames which were reflected in his eyes.

Jack let go of his hold on Pinny and raced on ahead into the back entry behind the street. It was deathly quiet there, but the bells of a fire engine could be heard getting closer.

Directly in front of him, suspended across the high walls like a bridge, was a heavy iron bench. On it were three men, still sitting there. The whole thing had been blown through the roof like that. It had not been the force of the explosion that had killed them. It had been the heavy sand bags. Their necks were obviously broken. The ambulance would have been too late in any case.

Jack’s stomach lurched into his upper ribs. His clenched fists began to bang compulsively against the tin of his helmet, his knuckles immediately raw. He could not take his eyes off the bodies on the bench.

He was still fixed in that position when the others caught up with him, Pinny’s face grey with pain.

‘Get them down,’ called the driver. ‘Get them bloody down off there.’

‘But...’ Jack was not allowed to finish his sentence.

‘But what? This place will be swarming with kids by morning. Do you want them gawping at that lot. Quick as you can or you’ll bloody know about it!’

Jack began to scale the right hand side of the wall, his feet uncharacteristically clumsy. The driver was close behind him.

‘We’ll go straight back to the prison after we’ve dealt with this. The other road might be clear.’

The return to the hospital was in the company of nine corpses stacked on to the stretchers. Jack and Pinny had to stand up. Jack was leaning against the back wall, the partition between the ambulance and the cab.

The drone of yet another wave of approaching bombers infiltrated the sombre dark of the contained space. And then a clatter-clatter-clatter-clatter.

Jack and Pinny hardly dared breathe as they listened for all they were worth, hunched in an attitude of alarm at each end of the ambulance. Where was it coming from?

The metallic clatter increased in intensity. It sounded so close as to be almost on top of them.

'My God! The buggers are machine-gunning us now!'

Jack was exhausted. Streaks of grime had found the weary creases in his face; around his eyes, on either side of his mouth. He was using the wall as support.

Pinny staggered along the length of the floor until he could pull Jack forward. He held on to the top stretcher with one hand, the other clutching at Jack's chest, jerking him into a clumsy embrace.

The rattling ceased.

'Machine-guns, my arse!'

The violent convulsions which were still shaking Jack's body almost had them both down on the floor. He was totally unaware that he was in that condition until Pinny brought his attention to it.

'Whoa, whoa there,' he kept repeating until Jack had steadied a little. 'It was your helmet, and your water bottle, you daft bugger. They were banging against the back. It wasn't machine guns at all. It was you, you daft sod! Where would machine guns be coming from? Unless it was our lot gone berserk.'

Jack turned his head awkwardly to stare at the wall; he could hardly believe that it was free of bullet scars. It was just a plain wall covered in dismal greyish paint.

He tried to release himself from Pinny's grasp, embarrassed, but Pinny would not let go of the front of Jack's coat. The situation was reversed. He was now supporting him.

They held on to each other in a kind of hopeless embrace until the ambulance reached the hospital. Then they did an immediate turn-round and went back to Walton Gaol.

Pinny never did get his broken foot attended to. It seemed of minor importance by the end of that ugly night.

* * *

Fran no longer went to the shelter in the key-park up the road. In the early days of the bombing she had, with Alexandra wrapped in a hooded cape that she had made for her from a blanket. She had made that after she had fallen down the stairs with the child in her arms, tripping over the trailing ends of a shawl. It had scared her, that accident, although neither of them was harmed. So she had made the cape as a safer option.

They were then living in a terraced house in Hanford Avenue. The shelter had been good, the neighbours had been good. They were cheerful company for her when Jack was on duty, which was three nights a week. But then, to her unmitigated fury, lots of people from Bootle had chosen to invite themselves to their shelter; invaded it almost. It had become overcrowded with children and babies and Alexandra had indeed caught the infamous impetigo which Izzie had warned against all those years ago. To make matters worse, she caught whooping cough as well. The child developed a reverse sleeping pattern and howled all night, every night. She kept everyone awake in the shelter and there were complaints. They were, in effect, asked to go elsewhere. The request had been couched in not quite such polite terms and Fran's prejudice against "Bootleites"as she called them, became further entrenched.

She took to huddling under the stairs in her own house, Alexandra clutched to her amongst the brooms and buckets, in-between which she had improvised a bed. She was glad to be there. She would not share a shelter with such people, not ever again. She was echoing her mother in that, and she knew it.

Dodo's accounts of the transformation of the cellar at Oakshot Road occupied her thoughts on more than one occasion. Fa had reinforced the ceiling, Dodo told her; her eyes wide with astonishment that such an array of extra supports was physically possible. Their mother had furnished the rooms down there almost as lavishly as it was upstairs, if you did not count the bunks which they all slept on. There were oil lamps just like the ones at Babyll, carpets on the floors, a proper stove. A store room crammed with tins of food. Everything. And their area, well beyond the docks, was not getting anything like the hammering that the city was.

Dodo had not meant to be boastful or unkind when she relayed such things, Fran was sure. It was quite beyond her to be a troublemaker of that sort and she was the only one in the family to risk regular contact, Fran reminded herself. Dodo wasn't defying their mother just to crow about being superior.

But as Fran hid under her eiderdown that night, she and the child alone, the whole house shaking above her until they were both deep in plaster dust and soot, she did argue with herself that perhaps the pride with which she viewed her own stand against the Reynolds might be, could be, interpreted as stubbornness. Maybe she had been in the wrong from the start?

Such thoughts were banished by the time Jack and Pinny arrived back, filthy, smoke-begrimed and almost catatonic with weariness.

Pinny staggered straight upstairs to his room. Jack was leaning against the dresser as she prepared breakfast, Alexandra, chattering away in indecipherable baby talk, perched on her hip.

'You look like a ghost,' she said.

But Jack was asleep standing up. Asleep on his feet, like a horse. She had to wake him when it was time for him to get ready to go to work. Then a bowl of porridge and he was off.

Pinny remained in bed, his mouth wide open with the pain in his foot, but he did not allow any sound to emerge.

It was at the R.A.F. Medical Board at the start of the war that the two had met up again. Jack had only been in touch with Pinny via the letters to and from the Seminary to Pinny's brother. He had occasionally sneaked in a note of his own but he was extremely wary of what he communicated. He suspected that censorship was in operation. Pinny had obviously felt the same as neither the family, nor Jack at the time, had received the faintest inkling that he had been rusticated for seducing the pretty daughter of the village post-mistress and had been summarily packed off in disgrace.

He had not gone home. War had been declared and he had immediately volunteered for the R.A.F. and had ultimately turned up in Queen Mary's Ballroom on Lime Street, scene of many a former conquest, but which now had been hastily transformed into a medical centre. There he had made the disconcerting discovery that his eyesight was failing rapidly. He did not pass the medical.

Jack had jauntily turned up at Queen Mary's at the appointed time, duly proud of the acceptance letter tucked safely in his pocket. He was slightly impatient at the need for the formality ahead of him. Disappointment of the first order was the result.

The necessity for the buying-up of virtually the whole stock of Boots No.1 by the week, a habit which had gone on for *years*, was at last explained. He had a duodenal ulcer; had probably had it for some considerable length of time. He was exempt from military service. The estimated recovery period was well into the next decade.

He had found this diagnosis puzzling as well as frustrating. On previous occasions, when he had actually collapsed with the severity of the pain in his stomach, most usually, and to his eternal embarrassment during swimming parties, he had ended up in hospital for 'observation'. Nothing as serious as an ulcer had ever been observed, let alone suggested. He had almost been made to feel that his symptoms were imaginary. At Lime Street it was spotted straight away and then confirmed by two other medics. A barium meal and an X-Ray had clinched it. Becoming a flyer for the R.A.F. had been as much a fantasy as Fran's dreams of being evacuated to Wales.

It was when he was emerging from the dance hall that he had come across Pinny sitting on the steps smoking a contemplative cigarette, as disconsolate as himself. Jack's overwhelming gloom was considerably lifted by this unexpected reunion with his friend and the sneaking sense of satisfaction it gave him to have Pinny back, once his friend's miraculous presence there had been explained. It proved that his doubts regarding the alleged vocation were vindicated and if they had not been in a public place he would have hugged him for it, serial fornicator or not.

He had joined him on the steps but their jubilation in having found each other again was somewhat marred by the appearance of Neville K.

In Jack's opinion, Neville K. was a bit of a devious bugger. He had always been aware that he was a drinking pal of Fa Reynolds. They belonged to the same club. Dodo had lacked the tact to refrain from boasting about it and Fran had passed it on.

It made Jack feel uncomfortable in his presence. He suspected that his every move and, more particularly his every utterance, was recorded for use as a conversation piece at the Burlington. He did not think that he was flattering himself by suspecting this. He knew that he had good reasons. The Reynolds were not attracted to the discussion of wider issues. They generally confined their immediate interest to the doings of other people. As the family was so large they did not have to look far for subjects for gossip. And books were conspicuous by their absence in the house at Oakshot Road. *John Bull* seemed to be the sum total of their reading. Philistine they were, according to his judgement. Philistinic busybodies.

Neville K. had not been invited to accompany Jack to the medical centre at Queen Mary's. Once he had learned, via Fran, that that was where Jack was headed, he had invited himself. Jack had the uncharitable thought that Izzie Reynolds had put him up to it. Neville himself had already been accepted into the Air Force. He had been passed as A1 and would soon be off to Bournemouth for training.

Neville was decidedly superior in his attitude once he had established that the two sitting on the steps below him were rejects. He refused their offer of a cigarette, claiming that he had to get back.

Jack intuitively knew that the details of his own ineligibility would be reported back to the Reynolds within minutes of Neville K. emerging from the railway station. There would be further reason for him being regarded as a *persona non grata* in that household, if they needed further reason, which he felt sure they didn't. He cursed his ill-luck. It did not occur to him to surmise that perhaps the bigoted small-mindedness which had led his mother-in-law to hound him and Fran in the first place might have contributed to the ulcerated condition of his duodenum and, in fact, been the root cause of his present dilemma.

He only blamed himself. It was his failure. Sneakingly, and with a deal of contempt for the tenacity of superstition, he thought that it was probably all his own fault. When he was small he had been told about lapsed Catholics. They would surely die in a state of mortal sin and go straight to hell. He had believed it. He had prayed for them at Mass; earnestly prayed for them. He had been in a state of acute anxiety if they happened to be the parents of someone he knew, like Danny McGuire, whose parents never went to church. He had pitied Danny. Now he was one of them and was paying the price. The state of his stomach could most likely be put down to divine retribution of some sort.

And then there was Pinny. His case must be even worse. He was to go gradually blind because of his sin which was patently worse than his own. He had manifestly cocked a snook at the priesthood!

But Pinny seemed to be oblivious of any such danger hanging over his head. He was leaning on his elbow, watching Neville K. hurrying towards the station.

'I can't fathom why they took him,' Pinny was saying, 'for one thing, he's a bloody bantam, if he's anything. Look at him, he'd hardly come up to my shoulder.'

'Yes, but he's got very keen eyesight, I can guarantee that, and a stomach made of iron by all accounts. That will make up for what he lacks in height. Anyway, he won't be flying,' said Jack, 'he is a meat importer. He'll apply for Catering or the Pay Corps or something.'

'Well, good luck to him! His pretty face won't help him much either, I can tell you.'

Neville had almost disappeared into the distance. Pinny had a strange, frowning expression on his face as he continued to watch him go. Jack looked at him sharply. He suspected then that something other than Pinny's irrepressible penchant for postmistresses had a great deal to do with his precipitate re-appearance in Liverpool. But he did not want to know any more than he knew already and would no more dream of asking. His own troubles were enough to be going on with.

With his usual good-nature he invited Pinny to stay with them at Hanford Avenue. Fran had welcomed him without a second thought and he was still there, a sort of unofficial lodger. He felt that he could not go back to join the family firm. His mother was adamantly refusing to have anything to do with him. She was so ashamed, so humiliated, that she ignored him if she came across him in the street. He got a job as a mechanic in a garage. Mechanics were in great demand, even Lou Bundenell was working on ambulance maintenance, but she did it on a voluntary basis. She also manned a reception centre for bombed-out families. She was there most nights.

She had been on duty the night of the Walton Gaol fire and her time had almost been as eventful as Jack's. Brownlow St. had been badly hit, the railway lines coming in to St. Michael's Station, Southwood Road, the prison, of course, and the Nurses' Home at Fazakerly, plus her own reception centre.

Some of the casualties there had been people who had been bombed out on the Monday night. A huge crater was left in the road just short of the church hall which was where they were all assembled, prior to moving in to the shelter. All the windows in the surrounding shops had been blown out and there were goods of every conceivable kind spilled over the pavements. A little higher up from them, sticks of bombs had wrecked the houses and undermined the foundations so that their fronts loomed over the crater like old medieval buildings. But these were not quaint old houses in even quainter market towns, these were tall city houses about to fall.

There was nowhere safe anywhere for her families, it seemed. Scores of people, mostly women and children, trying to exist in a tiny space, sleeping on floors, sharing one lavatory, living on hand-outs until the next raid, which maybe they would get through. Maybe not. There was nowhere safe anywhere and they joked and laughed and fought and blasphemed their way through it, as entertainingly as a turn on the Music Hall.

There was something very special about the spirit in Liverpool. It had been there even before the war, she recollected. And she was glad that she had not missed it, dire as things were. Portsmouth had a different feel altogether and she wondered whether it was because Liverpool had always been a vibrant merchant port as opposed to a centuries-old naval base with all that that entailed. And then of course, it lacked the Irish element. She was beyond defining the Irish element, despite the time spent in Dublin and her relationship with Tim. But she knew that if it was indefinable it was nonetheless what gave the city its uniqueness.

Her musings were interrupted by one of the Heaton daughters on her way to work.

'Oh, Mrs. B. Have you heard? All those firemen being machine-gunned last night?'

'No! When? Where?'

'Just up the road from here. They were trying to get people out, you know. It was such a bad raid. They had only stopped because they saw it happen just after they'd gone past. The whole junction went up and houses on all sides. They were on their way to somewhere else, but they'd stopped to help. Isn't it awful?'

The girl's face was stricken, her attempt to look grown up abandoned as she clutched bunches of her cardigan up to her mouth.

'It's just wicked, that's what it is.'

'But who was shooting, Carrie? Where was it coming from?'

'The air! They were shooting from the air. From the planes. You could not even see them, but they couldn't have been so high up. Oh, Mrs. B. it's coming to something, isn't it? It's really coming to something, you know.'

Lou put her arm round the frightened girl.

'When did you hear about this, Carrie?'

'Not long since. Dad heard about it from Reg Williams. He was with them. But he's safe; he's safe. He was inside one of the houses when it happened. He's back home now, but I'm telling you, he says it was murder. Plain murder. Mother's that upset, she knows most of them. At least she did. She's just beside herself, you know and I've had to go and leave her; I've got to get to the shop.'

'Carrie, you go on now or else you'll be late. And don't worry, I'll pop in to see your mother on my way. Don't worry now, there's a good girl.'

She stood waving to her as Carrie continued on her way. Then she turned abruptly and made for the Heatons.

'She's right. It bloody well is coming to something!' she muttered to herself as she broke into a run.

So Jack might not have been far wrong after all, when he thought that the ambulance was being machine-gunned. But, by that time, he had forgotten the incident. He was busy helping to sort out the wreckage that had once been his office.

* * *

Despite the bombing, life went on pretty well as normal. Lou, however, had lost her usual poise. She was inordinately excited about Stella's pending visit, the first that her daughter had agreed to make since her eventful return from Spain. Both she and Dee Mason had managed to get out via the Pyrenees after the fall of

Barcelona. They had only risked a train once they were safely on French soil; their papers having, overnight, turned into perilously incriminating documents on the peninsula. They had ultimately turned up on Maddy's doorstep where Stella had been ever since, Dee having volunteered for the Navy and commenced training as a submariner. He was conveniently close, stationed on the Solent, and Stella was coming up to discuss with her mother plans for her wedding. Lou was beside herself with joy.

Tim just laughed at her.

'Why on earth you set so much store on Stella being married is beyond me when you adamantly refuse to do anything about us,' he said, 'I could understand it if you were hell-bent on marriage to me!'

'Not now, not ever.' It was a constant refrain in their relations with each other.

Dee Mason's virtues had become the sole subject in Stella's letters. Her mother, instead of rejoicing because her worst fears were over regarding the dreaded spinsterhood of her one and only offspring, took to worrying about the dangers of submarines.

But when Dee managed to get leave and he and Stella came up together she came to realise that no-one could be more right. Added to that, they had survived so many dangers to date that going to war in a submarine seemed almost insignificant in comparison. Dee had evolved from a mop-headed, anxious-to-please little boy into a sensible, down-to-earth adult who was obviously capable of enormous courage. Lou had adored him as a very small boy. That she adored him even more having had her precious daughter returned to her from his obviously competent hands remained without saying. She admired what he had become and she welcomed him as a prospective son-in-law with all her heart. They made a fine looking couple, Dee and Stella; more importantly, they were good for each other. She was proud of her daughter's choice.

But she still caught herself worrying sometimes and she still rejected any notion of embarking on the married state herself.

She and Tim were lovers. It was not with the same desperate urgency as when Lou had gone to his bed as a girl, but she still loved to be with him. She loved him a great deal. However, some instinct had warned her, or perhaps it was the recollection of previous betrayal, not to allow him to think that she was beholden to him in any way. She lived her life separate from his and felt that she always must.

Yet again, Lou's judgement was flawed. For the first time since 1915, Tim Dundonald had found a meaning for his existence. The discovery of his daughter had given him a sense of purpose he thought had been lost forever. All the cynical womanising, all the irresponsibility, the casual, temporary nature of his way of living had fallen away. His gratitude for the salvation which Lou had brought about was very different from when she had actually rescued him from probable death. He had almost forgotten that. He had almost forgotten how she was as a girl. Now she was the focus of all his thoughts, his actions and his hopes.

And she kept him at arm's length, fearful of trusting him too much, of giving him too much of herself, wary of his desire to be a complete family.

But they often behaved as such. She had nursed his mother in Dublin and had only returned after old Mrs Dundonald had died just before war had been declared. When Stella came back for this wondrous visit, they all stayed in the house he had bought in Hightown; a big sprawling place with acres of wooded garden; inland, away from the beach. Lou was in her element there but she would never risk allowing herself to become mistress of it.

Yet it was a haven she took for granted when she needed to be away from Norton Street with its constant demands and the intermittent deafening, deadly, nocturnal symphony of bombardment. Apart from the noise of lazy aircraft on the occasions when they flew overhead, there was no inkling that a war was going on at all at the house in Hightown. In the summer it was all heavy air, drowsy with the humming of bees, and spacious cool rooms to rest in and in the winter, when it snowed, the view from every window was like the dreams she had as a child in India, of England being a magical, white land of be-silvered, glistening trees and mysterious shadows.

It became her retreat from the brutal reality with which she chose to surround herself on a daily basis. It offered a respite from the acuteness of her social conscience which Tim recognised as the driving force behind almost everything that she did. And he admired her for her unflinching, unfailing selflessness in that respect. He approved and he supported. He too could be found at the reception centre for victims of the bombing and he provided it with all manner of equipment: blankets, pots and pans, cutlery, crates of tea. She never asked where it all came from. But she knew that he was frequently at the docks and had become a popular figure with the men who worked there. She suppressed the promptings of her social conscience when she thought about the implications of black-marketeering. No-one had ever claimed that she was a saint, nor did she ever think of herself as one.

Stella was not to be married from Hightown, as she would have been under other circumstances. It was too risky to rely on the railways being intact. The railways had become a constant target during the bombing raids. They had decided that she would be married from the Lonsdales' house, having once accepted that whatever disaster Lonsdale brought down upon the day it would have to be accommodated. Plans went forward at a great rate and all kinds of manoeuvres worked out to foil the anticipated problems with rationing, transport and just about everything else.

The one sadness in all the excitement of the wedding plans was that the Jamiesons could not entertain the thought of travelling to Hampshire. Stella had wanted Fran to be matron-of-honour but that scheme was doomed to disappointment. Hampshire might as well have been the moon as far as the Jamiesons were concerned. It was frighteningly far, and to travel in wartime with a toddler was something that Fran was not prepared to consider, not even for Stella.

The truth was that Fran was somewhat in awe of Stella these days. Her long absence and the exotic nature of her adventures had placed a strain on their friendship. It had come to depend on letters. The difference in their surroundings was most evident in the content of these exchanges. Stella's were full of school news as she had, to a large extent, taken on Maddy's job at The Green and of Dee, of course, and their search for somewhere to live and how, wherever it was, it must have a copper beech tree in the garden. Fran considered herself lucky if she saw a tree at all that wasn't blasted to Kingdom Come, and she certainly wasn't fussy as to what variety it might be if she did. A slight hint of irritation with the Southerner that Stella was obviously reverting to ensued from receipt of such missives. More than a hint of exasperation occurred when often whole letters were devoted to the latest episodes in the ongoing saga of Lonsdale's misadventures.

Fran became heartily sick of Lonsdale. She could not understand how everyone put up with him or, more importantly, *why* they did. He was plainly and simply an upper-class twit in her book and she dismissed him as such. He bored her. Stella's devotion to him bored her. Her replies to Hampshire became a deliberate chronicle of the Blitz. Graphic details, with no deference to sentimentality. Stella needed to know that there were more important things to deal with than an idiot walking backwards into an open manhole or breaking his nose inspecting a sprung mousetrap when he was more than old enough to have known better. Such things as she had to contend with for instance. The intervals between their letters grew longer.

Fran, in truth, was in a state of suppressed terror and somewhere in her subconscious she knew that she was being unjust to Stella. She was using her as a scapegoat. She had been in this nervous condition since Jack had left the St. John's Ambulance. Then she had relied on the protection which the red crosses, so prominently displayed, had given him even though she had been well aware that it was a dubious dependence. He had joined the Fire Service. Pinny had gone with him and she had hardly had an easy moment since.

It was typical of Jack, the way that it happened. One of his colleagues on the ambulances, an oldish, grey-haired man who lived off Walton Road, had returned home the morning after the prison bombing to find his house flattened and his wife and three children killed. They had burned to death. A call went out for volunteers for the Fire Service and Jack had gone, Pinny soon after. It was a different experience altogether, for all of them.

But it was only during the nights when the men were on duty that dramatic happenings were likely to occur, otherwise their lives went on as normal. The devastation that they lived and worked amongst became commonplace. They hardly noticed it. And the raids were not always heavy, some nights there weren't any at all and Jack and Pinny would spend freezing hours up on the roofs of buildings, Jack's binoculars raking the empty skies for enemy aircraft which failed to appear. Pinny pretended to use his binoculars too but he could not see much. He knew perfectly well that Jack's sharp eyes were working for him as well. It was a fact that his eyesight was getting worse; a fact that he tried desperately to keep to himself. Even with his glasses, he could hardly see to read. He just made a show of doing so. He felt that it was better that way. He had always hated fuss.

Jack's sisters would visit when they could and then the house rang with laughter and lively news. It was through them that they learned that Auntie B. had sailed for America.

America was the stuff that dreams were made of. From Dodo, they heard that all the young boys, Fran's two younger brothers and a cartload of cousins, had been organized to go to a branch of the Mackenzies in Buffalo on the Canadian border, but they had not gone. The previous evacuation ship to theirs had been torpedoed and Izzie and her sisters had not dared to risk the loss of their boys. The fact that the girls had not been considered in this rush for safety did not escape notice, particularly on Jack's part. He never failed to be bemused by the favouritism shown towards the males in the Reynolds family. He chose instead to wonder what on earth Auntie B. would do once she arrived there. The Jamiesons had no convenient relatives to go to, as far as he was aware.

He had never managed to discover the real story behind the incident with Auntie B. His mother shut up like a clam when he tried to broach the subject. The fact that so much of a mystery was made out of it was all the more tantalising for Jack and Fran. They did feel that they had a vested interest, having suffered the most in the unfolding of the whole drama. An apology would have been welcome too. None ever came.

What did arrive was news of the eventual outcome and it could not have been worse. Auntie B. was the victim of a hit-and-run accident. She had hardly been in New York a month. After her death, the child was put on the first ship home at the Jamiesons' urgent request. He was now destined to be brought up alongside the younger ones in Monk Street. The driver of the vehicle was never traced and the mystery, far from being resolved, acquired even more of a legendary status. Jack and Fran, when they looked back, decided that they had better count their blessings. Whether she had met her end by accident or by design, they had got off lightly in comparison, they felt.

They began to filter back to Birkenhead after that. The family behaved as if the breach had never occurred. There was a war on.

Nobody bore grudges when there was a war on. There was too much else to think about.

On Fran's side, Fa's sister was good to them. Aunt Hannah made sure that she kept an eye on her niece and warmed to her and her little girl as if they were her own. She had never had the chance to have children herself. Her husband had been killed on the Somme in 1916, not long after their marriage. Three of her brothers had met the same fate. Fa was the only one she had left. But she didn't help his errant daughter just because he had asked her to.

It was obvious, certainly to Fran if not to Jack, that she was in constant touch with Fa regarding Fran's well-being, but it was a very different scene from the tale-telling indulged in by Neville K. Aunt Hannah was kindness itself and she would not have a word said against Jack whom she considered to be an admirable young man and a gem to be treasured.

Whether it was a direct result of this considered judgement on the part of his sister, or the fact that Fa was weary of his wife's neurosis where Jack Jamieson was concerned, he ensured that his erstwhile 'blue-eyed girl' was in receipt of a beautiful little piano delivered to Hanford Avenue. The piano stool which came with it contained all her old sheet music from the drawing room at home.

Fran was overjoyed. Many an impromptu little gathering ensued from the advent of the piano, especially if Monica and Clare appeared, because then, either one of them would have Alexandra on one hip, swinging to the music, freeing Fran to play. Their voices could be heard right to the end of the avenue if the windows were open. None of the neighbours thought to complain.

They chose all the tried and tested favourites: 'Stardust', 'The Birth of the Blues', and all the Ivor Novello latest hits. If she could not get the sheet music, Fran would play by ear. She had a good ear and was particularly fond of Charlie Coons and could imitate his style to perfection. She became a minor celebrity in the street because of this. People began to look forward to hearing her piano as they passed by. It cheered them up. It cheered her up to think that Fa had not forgotten her. But sometimes that thought made her cry as well.

Dodo came as often as she could. She missed Neville K. He was waiting for a posting. It sounded ominously as if it would be overseas and Dodo was almost frantic about that potentiality. Their brother Neville was already on his way to North Africa and young Charlie determined to join the Navy as soon as he was old enough. Dodo would creep round to Hanford Avenue for comfort, knowing full well that she was in defiance of her mother's orders.

She took advantage of Izzie's distraction after the departure of her eldest son to indulge in downright insubordination. She became quite clever at covering her tracks. When the weather was good at the weekends, for instance, she would ostensibly telephone one of her friends to suggest that they catch the earliest train to Southport on Sunday morning. Then Dodo would jump on at the Waterloo stop and search the carriages until she found Fran who would be waiting for her with little Alex and a huge bag of swimming gear.

They would spend the whole day at the lido. It spelt glamour, the swimming pool at Southport. It was huge and modern with sweeping terraces and an impressive-looking restaurant. They had no idea what it served in those days of rationing, they never tested it out, but it looked like something that one might see at the pictures and Fran loved it there. She much preferred Southport to going over the water to New Brighton. The pool there was not nearly so well-designed in her view. But they did go there if they were meeting up with her sisters-in-law. It was easier for them to get to New Brighton. Dodo did not always join them then. She found the boisterousness of Jack's sister Clare a bit intimidating. She preferred to make the plausible excuse that she could not get away and stay at home.

Fran also preferred Southport because it was perfect for Alexandra. There was a paddling pool and a slide and bubbling fountains in which she could play. On the occasions when Jack could go, he was solely intent on teaching her to swim. It was imperative that she became a strong swimmer. Memories of Molly's fate were uppermost in his mind whenever the child was near water. That was also the reason why they always went to either one of the big swimming pools. Fran was discouraged from allowing Alexandra to go anywhere near the beach. The Mersey Channel presented far too many dangers.

The beaches were out-of-bounds for other reasons too. Some of the shipping, and most recently the pilot boats out at the bar, had been blown up by mines. Miles of shoreline were cut off by rolls of barbed wire and there were gun placements at intervals as far as you could see and double rows of tank traps in case of invasion. The fascination of the seaside was a delight Alexandra was not to enjoy for a very long time.

But she enjoyed her father's efforts to turn her into an athlete. And she was precocious with it. Before she could even sit up he had her swinging from a broom handle. She could do somersaults and cartwheels almost as soon as she could walk. He was determined to remedy the bad start she had had when his constant fear had been that her survival was far from certain. The puny little creature she had been on her entry into the world was gone forever. Now she had such chubby cheeks that her eyes almost disappeared when she smiled, which she did a great deal when she was being put through her paces.

Her husband irritated Fran almost to death by insisting on doing gymnastics with his daughter whilst his supper dried up in the oven and she would grumble at him for the rest of the evening. She became expert at grumbling at Jack, did Fran, and he never took the blindest bit of notice. He knew that she didn't mean it seriously, it was just her way of dealing with things; it was just her way of coping.

She did cope with Jack's move into the Fire Service eventually. She got used to it as they all learned to get used to everything that in peace time would have caused a fit of the horrors.

He would come back with stories that made her laugh.

When he had first been appointed, he was asked if he would drive the Fire Engine. He had immediately imagined himself in a great roaring machine, helmet gleaming, racing through streets to the rescue. Real *Boy's Own* stuff it would be. His heart had skipped an excited beat or two in anticipation of it. Fran howled unrestainedly when he told her that the 'fire-engine' he was to drive turned out to be an ancient Buick car, trailing a tender.

His job was to drive the Buick to the great water store and pump water into the tender to augment the tanks on the real machines. The Buick then had its moment of glory as it raced behind the professionals. The big fire-engine would have its bells clanging, men to attention in their positions all along its sides, hatchets shining from their belts. The Buick, crammed to the gills with Jack's team, would bounce along behind it, the tender swaying with an alarming will of its own, but usually making it to the ultimate destination. Where the Buick had come from originally was anybody's guess. It had probably been donated by some wealthy toff from Blundellsands.

Jack's sense of being badly-done-to was assuaged however when he was made leader of the section. Fran's wasn't. He was absent all the more often, organising training sessions with his team. Every task was synchronised to the second, every contingency prepared for. He even taught them all First Aid from his Ambulance Service days. His team was the envy of all those who could not compete with their speed. Fran meanwhile, reminded herself that there was a war on and that she should not expect him to be at home playing with the baby. When he actually was, he made the most of it and Fran would be mollified for a day or too.

There was a fussy fellow on Jack's team who drove him mad. He was a veritable know-all and a show-off. He caused Jack, who disliked him for this, no end of trouble. He wore very good clothes off-duty: expensive suits, a Homburg hat, yet his daytime job was nothing to speak of. He got on Jack's nerves.

Petrol was rationed, of course, and if the number of raids had exceeded the average, there were occasions when the allocation was insufficient. Then they had problems. Jack would scour everywhere looking for fuel. The legitimate petrol was coloured red in an attempt to stop black-marketeering and prevent theft.

The particular incident which Jack related to Fran with a deal of venom, had at its centre the insufferable Know-All. He had insisted to Jack that he had found a source of clear-coloured petrol, not only available but cheap. 'Don't touch it with a barge pole,' Jack had warned. 'Keep well clear of that, it'll be trouble.' The Buick had become his pride and joy. He wanted no risks taken with it no matter how desperate they were. But the man took it upon himself to pour his 'find' in the tank. It was water.

'Venomous' is a bit of an understatement in describing Jack's response. However, it was Lou who sorted the problem in the absence of Pinny who was nowhere to be found. She came hurrying over, tool bag over her shoulder, and she stripped the engine there and then, draining the precious oil into someone's old baby bath which she had managed to scrounge, pursing her lips in agony at the terrible waste and joining Jack in colourful condemnation of the idiot who had caused such necessity, punctuated by grunts of effort as she went about her business with a variety of spanners and wrenching tools. The old car went better than ever as a result of her attentions which was a lucky break for the guilty party. It didn't teach him a lesson though. He was still as much of a Know-All as he had ever been.

Fortunately he had moved on elsewhere by the time that they were called out during one of the daylight raids when the Customs House was hit and all the big furniture shops at the bottom of Bold Street and Renshaw Street were on fire. Jack could not have done with him then, expounding his theories and mucking up the team's immaculate synchronisation.

The windows had been blown out of all the shops and the passers-by were dragging all the good stuff into the road to save it from being damaged in the burning buildings. The street was full of three-piece suites, cabinets, bedheads, ornate mirrors, all mixed up with fire hoses and pumps because the water mains had burst and water was everywhere, swirling around that absurd jumble of furniture in the middle of the road. Fire blazed on every side and right in the centre of the heap was a drunken sailor, unconcernedly playing a piano, as happy as Larry and no-one taking any notice of him as, like an army of dedicated ants, they got on with the job of dealing with the flames and the flood.

Fran's stories were not quite so tightly packed with event, but they did not lack drama for all that. Most of the things she reported to Jack she had gleaned from the neighbours who urged her to go with them to the proper shelter, instead of staying by herself when Jack was away at nights. But she never would. There was a fair bit of disorderly conduct in the public shelters, drunkenness, brawling and even worse... Her snobbery prevailed.

Well before it was all over the papers, Fran heard about the man who had attacked his wife because she had asked him for a separation. He was roaring drunk by the time they got into the shelter and had attacked her in front of everybody. Punched her black and blue. With the greatest difficulty someone had got her to the hospital; there were no ambulances available for such a contingency. That was the night that particular hospital was bombed. The wife never came back. It was the other wives who reported him to the police; had him put away.

Such stories appalled her. She would prefer to take her chances on her own rather than expose Alexandra to behaviour of that sort. So she sat in semi-darkness, night after night, not trusting the blackout at the windows to contain more than minimal light and when the choirs of sirens wailed she would creep under the stairs, the child hugged close, and wait for Jack to return.

16. Waterfronts 1941

AN EXTRAORDINARY interlude occurred in the spring of 1941, which took Jack away from the ordinary pattern of his life and gave him an insight into a world which had long intrigued him.

It came about because he had persuaded Pinny to join him over the water and have a drink in the McGuire's pub. Rumours had reached them that Danny McGuire had been lost at sea. At least everybody was of that gloomy opinion. He was last seen, so the story went, in an open boat, along with other officers and men, after their ship had been torpedoed.

They did know that Danny had been commissioned in the Royal Navy but they had not seen him for months, not since he had come to visit when he had last been on leave and it had become a good enough excuse for a party at Hanford Avenue. Now, it seemed, Danny was a gonner, or else a prisoner somewhere. But no-one had had any confirmation of any such thing.

Jack decided that he and Pinny must go to see the McGuires. The snag was that, whereas Jack would also fit it in with a visit to his family, Pinny was averse to crossing the water. He behaved as though he was in danger of being instantly stoned by any member of his family who might be encountered by accident, however distant the relative might prove to be. He had a great number of relatives in Birkenhead, he claimed. The McLaughlins populated the place, it was risky.

'Don't be so bloody soft!' Jack told him. 'What's risky about it? They can't kill you.'

'I know, but it'll be embarrassing. They'll tell my mother if they see me over there and she's cut me off without the proverbial shilling. It'll upset her. It's not on, Jack.'

'It's your attitude that's not bloody on. It's pathetic. And what's more, it's about time that you went to see your mother and got things straight. She can't hold it against you forever that you are not the priest she always wanted you to be. That's her problem, not yours. Besides, she can't be as frightening as all that.'

'She's not frightening at all. I'm the one who's frightened. Of causing more hurt. She was so proud...'

'What she was really proud of was being able to boast to the neighbours, *my* mother being one of them! Forget it then. I'll go to the McGuire's on my own.'

Jack looked at Pinny sitting miserably in the shabby armchair opposite him. He seemed to be trying to make himself as small as he could within its enclosed space, yet Pinny was a giant when he was in real danger: when he was surrounded by fire, manning the pumps like a maniac or heaving debris away on bomb-sites.

Jack ruminated on the attitudes of mothers. They wielded such power. They thought of their children as extensions of themselves. They never let go. 'We are always their children however old we might think we are. And there is this inalienable right they have to demand that they know what is best for us. They assume it; look at us, Fran and me.'

He never liked to remind himself of what had happened there, particularly in Fran's case. He forced his attention back to Pinny. His problem was a bit more complex than most, he supposed. He understood that and regretted his impatience.

But by the time that Jack had got himself organized to go, Pinny had changed his mind. They went across the water together. It was after they got off the ferry that Pinny began to hover in doorways and insist on Jack negotiating corners ahead of him, then lag behind because his lame foot meant that he could not keep up with Jack's stride. When they reached the church where they had both been servers and Jack a choir boy, Pinny's physical discomfort was much in evidence. Jack could only guess at his mental discomfiture. He suggested that they take a rest. They eschewed the church, deciding to go to the pub a bit further along, a bit of Dutch courage before they faced the McGuires being the excuse.

Sitting with a pint of beer in front of him, having peered round the assembled company and failed to recognise anyone, Pinny regained some of his composure.

'Sorry, Jack,' he said, 'I just feel so stupid.'

'It's not stupid you feel Pin; it's guilt-ridden.'

'Yes.'

They sipped the beer in silence, Jack surreptitiously keeping an eye on the main door. His friend's eyesight was not all that he claimed it was but he did not ever mention it. He knew that it was a sensitive subject. Jack thought about Pinny's machinations to escape the confines of the Seminary in order to join in the war, if that is what he had actually been about. He might just as well have stayed where he was. He would have been better off; he would, at the very least, have been getting proper treatment. It was obstinacy now that he was indulging in, as a sort of punishment; a variation on the old practice of self-flagellation. Monks, Jack had heard, still went in for it. An outlet for guilt. And he knew what the weight of guilt was all about, alright.

'The last time I went to Mass was the Sunday war was declared,' he announced, seemingly out of nowhere.

Pinny downed the dregs of his pint, his eyes shunting in Jack's direction as he did so. Otherwise he might just as well not have heard, his response being silent.

'I was walking back from St. Peter & Paul's on my own that Sunday. Fran had just heard it on the radio when I got in. Ultimatum up. I have never set foot in a church since.'

He did not know if this little confession was helping his friend or making the situation even more uncomfortable. What he was trying to do was to communicate to Pinny that he knew how he felt. Without saying it.

'I knew before though, that it was going to happen,' Jack went on, as if talking to himself. 'I was riding along Queen's Road the previous night and not one of the street lights was on. All I could think of was 'bloody fools; bloody, bloody fools.' Not much use in that though, was there?'

Pinny was examining the bottom of his empty glass, turning the base in a half-circle on the table. His response came suddenly and with no small degree of irony.

'The priests were all for rushing out and blessing the guns. That's when I seriously took up with Peggy the Post. The Cardinals did bless the guns as a matter of fact. No doubt His Holiness himself blessed the ones in Rome. I was not there long enough to find out after that.'

'You did right.'

'Did I?'

Jack got to his feet, swallowing the last of his pint as he did so.

'Another?'

'No. Let's be on our way. Do what we came to do.'

The McGuire pub was another quarter of a mile further on. It was full when they got there but they managed to squeeze their way to the bar through the crush and pay their respects to Danny's father. There was no news which could be said to be optimistic. There was no news of any kind regarding the whereabouts of Danny.

They were urged to elbow along to the end of the bar, if they could see their way to having a little word with Danny's Uncle Joseph before they left. He was sure to appreciate it. He would be pleased to see them. He had been very close to Danny.

They had to do it. It would have been churlish to say that they did not have the time. There was a sea of faces between them and the grey-haired Uncle Joseph propping up the end of the bar counter. They rubbed shoulders and pressed their chests into the backs of perfect strangers and old familiars alike as they struggled through, pint mugs held aloft for safe-keeping. 'Eh, la'! Watch wot yer doin'.' And then, a few bodies further along, 'How are yer Jack? Still playin' golf?' Beery enquiries were breathed straight into their faces as they bumped into erstwhile acquaintances. The usual platitudes were shouted above the general din and often cut short through a needy cough in the eye-stinging, throat-searing smoke which battled with the overriding smell of mothballs emanating pungently from the Sunday suits.

It was one of these coughers, an old chap from Preston who knew Jack's Dad, who accosted them next, pulling Jack towards him with his arm.

'Warra baht t'invasion, then?'

'What about it?' Jack was manoeuvring his glass tankard across the shoulders of the man in front with a degree of delicacy. He wanted to snatch a sip from it before the lot ended up in the sawdust where it was surely destined.

'What invasion?'

'As I 'eard it, there was a right carryin' on over't water. Them bells. That church at top a Bold Street. That what were bombed. St. Luke's, or summat like, that were it.'

'What was 'it'?' Pinny was giving him an impatient shove in the back to move him on. 'What was what?'

'T'invasion.' The old man and all those around him were laughing and coughing, eyes watering, unwiped noses dripping, and no thought of a proper explanation until the barmaid came to the rescue.

'Don't worry love, they're only 'avin you on. They've heard that story of the bells rolling down the hill and everyone thinking it was the alarm for the invasion. Everyone over the water, that is. We wouldn't be so daft over here!'

She was laughing then.

'First I know of it,' said Jack but joined in the joke at the expense of his fellow Liverpudlians. He reckoned it was going to be the only way they could get to the other end of the bar before closing time.

At last they reached Uncle Joseph. He had had his back to them all this while and was genuinely surprised to see them appear under his very nose. He was a big man, Uncle Joseph, and very Irish. A big round open face beamed at them and his voice when it came, was as soft and as deep and as rich as peat-bog. He was determined to get them another drink straight away even though they had not begun the ones they had already transported with such care above the heads of the Sunday, after-church crowd. They had had several more before they hit the fresh air outside when they had to go for the ferry. Jack also had a weekend's extra work ahead of him, on of all places, the docks.

Joseph McGuire was a foreman on the Liverpool docks. He had been bewailing his fate that a convoy was due in bringing long-awaited meat as its cargo and they were short-handed. It was a tricky business, meat. It could not be left in warehouses to go rotten. Jack had been commiserating with him when the idea had come up that perhaps Jack could be an extra hand, just for the weekend. The ships were expected in on Thursday, they would be unloading for days. Pinny had been invited to think about it too, and anyone else they might be able to recruit. The payment was fifteen shillings per day, tantamount to a small fortune. Jack said that he would see what he could do about getting Saturday off.

In the event, he got more than that. He had gone to his boss and explained the dilemma that the cargo coming in was meat and there was a manpower shortage. There would be problems unloading it. His boss, with somewhat undignified alacrity, allowed him to take Thursday and Friday off as well.

Pinny had declined the offer. The unattended break in his foot had healed so badly that it would be of little use up against the rigours of stevedore work. Jack was disappointed. This new experience was on a par with the night that they had spent in the hostel. It was even better, in fact. It was a chance to witness first-hand the working conditions of the men they had supported for so long in the political arena. And Pinny would not be with him.

As it happened, Jack was no longer active in the said political arena. All of that had come to a full stop at the outbreak of the war. He had more pressing calls on his time. Also, he was not so naive that he did not realise that the present conditions would be a far cry from his childhood when, for eight years, a whole community had been jobless. Having lived through that he knew that it had coloured his perspective. When he thought of the waterfront, he thought of the injustice of the tally system when men had had to take their chances with corrupt foremen who wielded the power to choose whether they worked or were sent away empty-handed; whether families such as the Heatons would eat or starve; whether the likes of Tom Heaton had the wherewithal to offer bribes and whether they would have resorted to it even if they had. It was a far cry from all that now. Now ironically, manpower was at a premium. But he only knew the half of it anyway. And in his innocence, driven by idealism, he wanted to know more.

On the following Thursday, he duly presented himself at the dockside; Gladstone Dock it was, an amateur, wearing his oldest clothes and still looking wrong.

There was no problem with the tally of course. He was handed his straight away from the very broad and calloused hands of Danny's Uncle Joseph, augmented by an enigmatic wink. For a moment he wondered whether he was being laughed at. It seemed not. An old hand was duly assigned to show him what to do.

The side of the ship which they were to unload was massively high. He had grown up alongside ships but this one was a veritable mammoth and it looked somehow incongruous against the background of war-shattered docks. It was a mountain of wholeness when everything else around it had the look of ancient debris. But amongst the debris there was rigid discipline and efficient organisation. The meat came up from the hold in a big net; the mammoth disgorging its innards high up above them on to the deck. It went up yet again, hoisted by a crane, and swung across the bluest blue of clear sky towards the storage bay where the dockers stood in a line waiting to receive it. Jack's neck ached with his determination not to miss a thing, but he was soon nudged into action and there was no time for staring then.

The line moved inwards, inside the building. His companion, a lean, wiry man with prominent buck teeth in a furrowed, yet still child-like face that looked as if it should not belong to him, explained to Jack how, when he got the heavy side of beef up on to his shouder, his head must bend over to the left otherwise he could be injured. When his turn came, two fellows lifted the thing on to his shoulder. It had swung through the opening, silhouetted against that incredible light. Despite the physical fitness that Jack tried so hard to maintain, he could feel his knees buckle underneath him for a second. Then he squared himself up and carried it across in the line towards the waggon-loaders at the far end of the floor-space, trying not to stagger and awed that they lifted it from him as if it had been a sack of feathers.

By mid-morning he was not afraid of staggering at all. He had got into the rhythm of it and the hulk of the ship became commonplace; nothing to warrant a second glance even. At midday they stopped and ate their pack-ups and one of his group darted across to a little shop opposite the dock gates and came back with buns; red jam smeared all over the top and something that looked decidedly like wood chippings sprinkled thickly on top of that. Jack accepted his, as a comrade should, and chewed through it in time with the others, composing his expression into what he hoped was infinite pleasure, but the concoction was barely on the borderline of edible by his standards.

Work re-commenced on the whistle. By the end of his shift Jack was stiffer than the sides of beef he had been hauling all day. His thighs felt as though they would fail to push the pedals round as he cycled home through the dusk, the keenness of the air after that bright day promising frost.

Alexandra missed her broom-handle hoistings that night. And the other three to come.

It was only afterwards that he heard about the theft. He had not seen anything of it. He had had no suspicions whatsoever. 'There's a war on, for God's sake!' he had angrily shouted at the particular edition of the newspaper he was reading, with the report from the Police Court in black and white before his eyes, 'A bloody war on! Would you believe it?' And then, 'It wasn't any of my crew, I can tell you that.' Loyalties did not take long to develop with Jack.

But he was set back a bit, disillusioned by the report. It had been carefully planned beforehand, the stealing. Sides of beef had been diverted into specially insulated vans and driven away to be sold to a butcher on the outskirts of the city. He was also to be prosecuted. 'The dodgy bugger!' Jack said.

And there was more. Petrol had been stolen from the stores, whether white or red Jack was unable to ascertain, and then the case of a foreman stevedore with a house full of the most extraordinary collection of property from the passenger ships: a woman's silver dressing set, travelling clocks, shoes, gloves, underwear, bedding, cutlery. Special cars had to be sent to his house to take it all away.

'Just listen to this,' Jack called in the direction of the kitchen where Fran was preparing supper, meatless suffice it to say. 'This fellow claims that he had to do it. He had to take his share like everyone else, otherwise he would not be one of them! I just can't believe it. They were all such decent types. I really can't believe it!'

'Well, you wouldn't,' Fran replied as she came in from the back kitchen, a bowl of steaming cauliflower held well out in front of her in order that the front of her hair did not go frizzy in the wet steam. 'You think that you are wordly-wise, but you are not that at all when you are mixed up in your Socialist thing. They see you coming, Jack. A lamb to the slaughter. Think yourself lucky that you've still got your shirt on your back. Do you want white sauce with this? There's no cheese.'

The cauliflower was being dished out on to the plates. 'The extra money is nice to have though. What shall we do with it?'

'I thought it would buy a decent wedding present for Stella. What do you think?'

Fran drew her lips together. For that moment she looked just like her mother and Jack almost flinched. But Fran was on her feet, supper abandoned; he could hear her going upstairs. On her return she was carrying something folded in brown paper and underneath that, white tissue. When she opened it out it was a beautiful drawn-thread table cloth with delicate embroidery in each corner, one of which was not quite complete.

'I've been making this for her. I have to have something to do all the times when you're out. Will it be alright, do you think? Will it be good enough?'

Jack looked at it, lost in admiration, 'It's exquisite!' he said. 'But how you've managed it with everything else going on, I don't know.'

Fran resisted saying that most of what went on, went on with Jack, not her. Instead, she asked him if he thought that Lou would be able to take it with her to Hampshire, when it was finished. She still had a little bit to do, but it would be sure to be ready before the wedding.

'I'm positive she will,' he replied. 'She'll be delighted to.'

So the extra earnings went into the bank and were forgotten about in the eventful months to come.

* * *

Jack was never again invited to augment the workforce at the dockside even if he had been willing to go. The decision had little to do with Joseph McGuire or any of the other stevedore foremen.

The port of Liverpool was the place from where a good deal of the armaments destined for North Africa were shipped. With the Germans moving into that area of battle in force, the British were most definitely in difficulties. Liverpool became very busy indeed, but it was guns that were hoisted in the nets and swung across the sky to the holds. It was skilful loading that was required and an amateur had no place there any more that spring.

The railways fed the docks; heavy goods trains pounded the lines into the port by the hour.

Everyone knew that there was overcrowding at the bar, berths being prioritised for vessels bound for Africa; incoming ships had to queue. It came as no surprise therefore that enemy aircraft would be attracted to such enticing prizes and they came droning over the sea like so many deadly flying insects towards a honey pot. They came, as usual, by night.

Jack and Pinny were in the sector post having a cup of tea with the Fire Wardens when the siren sounded on the second consecutive night of raids. It was early May; the first touch of summer was just a hint promised in the darkness.

They had been assigned to fire watch and the post was high up on a roof. They were among the relief shift. The explosion was sudden. The cups they had been drinking from vanished. A packet of ten Park Drive belonging to the chap sitting next to Pinny vanished; disappeared into thin air and he had been just about to help himself to one. 'Sod it!' he shouted furiously. 'Them were me bloody fags! I were lookin' forward to that smoke.' But his complaints also hit thin air. The others were gawping in astonishment as all the buttons on the chief warden's coat blew off in one go, transforming themselves into stinging missiles. 'Out of 'ere! Let's be 'avin' yer!' They galvanized into action, out to their respective duties, Jack and Pinny joining the rush for the opening in the sand bags.

It was a heavy raid. It looked as if it was going to be as bad, if not worse, than the previous night. One look made that obvious. Incendiary bombs were dropping in their hundreds, interspersed with the swish and whistle of high explosives. They were aiming for the railway bridges and hitting everything within miles. The whole city was going up. The familiar smell of cattle-cake from the warehouses had become scorched, fired. It stung their nostrils and made their eyes water with the intensity of it; up high as they were, the stink was suffocating.

Pinny was winding up his field telephone in order to be ready for Jack who was scanning his designated area with binoculars. Another wave of bombers was approaching across the water.

‘Lord Street’s got it again. Renshaw Street, it looks as if Blacklers is up. Paradise Street. Come on, come on!’

‘Hang on, Jack. This bloody thing isn’t getting through.’ Pinny’s glasses kept slipping down his nose and irritated jerks of his upturned wrist punctuated his frenetic windings as he tried to right them. ‘Ready!..Lord Street, Blacklers, Paradise Street...’

‘St. George’s Hill now...The Museum...Library...The G.P.O....Victoria Street...William Brown Street...’

The binoculars edged round as Pinny’s voice echoed Jack’s into the telephone.

‘Government Buildings...Hang on...Yes. It’s The Customs House.’

‘Jesus! Why don’t I just say it’s the whole bloody lot and have done with it?’

‘India Buildings...Because they want us to pinpoint...Dock area... Ask them if they want them named.’

‘Do it Jack. Just do it! I’m not risking this thing cutting out again.’

The list went on, Jack’s voice monotonously level, as if in another circumstance, another world, recounting a relentless inventory of somebody’s assets having a bad day on the stock market. Jack was totally concentrated on the job in hand but deep inside his head he was numb with shock. It was to be total annihilation then, this night.

‘Prince’s...Duke’s...Canning...Salthouse...

And he was up here on a roof and his wife and child were somewhere else. On their own. In the middle of this. And if he went on thinking he would surely go mad with the anguish of it.

‘Stewart’s Warehouse...North King’s...number 2 dock... Hadfield’s Fertilizers...’

The men posted on the other side of the roof were relaying their own list: Telephone Exchange, gasworks at Atholl Street, railway sidings...ammunition train on fire...

And on some other roof someone would be detailing the serious conflagrations in the Kirkdale and Walton area, Orrell Park where Hanford Avenue was. He must not *think*. It was fatal to think.

The waves of bombers kept on coming. Tracer bullets swept through the sky from below, the Ack Ack gunners on the shoreline belting out round after round of ammunition. But there were others, in the city itself, racing up and down the streets, amongst people's homes, the force of their barrage blowing out whatever doors and windows still remained. Ordinary houses where milk would have been delivered that morning, now shuddering at the foundations with the heavy trundling and turning of wheels that really had no place there at all, carrying guns that spouted metal, like rain.

Fighter planes, at last, were noisily in evidence and they added their own rain to that otherwise balmy May night which seemed as if it would never end.

When morning did eventually come, some of the fire watchers were still on what was left of the rooftops, Jack and Pinny amongst them, waiting for the signal that would release them from duty, now that the All Clear had sounded. The scenes of devastation below them did not invite comment. They preferred instead to look out towards the horizon, daring another enemy bomber to reveal itself but knowing that there wouldn't be anything there. The job had been done. They looked out because neither of them could bear to register what lay below in those first minutes of exhausted relief.

Fires were still active, although not raging as they had been during the night, but all around, both on land and on water. Several ships were still ablaze, one of them the S.S. Malakand, loaded with ammunition.

Pinny was wearily cleaning the lenses of his glasses on his sleeve, the radio placed safely between his feet. Since his binoculars had been taken away from him, he took his new responsibity very seriously. Jack was remarking on the fact that there was still a great deal of activity down there with fire hoses and engines.

'They'll be needing the emergency water pumps,' he said. 'I hope to God there's some left intact. There's a couple of ships still on fire and there's oil in the sea water.'

'What?' Pinny turned to look in the direction of Jack's gaze, 'Poor sods!'

At that moment, despite the efforts of the desperate men fighting the fire, the flames reached the hold of the Malakand. The explosion was as if all the events of that terrible night had conspired together to produce the nearest thing to a volcanic eruption. Shrapnel: shards of metal from what had been the ship, exploded ammunition, parts of the dock itself with huge splinters of wood from the surrounding wharves, all cascaded in a deadly shower hundreds of feet above the wounded city.

Pinny had shoved his helmet back to put his glasses back on.

'Pin!' Jack shouted in warning as he ducked to avoid the murderous hail coming with ferocious velocity in their direction. And then as his friend fell backwards, 'Pinneeeeeee!'

The sound was echoed by the seagulls screaming round, circling wildly in the air, as if in mockery.

'PINNEEEEE?'

The other wardens came running across to where Jack was crouched over his stricken friend.

'Come on now. There's nothing more you can do here. We'll bring him down.'

And the chief warden, his buttonless jacket gaping open, hurriedly led Jack towards the door to the stairs below.

* * *

Fran heard the explosion as she struggled to push the pram along. She was down on the dock road by then, trying to make her way amongst the ruins of a city razed to the ground, firemen and rescue workers busy all around her; figures dimly moving in and out of her limited vision in the pall of smoke. Water from the fire hoses swirled around her ankles but she waded through it undeterred, her shoes soaked and slipping from her heels as she stumbled on. The hoses themselves were criss-crossed all over the road, fat and bloated, rising up in the water like black, grainy snakes. She hauled the wheels of the pram over them and bounced it down on the other side, her arms aching from the continuous effort. She did not care. She had to get Alexandra to safety. Her skirts were splashed with filthy mud almost to her waist.

She had made the decision during the night. She had come out from under the stairs when the front door had blown out. She had seen the wheeled platforms of the guns fill the opening as they hurtled by. She knew that the faces of the gunners would be as deranged as hers was. And then Bryant and Mays had gone up. It had to be the match factory because of the blinding light. Nowhere else could have produced such incandescence. And add that terrifying roaring to the already deafening noise.

She had run back inside and manhandled one of the fireside chairs across to where little Alex was huddled under the stairs, pulling it upside down over them both as extra protection. But they would be killed. She was convinced that they would be killed. It was then that she decided. If they got through this night, she had to go back home. If she didn't, they would both die, tomorrow or the next night. The city was a death trap.

'Mummy not cry,' Alexandra had tried to say in her yet-to-be-articulate way, 'Mummy not cry!'

And the child cried with her, in sympathy, but with no real idea of the cause.

Even before the All Clear sounded, as soon as she felt that it must be over, or as good as, Fran struggled out and pushed Alexandra into the pram, throwing a coat over her which she grabbed from the peg as she went. Then she ran back inside and scribbled a note to Jack.

The street outside was a mass of fallen debris. There was no time to notice. She knew the way she had to go and she set off, weaving round the heaps of rubble, trying not to see the state of her neighbours' houses. She must not be held up.

The aftermath of the bombing was all around her. Even shelters had been hit, she could not ignore that, and scores of ambulances were still in action at every corner she turned. One had been hit itself at some time during the raid. It was just a mass of twisted metal at the side of the road. She shut her eyes to the implications of it and hurried on through the devastated streets. It became difficult to get her bearings. At one point she had to ask a group of rescue workers where she was. They were dealing with a man who had obviously been bombed out. 'Where's your house?' they were asking him as he stood, wrapped in blankets, looking dazed. 'Where's your house, mister?' He looked down the road and pointed in disbelief, 'Where that big hole is!' He had stayed in bed when the siren went, he said, and woke to find himself lying in mid air. The rooms below had collapsed and the bed was supported by three joists in what had been the bedroom floor. He had been given a fireman's lift to get him down and he still could not fathom the extent of his luck.

When they turned to Fran, they were smiling.

But she got more than directions from them. She was lectured on the hazards of being out so early, particularly with the child. She was advised to return to her home. People were only just getting their breath back and there had not been time to attempt to make any of the damaged buildings safe. It was very dangerous. Four of the hospitals had been hit. She could not rely on help if she got hurt.

She feared that. As she pushed on, she had feared that all the time, that there would be no help. She was on her own. Jack must be dead. He could not possibly have survived, being out in the worst of it. He must be dead and she was on her own. Now she had to get where it was safe. But she had to cross through the horrors of the dock road first.

When the explosion happened behind her she jumped with fright, almost allowing the pram to topple off the swollen hose she was negotiating. She righted it clumsily and looked up, turning this way and that, frantically trying to see where the danger was. A huge fireball was colouring the sky behind her, debris hurtling in demented arcs on all sides. She turned then and half-ran, half-stumbled, away.

It was eight miles that she had walked by the time that she reached Oakshot Road, dirty, mud-splashed, tottering with exhaustion Her mother was waiting on the top step and came running down towards her as soon as she had turned the corner from South Road.

'Oh, Fran! Thank goodness you're here. We've been trying to telephone all morning but the phones are dead. Fa's gone to get you. He knew all the time where you were! Oh, Fran.'

They had reached the house and were struggling to get the battered pram up the steps.

'He will be looking for you. We are not staying here tonight. We are driving out to Maghull, the van's already loaded. He would *not* go without you.'

Fran paused on the broad top step, casting a bleak look back at what remained of the city.

'And Jack!' she said. It was an ultimatum, not a question.

'And Jack,' came the immediate reply.

They moved inside the infamous porch, Fran took Alexandra from under the soot-smeared coverings on the pram and held her in her arms.

'Alexandra. This is your grandmother,' she said.

Izzie looked at the golden-headed, dirty-faced child, snuggling against Fran's shoulder and immediately reached out to take her.

Little Alex smiled.

* * *

That same May morning, way down on the South coast, Stella was a solitary figure on the beach below Hill Head. She and Dee had stayed at the little hotel there during his short leave. It was near enough to the submarine base at H.M.S. Dolphin where he was stationed.

But they had spent the first day at The Green. They both felt that they wanted to be there together for one last time before he sailed. Although nothing specific had been said about a sailing, she knew in her bones that that was why Dee had expressed a wish to come down and why he had pretended that the visit to the hotel was a little celebration because they had been married for a whole month. She had instinctively seen through his ploy. He would be gone within forty eight hours, an inevitability she had long expected.

They had stood, framed against the massive bulk of the beech tree, looking with nostalgia at the front facade of the house with its white-pillared porch and the steps going up to the big red front door.

'It's always been my real home, this house here,' she said, 'I always felt that I did not belong anywhere else. This is where I was the most happy, felt the most loved, growing up here with you. It was always here that I would think of when things got bad.'

He squeezed her hand, 'Me too. And your Mum roaring up each weekend on that motor bike of hers. You've no idea how I looked forward to that!'

'Yes! It was a monster of a machine really. She loved it though, you know, I can't think why. And then of course...'

She laughed but he could sense her whole body tense up, coil under his touch as he put his arm round her shoulders.

'I'm sorry,' she said.

'None of that matters now, you silly old thing, not one bit of it. It's all over, as if it never happened.'

'I know,' she said, rubbing her nose on her sleeve and blinking madly so that she could see properly.

'Come on. I'll race you round the village, just like we used to.' And he caught her by the hand and they ran, breathless, up the hill, as far as the little schoolhouse. On the way down, each house door had to have its knocker banged or its bell pulled. It was a ritual that had been set up long before they were old enough to know that there were other rules to break.

Afterwards, feeling foolish, they crept in through the back way hoping that their escapade had gone unnoticed.

Two idyllic nights and two days they spent in no-one's company but their own in a cosy room which looked out over Southampton Water, just far enough away to be able to indulge the fantasy that there was no war at all. Unbelievably, the bombers had spared them a visit. Obviously, it had been someone else's turn, poor souls. And then he had left early, before dawn, to go back to Gosport.

Now she had made her way down to the beach, and stood patiently, her shoes sinking in between the sandy pebbles, looking out across the water, the Isle of Wight green and glittering in the early sunshine. She was waiting for the sight of a submarine on the surface; waiting for it to creep silently into her view. She had not brought binoculars, nothing to draw attention to herself. The movements of submarines were top secret. They had to be. She was not absolutely certain that it would come through the Solent at all but she could not have gone to Gosport. The families of submariners did not congregate on the quayside to say goodbye. They were not told when or where their loved ones were going. There was nothing like that.

So she had left the hotel and walked through the still-sleeping cluster of houses and made for the shore, prepared for a long wait, oblivious to the breeze rustling the scrubby grass behind her or the calls of the birds as they warned each other of her presence. She was just waiting. Alone in the morning.

She was waiting because when she did see what she was looking for, she would know that Dee would be in that ship. Dee, with whom, in the escalation of madness which surrounded them, she had found sanity; he, who had brought her solace when she had been incapable of believing that any such thing was within her rights. And beyond infinite price, it was through him that she now felt able, but only just, to receive the most important gift of all. The ability to forgive herself.

She would watch until the ship came. She would watch for however long, until it submerged way out, and it would be her last contact with him until he had returned from the deeper waters he was under orders to cross.

Until she had seen that, she would wait on the shore.